"I WANT YOU,"

he murmured, his voice thick with passion.

She opened her eyes and looked at him. His hot black gaze was devouring her body.

"I love you," she whispered, and he swept her to him, kissing her deeply, passionately.

"Let me," he murmured, his breath hot and panting. "Let me make love to you."

She watched him as he stripped off his shirt and boots and trousers.

His breath hissed out of him and he said in a choked voice, "Enough. I cannot bear it anymore."

He pulled her down with him onto the thick rug and began trailing kisses across her neck, turning her aflame.

* * *

Praise for Candace Camp's *Rosewood*:

"Candace Camp takes you on Millie's journey from spinsterhood to sensual awakening. I loved every delicious step."

—Sandra Brown, bestselling author of MIRROR IMAGE

Also by Candace Camp

Rosewood
Light and Shadow

Published by HarperPaperbacks

CANDACE CAMP

ANALISE

PREVIOUSLY PUBLISHED UNDER THE
PSEUDONYM LISA GREGORY

HarperPaperbacks
A Division of HarperCollinsPublishers

HarperPaperbacks   *A Division of* HarperCollins*Publishers*
10 East 53rd Street, New York, N.Y. 10022

Copyright © 1981 by Candace Camp
All rights reserved. No part of this book may be used or reproduced in any manner whatsoever without written permission of the publisher, except in the case of brief quotations embodied in critical articles and reviews. For information address HarperCollins*Publishers*,
10 East 53rd Street, New York, N.Y. 10022.

This book is published by arrangement with the author.

Cover photograph by Herman Estevez
Quilt courtesy of Quilt of America, Inc., N.Y.C.

First HarperPaperbacks printing: August 1991

Printed in the United States of America

HarperPaperbacks and colophon are trademarks of HarperCollins*Publishers*

10 9 8 7 6 5 4 3 2 1

ANALISE

SABOTAGE

One

The pride of New Orleans was out in full force that night; there was hardly an old or distinguished or wealthy family in the city that was not in attendance. It was late in February, and everyone was anxious to celebrate the passing of the winter, slight and brief though it would seem to their more northern neighbors. Lent would begin in a few weeks, and despite the fact that the Bishop had lifted the Lenten restrictions because of that odious blockade of Mr. Lincoln's, there would be few parties in the coming season of fast in this predominantly Catholic city. It was a perfect time to celebrate, therefore, before Lent began, and there was no city in the Confederacy better at celebrating than the French-flavored New Orleans.

In only two more months, the war would have been going on for a full year, and still New Orleans had seen not a hint of fighting. The town, like its new country, was smugly confident that it was invincible. And if the tables of food at the end of the room were lacking in many delicacies that would once have been shipped in, and if the lovely ladies twirling in the arms of their cavaliers wore dresses that had seen more than one season, who could tell it in the soft candlelight, and who would miss the food with all the cheerful gaiety bubbling around them? As one wit put it, "Why should we miss French champagne, when we have all those intoxicating beauties around us?"

The most intoxicating beauty of all was the daughter of the house, who stood now in the midst of a knot of admirers, the object of more than one admiring glance from the males of the company and quite a few glares from less fortunate belles and their aspiring mamas. Analise Caldwell was the only child of the scion of a wealthy American sugar plantation family, John Caldwell, and a lovely dark-haired Creole widow, Theresa duBois Fourier. Her name and fortune alone would have won her a soft spot in the heart of many a dashing Creole aristocrat, but she had also been blessed with a cloud of raven-black hair, a delicate heart-shaped face, and a slim, full-breasted figure.

Her most arresting feature, however, were her large, midnight-blue eyes, ringed with long smoky lashes. These she was now using with noticeable effect on her knot of suitors, flirting audaciously with them all over the top of her ivory fan, as she modestly declared her complete and girlish inability to choose between them.

"Robert," she teased, "how can you be so outrageous? I have danced with you twice tonight, and if I do so again, you know my reputation will be in absolute tatters."

"Oh, no, Miss Analise," her swains protested, almost in chorus, and Analise's steadying sense of humor made her almost giggle at their similarity. More than once she had suspected that her popularity was due as much to the vast competitiveness of the Creole male as to her own attributes. In a city where duels were fought over a few careless words and fortunes were won and lost with cool indifference on the turn of a card, no one wanted to be left out of the race to win any girl judged to be a prize worth having.

While the cluster of men around her sought to reassure her of her unassailable reputation and their own merits as her next dancing partner, Analise glanced above their shoulders and around the room. It was strange that she would feel bored at her own party, which had turned out to be such a success, with the triumph of having half the eligible males of the city competing for her, but boredom was precisely what she felt. Even while she smiled and flirted automatically, she found her mind sliding to the papers on her desk: the plans for the spring planting, which she was itching to start on tomorrow. Nor could she keep from reflecting on the damage to their economy done by the Union blockade. Last year's crops had lain rotting on the wharves, and not a penny to show for all their effort and expense, because the Union navy kept the merchant ships effectively bottled up in the harbor. If the same thing happened this year . . .

With irritation, she tried to shove the thought out of her mind. The blockade was hardly something to be thinking about at a party; besides, it had to be lifted, it simply had to. Any other alternative was too unbearable to think of.

She caught sight of her brother Emil by the open doors to the side verandah and grimaced inwardly. He was talking intimately to a pretty blonde girl who laughed up at him with a sparkling smile and flashing blue eyes; the expression on his face was warm and intent. Analise could have cheerfully hit him, despite the fact that Emil had always been her hero. Why did he have to be like all men and prefer the vapid blonde good looks of someone like Becky Oldway when he had the love of a warm, sweet girl like Pauline Beauvais? Emil was actually her half-brother, not full blood, for his father had died of yellow fever when he was a baby and his mother had married John Caldwell. John Caldwell was the only father he had ever known, and to Analise he had always been her adored older brother. Since she loved him dearly, she dreaded the thought of his marrying Becky, whom she thought shallow and selfish. She would only make him unhappy, whereas the plain Pauline would worship and care for him.

Still frowning at her brother's preference in women, Analise turned her head and surveyed the room. Suddenly she felt that someone was looking at her, could feel the sensation of eyes boring into her. Then she saw him, and her eyes stopped; Analise knew immediately that it was this man who had drawn her gaze.

He stood on the staircase, leaning negligently against the white-railed banister, seemingly a study in lazy indifference, but there was a tension about his well-disciplined muscles, much like a panther gathering to spring, and his hot, black eyes burned steadily into Analise's. She felt a shiver run through her as she met his look, and although she was not quite sure why, she knew at once that he was dangerous. Dangerous and wild and untamable, like the sleek black stallion, Lucifer, that Papa had once owned, which even the daredevil Emil could not ride. Lucifer—the fallen Angel; that would be an appropriate name for this man too. With his thick black hair and swarthy skin, he was as cold and dark as Lucifer, and his firm features as handsome and full of pride.

Firmly, Analise pulled her eyes away from him and

returned to her bevy of admirers. She could still feel his gaze on her, and she felt foolishly flushed and confused. Who on earth was he, and what was he doing here? She was positive she had never seen him before; he could not possibly have been invited to their party.

The band was striking up another waltz, and she said with mock severity, "Now, hush, all of you, you know you are not being fair at all. I have already promised this dance to Lieutenant Carrière. See, his name is here on my dance card; shame on you to think my card was not already filled. Why, I do believe you must think I am some sort of wall-flower, to still have a dance available."

"Not at all," Lieutenant Carrière exclaimed, readily stepping forward to claim her hand. "They just hope to persuade you into letting one of them take my place. Poor devils—don't be angry, Miss Analise; rather pity them."

Analise laughed out loud; the lieutenant was always so extravagant in his praise that she hardly knew whether he took himself seriously or spent his time laughing up his sleeve at those who did. At least he was a poor enough dancer that trying to follow his steps would keep her mind well occupied for a while—and off that strange dark man on the steps.

As she sluggishly made her way around the room in the Lieutenant's less-than-skillful arms, she could not keep her eyes from straying back to the staircase. It was empty now, and for a startled moment, Analise wondered if he could have been a figment of her overtired mind. Cautiously, trying to look casual, she glanced about the room and found him at last, lounging against the wall, his arms folded, deep in conversation with Perry Malenceaux. She nibbled pensively at her underlip—an unladylike habit she resorted to when deep in thought, much to her mother's exasperation—and wondered if he could have come with Perry. Perhaps he was some distant Malenceaux cousin; they had seemingly thousands of them up around Baton Rouge.

When the dance ended, Analise quickly worked around the room to where Pauline Beauvais stood against the wall beside the hawk-faced cousin who chaperoned her tonight. Pauline was one of the wallflowers who drifted here among the chaperones, staying close to the crowd for purposes of camouflage, though certainly she had far less need of chaperonage than did the beautiful butterflies who twirled about the dance floor. Actually, Pauline would not have come tonight had the party not been given by her dear friend Analise; she really preferred a quiet evening at home with her books, especially when she knew that she would be forced to witness Emil Fourier's eager courtship of Becky Oldway.

"Hello, Analise," she said now, with a small, grateful smile at her friend. Standing in conversation with the belle of the ball somehow made her own lack of swains less painful. "It is a lovely party."

"Yes!" the hawk-faced cousin interjected and cleared her throat ostentatiously. "And don't pretend to me that it was your mother who planned and produced this affair. I've known Theresa duBois since she was in short skirts, and she never had the sense to bring off something like this. All she was ever capable of doing was choosing a piece of material to show off her complexion and chattering about the latest scandal."

Pauline flushed and shot a pleading look at Analise. Her Cousin Jeanette was an autocratic old soul who claimed kinship with half the good Creole families in New Orleans, among them the Beauvais, the Beauregardes, and the Carterets, and she felt that her position gave her the right to make rude comments whenever and about whomever she chose. It was often mortifying to be with her, but Pauline's mother was dead, and she could not be too picky about choosing a chaperone, what with her family's financial straits.

Analise merely laughed at the withered old woman; she knew her mother's frivolous character probably better than Jeanette Pacquet did, and she was too honest to deny the remark and too blunt herself not to be amused by it. "Now, Cousin Jeanette," she said with the easy familiarity of a long-time family friend, "don't be spiteful. What else, pray, should Mama need to know? That was enough to catch her two well-endowed husbands."

The old lady drew her mouth up and made a fortunately unintelligible noise, but she smiled a little. She belonged to an earlier, franker age, and she liked the Caldwell girl for her spirit and forthrightness, even if she had the misfortune to be half-American. It was just too bad that some of her exuberance did not rub off on Pauline.

"Pauline," Analise said, taking her friend by the elbow and pulling her away from the gaggle of duennas, "I must ask you something. I have just seen the most unusual man, and I want to know who he is. You know all the families around here."

Her friend's interest was piqued. It was most unusual for Analise to be anything but indifferent about any man; she had always had so many suitors that none had been important to her, like a child overindulged with toys.

"Who are you talking about?" Pauline whispered back.

"That dark man over there, the one talking to Perry Malenceaux, against the far wall. Do you know him?"

Pauline narrowed her eyes uncertainly; years of reading had made her vision poor at anything but close range. "I don't think so . . ."

Analise sighed. She had been counting on Pauline's connections with all the old French families to identify her stranger. He could hardly be from around here and not be known by Pauline.

"I thought perhaps he was one of Perry's interminable cousins," she prodded.

Now Pauline outright squinted at the man. "There isn't the Malenceaux look about him; they all have those long, horsy faces. Of course, most of his clan live up around Baton Rouge; I'm not very familiar with them."

"Neither am I," Analise said, chewing at her lip.

"But, wait," Pauline said suddenly, turning to look at her friend in surprise. "This is *your* party. Don't you know him?"

"No, that is why I wondered who he was. I didn't invite him; that's certain."

"Well, I think you are going to get our curiosity satisfied," Pauline remarked drily. "They seem to be coming toward us."

Analise barely suppressed a gasp, and her stomach twisted in the strangest way. Why, she thought to herself, I am acting like a girl at my first dance. What on earth was it about the man that had such an odd effect on her?

She did not have long to ponder this thought before the two men were upon them. Malenceaux made a bow with his usual flourish and said, "Miss Analise. Miss Pauline. Are you two hiding over here from your beaus?"

Analise smiled faintly at his witticism. She could feel the other man's eyes raking her body, as warm and tangible as a hand, and her breath caught in her throat.

"Miss Analise, I hope you won't think it too bold of me," Perry continued, "but I brought along a friend of mine tonight who most particularly wants to meet you. Ma'am, this is Captain Clay Ferris, from Savannah way. Now, don't you go breaking his heart and give him a bad impression of our city."

"I would not dream of it," Analise murmured, returning the man's formal bow with a brief nod of her head.

When Analise seemed inclined to say nothing else, Pauline jumped into the breach, saying softly, "Tell us, Captain Ferris, what brings you to New Orleans?"

"Yes, Captain, I believe the fighting is a little farther north, is it not?" Analise asked coolly, ignoring Pauline's startled look at her rudeness. Analise did not understand it, but she had felt an immediate antagonism to this man, as strong and inexplicable as the leap of her heart when he bowed to her and smiled that warm, lopsided smile.

The Confederate officer looked at her steadily for a moment, until Analise grew nervous under his flat stare. Her remark began to seem rude and stupid, not pert as she had meant it to be.

Finally Ferris said, "Well, like the brave soldiers here in New Orleans, I realize the importance of our port cities. Although I am sure that they, like I, would rather be wearing our uniforms in battle, defense of New Orleans and Savannah and Charleston must be uppermost in our minds. Should we lose our ports, we would be virtually crippled. But, of course, being a lady, you would not worry your little head about such things."

Two red spots of anger flared in Analise's cheeks at his words, spoken in a tone so carefully polite as to point up her own unfair remark. She felt foolish and bested in an exchange, something she was unused to, and she would have liked to let her temper fly, but she gulped back the hot words that rushed to her lips. She would not give him the satisfaction of making her heedlessly angry. "Why, Captain Ferris, as if I did not know how brave all those men are for defending our city. I vow, I would feel quite scared if they were not here to protect us. What I meant was: I cannot quite understand why we in New Orleans need the help of a Savannah man to protect our city."

A spark of amusement flared in his dark eyes and he smiled at her as if to acknowledge her skillful parry. "No, it is I who need their help. You see, I am here to observe your defenses with a mind to improving Savannah's. New Orleans really has quite an excellent obstacle course set up for the Yankees."

Puffed up by this remark, Perry chimed in, "Quite right. Not many places will you find torpedoes like the ones we have."

"Indeed, quite ahead of the time," Ferris responded and tried to turn the conversation. "But no doubt we are boring the ladies with such talk."

Malenceaux merely laughed, not to be diverted. "Then you don't know our Creole belles. They are quite informed on the subject of this war. Why, Miss Analise's father is the man who invented those torpedoes."

Hastily Analise broke in. "Now, Perry, you will have the Captain thinking that we New Orleans girls are book-worms like all those Yankee girls." Malenceaux was a fool, always had been—imagine blabbing something like that right here at a social gathering, in front of a stranger, when the torpedoes were supposed to be so terribly secret. "Indeed, Captain, I have to confess that most of the time our discussions on the war concern the blockade and the way it is ruining all the parties this year."

That remark turned Malenceaux to the subject of the enemy blockade and the inconvenience it had imposed on all of them. "It galls me," he said pompously, "to see our lovely ladies forced to wear last year's dresses and hats. Criminal, absolutely criminal."

"I think it is of somewhat greater concern that the blockade is choking the South's commerce," Ferris said drily, and Analise had to hide a smile.

"Is it doing that?" Pauline asked, her interest caught. "I mean, is it as bad in the other ports?"

"Why, yes, ma'am. Charleston, Savannah, Wilmington, Mobile—everywhere it is the same. Cotton, sugarcane, rice, indigo, all the crops are sitting rotting on the docks for lack of transport," Ferris replied.

"What does that matter?" Malenceaux said impatiently. "Ole Abe doesn't know us very well if he thinks he can bring the Confederacy to its knees by hitting us in our pocketbooks. Only a Yankee bleeds from there."

The Captain turned his flat black gaze on the other officer. "Indeed? Pray tell me how the South is to fight if it cannot finance its army and navy. Do you think England and France will give us cannon and guns in return for promises of breathless glory?"

"A little pessimistic, aren't you, Captain?" Analise needled him, although she could easily see the logic of his words.

His smile was grave. "Just realistic, ma'am. I would like

to make the government see the vital importance of our port cities. Victories in Virginia are all well and good, but what we need is a strong navy. My friend Malenceaux here would tell you that Southerners are natural fighters and cavalrymen. Well, they are natural sailors, too; the South was built on shipping as much as on crops. All that is needed are enough ships and the cannon to defend them, and we can break the blockade.''

"Pardon me," a suave masculine voice interrupted them, and Analise tore her eyes away from the Captain's magnetic gaze to look beyond him at Richard Helms. "Miss Analise, I believe this is my dance. . . ."

He paused and Analise fumbled for her dance card, not really wanting to end this interesting conversation; this was the most intelligent talk she had ever had with a man.

Then Ferris said coolly, "No, there you are wrong, sir. Miss Caldwell has promised this waltz to me."

Helms stared at him open-mouthed and Pauline's eyebrows flew up in astonishment as the Georgian firmly grasped Analise's arm and led her onto the dance floor.

"How dare you!" Analise spluttered, flushed with outrage at his high-handed treatment of her. "This was Mr. Helms' dance, and you know I never promised you a dance this whole evening. I shan't dance with you!"

Ferris took her firmly in his arms and swung her out onto the dance floor. He said coolly, "Too late. You cannot do anything about it now without creating a scene. Just relax and enjoy the music."

Analise's blue eyes flew wide open with fury, and she hissed, "Of all the unmitigated gall! I declare, Captain Ferris, you are the rudest, most conceited man I have ever met. I have absolutely no wish to dance with you; you did not even ask my permission. Please return me to my friends at once."

He smiled and his hard face softened with charm. "How could I ask you? You have been surrounded by men all evening; that was the first chance I had to be alone with you. Besides, you know as well as I that your dance card was filled within ten minutes of the first arrival."

Despite her anger, Analise could not control the peculiar flutter in her stomach at his smile, and the angry words that had been boiling inside her curiously seemed to have fled her mind. She could only say, with a slightly petulant air, "You were not even invited, Captain Ferris."

His laugh was rich and deep. "You have me there, Miss Caldwell. But, having come here uninvited, it seems a small sin to steal you for a dance."

Analise had to laugh. "I suppose that is true. In for a penny, in for a pound, so they say."

He was a superb dancer, and he guided her smoothly, firmly across the floor. Analise felt as though she was floating in his arms, but at the same time she was supremely aware of every point where his flesh touched her: the back of her waist where his palm pressed firmly, the warm grip of his other hand holding hers, the hard muscle and bone of his shoulder beneath her hand. Even through their clothes, her skin was hot and tingling where his lay.

Analise looked up at him and saw mirrored in his black eyes the same awareness of their physical closeness. His eyes blazed with something strong and elemental that she could not recognize but that her body responded to without thought. No man had ever had that effect on her; none had made her feel breathless and dizzy.

Ferris guided her steps toward the wall of narrow doors

that led onto the verandah, and as the music stopped, his hand gripped her arm and propelled her onto the porch with him. Analise protested feebly, but now his hard arm was around her waist, drawing her inexorably to the rail of the porch.

"I promise I will not assault you," he said amusedly, as he settled himself upon the broad railing. "I merely wanted to talk to you, and that is almost impossible in there with all those admirers and chaperones."

"But everyone will notice that I am gone," Analise protested. "It will be quite a scandal."

"Even though we are standing three feet apart, farther away than when we danced?"

"Yes, well, no one *knows* that," Analise said flatly. She knew that the only proper thing for her to do was to leave immediately and reenter the ballroom. Mama might be a flibbertigibbet, but if there was one thing she knew, it was the conventions of society, and any deviation from propriety was enough to send her into spasms. Why, she even kept secret the fact that her daughter was largely responsible for running their plantation, for fear that everyone would think she was appallingly smart, unfeminine, and—worst of all—improper. No lady would ever think of poring over the plantation account books, staining her fingers with ink and muddying her mind with things better left to men.

Perhaps it was that thought that made Analise stay; she despised her mother's confused, meandering lectures on her improper behavior, and simply the thought of them had the adverse effect of making her want to annoy the woman. Then, again, perhaps it was not that at all, but something about this man. Nervously her mind shied away from that thought.

"What did you do before the war, Captain Ferris?" she asked, trying to reestablish formality.

He grinned, knowing that she had capitulated and would stay, and Analise thought with a slight shiver that his grin was nothing short of devilish.

"Oh, a planter. Coastal Georgia is quite similar to this area, although we grow rice and indigo rather than sugarcane." He leaned back against the verandah column and studied her for a moment.

Analise dropped her eyes to her hands under his steady regard. "Really, Captain," she said lightly, to cover her strange shyness. "I feel as though I were one of your crops and you are watching me, waiting for me to get taller. I cannot imagine what you find of such interest in my face."

He chuckled briefly and said, "Can't you? I doubt this is the first time you have found yourself the object of a man's attention."

"Of course not," she replied tartly, "but few are so impolite as you!"

"I was never a very successful student of manners, I am afraid. You are a lovely woman, and I enjoy looking at you. Is that too honest for your maidenly sensibilities?"

Analise looked at him and raised her eyebrows. "Sir, I think 'maidenly sensibilities' and numerous other polite myths are made more for the benefit of the male than for us women."

He laughed, his voice surprised and faintly amused. "Indeed?"

"Yes, indeed!" Analise retorted hotly, stung by his superior air. "Gentlemen are absolutely horrified to hear a lady mention the presence of quadroon mistresses; such things, you see, are not 'proper' for a lady to hear or speak of. Yet it is perfectly all right for the gentlemen to keep quadroon mistresses. And that, sir, seems to me the height of hypocrisy and clearly a code created by men, not women!"

For a moment he stared at her in silence, and suddenly Analise realized what she had said in her anger and felt mortified. Whatever must he think of her, saying shocking things like that to him, things even husband and wife did not discuss with each other, let alone a single young girl to a perfect stranger!

Then that charming smile of his touched his mouth, and she saw that his eyes danced with delight. "My dear Miss Caldwell," he drawled lazily, "more than one person has told me that I am shockingly blunt, but I think in this regard I must hand the honors over to you."

Analise blushed, even more embarrassed by the amusement in his voice; no doubt she had made a very entertaining spectacle of herself for this Savannah gentleman. Stammering a little, she began, "I beg your pardon. Heaven knows what you must think of me. I am afraid my tongue has run away with me again, and I apologize. Now I think I really must go in."

She turned to flee to the haven of the lighted room, but the man reached out swiftly and grabbed her wrist with one hand. Analise tugged, but his grasp was like iron, and she could not escape him.

"No, wait, Miss Caldwell. You have not done anything to run away from. I do not deplore your honesty—quite the opposite, I find it refreshing and utterly enchanting. As it happens, I quite agree with what you said. I have never seen the sense in a woman having to be deaf, dumb, and blind to qualify as a lady." He paused briefly and then said in a different tone, his voice slightly edged with bitterness, "I have long known that women are not saints. And why a man should want a saint for a wife and bed partner is beyond my comprehension. I like my women to be flesh and blood."

His hand dropped away from her wrist, but Analise stood still, as though rooted to the spot. Her eyes searched his dimly lit face, looking for sarcasm, and all the while her heart pounded fiercely. He could not mean what he said; she could imagine no other man saying such a thing. But then what other man would have spoken to her in that blunt tone and used such inelegant words? She could almost hear her mother saying primly that he had no respect for her, and yet . . .

At last her companion broke her stunned silence. "It seems I have shocked you more than you did me. Shall we call a truce and agree to forget genteel amazement between us?"

"What are you suggesting?" her voice was stiff and cautious.

He laughed. "Nothing improper, I assure you. I am simply asking your permission to call on you."

Analise said hesitantly, "I—I don't know. I scarcely know you, after all. Mama might not approve."

"Why do you dislike me, Miss Caldwell?" he asked suddenly.

Analise swallowed. She was intensely aware of his lean body, though he was several feet away from her, more aware than she had ever been with any of the men she had danced with. She did not like him really; he was too abrupt, too confident, too uncomfortably in control. But neither could she say she disliked him and did not want to see him again. Rather, he disturbed her, upset the equilibrium of her world. He made her insides quiver strangely, and she could not help wondering what it would be like to kiss him; and yet—and yet he scared her.

"I don't dislike you," she said, her voice strangely uncertain.

"Then what is it?" he asked. She shook her head helplessly.

Before she realized what he was doing or could even draw breath for a gasp, he was off the railing and standing so close before her that the coat of his uniform brushed against her breasts. Taking her by the shoulders, Ferris pulled her against him and kissed her thoroughly, leisurely, his lips lingering on hers. Analise stiffened, shocked; no man had kissed her without her permission, and none of the ones to whom she had given modestly blushing permission had possessed her mouth so demandingly. His lips were hot and searing, insistently forcing her lips apart. Then his tongue was inside her mouth, softly exploring that sweet cavity, and his arms went tight around her, crushing her into him, until she could feel the full, hard length of his body against hers even through their clothes. A shiver shot through her like icy fire, and involuntarily she responded, her body melting into him and her arms creeping up around his neck while her lips met his, warmth for warmth.

Suddenly he released her and stepped back. His black eyes glittered, and his chest rose and fell heavily. Analise stared back at him in silence, savoring the sweet, heavy taste of passion still in her mouth. She knew she ought to slap him hard and call him a scoundrel, but she did not;

neither did she do what her blood urged her—throw herself back into his arms. Instead she looked at him with mute appeal, her blue eyes huge and dark, her mouth trembling a little; then she turned with a flash of skirts and ran into the ballroom.

Her companion did not follow her, but turned back to the railing to stare out into the damp blackness and suck the heavy Louisiana air into his lungs. "Damn," he muttered, and fumbled for a cheroot and lit it. "Damn." What a delightful, and dangerous, spice had been added to his mission.

Two

*A*nalise bent her dark head over her desk and attempted for the third time to plow through her overseer's letter. In spite of the man's atrocious spelling and even worse grammar, she usually did not have this much trouble deciphering his writing. The problem she was having this afternoon was her own inattention. She simply could not seem to concentrate on the man's suggestions for the spring planting, which she had been looking forward to so eagerly last night.

The paper drifted from her fingers as she raised her head and stared out the verandah doors. As they had been all day, her thoughts drifted back to the evening before with Captain Ferris and that wild, exciting kiss he had given her. What an unusual man he was; she could not decide whether she liked him or feared him or despised him. No gentleman would have kissed her like that. But, then, no gentleman had ever managed to stir her emotions, either.

"Ah, there you are, my dear!" a man's voice cut into her thoughts, and Analise turned to see her father peering in at her around the edge of the door, a smile on his lips and his expression the vague, bemused, slightly anxious one common to the near-sighted. As always, his cravat was slightly askew and his hair rumpled; he did great damage to his valet's careful toilette under the duress of his thinking process.

"Yes, come in, Papa," Analise said affectionately, "and do put your spectacles on."

"What? Oh, yes." Mr. Caldwell felt the top of his head carefully until he came upon his eyeglasses. "There, that's better." He beamed at his daughter and came over to plant a fatherly kiss on her forehead. "How did you like the dance last night? Did you enjoy it?"

"Oh, yes, it came off perfectly," Analise replied and could not help adding a good-natured dig. "You should know how the party came off. After all, you were there."

"Ah, yes, well." John Caldwell grinned at her sheepishly. "I have to admit that I got into a conversation with Colonel Chalmers. We retired to my study and stayed up until one o'clock discussing the feasibility of an underwater, power-propelled boat." He stopped and looked at his daughter; seeing that her blue eyes brimmed with unspent mirth, he began to laugh. "Well, I can see that I don't have to tell you that."

"No," Analise agreed, "and it did not surprise me in the least when I saw the two of you sneaking off to your study for some bourbon and conversation."

Analise loved her father dearly and she would have defended him to the last had anyone criticized him, but neither was she blind to his character. He was a bright man, with a scientific turn of mind, one of the best inventors of the day. He had indeed invented the torpedoes that would be used to defend the city against the Yankees, as Perry had so blunderingly pointed out last night. He had also drawn up quite a few more plans for the army and navy, including the underwater boat so dear to his heart, which they had not had the money (or trust) to manufacture yet. However, for all his cleverness, he was a hopeless case when it came to the practicalities of everyday life—worse, if possible, than her mother. His family had long ago given up relying on him to remember meetings and parties and special events or to arrive anywhere on time or to not get so involved with an interesting discussion that he ignored everything else going on around him. Analise loved him and respected his mind, but she never went to him for help with a practical problem or depended on him to guide her gently through life, as other girls did their fathers. Instead, she loved him for his quaint ways and shielded him from the realities of life, often feeling that she was more the parent than he.

"I am afraid I am not much use to you, am I?" Mr. Caldwell said suddenly and sighed.

"Oh, no, Papa, don't say that!" Analise exclaimed and jumped up to hug him. "Why, you are the very best father in the world. I could not ask for a kinder, more intelligent man than you."

"I know, you are always kind enough to praise me, my love, but I can see my shortcomings. I have not been the kind of father to you that I should. No, nor the kind of stepfather Emil should have had, really. He needed a man's firm guidance; he has grown up far too hot-headed and heedless, with no regard for true worth, only that insane Creole 'code of honor.' And you—you should not be in here, poring over Belle Terre's books and worrying about the crops and the slaves and the finances, wrangling with hard-bitten merchants, and having to deal with common overseers. You are the most beautiful girl in the world. Oh, yes, I'm not that blind and deaf to the outside world. I know a real beauty when I see one; after all, I married your mother, didn't I, and God knows, all she has is beauty. You should be out in the parlor, flirting with some young blade, not in here, ruining your eyesight over MacPherson's writing."

"Papa, no, I won't let you say such things. Why, I love running the plantation. I could not bear it if all I had to do all day was sit and embroider and gossip about this gentleman or that couple, as all my acquaintances do. That is deadly dull, believe me, and I look forward to bargaining with the merchants over my crops and planning the crops and working on the books. You know how much I like to run things. Why, just think," she teased, "if I did not have the plantation to run, I would probably spend all my time trying to run you!"

John smiled weakly. His daughter was, as always, very persuasive, and it would be so much easier to give in to her and let things slide, as always. But last night his wife had let him know in no uncertain terms that Analise had disappeared for all of two dances, and not a soul knew where she was or whom she was with—thank God no one had noticed—and that her unbecoming waywardness was all the result of his paternal neglect. Normally Theresa Caldwell was the most placid of people, quite happy to let him do as he wished, as long as she could content herself with her clothes and hairdos and imported chocolates, but there was one thing on which she was firm—her deeply entrenched Creole sense of family honor and name. If Analise wanted to do such unfeminine things as she did, that Theresa was willing to overlook, but when she let the headstrong side of her personality threaten her reputation, Mrs. Caldwell was determined to stop her.

So Caldwell, by nature a pacific man, had refrained from pointing out that Theresa herself had been as happy to unload the running of the household bother here and at Belle Terre on her young daughter as he had been to give up the mess he had made of the plantation's books, and he promised his wife to admonish Analise about her abnormal behavior.

Remembering his wife's Gallic wrath, he drew breath and began again. "But, Analise, my dear, it simply is not right. I know you say you love doing such things, but that is not the point. It is not ladylike; you should be concerning yourself with dresses and parties and men; you should be engaged or married. A beautiful girl like you and already twenty; after three seasons, it is not right that you are still single. It was wrong of me to let you start acting as my secretary when you were fifteen, although then it seemed innocuous enough; and then when you began *doing* the correspondence and then handling the books and directing the overseer—well, I should not have allowed it. It just seemed to creep up on me, all so gradually, and it was so much easier to let you do it that I just did not have the heart to object."

"And there is no reason why you should," Analise said. "There is no sense in your doing something you loathe when I can do it better and love it, besides. And it has not exactly turned me into a withered old maid yet, has it? I know plenty of girls who did not get married until they were twenty-one or twenty-two; it isn't as if I haven't had lots of offers. I just have not wanted to marry any of them. I do not spend my time crouched in here like some mole;

I receive callers every afternoon, and I can assure you that my appearance and wit are no disgrace to you."

Her father sighed, feeling the insidious spread of defeat. He had never been able to outtalk Analise; no wonder she was such a success with those traders. Well, at least he had done his duty and could tell Theresa that he had spoken with their daughter on the subject. Let Theresa try to move her.

Analise hid a smile at the obvious relief on her father's face as he retreated to the safety of his study. Poor Papa. Mama must have set upon him the night before about Analise's absence from the party for a few minutes. It was galling, really, the way you had to be in everyone's full view all the time if you did not want to set the city gossiping— and not at all fair, either, since men could go about anywhere they pleased, whenever the mood struck them and with whomever they chose. One would think that all gentlemen were in continual pursuit of an opportunity to ravish a young lady, even in her parents' parlor or just outside a crowded dance floor. And, for that matter, it was ridiculous to think that her pretty, plump, fluffy mother would be able to do anything should some gentleman take it into his head to attack Analise. What practical good was a chaperone?

In the past, Analise had not particularly chafed at such restrictions. She frankly had not had that great a desire to be alone with any of her beaus. But now, suddenly, it seemed a rather large injustice. With a sigh, Analise strolled across the room and leaned against a doorjamb, gazing cloudily out over the side garden. Was it because of Captain Ferris that her restrictions now seemed burdensome? Was it because she wished to meet him without the watchful eyes of a chaperone upon them? A blush rose in her cheeks as she recalled his kiss; that was precisely what a chaperone was there to prevent, and she should be grateful he would not have the opportunity to do that again. It had been wicked of him to kiss her so. A smile curved her mouth; she had to admit that, wicked or not, she was aflame with curiosity and eager to experience it again.

Her thoughts were interrupted by a maid's gentle tap on the door. "Miss Analise?"

"Yes, May," she said, turning, and a small, turbaned black woman entered the room.

"Company, Miss Analise, to see you. A gentleman I never seen before." Her face was openly curious.

Analise's heart gave a wild leap and settled into loud, rhythmic thumps. Captain Ferris! Carefully she schooled her expression to one of faint, polite interest and followed May out of the room.

When she entered the parlor, a gracious smile on her face, Captain Ferris and her father both rose to greet her. Analise felt a stab of amusement—apparently her father felt such guilt (or such pressure from his wife) over his parental neglect that he had chosen to sit in on this call, something he usually avoided like the plague. Her amusement quickly vanished as she turned to the officer and met his fiery dark eyes; her knees went weak as he took her hand in his firm, warm grasp and gently brushed his lips against her hand. It was no more than a polite gesture extended to her countless other times by other men, but now she felt shaken and caught in an intimate moment.

"Captain Ferris," she said, striving for composure. "Have you met my mother and father?"

"Oh, yes, I had the pleasure of making Mrs. Caldwell's

acquaintance last evening. I believe Miss Beauvais introduced me to her." Analise glanced nervously at her mother
and was relieved to see that she was smiling merrily, her
eyes bright with excitement. Of course, she could not
know that the Captain was responsible for the reprehen-
sible absence of her daughter from the party last night; no
doubt she was simply brimming with curiosity about the
stranger and hopeful that this new man might spark Analise's interest.

Ferris continued politely, "However, I did not meet
your father until just now, although I have been quite
anxious to. I have heard splendid things about you, sir."

Mr. Caldwell looked astonished, and Analise quirked a
sarcastic eyebrow at their caller. "Come, now," she murmured, her voice amused, "coming it a bit too strong,
aren't you?"

Theresa shot her daughter a despairing glance at this
blatant rudeness to a guest, but the man smiled, unper-
turbed. "No doubt that sounds like exaggerated manners,
but in fact it is true. More than one person has told me
what an ingenious inventor you are."

Caldwell squirmed, looking embarrassed, and admitted,
"Well, I do dabble a little in that sort of thing."

"That is fascinating," Ferris encouraged him. "Where
do you do your work, sir?"

"Oh, here and at Belle Terre, our plantation; I have a
study at both places exclusively devoted to my work."

"And what sort of things do you invent?"

Thus encouraged, her father launched on a recital of the
peacetime inventions he had made, until Theresa was posi-
tively glassy-eyed with boredom. Even Analise thought
that her suitor was going a bit too far in his effort to

ingratiate himself with her father; Papa could talk for days about his gadgets, even when he was being careful to avoid the taboo area of his military creations. And if he decided Ferris was trustworthy enough to tell him about those, there would be no stopping him.

She was grateful, therefore, when the butler announced the arrival of another visitor. Becky Oldway would no doubt drive Papa away within seconds after her arrival. Analise had to hide the laughter that sprang into her eyes at the expression of horror on her father's face when Becky swept into the room, all smiles and flutterings and sugar-sweet words. Almost as soon as she was seated, he sprang to his feet and announced that he must get back to his work.

Surprisingly, Ferris stood also and said, "I wonder if it would be too impertinent of me to ask to look at some of your sketches. I am very interested in some of the things you mentioned, particularly the harvesting machine."

A look of consternation crossed Caldwell's face; Analise knew he was torn between the extreme secrecy of the torpedo and underwater boat projects and his desire to show off to one of the few people who actually seemed interested in his hobby. Rather reluctantly, he said, "Ah, delighted to show you, but I can't, you see. Uh—most of my farm plans are out at the plantation. Some other time, perhaps. Excuse me."

Ferris continued to look at his retreating figure as he left the room and hurried down the hall. The Captain's expression was strangely closed and guarded, and Analise felt a stab of disquiet. There was something watchful and dangerous about the man, as if he were constantly on the alert, coiled to strike. Even here, in the overwhelming ordinariness of their parlor, paying an innocuous social call, there was a faint tinge of excitement to him, a tension that showed in the sharp angles of his face, the controlled strength of his muscles. Analise sensed that he was a man at home with adventure, and she wondered uneasily what he was doing here on such a citizen's errand, far from the real action of the war.

He smiled now at Becky, a suave, consciously sensual smile, and complimented her on her dress; the momentary mood was broken. Analise chided herself for a romantic; the way he was flirting with Becky—no doubt the danger about him was that he was an adventurer on the lookout for a rich wife.

"Why, Captain Ferris," Becky replied to his witticisms, "I declare, you are a most terrible man." She batted her eyelashes at him artfully, although her eyes slid hopefully, surreptitiously to the hallway.

Analise knew she was hoping Emil would appear, and it gave her a perverse joy to know that Emil had gone to a coffeehouse with friends and would probably be gone all afternoon.

Becky was a pretty girl, with dainty features, round blue eyes, golden, clustering curls, and a prettily rounded figure that promised obesity when she grew older if she did not watch her sweets. The look she strove for was one of sweet innocence, and she was given to flowery declarations of great friendship with Analise. Analise was familiar enough with her to know, however, that while Becky was not overly intelligent, she was shrewd enough to cultivate Analise's friendship as a pathway to Emil. Otherwise, her vanity would never have permitted her to linger in the company of a woman whose dark, vibrant beauty made her look pale and insipid by comparison.

Becky desperately wanted Emil Fourier, not only for his wealth and good looks, but also because his family was one of the oldest, most respected in Louisiana. Her father wanted her to marry position, and Becky warmly agreed. Although Mr. Oldway was wealthy, he had climbed to that estate from a poor Alabama family, and more than once Becky had been subjected to small slights and snubs from old-line New Orleans matrons, too often not invited to the really exclusive parties. But once she married a Fourier, she felt certain that she could be a leader in society.

The butler announced Armand St. Jean and Robert Delacourt, and suddenly the gracious parlor seemed crowded and far too public a place for any sort of reasonable conversation. Analise felt a pang of disappointment and realized that she had been looking forward to another personal talk with Ferris. Again she inwardly reviled the multitude of stiff social customs that prevented them from meeting in private. It occurred to her for the first time how ridiculous it was that a man and woman could pass through a courtship and engagement and never really be alone until they were actually married. And then it would be too late to discover that they bored each other thoroughly!

Ferris also clearly disliked the lack of privacy, and he soon stood to take his leave. As he bent over her hand, he shot her a warm, intimate glance, which Analise felt down to her toes, and she knew without his speaking that he would find a way to see her again alone.

It did not take Ferris long to prove Analise's suspicions correct. The next day, as Analise left the hospital after her hour of rolling bandages for the soldiers with the other women of the Ladies Auxiliary, and stood looking for the familiar figure of Sam, their coachman, perched on the high seat of the Caldwell open carriage, she felt a firm hand take her arm. She turned to find herself staring into the coal-black eyes of Clay Ferris. All at once it seemed as though her nerves came alive, and for an instant she could not summon the breath to speak. Damn the man, she thought, for the effect he had on her.

With effort, she kept her voice cool as she said, "Captain Ferris, what a surprise. I never expected to meet you here."

He grinned, not at all disconcerted by her tone. "Didn't you? Well, I certainly expected to; I have been waiting for you here since eight this morning."

Analise raised her eyebrows at his words, but said nothing and started for her carriage. The Captain, undaunted, fell in beside her. "Allow me to escort you home, Miss Caldwell."

"Thank you, I have a carriage, and I think our coachman is quite enough protection."

"One old slave in these troubled times?" His voice was low and mocking. "Hardly a fit retinue for a beautiful maiden."

"Please, Captain Ferris, I am not one to be taken in by smooth words."

His hard hand on her arm pulled her to a stop, and she was forced to look up at him. "Then what do you prefer?"

"The truth," Analise said bluntly. "You are an odd man, Captain; you seem out of place."

"I am a stranger to New Orleans," he admitted.

"I think you would be unusual anywhere," Analise said

honestly, and her tone gave her away more than she knew. "Captain Ferris, what do you want with me? Why have you begun this constant pursuit of me?"

For a moment he stood looking down at her without speaking, and Analise saw that his eyes were murky and troubled. "I don't know," he said, his voice almost bleak. "Sometimes I think I should not. You are danger, lady."

"I?" Analise repeated in amazement.

"Yes, you; you are a threat to everything I am." His dark face was harsh, almost bitter, and for a moment he seemed very far away. Then the sharp angles of his face shifted, and he laughed. "You are a threat to any bachelor, ma'am."

"That is not what you meant," Analise accused him, and he shrugged.

They had reached the carriage. Ferris helped her into it, then in one fluid motion pulled himself into it beside her. Analise motioned to Sam to start. After all, what could happen in an open carriage in full view of the people of New Orleans?

"You intrigue me, Miss Caldwell," the Captain said, his dark eyes intent on her face. "Why is that?"

"How am I to explain your intrigues?" Analise countered.

He took her hand in one of his and gently caressed her fingers. "You are lovely. Like fine porcelain or delicate Irish lace. Beautiful, expensive, and protected."

Analise blushed, feeling uncomfortably that he mocked her.

"When I saw you the other night at your party, when I looked across that sea of frilled, beribboned, frivolous females and saw you, I wanted you more than I have ever wanted anything in my life."

She cast him one brief, astonished look, shocked by his boldness, and quickly transferred her gaze to the street outside their carriage. "Please, Captain, you should not speak of such things."

"Why not? You said you wanted honesty. It must be what every man thinks about you. Why not say it openly? I saw your hair, black as night, and the proud way you hold your head; I saw your eyes like sapphires and the sweet swell of your breasts. And I wanted you in my bed so badly that it made me ache."

Analise knew that she should stop the carriage and order him out of her sight forever for the improper things he had said, but his words ran like liquid fire through her, and she knew she did not want to cut him off.

"Captain Ferris, you are mad," she said breathlessly.

"Because I feel such things? Or because I have the nerve to admit them?"

"No one has ever spoken to me like that. I ought—" she broke off, confused, trapped by his fiery dark gaze.

"You ought to what? Toss me out? That would be good form, no doubt. But you are different, aren't you? That is what makes you so dangerous. I fear I am falling in love with you, and that would ruin all my plans."

The air was stifling suddenly, and Analise could hardly breathe; his eyes were magnetic, drawing her to him, until she felt her very soul might be swallowed up in them.

"Analise." His grip on her hand was steely, and there was a low, almost desperate quality to his voice. "Don't go home yet. Drive with me a while. I want—to know about you, everything about you. I want to talk to you, laugh and tell stories, gossip—I don't care what. I want to be with you alone."

For a moment Analise paused, torn by indecision. She should go home; she should not be alone with this man. She should. She should . . . Fiercely she swung and called to Sam, "No, don't go home yet, Sam. I have promised to show Captain Ferris the sights of New Orleans. Drive through the Vieux Carré and up Esplanade Avenue."

She turned back to Ferris and met his blazing smile with one of her own. They began to talk then, Analise for the first time she could remember freely telling a man of her interests, talking about her maps and crops, her plantation books and household books, her budgets, her tussles with the merchants. He watched her, his black eyes alight with interest, and now and then encouraged her with a laugh or teasing remark. Once she turned as she spoke and surprised a peculiar look of pain and affection and, yes, remorse, too, on his face, which vanished as soon as she saw it.

It was then that her flow of words at last was stemmed; suddenly she felt confused and shy. They had reached the old Bienville estate, and she called to Sam to drive to the Dueling Oaks. She pointed out the oak trees where young Creole aristocrats through the years had come to settle their points of honor in a bloody way.

"Earlier, they used to meet in St. Anthony's Garden, behind the Cathedral. I guess the Oaks are less sacrilegious, at least. And would you like to see the Suicide Oak?"

He smiled lazily. "But of course. These trees seem to have a wicked history."

"Oh, yes," her eyes twinkled as she spoke. "But aren't they beautiful?" She leaned back to look at the great spreading trees, their branches dripping silver-gray, feathery moss. Then Sam stopped, and Analise walked with

Ferris over to the huge, splitting tree, its low, thick branches gnarled grotesquely.

"It looks aptly named," he joked, and Analise nodded. "It looks like evil was done here, doesn't it? The legend is that a young man hanged himself from one of these branches."

Ferris turned to look at her, and the flicker in his eyes reminded Analise uncomfortably that the low-hanging branches hid them from the view of the carriage. Slowly his hard eyes explored her body, lingering over the soft curves, and Analise found it oddly exciting. None of her suitors' soft compliments had the honesty and elemental impact of his frank, hungry gaze. Somehow this fierce, dark man awakened the wantonness in her that no other man had touched. He was wild and dangerous; she could feel that clearly, and something in her told her to flee, but something stronger held her, some matching wildness that rose up in her to meet his.

Ferris, watching her, saw the change in her face and the answering spark in her eyes. It made his breath come short and quick. "Analise," he breathed and went to her.

Without thought or plan, she stepped forward to meet him, and he swept her into his arms. Hungrily his lips descended on hers, pressing into them, opening them to his demanding tongue. Analise melted into him, weak and breathless from the force of his passion; shyly, tentatively, her tongue answered his.

A tremor shook him at her response, and he wrapped his arms around her even more tightly, as if he would meld her into his own flesh. For a moment, they were aware of nothing but their intense, driving need for each other. Then one of the waiting horses stamped, making the harness jingle, and the sound whipped through Analise like a shot. Hastily she tore away from Ferris' grasp, and they stood facing each other for an instant. Then Clay held out his hand and rigidly escorted her back to the carriage.

As they rode back down Esplanade Avenue, Analise kept up a busy chatter. "This is where all the wealthy Creole families are moving. I am afraid the French Quarter is rapidly losing ground. Only the families who are too bound by tradition stay there, or the ones that lack the money to move." That was the category her friend Pauline's family fit into, too strapped for money to leave their pale, lovely, iron-trimmed house in the decaying Vieux Carré, too proud to work for a living. "And now we are going back into the Quarter. It lies between Esplanade and the Garden District, where I live. That is the American side; once there was a tremendous rivalry between the two. Esplanade Avenue was the answer to the Americans' big, brash houses. Of course, it is not so segregated now. My father is American, and Mama is Creole; so you can see they are not so far apart any more. There is the convent, where I went to school. And legend has it that here was a tavern where Jean Lafitte himself once met his cronies."

Laughing a little, Ferris took her hand. "Wait, slow down; you do not need to keep me away with words. I promise you I shall not intrude upon you again."

She blushed, and her dark blue eyes searched his face. "Who are you, Clay?"

He frowned and again that murky look covered his eyes. "I? Why, I told you: I am a planter from Savannah."

"But surely not always. There is something so—I don't know—hard, I guess, about you."

He paused and looked away from her, and when he

spoke, his voice was brittle and light. "Oh, yes, I have done other things. I was born to the role of a planter, but when I grew up, I chased my fortune all over the world. Let's see, I hunted for gold in California; I dabbled in the Oriental drug trade; I fought in the army of a Chinese war lord and once for a prince of a small Serbian country. I gambled in the resorts of Europe, and I even once managed a Ceylon tea plantation."

Analise stared at him, fascinated, a little frightened; at last she said, "And why did you return home?"

He turned to her, his face set and blank, a gray bleakness in his eyes. "I have found that you cannot escape your birth."

Analise frowned, and then he said, his voice low and harsh, "I am as dangerous for you as you are for me, Analise. Perhaps it would be best if we do not see each other again."

Now her eyes widened at the rebuff, and she choked back the tears that rose in her throat. Sam pulled up in front of the graceful, pastel Caldwell house, and quickly Analise scrambled down from the carriage, before Ferris could move to assist her. Almost running, she opened the low wrought-iron gate and went down the walk to the spacious, airy house. Behind her, the Confederate soldier got out of the carriage and stood watching her. When she closed the door firmly after her, without once looking back at him, Ferris turned and, tossing a casual tip to the coachman, strode off at a rapid pace.

Three

In the solemn hush of midnight, a dark figure moved along the low iron fence of the Caldwell house, then paused in the encompassing shadow of a magnolia tree to look up at the dark structure. The flowers were beginning to come out, and the heavy night air was redolent of the lush, blooming vegetation. How like Savannah it was . . . he had almost forgotten that ripe, sensual smell of riotous flowers.

He remembered countless nights of lying on his bed beneath the mosquito netting, the humid air pressing like a weight upon his chest, and the thick smell of honeysuckle hanging over everything, hearing his mother's laugh, tinkling and clear as crystal, floating up in the hushed night from her bedroom below. Then would come the lower rumble of a masculine voice, soft and slow and Southern. The boy he was then would clench his hands in futile anger, knowing it was wrong, wicked, that it was this that had driven away his father. His chest would swell with tears, and he wanted to have his father's crisp, nasal New York accent back again. But at the same time, he was intrigued, fascinated by what went on below, and his blood would race as he tried to envision what transpired between his mother and her latest lover. He wanted to feel it, too, was drawn by the lush, seductive world, even as he railed against her for being lured by it. Thalissia. Beautiful, sensual Thalissia Ferris Schaeffer. He had never met a woman who equaled her beauty—until Analise.

With an angry shake of his head, Mark Schaeffer ejected that thought from his mind and stealthily stepped over the low fence. Cautiously he crept down the side garden, blending in with the shadows, still as the night. At the party here the other evening, he had gotten a fair idea of the layout of the place; like most houses in this humid climate, it was built for ventilation, with covered porches on three sides, a wide central hallway, and an enclosed breezeway running the length of the back. Every outside wall contained a bank of narrow, shuttered doors that could be opened to admit the maximum possible breeze. The parlor and dining room lay on the right and on the left was the ballroom; behind it were two cubbyholes of offices. The slaves slept in separate quarters on the back of the lot, and the second floor was where the members of the family slept.

He moved from the cover of the trees and swung himself lightly over the rail of the verandah. Softly he went to the doors of the first office; the shutters were closed, but the doors behind them stood open. He pulled back a shutter and slipped in, waiting in the dark for his eyes to adjust to the moonless room. Gradually he saw a small desk and chair; they seemed rather feminine, and he decided that this must be where Analise did her work. He gave a cursory glance to the bookshelves and papers; this was not what he wanted.

Cautiously, Schaeffer opened the door into the inner

hallway, listened a moment for sounds, and then glided down the hall to the second office. It was locked. That was the one he wanted, the one where the plans would be, safely locked away from prying eyes. Mark went down on one knee and pulled a tiny tool from his inside coat pocket and set about jimmying the lock. It was an old lock, not built to withstand much pressure, and it broke easily. Letting out a pent-up breath, Mark pocketed the tool and entered the study, softly closing the door behind him.

Here he had to light a candle, praying that the closed wooden shutters would conceal the glow. Then slowly, methodically, despite his stomach churning with tension, he began to explore the room. The desk was littered with papers, which Mark quickly rifled through. None related to torpedoes. The drawers of the desk were locked, but again he broke the fragile lock and searched the drawers; his efforts were fruitless.

Schaeffer straightened and glanced around the room. Two walls were lined with books; one wall consisted of the verandah doors; and against one wall stood a row of wooden cabinets. Mark went to one and opened it; inside in neat rows stood a number of long rolls of paper that resembled rolled maps. Eagerly Mark pulled one out and unrolled it; it was a drawing of some sort of pulp-crushing device, an invention for squeezing sugarcane, no doubt. His heart began to thud; he was finally getting close. Mark closed the door and looked at the other cabinets; the one at the north end was locked. Almost shaking in his haste and excitement, he pried open the lock. Inside lay several similar rolls. The first one was a drawing of an ironclad boat and the next seemed to be a vehicle that operated underwater. Vexed, Mark pulled out another roll. As he undid it, a smaller paper fell out of it, and Mark picked it up and glanced at it. It was a map in great detail of the Mississippi River below New Orleans. There were two X's at points about thirty yards apart. Written in one corner of the map were the words: "giv'n me by Col. Chalmers 2/24/62—loc. of my weapons."

Heart pounding, Mark unrolled the larger scroll. There, in John Caldwell's hand, were the blueprints for the torpedoes that could mean failure to the Union's plans to gain New Orleans. The torpedoes that protected the gateway to the Mississippi River. The torpedoes he had been sent to destroy.

Schaeffer longed to sit down and study the plans, but he knew he could not press his luck. The longer he stayed here with a light burning, the greater were his chances of discovery. So he folded both papers up as small as possible and tucked them inside his coat. He blew out the candle and left the room, then paused in the hall.

His thoughts flew to Analise, no doubt lying safely asleep in her room upstairs, and he wanted desperately to take one last look at her. It was insane, he knew, and increased his chances of getting caught, but reason held little sway where Analise was concerned.

Damn that girl. Never in his wildest dreams had he imagined that this might happen to him. Since he had left his mother's home at fifteen and joined his father in New York, Mark Schaeffer had despised Southerners: man, woman, and child. He hated the superficial code of honor beneath which lurked the dark cruelty of slavery; he hated the lying, faithless women, like his mother. He had joined the Union army gladly when Secession came; nothing would please him as much as defeating those stiff-necked Southerners and abolishing the malignancy of slavery. Of course, he had managed to get in a tangle with his Major over the Major's wife, and had been exiled to Ship Island, below New Orleans. In that remote spot, he had been given the greatest opportunity of the war: to enter New Orleans secretly, disguised as a Confederate, and discover the plans and location of the torpedoes it was rumored the Rebels had built, then destroy them. It was with inner amusement that he had chosen his middle name Clayton and his mother's maiden name Ferris for his Confederate alter ego.

At the inception, the inventor's daughter had been part of the plan. He was to woo her and win her, in his usual cavalier way, and gain entry to her house, then persuade her or her father to reveal the plans. Caldwell had proved infuriatingly close-mouthed about his military inventions, and Analise . . . Analise had turned his world upside down. He had fallen in love with her. He, Mark Schaeffer, exiled, Southern-hating, Union captain, had fallen in love with a New Orleans belle.

He closed his eyes against the pain. Dear God, what would she think of him when they discovered what had happened? She was bound to put two and two together and realize that the Georgian Clay Ferris was an imposter and that she had been deceived. She would hate him.

His gaze crept involuntarily to the stairs. Sweet Jesus, he would have done anything in the world for her, he thought, except this: he could not turn his back on the Union and let their entry to New Orleans be a bloody one, just because he had foolishly fallen in love.

He had taken many women casually, coolly, but he had

not thought it was in him to love a woman. And now he wished he did not. Once he had planned to make love to her, to gain entry to the office by using her. He had not been able to hurt her that way; instead he had taken the more dangerous way, breaking into the study at night. And here he was, wanting to endanger his mission even more by slipping upstairs for one last, longing look at her.

Mark turned away from the staircase, then froze at the soft sound at the top of the stairs. He looked up, and there stood Analise, her eyes wide with fright, her black hair loose upon her shoulders, her thin nightgown billowing in the slight breeze.

For an instant they stared at each other in mutual consternation. Mark's stomach seemed to hit the floor; there was no reason in the world for him to be here in the middle of the night. She would know; she would figure it out, and rouse everyone.

Analise raised one finger to her lips to indicate silence, then slipped softly down the stairs, and, taking his hand, pulled him into her office. She closed the door and turned to him, her voice a stage whisper, "What on earth are you doing here?"

Mark's throat felt as dry as dust; his lie had better be good this time—it was worth his life. "I wanted to see you. What I said this afternoon about not seeing you again— well, I was frightened of the way I felt about you. Then I realized that I could not bear to not see you again." Mark looked down at the floor, avoiding her clear blue eyes. He despised himself for the way he was using the beautiful truth of his feeling for her to cover his lies. Yet, he knew he had to; for the one ideal he had held in his life, he had to get away from this house without detection and get to the torpedoes.

He raised his head and looked at her. "I want you," he said simply and told himself there was no lie in that. Seeing her in her soft, clinging nightgown, her breasts thrusting proudly against the flimsy material, he felt passion tightening his loins.

Analise stared at him, her eyes wide, her lips softly parted. His hot black eyes held her, mesmerized her; she could hardly breathe, let alone think. He reached out and took her hand, pulling her to him, and his mouth fastened on hers with sweet domination. Eagerly, honestly, she returned his kiss, and Mark groaned softly with pleasure. He tore his lips from hers and began to kiss her face and ears and neck; his soft exploring lips sent tingling waves of pleasure through her. Pressing his body into her, he trailed fiery kisses down her neck to the soft swell of her breasts above the neck of her gown.

"Oh, Clay, Clay," she murmured, her voice warm with passion, and Mark recoiled inside at her loving use of that name; desperately he wished that it was his real name she was using.

He stopped her words with a kiss, and his hands moved over her body, cupping and caressing her breasts, sliding down her stomach and around her back. With shaking fingers, he fumbled at the buttons of her nightgown, opening it to reveal her naked breasts. Gently he squeezed her breast and teased the nipple to hardness with his fingers. A low moan escaped her throat at his intimate touch. Mark looked at her: her head was flung back, her eyes closed in pleasure, the soft throb of her racing pulse in her throat, her full, rose-tipped breasts washed with moonlight streaming through the doors. Just the sight of her made him throb with desire.

"I want you," he repeated, his voice thick with passion.

Analise opened her eyes and looked at him, luminous and proud, making no attempt to cover her naked breasts. She knew she should feel shame at the way he looked at her, his hot black eyes devouring her body, his mouth heavy with desire, but she did not. She was conscious only of pride in her body and its ability to stir him. In that one blazing moment it came to her: She loved him and wanted him, as he did her.

"I love you," she whispered, and Mark swept her to him, kissing her deeply, passionately.

"Let me," he murmured, his breath hot and panting. "Let me make love to you."

"Yes, oh, yes," she responded, past thinking or caring, knowing only her love, her desire.

He pulled her nightgown from her body and studied her, his eyes roaming the delicious swells and curves of her figure. Then, swiftly, he began to disrobe.

Analise watched him, admiring the graceful economy of his movements as he stripped off his shirt and boots and trousers. She stared, intrigued, at his lean brown body; he was trim and spare, like his movements, but muscular and hard. Something tightened in her loins as her eyes traveled down him, taking in the V of black, curling hair on his chest, the long white scar that curled around his lower ribs, the flat, hard abdomen with its trail of hair plowing down inexorably to that place where she most longed to look and yet dared not.

His chuckle was warm and loving, and he said, his voice vibrant with desire, "Go on, it's all right for you to look.

I want you to know me as much as I want to know you."

Cautiously Analise let her eyes stray to that most forbidden place, where his manhood hung, engorged and stiff with his passion for her. She gulped and quickly glanced away, but something jumped inside her, causing a curious compelling ache between her legs, and almost involuntarily her gaze returned to his swollen shaft. How massive it was, how frightening—and yet, she realized in astonishment, she yearned to feel its force.

Mark's breath hissed out of him and he said in a choked voice, "Enough; I cannot bear it any more."

He pulled her down with him onto the thick rug and began to kiss her again. His mouth slid lower, trailing hot kisses across her neck and chest, while his hand crept down her abdomen and between her legs, teasing them open. Gently his fingers explored her, probing and caressing the hidden well-spring of her femininity, turning her aflame. His mouth claimed her breast, suckling her nipple to a taut point of pleasure.

A moan escaped her, and Analise began to run her hands over Mark's body, pulling him against her, digging her fingers into his skin.

"Oh, Clay, please, Clay," she whispered, her voice throbbing.

Stirred past reason, he rolled on top of her, shoving her legs apart and pushing the staff of his love into her. Analise felt a sharp stab of pain and then a glorious satisfaction as he filled her. Her brief cry of startled pain turned to a muffled, fulfilled groan, and the sound sent desire pulsing through Mark. He began to move within her, driving into her with all the wild force of his need. Analise wrapped her legs around him, tingles of pain submerging in the deep waves of pleasure coursing through her. Never had she felt such intense, mind-numbing delight as now, as his sweating body strained against her. Something raw and elemental built up in her, growing with each thrust, until at last she reached the peak and passion rocked her, shaking her body with spasms of pleasure. At her involuntary movement, Mark shuddered and cried out, then collapsed against her.

They lay entangled, satiated and drenched with sweat, stunned by the primitive, abandoned passion they had shared.

"I love you," Analise murmured.

"And I love you," Mark answered huskily, rubbing his cheek against her hair. "Always remember that—I love you."

For a moment Mark closed his eyes and wished that he did not have to move, that he could just stay here like this with Analise and revel in the love they shared. Then, with a sigh, he kissed Analise lightly on the mouth and sat up.

"I must go," he said and she smiled at him, her eyes soft and shining.

"Yes," she agreed, "someone might come down any time."

He dressed swiftly, keeping his head turned so that he could not see the trusting glow of love in her eyes. Surreptitiously he felt in his coat pocket for the maps, then turned back to Analise. She had risen and now stood before him, her body gleaming palely in the moonlight. Mark swallowed the lump rising in his throat and pulled her to him in one last, bone-crushing embrace.

"I love you," he whispered again, his voice shaking with

emotion, and then swiftly he released her and slipped through the narrow door onto the verandah.

Analise followed him to the door and watched as he swung lithely across the porch railing and vanished into the dark shadows of the garden. A soft smile playing on her lips, she drew her nightgown on over her head and softly crept back up to her room.

Hazy and limp with lovemaking, she crawled into her bed and fell quickly asleep. Once, in the middle of the night, a distant noise awoke her and she blinked, her mind groping groggily for what had brought her to consciousness. Then, again it came, a muffled boom, and she frowned, but her sleepy mind refused to grasp it and she slipped gently back into her dreams.

Four

Analise awakened slowly and looked around; she felt different, confused; everything looked the same, and yet . . . With a start she remembered and blushed. Clay had been here last night; the warm, male scent of him still clung to her skin.

She folded her hands behind her head and dreamily contemplated the ceiling. Lingeringly, she went over the previous night, remembering every word, each kiss and caress. She thought of his slender, muscular body, the way it had felt beneath her hands and the delicious weight of it against her own body. The memories stirred her passion and she smiled, wondering when she would see him again. Surely he would come to call on her this afternoon, and they could make arrangements to meet again tonight. No longer did she feel any fear, only eagerness. Their love was too great, too powerful, for fear or convention. No doubt her mother would swoon if she knew what Analise had done. But Analise felt no guilt: she and Clay Ferris were two of a kind, different from the others, stranger, bolder, not shackled by society. No doubt they would marry later, but right now that did not matter—all that really mattered was the wonder and glory of their love and the beautiful, shattering expression of it.

Her thoughts were interrupted by a gentle tap on the door. May, her maid, glided in, balancing a small tray on one hand.

"Morning, Miss Analise; I've got your coffee and beignets here."

"You mean what passes for coffee now," Analise said with a grimace, but her tone was too light and happy to express real distaste.

"Yes'm," the black woman said noncommittally, setting the tray on her bedside.

"Isn't it a beautiful morning, May?"

"My, you're in a good mood this morning, Miss Analise. You thinking about that handsome Captain Ferris?"

Analise giggled. "Nothing gets past you, does it, May?"

"No, ma'am, not when a gentleman comes calling on you with that look in his eyes, it don't. And it ain't hard to see the look in your eyes, neither."

Analise smiled secretively and changed the subject. "What was that noise I heard last night? That big boom. It awakened me."

"There was two of them, miss. Some things in the river blew up."

" 'Some things in the river?' " Analise repeated, mystified. "What do you mean? A boat?"

"No, ma'am, not a boat. Just something in the water."

Analise frowned and shrugged. It did not make much sense, but obviously there was nothing more to be had from the slave grapevine. She would have to wait until her afternoon calls to find out.

She did not have to wait that long. Shortly after she

dressed and went downstairs, the butler announced the arrival of Colonel Dumare.

"Who?" Analise asked.

"I don't know him, Miss Analise. But he says it's urgent that he speak to you."

"All right, show him in," Analise said and waited curiously.

A small, dark man dressed in the gray uniform of a Confederate Colonel entered the parlor on the butler's heels.

"Colonel Dumare, ma'am," the butler intoned and left the room.

"Miss Caldwell, I am most sorry to disturb you, but I am afraid this matter is too important to wait. Do you have any knowledge of the whereabouts of Captain Clayton Ferris?"

"Clay!" Analise repeated, stunned. "What on earth—"

"Miss Caldwell, this is extremely important. Last night the torpedoes in the river—your father's torpedoes—were set off and destroyed."

"So that was the sound I heard. But how? Who—?"

"We have reasons to believe that it was Clayton Ferris."

"You must be insane!" Analise exclaimed, springing to her feet. "Why on earth would Clay Ferris set off the torpedoes?"

The man swallowed. This would be a difficult thing to say. It was obvious from her stance and the angry glint of her blue eyes that the girl was outraged; apparently she was quite taken by the imposter Ferris.

"Ma'am, from information we have received, we have reason to believe that Captain Ferris is a Yankee spy and saboteur."

Analise stared at him, too stunned and angry to speak.

Dumare hurried on. "You see, Lieutenant Daniels, who has cousins in Savannah, met Captain Ferris a few days ago. He became rather suspicious because he has visited his cousins often and knows many Ferrises there, but none is named Clayton. He talked to his mother about it, and she, who is originally from Savannah, was convinced that there was no Clay Ferris."

"As if one woman knew every resident of Savannah!" Analise scoffed.

"It made us suspicious enough to telegraph Georgia, seeking information on the man. He claimed to be from the Fourth Georgia Cavalry, but Georgia telegraphed us that there is no Clayton Ferris in the Fourth Georgia Cavalry."

"Oh, fiddle!" Analise snapped. "An error in their records. You know as well as I do that our army records are sloppy and incomplete."

"You may have a point," the Colonel said evenly, "if it were not for the fact that Captain Ferris has disappeared."

"Disappeared?" Analise repeated dazedly.

"He never returned to his quarters last night."

Analise's brain whirled. She knew where Clay had been part of the night, but after he left her, where had he gone? Why had he not gone back to his rooms?

But staunchly she came to his defense. "Have you never heard of a gentleman staying out all night drinking and playing cards—or following other, less mentionable pursuits? Besides, even if he were using a false name, why should that brand him a saboteur?"

"Because," he said pointedly, meeting Analise's fierce

glare straight on, "ever since the man came to town he has been showing an unmistakable interest in the daughter of the inventor of the torpedoes."

Her stomach lurched, but Analise replied steadily, "And you think a man's only reason for courting me would be to get at my father's torpedoes?"

"Hardly. However, courting one's daughter is certainly a safe way to gain access to one's house. Tell me, Miss Caldwell, where are your father's plans kept?"

"In his study."

"Would you mind checking to see if by chance anything is missing from his study?"

Raising her eyebrows, Analise said, "Certainly not."

Stiffly, she turned and went down the hall to her father's study, a cold anger burning inside her. How dare they accuse Clay? It was absurd—the very idea that he had said he loved her and pursued her just to worm her father's plans from her! She was hardly some dried-up old spinster without any other attractions for a man. That business about the name was all very odd, of course, but she was sure there was some reasonable explanation for it. She knew that Clay had not lied to her.

Analise reached the door of his study and turned the handle to show that it was firmly locked. She gasped as the door opened easily, and snatched her hand back as if it had been burned. Dumare knelt and examined the lock; he said nothing, merely pointed out the scratches around the keyhole. Analise pushed past him and ran into the room, straight for the one locked cabinet. She stopped stock still and stared at the cabinet door: the lock was clearly broken.

Her mouth felt as dry as dust. Dreading it, knowing what she would find, she reached out and opened the cabinet. One by one, she unrolled the drawings and let them drop to the floor; the sketch of the torpedoes was not there. Slowly she turned to face the Colonel, shock and pain stamped plainly on her face.

"They're gone. The plans are gone—and the map, too," her voice came out hoarsely.

Dumare felt a wave of pity. It was obvious from her face that she felt more than wounded pride. Clearly she had cared deeply for the scoundrel—and trusted him completely.

"Your father had a map, then, showing their location?" he asked.

"Yes, the officer who placed them gave him a map; they are good friends, I believe. My father was very interested in the actual utilization of the weapons," she replied, her voice dull.

"Miss Caldwell, do you have any idea where Ferris might be?"

She looked at him, her blue eyes cold and bleak. "No. I imagine he must have escaped."

"Well, thank you, ma'am. I am sorry to have disturbed you. I shall take my leave now."

The Colonel bowed and left. Analise closed her eyes and leaned weakly against the cool, smooth wood of the cabinet. Clay Ferris had stolen the plans to the torpedoes. No—that was not even his real name. She had thought he loved her, but he had not even told her his true name. The man she loved did not really exist. In his place was just a cold, lying Yankee spy.

Dear God, he had lied! Lied about everything. It all slid into place now with a sickening logic: his swift avowal of love for her, the questions he had asked her father about his inventions, even his presence in the house last night! No doubt she had surprised him just as he was making his escape with the plans.

Hot tears of shame rushed to her eyes as she remembered the things she had said and done last night, foolishly certain of their love, and all the while he had been coldly, calculatedly deceiving her, using her love and gullibility to make his escape. No wonder he had not been repelled on their ride through the city when she talked of her interest in business and plantations. He would not have been deterred in his courtship if she had had green hair and crossed eyes!

Pain tore through her chest, and Analise felt as though her heart must break from the anguish of it. Clay did not love her. Clay did not even really exist. Sobs wracked her body, and she leaned against the cool wood of the cabinet, crying helplessly, hopelessly.

Rumors spread through New Orleans like wildfire, and it did not take long for everyone to be gossiping about the mysterious disappearance of Clay Ferris on the same night that the torpedoes in the river had been destroyed. Nor was anyone reluctant to surmise that his assiduous attention to Analise Caldwell had been a ruse to get the plans of her father's torpedoes. And, as if all that was not juicy enough, the beautiful Analise was so wan and listless, so reluctant to talk about the whole matter, that it was obvious she had fallen in love with the man. Imagine that: the proud, beautiful, vain Miss Caldwell, who had the hearts of half the men in New Orleans in her hands and who returned no one's affections, had fallen in love with a spy who was merely using her to get her father's secrets.

It was poetic justice, some men who had pursued her so hopelessly said. Belles who had been outshined by her talked with relish of her comeuppance. Becky Oldway, like many others, came to offer Analise consolation, but she did so with such an arch expression and amused gleam in her eye that Analise longed to slap her smug face.

Predictably, when Emil heard the news, he came storming into Analise's room, his handsome face thunderous. "The blackguard," he snapped in the thin, tense voice of real anger. "The traitor."

"Not to his own country," Analise said with a smile, trying to deflect Emil's wrath. She did not really want to discuss with him a subject so painful to her.

"Perhaps not, but he is a scoundrel, all the same." Emil was not to be sidetracked. "To put you in such a position, to make your name available to all the scandalmongers—it is unforgivable."

"What does it matter, Emil?" Analise said wearily. "There are worse things."

Emil looked at her, his face a little shocked. "I suppose so. He could have—had his way with you and left you to face the scandal. But don't you see? That is what people will whisper: that you succumbed to him. Particularly since you have taken to being such a recluse. You must not, you know; you need to face everyone, show them how little this thing has affected you."

Tears brimmed in her eyes and she turned her face up to her brother. "But, Emil, it has affected me. You see: I fell in love with him."

He stared at her, aghast. "You can't mean it. But you knew him such a short time." Analise shrugged and he paused, nonplussed, for a moment, then picked up again,

"Well, even so, you must pretend. You don't dare let them know how you felt about him."

"Why? What does it matter? What do I care what they think?" Analise exclaimed heatedly. "You are just like Mama. All she cares about is the 'family name,' as if my feelings were of no importance! When she heard about it, she merely said to me, 'Well, thank Heavens you did not do anything foolish and fall in love with him, like that poor McCuin girl did with the gambler last year. How her family suffered. I don't think I could ever live that down.' That is all that mattered to her. Well, frankly, I really did not expect anything else from Mama. But you, Emil . . ."

Emil frowned, his eyes puzzled, and suddenly Analise realized that he was like their mother, like everyone, really. Name and reputation were all important here. She sighed and blinked away her tears. It was foolish of her to expect them to be any different; it was she who was the odd one, the one who did not seem to fit any more.

"I am sorry, Emil," she said kindly. "I should not have spoken to you that way; I am afraid my nerves are a little on edge."

"Of course," he smiled and patted her hand sympathetically. Nerves in a female were something he was familiar with and capable of dealing with. "What you need is a quiet little rest. Why don't you just go upstairs and lie down for a few minutes?"

Analise followed his advice, not so much because she agreed that she needed a rest, but because she wanted solitude. No one understood her feelings, except perhaps Pauline, who suffered herself from unrequited love. But even to Pauline she had not revealed how deeply her wound went. She was too ashamed to admit that she had been so deceived by that saboteur that she had given herself to him. It made her burn with humiliation to think how easily she had fallen into his hands, like a ripe plum. No doubt he jested with his Yankee comrades about the easy virtue of his Southern belle, who had responded to his false lovemaking like a bitch in heat. Oh, how she hated him now for his deception! And how she despised herself, for being so easily fooled.

John Caldwell soon decided to precede his family to Belle Terre, where they commonly spent the hot summer months, ostensibly to see that the plantation house was in readiness for their arrival in a month or two. Analise, knowing how little he would notice the state of the house, let alone harry the servants to clean and repair, guessed that he did it just to escape Analise's unhappiness. Her father did not deal well with troubles, and it saddened and frustrated him to see his beloved daughter so unhappy.

Analise did not mind his going; no one was able to bring her much solace these days, it seemed. She only wished that he had taken her mother with him. Theresa's vanity and silliness irritated her now more than ever. Analise took to retreating more and more into her books, even in her mother's presence.

On Good Friday, April 18, as they sat in the ladies' sitting room upstairs, Analise immersed in a book and Theresa luxuriating in a box of chocolates Emil had bought her from a daring blockade-runner, a distant noise disturbed their quiet.

"What was that?" Theresa exclaimed, eyes round with fright, her hand flying dramatically to her heart.

"What was what?" Analise looked up from her book, frowning.

"Good gracious, don't tell me you did not hear it! That strange noise."

There was a faint muffled boom in the distance, and Theresa said triumphantly, "That! There it is again."

Analise shrugged. There followed a muffled rumble. "Thunder," she said and went back to her book.

The noise came again; Mrs. Caldwell strolled out to the verandah and back.

"It can't be thunder," she announced. "There's not a cloud in the sky."

"Well, it sounds a long way off, Mama."

"It is gunfire," Theresa said emphatically. "I am certain of it."

"Gunfire!" Analise snapped. "Why, there isn't any fighting within seven hundred miles of us."

"Nevertheless, I am sure that is what it is. It sounded just like the time that hero, what was his name, sailed into New Orleans, and the guns at Fort Jackson sounded a salute to him. Now what was his name? Do you remember? No, of course, you weren't even born then."

Analise straightened and closed her book. Now that she really listened to it, it did not sound quite like thunder. It was too rhythmical and constant.

"Mama, do you suppose—could the forts be firing on the Yankees? Could the Yankees be trying to sail up the river?"

"Sail up the river?" her mother repeated, her eyes wide and round. "No, don't be silly. They could never get past the forts; surely they would not be foolish enough to try."

"Yankees will try anything," Analise said, bitterness

tinging her voice. She pulled the bellcord, and when a maid appeared at her summons, she said, "Jewel, send a boy to town to find out what that noise is. No, wait, tell Josiah to go; I don't want to get it all garbled and wrong."

"Yes'm," Jewel said and curtsied. For a second, Analise thought there had been a strange look in the black woman's eyes, but she dismissed it. Jewel was just jumpy about the noise too.

Before long, the noise stopped. The silence caught their attention, and the two women looked at each other.

"Now what do you suppose is going on?" Analise asked.

About thirty minutes later, Josiah, the butler, entered the room, and Analise looked up expectantly.

"It's the forts, Miss Analise."

Mrs. Caldwell gasped, her hand flying to her throat. Her daughter ignored her and said. "Are the Yankees trying to pass the forts?"

"No, ma'am, it's the Yankees that are shelling the forts."

"What?"

"Yankee gunboats, Miss Analise, they sailed up and started shelling the forts."

"Thank you, Josiah."

After he left the room, the two women stared at each other. The older woman began to nervously twist her handkerchief.

"What are we to do, Analise?" she cried at last. "Shall we go upriver to the plantation?"

"Don't be so nervous, Mama," Analise said. She felt a thrill of excitement and a touch of her mother's fear as well. But it was the first time any feeling at all had managed to penetrate the dull ache inside her. "They are just shelling the forts; that's a far cry from their entering the city. Why, the forts are way downriver. Besides, the gunfire has stopped already; the forts probably sank the ships."

Her words of reassurance were belied a short time later, when the distant boom started up again. It continued without letup, day and night. The very constancy of the sound was nervewracking. Analise hated to think how horrendous the noise must be inside Fort Jackson and Fort St. Philip. For the first time since the war began, Analise felt real fear of the enemy. Finally, it had become something more than the deprivations of the blockade or the reports of victories on the faraway battlefields of Virginia.

The enemy was suddenly at their gates, steadily pounding away at New Orleans' protecting forts. Could they stand up under this heavy bombardment? What if the Yankees got past the forts? Well, there were the chains across the river and the fortifications at Chalmette, the famed battlefield of General Jackson's victory over the English in 1814. But if the forts could not hold them, how could those smaller fortifications do it? And she remembered Pauline's father once saying scornfully that the chains were too deep to hit the shallow hulls of the Yankee gunboats. What then? There was the vaunted ironclad *Mississippi*—but one ship against so many. Gone were the torpedoes, thanks to Clay Ferris and her infatuation with him. She knew her father's submarine boat was not yet finished. There was little to keep the Yankees from steaming straight upriver to the city's docks. And once they arrived? Well, New Orleans itself had no guns, no fortifications. They could go straight from the ships to the streets of the city. Then the only defense were the soldiers stationed here—fighting in the streets of her city? She could see hordes of blue-coated men charging through Canal Street.

It was wild, insane! Surely it could never happen. And yet—the only thing to stop them was the fort, now under such heavy fire.

Easter Sunday came and went, with the forts still under continuous bombardment. Analise, her mother, and Emil went to Easter Mass at St. Patrick's. There, as at the other churches in the city, the parishioners were anxious and gossipy. The firing was getting on everyone's nerves; and rumors abounded. Some said the Yankee ships had slipped past the forts; others said they had done little damage to the forts and were on the verge of leaving. There were dire warnings of slave uprisings on the river plantations; it was rumored that New Orleans was rife with Yankee saboteurs. Some claimed the soldiers were about to pull out of New Orleans; others swore that Lovell had telegraphed for reinforcements, which were on the way.

As they rode home from Mass, Mrs. Caldwell was babbling in fright. "We must go upriver, Analise. We can't stay here—the Yankees will be upon us any day now. We simply have to get out, get to Belle Terre."

"Mama, don't be hysterical," Analise said firmly. "We don't know anything; all we hear are rumors. What if it is true that the slaves are rising on the plantation? I would sooner face the Yankees here than rebelling slaves at Belle Terre. Wouldn't you?"

"Oh, your poor father. What shall we do?"

"Be sensible, Mama. What could you and I do to protect Papa? He would be a lot better off without us to worry about. Tell her, Emil."

"That's true, Mama. Papa John would not want you to

come there if there is danger. And I forbid it too. You are better off here, where there are soldiers like me to protect you. Besides, it is all poppycock, what they say. The Yankees will never get past the forts."

"If you say so, Emil. But what if the army leaves us? Then what will Analise and I do? I shudder to think of it: all those horrid, savage men, running wild through the streets, looting and killing and—" she stopped, unable to say the dreaded word.

"Raping," Analise said crisply. Suddenly her mind turned to one of those savage, blue-coated men, and she saw him clearly, his thick black hair and scorching black eyes, his angular face and sensual mouth, the subtle power of his body. And she remembered, too, that one sultry impassioned night with him, when a Yankee had had his way with her flesh. But you could not call that rape. No, not rape. Tears stung her eyes; she blinked them away and said flatly, "Hush, Mama, we are not going to run. I will not be a coward. We are staying right here whether New Orleans stands or falls."

A slow, agonizing week dragged by as the heavy bombardment of the forts continued. Analise was beginning to think it would go on forever. It seemed a fitting background to the constant pain inside her.

Few people in New Orleans shared Analise's lethargy. Since 1814 no enemy had threatened them; they were a prosperous, secure people. But now the wolf was at the door, and panic pervaded the town. Many people fled to their plantations early; those without land left to visit relatives in more remote towns. The military lost their general air of gaiety and playing at arms. Soldiers such as Emil, who had heretofore lived in a relaxed atmosphere, quartering at home and drilling now and again for show, were suddenly faced with grim reality. Soon they might have to defend the city, to fight and kill or be killed. For many of the hot-headed young Creoles, the thought was exhilarating; ever since the war began, they had been champing at the bit for some action. However, others, such as the colorful gamblers' companies, unobtrusively disbanded and returned to their homes.

On April 24, a full week after the bombardment began, a sudden quiet filled the air. Analise, who was mending a ruffle in her petticoat, lost the rhythm of her sewing and stabbed her finger. Shaking the sore finger, she looked up and grew still. Something was wrong. The noise had stopped!

She leaped to her feet, her heart thudding furiously. In the silence, there was a heavy ringing in her ears. Her mouth felt dry, and her stomach contracted. What did it mean? What had happened? Had the Yankees retreated or were their gunboats even now gliding smoothly as death toward the city?

Analise ran to the hall and threw on a bonnet and gloves, then hurried out the front door, heedless of convention. She had to know what was going on; she had to find out. Anxiously she hurried down the street until she met a teenaged boy running in the other direction.

"What is it? What's happened?" Her voice sounded strange and cracked to her ears.

"Gunboats, ma'am—they're coming for New Orleans. The Yankee ships just passed the forts!" he cried and ran on.

"No! No, it can't be true!" Analise exclaimed and turned, uncertain what to do.

Suddenly the bells in Christ Church began tolling the alarm, immediately joined by St. Patrick's and First Presbyterian. Analise raised her hands to her ears against the din. No, it couldn't be true. It just couldn't! But why else would the church bells be sounding the alarm? Panic, she told herself, that's all it was. She had to find out the truth.

She picked up her skirts and ran for town. The closer she got to the center, the greater grew the noise and confusion. People milled around with no goal or direction. At Canal Street, Analise had to jump back to keep from being run over by a heavy dray. It was followed by several more, all filled with cotton bales being rushed to the levees. Analise watched in horror. It was all so unreal—the panicked, aimless crowds, the plunging horses, the hoarse cries of the drivers.

"Analise! Analise!"

She whirled at the sound of her name and saw Pauline Beauvais waving to her frantically.

"Pauline!" Analise pushed through the crowd to her friend. "Pauline, what's happening? Is it true?"

Pauline's face was dead white, her eyes wide with fear. "Oh, Analise, it's true; they are coming. The Yankees have passed the forts."

"Are you sure?" Analise gripped her friend's shoulder tightly.

Pauline nodded absolutely. "Cecile Moise told me—you know, the attorney general's daughter. She was with her father when they received the report from the forts."

Analise's mind reeled at her words, and she stepped back. It was true. It was actually happening.

"I must get back to Mama," she said mechanically and turned to run back to her house.

At home, she found everything in a panic. The carriage stood outside their house, and servants scurried everywhere, packing haphazardly. Boxes and trunks were scattered all over, half filled, and her mother stood in the central hall, crying and waving her handkerchief and calling out conflicting orders to the harassed slaves.

"Stop it!" Analise's voice cracked out. "Stop this at once!"

Everyone stopped in mid-motion and stared at her. For a long time Analise had been the authority in the house, but never had they heard her speak with anything other than ladylike quiet.

"But—but, Analise," her mother began to sputter, "the Yankees are coming! Everything is lost! Lost!" Her voice rose hysterically.

"Hush! Just sit down and be quiet. We are going nowhere. Josiah, get everyone here in order, unpack the carriage, and put everything away. We are staying right here." Her voice was crisp and cool, at odds with her fluttering insides. She was frightened, but she knew only one way to deal with things: to meet them head-on. She hated the Yankees and she was not about to run from them; she would stay right here and meet them, head high. And never would she let them know that she was afraid.

"But, Miss Analise, the Yankees are coming," Josiah protested.

"Well, I don't know what you have to fear, Josiah, since their express purpose is to make us bow to an abolitionist government."

"But, Analise—" Theresa wailed.

"Hush, Mama. This is doing no one any good. We are not cowards; we are not going to run. We are going to stay right here and face them."

"Oh, dear, oh, dear." Her mother sat down weakly in a chair. "I wish Emil were here. Where is he?"

"I am sure he is with his troops, as he should be. You forget, Mama, that he is a soldier."

"He should be here. He should be with me," Theresa insisted petulantly, like a child, and Analise could have slapped the woman for her shallow selfishness.

"Mama," she said sternly, "Emil is with his men, where he belongs. He and the other soldiers must defend us, and this is no time to be trying to pull him away from his duty."

Theresa clouded up at her daughter's scolding tone, but Analise ignored the approaching tears and tried again to put some starch in Mrs. Caldwell's backbone. "I am not going to join that panic in the streets. There is no telling what might happen on our way to Belle Terre. For all we know, the slaves may be in revolt, and, frankly, I would rather face the Yankees. Besides, we cannot just leave our house and possessions and the servants to the Yankees."

"I don't care! The darkies can look after themselves; they always do. I can't bear to face the Yankees. I can't and I won't."

Analise sighed. Had her mother always been so callous and superficial, and she just had not noticed? Or had the war, with its deprivations and frights, weakened her character to such a point? Well, it did not matter. Nothing was going to induce Analise to leave now, and it was her the servants would obey. Theresa would just have to learn to live with it.

Under Analise's calming influence, the servants soon

had the house in order again. Theresa went up to her room to indulge in an attack of the vapors, and Analise sat down to take up her mending again. But no matter how successfully she strove to appear calm, her stitches were uneven and her mind ran in circles. Outside in the street she could see the constant movement of people, and it increased her nervousness. Carriages and wagons filled with all kinds of people and goods rolled past. Late in the afternoon, Analise got a whiff of something burning, and she knew she could stand it no longer.

She donned her hat again and joined the crowd on the street, traveling against the current as she moved toward the downtown area. As she drew closer, the crowd became more aimless and grumbling, like a huge, amorphous organism.

Now she could see flames shooting up and black smoke billowing; it seemed to be coming from the docks. When she reached Canal Street, she saw a vision from a nightmare. The bales of cotton, which she had supposed had been piled on the levee as protection for soldiers and guns, were being set on fire. All the products of the plantations—corn, rice, and sugar—that had been piled up so long on the levee had caught the flames. The whole levee, the riches of the South, were ablaze. Looters darted in and out, carrying off in wheelbarrows piles of corn, rice, and sugar that had not yet caught fire, while above and in front of them the orange flames danced. Analise watched, mesmerized; it was like a scene from Dante's *Inferno*.

A rough hand grabbed her arm, and she turned to see the leering face of a strange man. His clothes were ill-fitting and some liquid stained the front of his shirt. His face was pockmarked and needed a shave, and his breath smelled strongly of alcohol.

"Who are you! What do you think you are doing?" Analise tried to pull her arm away.

The man laughed. "Oh, you're a pretty one, all right, and mighty high and fine you are too, aren't you? Well there ain't no rich folks any more, honey, ain't no good names. The Yankees are coming, and pretty soon you'll be in some blue-belly's bed. So there's nothing to stop my having a little fun—"

His hands dug into her arms and he pulled her roughly forward. For a moment, shock held her motionless, but then instinctively she threw up her hands to ward him off and began to struggle. She landed a good blow or two on his face, but she could not deter him. His leering face crept closer and closer, and her stomach turned at the realization that in another moment his mouth would be upon hers.

Suddenly he was gone, flung from her with great force. An angry Creole voice said, "God damn you, how dare you put your filthy hands upon a lady! I ought to shoot you on the spot."

The man scrambled away hastily, all his bravado gone, and Analise turned to thank her rescuer. Surprise flashed across their faces at the same instant.

"Perry Malenceaux!"

"Miss Analise! Whatever are you doing down here?"

"Oh, Perry, I'm so glad to see a normal face. I was beginning to feel the whole world had gone mad. The levee looks like—like purgatory."

"Miss Analise, you better get home; this is no place for you. Lock yourself up in your house; God knows what will happen when we leave."

"When you leave?" Analise repeated stupidly. "What do you mean?"

"Why, we are pulling out. Don't you see?"

Analise looked around her and for the first time noticed that pushing through the crowds was a steady flow of gray-coated soldiers, all moving in the same direction.

"Where are the soldiers going?" Analise asked, her stunned mind unable to take in this final horror.

"To the depot. We are leaving."

"The soldiers? All the soldiers? You mean the army is deserting us?"

Malenceaux blushed at her tone. "Well, not all, just the regular army. General Lovell and the militia will still be here."

Analise stared at him. "But you are leaving us almost entirely without protection!"

He shifted uncomfortably. "I'm sorry, Miss Analise; I wish it were different. When I think of what those devils might do, and all you women and children here—but what else can we do? We can't let the army get trapped and slaughtered here." His face twisted in anguish and disbelief. "Sweet Jesus, I never dreamed they could pass the forts."

The thought of Clay Ferris flashed through her mind: The strong, hard lines of his face, the black, unreadable eyes, the carefully leashed power of his body. She said, "Sometimes I think there is nothing they can't do."

Her former beau sighed and said, "Why don't you go back to Belle Terre, Miss Analise? I think you would be safer there."

Analise gave him a half-hearted smile and said, "No, I think not. Thank you, Perry. Goodbye. Be careful."

Slowly she turned and walked away. With dragging steps she returned to her house, wondering how she would keep her mother from completely dissolving into hysteria. When she reached the house, she found she need not have worried. Emil was there, and Theresa had passed from hysterics into a white-faced shock.

"I presume you have come to say goodbye, Emil," Analise said dully.

"Yes, I am afraid so. We are pulling out immediately. Mama has taken the news rather badly; Analise, please, take good care of her."

For the first time she could remember, Analise saw her brother's face etched with sorrow and frustration. She smiled in reassurance, and led him toward the front door.

"You know me," she said lightly. "I am quite capable of looking after things. Don't worry about us; you just look after your own safety. That is what will most please Mama and me."

His face brightened boyishly, and he said, "Oh, you need not worry about me. I shall be just fine; a Yankee bullet hasn't been made that can harm me. Just you wait, we'll be back. You will see. We shall wait for reinforcements, and then we will come back and storm New Orleans. We will regain it within a month."

Analise smiled a little sadly. Poor Emil, he really did not know; he thought he and the South were invincible. But if the army could not even defend New Orleans, what hope did they have of routing the entrenched Union troops? She knew, with calm, despairing certainty, that New Orleans was lost forever.

"I shall look for you then," she said lightly; there was

no point in letting her pessimism cloud his outlook. "Take care, big brother."

He smiled gaily. "Take care, little sister."

It was all a game to them, Analise thought bitterly, watching him walk down the sidewalk. He was actually happy to be going, hoping to get a chance to fight. For him and all men, it was just a game: war, spying, sabotage. North or South, Emil or Clay Ferris, it meant nothing to them. It was they who played and the women who got hurt. Her brother smiled and went off to shoot at the man she loved, while her entire world crumbled around her.

Analise swallowed and pulled herself upright. She closed and locked the door, then dragged herself wearily upstairs to her bedroom. She felt exhausted, almost too tired to undress and tumble into bed, although that was all she longed to do. Instead she went out onto the verandah and trailed slowly along it, stopping at the corner and resting her cheek against the cool wrought-iron column.

Her gaze drifted toward the river. She could not see it from here, but she knew it lay beyond the houses, still and silent like a giant serpent. Somewhere down that river lay the Yankee ships, waiting in the dark, gathering for their final spring tomorrow. The wolf was at the door. She wondered if Clay had left for some other deceitful mission, gone to break another poor girl's heart to get another secret for his army.

Or had he stayed? Was he lying out there on one of those ships, waiting to seize New Orleans? She wondered if she had vanished from his thoughts entirely, gone and forgotten. Or did he sometimes think of her as he lay upon his narrow army bed?

She blinked away the tears and turned back toward her room.

The next morning, Theresa Caldwell chose to keep to her bed all day to express her complete disapproval of the whole thing. Analise made no effort to urge her to rise. Things were much easier without her fluttering around, making silly demands and swooning.

Suddenly, the sound of gunfire ripped through the air, and Analise dropped her pen, sending ink splattering all over the page of her account book. It took her a moment to realize that it was not the sound of rifles in the street, but heavier gunfire. It had to be the fortifications at Chalmette. That meant the Yankee ships had started upriver again.

Quickly she tied on a hat and left the house for the levee. She was becoming quite used to venturing forth on the street by herself, and she found she enjoyed it. Analise hurried down to the levee, where crowds of people stood watching the river, considerably more subdued than they had been the previous day. Blackened remains of the burned crops lay on the levee, their charred smell still tainting the air. The ships in the harbor had been set afire too; some still blazed.

"There they are!" the excited whisper spread through the tense crowd.

Analise looked downriver to see the Federal ships gliding ominously into view around Slaughterhouse Point. There was a gasp from the crowd, and she swung to see the ironclad *Mississippi*, the hope of New Orleans, float past them ablaze. Useless against the number of enemy ships, it had been destroyed to keep it from falling into Yankee hands. Tears of frustration stung Analise's eyes. The Confederates had failed miserably. Why had they relied so heavily on the protection of their forts? Why had no real defense of New Orleans been set up? Even had the torpedoes not been destroyed, they would not have saved the city. They could have hurt the enemy, but not crippled it; only if there had been some sort of navy to oppose the Yankees as well could the torpedoes have made much difference.

Now she watched the ships come like doom toward the city. Stubbornly she stayed until the ships came to a halt, dropping anchor in front of New Orleans. Softly it began to rain. Analise stared in horror at the sight. Enemy ships in their harbor. It had been a long time since she had seen the candy-striped flag that hung limp in the rain from the ships' masts. With a choked sob, she turned and went home.

It was not until the next day, when Pauline came to visit, that she heard what had happened the rest of the day, while she remained shut up in the house.

"Well, some of their officers came ashore," Pauline said, recounting the eyewitness account of her twelve-year-old Cousin Henri. "You can imagine how the crowd reacted to them—calling out threats, hissing and spitting. Henri said that he thought at any moment the crowd would fall upon them and tear them limb from limb. He said that never had he seen a group of soldiers so brave. And one of them was a dark, cold man, who Henri thought looked like—" Suddenly she bit off her words and flushed.

Analise said nothing, only looked away. So he was here. He had remained with the troops and now came to gloat over their defeat. Brave? Oh, yes, certainly he was; she did not doubt his courage. He would be perfect for the job of demanding surrender: brave and totally without compassion.

"Anyway, they marched to City Hall and demanded that we surrender. Well, of course it was refused. In the meantime, the mob outside had grown so large and angry that the Yankees had to be sneaked out the back way and escorted by some of General Lovell's soldiers, for their own safety."

"Do you think we will surrender?"

"I can't see how we can keep from it."

"There are advertisements in the newspapers for volunteers to board the ships and fight them."

Pauline laughed shortly. "Well, asking for volunteers is one thing, but getting them is something else entirely. Who would go? There's no one left but old men, boys, and scoundrels."

Analise sighed. "No doubt you are right."

Pauline's prediction did, indeed, turn out to be true. No volunteers boarded the ships. General Lovell decided to pull out his troops, and the last fragment of protection for New Orleans was gone. Despair hung over the city like a pall. Surrender seemed inevitable. The only hope lay from the forts, which the Union navy had bypassed but not conquered. Some people rested their hopes on the soldiers of the forts marching to New Orleans' rescue.

Analise was not so naive. Obviously, it was all the fort soldiers could do to keep the enemy at bay. They could not possibly break loose and save New Orleans. They were doomed. Deep down, Analise could hardly believe it. Never since the war began had she dreamed that this could happen. Innocently she had believed that the blockade was the worst that could happen. But now they were about to be conquered. God only knew what would happen to them then. In ancient times, they would have been enslaved. Briefly her mind held an image of herself, bound hand and foot, standing naked before a leering crowd, watching as a dark, fierce, cold-faced man bid on her. She shivered, not knowing whether from fear or anticipation.

Would he come to her? Sternly she thrust back the idea she had been striving so hard to suppress, but it popped back into her head. Would he come and claim the dues of a conqueror? Take her as his property, his particular spoils of war? Even as she vowed that she would shoot him if he ever came to the house, she felt a thrill of desire. At night, she dreamed sweating, tormented dreams wherein he came to her and roughly tossed her down and raped her, but in every dream she was seized by such a sweet burst of pleasure that she awakened and lay trembling and shocked by her reaction. Surely she could not want that, could not actually desire to feel his touch again, to be further humiliated and defiled by him. No, she hated him! She knew she did— she hated him and all the other Yankees who had so destroyed her life. And if she ever by chance saw him, she would be as cold as ice to him. But, then, it was foolish to even think of it. No doubt he had no desire for her. She had probably just been a tiresome obligation for him.

There was little else to occupy her thoughts, however, as the city waited numbly to be occupied. All normal activities had come to a halt while negotiations for surrender crept on. Capitulation was obvious; the only thing in controversy was the Louisiana flag, which hung from City Hall. The Union navy commander, Farragut, demanded that the state's flag be hauled down and the U.S. flag run up in its place. The proud Orleanians balked at this final humiliation.

In a rage Farragut threatened to fire on the city unless they removed the flag, warning the women and children to leave the city. However, New Orleans stood firm, despite that threat and despite the rumor that the slaves in the Third District were in revolt. The women of the city, Analise among them, agreed firmly that they wouldn't leave. They would stand up to Farragut and declared that it would be on his head if he slaughtered innocent civilians. Farragut's guns remained still.

On April 29, New Orleans learned that their last hope was gone; the forts had surrendered. An uneasy agreement was reached on the subject of the flag. Crowds gathered to watch as once again Federal officers landed and marched to City Hall. Analise, her heart in her throat, recognized, even at the great distance from which she saw him, one of the flint-eyed Yankee officers. Her mind would always know that face.

The crowd rumbled and grew threatening as the officers passed: when one of the Yankee soldiers appeared on the roof of City Hall, the crowd's rage increased. Analise expected at any moment to hear a shot ring out and see the lone blue-coat crumple from a sniper's bullet. She found herself praying that it was not Clay Ferris on that roof, then stopped herself with an angry denial. What did she care if he fell?

With icy nerve, the officer hauled down the Louisiana

flag and with his sword neatly sliced it from the rope. A hush fell over the crowd as he dropped the state flag and ran the U.S. flag up in its place. Showing no sign of haste, the Yankee left the roof. Analise watched the once-familiar flag catch the breeze, and numbly she turned away, barely able to see for the tears in her eyes.

SURRENDER

Five

$\mathcal{I}$t was April 30 when General Butler landed his troops in the city of New Orleans. While the band played the strains of "Yankee Doodle Dandy," the blue-uniformed soldiers marched up the streets past a sullenly watching crowd.

Analise did not venture out. She had no desire to see the soldiers take over the city she loved; she wanted to avoid seeing one soldier in particular. Besides, she knew it would not be safe for a lady. So she contented herself with sitting at home, trying to calm her mother's resentful, exaggerated fears. All day long she felt as though she were waiting for something to happen—exactly what she was not quite sure. But the day went peacefully enough, until close to midnight, after everyone in the house had gone to bed.

A loud, imperious knock sounded at their door, and Analise, in bed but not asleep, crept silently onto the verandah to peer down and identify their visitor. The sight of the blue coat set her heart pounding in fear; then the man turned slightly and she recognized the features of Clay Ferris. Her heart seemed to leap into her throat, and she retreated quickly into her room. Mind whirling, she hurried to the top of the stairs.

"May, wait," she called to the maid who had come sleepily to answer the door. "Tell that man that I am asleep, that I refuse to see him, that I never want to see him again. Understand?"

Eyes wide, the maid nodded, then went on to the door. Analise crouched down by the banister so that she could get a glimpse of the conversation and still remain hidden from view.

May opened the door. "Yes, sir?"

"I want to see Miss Caldwell," Mark said, and the sound of his deep, softly accented voice stabbed through Analise's heart.

"I am sorry, sir," May replied cooly. "Miss Caldwell has retired. She specifically said she would receive no visitors."

"She will see me," he said firmly.

"No, sir. Miss Analise told me she would most particularly not receive you. In fact, she told me to inform you that she did not wish to see you again."

Mark sighed and seemed to hesitate for a moment, then made an angry exclamation and pushed through the door, sending May stumbling back.

"Sir!" she exclaimed, grabbing at his sleeve. "You can't come in here."

He turned, weeks of pent-up longing surging through him, and snarled, "Damn it, I'll do as I please, and I suggest that you stay out of my way."

May gasped, and Analise quickly came down the stairs. At the sight of her clad only in her nightgown, the outline of her naked limbs faintly visible through it, Mark stopped dead in his tracks and stared. The repressed hunger for her sent long running shivers of desire through him, and greedily his eyes swept over her, taking in every detail.

Analise blushed at his look and felt a treacherous warmth spread in her loins. Angry at her own response, she said icily, "May, please close the door. Then you may go. I will talk to this—" she paused just long enough to make it sting when she continued—"gentleman."

"Shall I get Josiah, ma'am?" May asked nervously.

"No," Analise said firmly, excitement coursing through her—the excitement of doing battle, she told herself. "I cannot let him hurt one of you."

"Analise, please," Mark said, stiff from the effort of subduing his raging passion for her and controlling the anger her barbed remarks set off in him. "I am a Unionist."

"And I am a Rebel," she shot back.

"God damn it, woman, will you listen to me?" he barked. "I am a soldier in the United States army, and I have a duty to obey orders. I was ordered to destroy those torpedoes. But more than that, I wanted to destroy them, had to destroy them for myself, because I knew we must take New Orleans to win the war, and I am firmly convinced that we must win this war. I believe in abolition; I despise slavery; and I am committed to the Union winning this war."

"How noble you are," Analise said sarcastically.

"Don't mock me, Analise; you are pushing me too far. I lied to you so that I could destroy the torpedoes; otherwise, I could not have been true to one of the few principles I consider worthwhile. Union victory is one of the two things in the world I value. The other one is you."

Slowly he moved up the stairs as he talked, and Analise watched him, mesmerized by the sweet drone of his words. "I did not lie to you about my feelings, Analise. There was nothing false in my kisses; my hands never lied when they touched you. I burned for you; I still do. I did not sleep with you to get that plan. I already had it in my possession. I made love to you only because I wanted to. I could not bear to leave you, maybe to die and never see you, without tasting your sweet flesh just once.

"And ever since, I have done nothing but dream of you and think of you: your sweet mouth, your tender breasts, the flat plane of your stomach—woman, I have ached for you, yearned for you since I left. Dear God, Analise, believe me. You told me you loved me. Remember that night, when we made love, remember how you rose to meet my passion with your own. That meant something to you, surely; you loved me then. Won't that love give me a chance? Let me prove my love to you. Marry me. Let me—"

He reached out and pulled her against his chest, his eager mouth seeking hers. Weakly, Analise clung to him as his arms encircled her, pressing her breasts into his chest. His mouth ravaged hers, his tongue possessively roaming her mouth. Analise felt as though she were falling, slipping down into the wild, dark vortex of her love for him. Frantically, she clawed to stay above it—what power he held over her! She felt possessed by him, held in thrall by her passion. She realized with fear that he was persuading her, that she was about to abandon herself to his lovemaking once again. He could do anything to her he wanted, and he obviously realized it. That was why he had kissed her, knowing his expert mouth and hands would overcome her reasoning power. She would be lost, lost.

"No!" Analise tore herself away from him, pushing at him as hard as she could. Mark stumbled backward down the steps and caught at the rail to keep his balance. He stared at her, his breath coming fast and hard, so blazing with desire that it took him a moment to comprehend her rejection.

"I loathe you!" she cried wildly, hurling her last, desperate attack. "I despise you, don't you understand that? I hate the very sight of you. I loathe you and all the other Yankee vermin you run with!"

He swallowed against the bitter bile flooding his throat. Had he gone to her and taken her in his arms again, she could not have resisted him a second time. But he did not, for her scathing words, slashing through the heat of his passion, cut him to the quick.

In his head he heard the echo of his mother's hysterical, alcohol-tinged voice crying at his father, "Go on then, damn it, Mr. Prim-and-Proper Schaeffer! I despise you, hate you and all you frozen Yankee men!"

"Southern bitch!" he shouted at her, and slammed down the stairs and out of the house.

Shakily, Analise sat down on the steps. Her legs felt like water, and she was trembling violently. It had taken all her strength not to give in to him, and now she felt as weak as a baby and desolate. Leaning her head against the railing, she burst into a storm of tears.

Mark strode angrily down the street, his emotions in raging turmoil. He had thought she was different, thought she would listen to reason, but, no, she was just a shallow Southern belle, like all the others. Like his mother. She refused to even listen to his explanation; she had already tried and convicted him without waiting to hear his side. That was some love she had for him, that she had no trust in him at all, but believed the worst about him. She cared nothing for the anguish and conflict he had felt, made no effort to understand the strong principles that motivated him. No, all she cared about was herself; her pride had been wounded; she had been unhappy. And nothing in the world mattered next to that.

But, damn it, he loved her! Even his hurt and anger could not do away with that feeling. Just the sight of her had made his insides a quivering mass of jelly. He still longed for her as much as before, still ached to possess her. Obviously that was not to be; she clearly wanted no part of him. But, dear God, how was he to bear it! He stopped still and faced the thought of never again seeing her face or hearing her musical voice, never again sinking his hands into that raven black hair and tilting her face up for a kiss.

At the thought, he began to walk again, hurrying from the idea of life without Analise. He headed for the taverns and whorehouses of the Quarter; there, surely, he could find surcease from his pain in a bottle and the arms of a willing woman.

Mark managed to lose himself for three days in alcohol and sex. Only the loyalty of his subordinates, who lied cleverly and often while they ransacked the brothels of New Orleans looking for him, kept him from losing his newly won promotion. Eventually he gave up the effort and stumbled back to his men. His head ached and his mouth tasted like cotton; he was exhausted from the marathon lovemaking he had engaged in in an attempt to satisfy his desire. He felt half-dead and wished he were, but still he had not erased Analise from his mind. The pain, the anger, the rejected love, the thirst of passion that only she could slake still haunted him.

His men were among the troops to be left in occupation

of New Orleans. Mark did not relish at all the idea of spending his days guarding against a most unlikely counterattack and subduing the resistance of old men, women, and children. More than that, he wanted to get away from the place where he was haunted by memories of Analise.

He felt that he could hardly bear it, and he begged to be assigned somewhere else. He wanted to get back into battle, as far away as possible. His request was denied, since General Butler believed that Mark, being half-Southern, would be better able to deal with these obstinate, stiff-necked New Orleanians. So he was condemned to remain in his torturous prison, growing more frustrated and vile-tempered every day.

After her confrontation with Mark, Analise felt bereft. For a long time she had thought about and dreaded and anticipated that meeting; now that it was over, her world seemed suddenly empty. She had hated him, wanted to hurt him as he had hurt her; she had wanted to spew out her venom at him. But now that she had done it, she felt no better. It had given her a fierce joy to see hurt flame in his eyes. It was like prodding a lion with a sharp stick—dangerous, exciting, a release of her seething vengeance and anger. However, she found that it left her worse off than before. Seeing him, feeling his touch and the sweet force of his kiss, hearing his voice—it all brought back too forcibly the extent of her love for him. Love and desire for him tore at her more fiercely than ever. It hurt her, but, more than that, it frightened her. Was she to feel this way forever, always hungering after the taste of his lips, always yearning for the sight of him? She could not bear that; it was frightening to think of having to deal with such feelings the rest of her life. More terrifying, though, was the feeling of being out of control. She was putty in his hands; had he tried once more with her that night, she knew she would have melted into his arms. Analise feared that if he came back, she might give in, and from then on he would be able to do with her as he wanted. He could bring her to her knees quite easily, break her to his will; and her traitorous heart and flesh would aid him.

So, still loving, still hating, fearing him and herself, and anxious for another chance to pay him back, she secretly yearned for another visit from him. When it did not come, her relief was tinged with anger. So much for his mighty protestations of love for her, his burning desire to marry her. He certainly accepted defeat easily for one who claimed such strong emotions. Obviously, what he had said to her must be false, or he would at least have tried again to convince her.

Yet—why had he said he loved her and asked her to marry him? No doubt it was some trick, but she could not see any advantage for him in it. No, she would not let herself think that way; if she did, before long she would persuade herself back into his arms. Far better to accept reality: No longer was she a wealthy, beautifully gowned belle living a pampered life and surrounded by her admirers. Now she was a woman dressed in worn, outdated dresses, with her wealth, beaus, and servants gone. And Mark Schaeffer, alias Clay Ferris, had deceived her and did not love her.

She tried to accept the new pattern of her life, but she found it difficult. Like most of the people of New Orleans, she was far too proud to adjust readily to being a con-

quered subject, ruled by an occupation force of the enemy.
It was humiliation enough to walk down the familiar streets
and see the blue-coated soldiers walking and lounging
about or to look at City Hall and see the American flag
flying there again. But there was worse than that: The
Yankees lacked courtesy and showed little respect for ladies, as if they were common women. A lady could hardly
walk down the street without being subjected at least to
rude, appraising stares from the soldiers. Often there were
leering grins, catcalls, open requests to share their favors.
Rumors of rapes and near-rapes were rife in the city.

Privately Analise suspected that a great many of the
incidents sprang mostly from anger and resentment or a
desire for excitement. She doubted that any group of men
was quite as sex-crazed as the New Orleans ladies painted
the Yankees. However, she had herself run into more than
one discourtesy and even one shockingly indecent proposal. It made her feel suddenly, frighteningly defenseless.
Always before, she had been secure in the protection of her
hot-blooded Creole brother—and of half a dozen beaus as
well. Now there were no gentlemen to protect her and the
other ladies; the new vulnerability was unnerving.

To make matters even worse, many of the slaves had
taken advantage of the occupation of New Orleans to run
away into the swamps. There was no one to pursue them
now. Several of the Caldwell slaves were among the run-
aways; only Josiah, May, and May's daughter remained.
Analise remembered the strange look she had glimpsed in
Jewel's eyes when the Yankee attack was being discussed;
now it made sense to her—Jewel had been eagerly praying
for a Union victory.

The numerous defections meant that Analise and her

mother were forced to take over many chores they had never before faced. All the mending and housecleaning fell to them, and Analise assumed the chore of buying food from the Market. The Market was a noisy, jostling place, and Analise found it exciting. In fact, despite the noise and smells and the dickering over prices, which Analise was still a novice at, she found that the visit to the Market was the highlight of the day. She soon came to enjoy pitting her skill in trading against that of the vendors. It was a challenge to her to try to feed her mother and servants on as small an amount as she could.

One day, as she turned from a vegetable stand, putting her purchase in her basket, she looked up and saw Mark Schaeffer standing only a few feet from her, buying a handful of strawberries. Quickly she looked away and tried to melt into the crowd, but he had seen her and was instantly at her side. Firmly he grasped her by the elbow and propelled her out of the crowd.

"Let go of me!" she hissed. "What do you think you are doing?"

"I am trying once again to get through that hard Rebel head of yours. Analise, would you listen to me this time?"

She looked at him with icy blue eyes, stung by his words. "I cannot think of anything you could possibly have to say that would be of the slightest interest to me."

"I want to marry you. Does that mean nothing to you?" His voice was tight, constrained. "We love each other; there's no reason for us to live like this, walled off from each other and happiness."

"I don't know what devious game you are playing, Clay Ferris or Mark Schaeffer or whatever you are calling yourself now. Frankly, I don't even care. What you do and say is of no concern to me. I don't want to see you or hear from you again. Once I was fool enough to love you, but that is all past now. I no longer have any tender feelings toward you."

His eyes went as cold and hard as marbles. "I see. Then I shall not trouble you with my presence any longer. I only hope that when you are lying in your cold, solitary bed, you will remember your passion and your enjoyment of my touch. And ask yourself if your pride is worth it."

Analise flushed at his words, humiliated at his knowledge of her body and her eager passion. How secure he was in his power over her. How she hated him for it.

To stab back at him she said, her voice falsely sweet, "What makes you think my bed is solitary?"

She saw rage flame in his dark eyes, and she turned away triumphantly. At the edge of the stalls area, a Union soldier reached out to put a hand on her arm.

"Hey, now, ain't you a nice little thing?" His voice was nasal, grating, and his face flushed with desire.

Angrily, Analise jerked her arm away from him and snapped, "Let go of me, you baboon!"

He shrugged and retreated. Analise marched on angrily. Damn Yankees! She despised the whole filthy lot of them.

Six

The rapping on the door was soft, but insistent, and finally it dragged Analise from her sleep. Groggily she sat up and looked at her clock: one o'clock! Who on earth would be tapping on the door at one in the morning? The only one she could think of bold enough to do that was Mark Schaeffer. She grimaced; if it was he, he could stand out there all night knocking, for all she cared. Finally, however, as the gentle noise continued, curiosity overcame her, and Analise went softly from her bed onto the verandah and peered down over the side.

"Emil!" she exclaimed and hurried downstairs.

When she flung open the front door, he slipped quickly inside and closed it softly after him. Analise threw herself into his arms and he enveloped her in a bone-crushing hug.

"Analise, oh, you have no idea how good it is to see you. God, I have worried so about you and Mama, left here all alone with those rascals."

"Emil," Analise said, stepping out of his hug, "whatever are you doing here? Why, if anyone saw you—the Yankees are suspicious of any civilian of your age. If they caught you, they'd hang you as a spy, for sure."

Emil laughed. "Don't worry, little sister. Do you really think I can't outsmart a few Yankees?"

"But, Emil, the town is swarming with them. They are everywhere; it would be so easy for one of them to see you."

"Hush, now, it is done. I am here, and there is nothing to be done about it. So stop your worrying; you are worse than Mama."

"That's because I have more sense than Mama," Analise retorted, but she had to smile at him. It was hard to resist Emil's daring charm.

He smiled back, knowing he had won her over. "Come, now, let's sit down, and tell me how everything is going."

"Oh, we are managing fairly well, actually. The worst thing is that most of the slaves have left, so Mama and I have now become house cleaners."

"Oh, no; oh, Analise. I cannot bear it. That you should have to be a scrub woman—"

Analise giggled. "Well, it is not quite that bad, Emil. Actually, we just do the dusting and mending and light housekeeping. May and Josiah do all the heavy work. And I do the shopping for food, which I have to admit I enjoy."

"How like you to make light of your troubles."

"Well, Emil, I have never been quite the fragile flower you thought, you know. And it is not as if we have been thrown out of our homes or anything, or subjected to rape or torture."

"We hear that there are those who have been," Emil said worriedly.

Analise frowned. "Yes, the Yankees have taken over some people's houses, but mainly those of people who have fled. And I have heard of rapes, though I do not know anyone who has actually been—"

"Analise, you sound as if you were defending those scoundrels!"

"Of course not. I am only trying to reassure you that we are all right. It is not the most pleasant thing that has ever happened, believe me, but neither are we in constant danger. Emil, when you are facing battle, it is no time to be worrying needlessly about Mama and me. We hope that you will recapture the city soon, but until that happens, you must not worry so about us. We will get along."

Emil flushed and looked down at his hands. "Well, that is one reason why I came, Analise. The army is pulling out; we are not going to regroup and wait for reinforcements to attack the Yankees and take back New Orleans. We are being moved to Vicksburg. That is why I risked sneaking back here to see you one last time before we go."

"You mean the army is abandoning us to the Yankees?"

Emil sighed. "For those of us from here, it is the hardest thing we have ever had to do. But apparently, they feel it is better to defeat the Yanks in battle elsewhere and make them sue for peace. Then, of course, we will make them turn New Orleans back to us as part of the peace settlement."

Analise looked at him, but said nothing. A cold wave of fear washed over her; surely this was no way to win a war, giving up the country's major port without a fight. New Orleans' capture bottled up the Mississippi River, and without the river, Southern commerce was destroyed even more than it had been by the blockade. And a country without money could not win a war. She knew then what it would takes years for others to accept: the South would lose the war.

However, she knew such logic would carry no weight with her brother, so she said nothing. Besides, what else could he do but fight for his country, even if it was doomed to defeat? There was no sense in worrying him with pessimistic thoughts.

"Well," she said with a brightness she was far from feeling, "I am certain that will happen soon; until then, we can hold out. As I told you, nothing desperate has happened to us yet. Let's talk of happier things. How long can you stay?"

"Only until tomorrow night, I'm afraid. I had a hellish amount of trouble getting leave for even that long. And, of course, I had to tell them I was going to see relatives in Baton Rouge; they would never have let me come back here."

Privately, Analise thought that his superiors had by far the smarter idea than Emil, but she was too happy to see him to care. Emil would be all right; he always managed to pull himself out of tight situations.

"How about some food? Is there anything in the kitchen? I am starving to death," he said, and laughingly Analise led him to the kitchen.

Major Mark Schaeffer listened to the report of the officer in front of him without a change in expression. He was rather doubtful about what the man had to say; there were reports of spies constantly, most of them totally without any basis.

"So this suspicious young man in civilian clothes— where did he go? Did your man follow him?" he asked.

"Yes sir, he did. And the man went to one of those fancy houses over on Camp Street. Two hundred Camp Street—it belongs to a Mr. John Caldwell, who—"

Mark stiffened at the address and said, "Yes, I know; I am familiar with the family that lives there."

"Well, sir, he went there and knocked on the door real quiet. Kind of a strange time to be calling on folks, don't you think? Anyway, the door opened and he went inside and did not come back out. There was a light on in the kitchen a while; Sergeant Benson crept up and peeped in, and there was a real pretty girl in her nightgown sitting with this fellow at the table. He was eating and they were talking and laughing. Benson said he looked right at home."

Talking to a man while she sat around in her nightgown! No respectable woman would do that unless the man was a very close relative—or unless she was intimate with him.

"What did they do after that?" he asked gruffly.

"Why, they blew out the light, and no more lights came on," the man said, a little taken aback by the sudden fierce frown on the other man's face. "But the man did not leave the house," he added significantly.

Jealousy tore at Mark. He tried to fight it back: Analise was not the promiscuous sort his mother had been. Until she met him, she had never been intimate with a man. She had not come to him loosely, but out of love and with trepidation. However, he remembered her passionate response to him; perhaps, once awakened to the joys of lovemaking, she was more willing to indulge in it, with or without love. Perhaps in her fury and hurt at his defection, she had turned quickly to another lover, as an act of spite.

"You say he is still there?"

"Yes, major."

"Well, I suggest we pay a little visit on the Caldwells and find out exactly what this young man's business is."

Analise, her mother, and Emil were seated in the upstairs sitting room, chatting, when a loud knock sounded at the door. Analise cast an anxious glance at her brother as she rose to answer the door.

"Perhaps you had better hide, Emil," she said.

"Oh, Analise, you are such a worrywart. It is probably just some friends coming to call on you."

"Please, Emil," Mrs. Caldwell added.

"Just in case."

Emil sighed and said, "All right, just in case. I'll hide in the wardrobe in your room, but don't you leave me in there too long."

Analise smiled at his joke and hurried downstairs. For some reason, she had a strong sense of foreboding. When she opened the door to see five blue-uniformed soldiers, led by Major Mark Schaeffer, her heart plummeted and she knew her fears had not been in vain.

"Miss Caldwell," Schaeffer said, his face stiff and cold. There was an odd, dangerous glint to his eyes that unnerved Analise.

"Major Schaeffer," she returned just as coolly.

"I understand you have a visitor?" he said, and her heart began to pound violently.

She hoped he could not see the way her pulse was jumping in her throat. "I beg your pardon? I am afraid that you are our only caller today."

"Then you won't have any objections if we search your house, will you?"

"I most certainly will," Analise returned hotly. "A person's home is protected from search and seizure—or haven't you read your Bill of Rights?"

Mark smiled thinly. "I am afraid you forfeited the Bill of Rights when you chose to form a new country. You are under martial law now, Miss Caldwell, and I must insist that we search your house."

Silently, Analise stepped aside, allowing them to enter. There was nothing she could do to stop them, and any further resistance would only make them more suspicious. She could only hope that Emil was well enough hidden that they would not find him.

Mark motioned to his men, and they quickly moved into the house and spread out in all directions. Looking down the long central hallway that split the house, Analise could see more soldiers standing guard in the back yard. He was taking no chances; he had cut off any escape route. Looking at Schaeffer, Analise felt her heart sink. His angular face was as cold and closed as stone. She knew with certainty that he would find her brother.

Anger and fear churned in her stomach. Mark was doing this just to get back at her, she knew. Doubtless he had had her house watched to see if he could come up with anything against her or her family. He wanted to defeat her, break her to his will. Well, that would never happen, she vowed—no matter what he did to her. Pointedly, she turned away from him, but his only response was a harsh, humorless laugh.

There was a triumphant call from upstairs, and Analise's stomach lurched. They must have found him. Her hands went cold as ice and the blood pounded in her head. She had to do something—but what? How could she rescue her brother from a group of soldiers? There was the sound of footsteps on the stairs, and she looked up anxiously.

Mark carefully watched her expression as the men descended. The first man down the stairs, his hands behind his back and the soldiers' gun pointed at him, was a darkly handsome man dressed in civilian clothes. He was a proud-looking devil, Mark thought: you'd think he was going to the opera or something, instead of being caught hiding in a woman's house. When Analise saw him, she went deadly pale and began to tremble.

"Emil!" she cried out, her voice full of love, and the cry cut through Schaeffer like a knife.

She ran to him and flung her arms around him, breaking into tears. The man leaned his head against hers comfortingly and whispered something to her. Mark's fingers itched to reach out and tear them apart.

"Damn it, Analise, stand aside," he rasped out.

She turned to him and said fervently, "I hate you!"

"How dare you call her by her first name!" Emil snapped in outrage.

Mark laughed briefly—what a typically Southern remark. "I think you have far worse things to think about than discourtesy to a lady, sir."

"Emil, please, I know him." Analise said to keep her brother from getting himself into worse trouble with the Yankee.

"Know him!" Emil repeated incredulously, staring at her. "You know a Yankee on first-name terms? Analise, my Lord—"

"Well, when I knew him, his name was Clay Ferris," Analise retorted.

Emil turned to the Union major, his face livid with rage. "You are the blackguard who—I ought to horsewhip you."

"A rather unlikely possibility in your present state, I should say," Mark said, his voice coolly amused. "Now, if you would be so good as to accompany me, Mr.—?"

"Fourier. *Lieutenant* Emil Fourier, C.S.A.," Emil said stiffly.

Jealous rage washed through Mark, and for a moment he could not speak. The different last name proved him no relative. There was no avoiding the fact now: She was sleeping with another man. It was all he could do to keep himself from going after Fourier with his bare hands and choking the life from him.

Without looking at Analise, Mark swung around and walked from the house, barking at his men an order to bring Fourier to headquarters for questioning.

"No!" Analise cried, her eyes wide with horror. Surely this could not be happening. The man she had once loved could not be taking her brother away to certain death as a spy. "Please, no!"

She ran after him onto the verandah, but Mark was already through the gate and moving swiftly down the street. He did not turn or even look back at her heart-rending cry. Analise grabbed the white wrought-iron post to keep from sinking to the ground. Dear God, was Mark really this cruel? With disbelief, she watched as the men marched her brother past her down the steps and out into the street. When he was out of sight, she sank slowly down onto the porch and dissolved into a flood of tears.

It seemed as though she cried out every tear she had

there on the porch. When she was finally through, she rose shakily and went back inside the house. She was numbed inside, and she thought to herself that she had expended her last feeling.

Inside the house, she found her mother having hysterics over Emil's capture. "Analise!" she cried, catching sight of her daughter. "You must do something. You cannot let them kill Emil."

"What? What can I do?" Analise moaned in despair. "What can I do against a whole army?"

"Oh, what shall I do?" Theresa wailed, ignoring her daughter's answer. "My only son! Oh, Emil!"

Listlessly, Analise sank down on a sofa. What could she do? There must be something; surely that snake had some purpose in arresting her brother. If only she knew what he wanted . . . Suddenly, her head snapped up. But, of course! This was a scheme to force her to marry him. He had been quite insistent about wanting to marry her. And not only that—to humiliate her by making her come to him and beg him to marry her so as to save her brother's life.

She stood up. That had to be it. Why had she not thought of it before? Well, she would show him: She would go down there and agree to marry him. After all, what did she care? She had nothing left to live for now, anyway. She might as well throw it all aside and marry him. At least that way she could have some revenge. She could make his life miserable; he would rue the day he had ever decided to force her to accept his proposal. She would spend his money like water and drive him to penury; she would be utterly faithless to him; she would make him a laughing-stock.

Smiling grimly, she hurried upstairs to wash the tear

stains from her face. Then she carefully arranged her hair and changed into her prettiest, least worn frock. She could not go to her future husband looking like a tear-blotched serving girl. Then, with the light of battle in her eyes, she sailed down the stairs and out into the street.

However, her courage began to fail her as she neared the Union army headquarters and realized that she had no idea where Mark and her brother were. She would have to ask for him, endure the curious stares of the Yankee soldiers. For a moment she halted, wondering if she would be able to go on. Then, squaring her shoulders and taking a deep breath, she walked forward. She would just have to face them all down; put a superior, accustomed-to-command look on her face, and face them down.

As she had feared, there were soldiers all about the headquarters, and all of them turned to look at her, plainly curious about her presence here in the Northern male stronghold. On many the curiosity was mingled with a certain hot, speculative look that she knew meant they were pondering her virtue and station in life. Belligerently she raised her chin.

Going up to one who looked less frightening and younger than the others, she said imperiously, "I wish to see Major Mark Schaeffer."

"Yes, well, that is—are you expected?"

Analise allowed a faint, derisive smile to curl her lips and said, "Yes, I think so. Now where is he?"

"Down that hall and up the stairs at the end. Third floor."

She favored him with a brief smile and followed his directions, her heart thudding—whether with anticipation or fear, she was not sure. On the third floor, she had to ask again where he was; this time she was shown to his office by one of the men who had taken Emil away in the morning.

He opened the door and said, "Lady to see you, sir."

The soldier stepped aside and, head high, Analise swept into Mark's office.

As the hours passed, Mark's quick rage had turned into deep, icy anger. At headquarters, he had questioned the furious Southerner, trying one last time to clear Analise of his suspicions. To all his questions, Emil maintained a steady silence. The only one he had answered was Mark's inquiry as to his connection with the Caldwell family.

Coolly, Fourier had looked at him and said, "I have none." It was the only way Emil saw to protect his mother and sister—to deny all connection with them. He had to keep the Yankees from thinking that they were part of some spy plot. "I saw your soldiers and I sneaked into their house and hid."

Mark's face twisted with disgust. Obviously he did not know that a soldier had seen him enter the house the night before, had seen him sitting with Analise in her bed clothes.

"It's clear to me that you are lying. You say you are a soldier, but your presence here in civilian clothes marks you a spy. I am sure that as such you will be hanged. However, that is for a military court to decide tomorrow." He opened his door and said to a soldier outside, "Corporal, take this man to his cell."

After Fourier was gone, Mark sat slumped at his desk, his head whirling with bitter, angry thoughts. So she was like his mother after all, like all Southern women, so shallowly devoted to the appearance of virtue, but without a shred of faithfulness. She had claimed to love him, but as soon as he was gone she had immediately fallen into another man's bed. He laughed bitterly, thinking of all the anguished nights he had spent yearning for her, worrying about what she thought of him. It was more than obvious that she had no feeling for him at all.

His eyes snapped open at his Corporal's announcement of a female visitor, and he watched Analise walk proudly into his office. He swallowed, unable to speak for a moment. All he could think of was how beautiful she looked, so proud in the lovely blue dress. Her jet-black hair curled prettily around her face; her blue eyes shown brightly with barely suppressed anger; her cheeks were ablaze with color.

"Analise!" He breathed, standing up. Dear God, how beautiful she was in person, so much lovelier than even his memories.

Analise closed his office door to ensure their privacy and give her a moment to regroup her thoughts. It seemed as though every time she saw Mark her mind went off in all directions.

"What do you want?" Mark asked, a small flicker of hope rising up in him—perhaps she had come to somehow exonerate herself.

"What do I want?" she repeated in amazement. "As if I could think of anything else at this moment except Emil. I came to ask you to save Lieutenant Fourier's life."

Mark's eyes turned hard and he sat down, feigning an air of disinterest. "Mr. Fourier will be tried tomorrow as a spy; there is nothing I can do in the matter."

"Don't play games with me," Analise returned hotly. "You know as well as I that at your order, Lieutenant

Fourier would be released from jail. He would not have to stand trial."

"You are asking me to let a spy go free?"

"He is not a spy. He is a soldier who wanted desperately to see us before he was sent to fight. Is that so wrong?"

Mark shrugged and said nothing. He set himself against the soft entreaty in her eyes. He refused to give in to her wiles; she would not be able to use him to set her lover free.

At his silence, Analise sighed and said, "All right; you win. I will buy his freedom from you. If you will set him free, I will marry you as you asked."

Mark froze, staring at her. What painful irony—she was offering him what he wanted, but as payment for freeing her lover. Cold anger gripped him. He said, his lips curling into a sneer. "My, you have a high opinion of your worth, Miss Caldwell. Do you really think I am that anxious to marry you?"

Analise stared at him, numb with shock. Surely, that could not be; after humiliating herself before him, surely he could not refuse to set Emil free. "But—but you said . . ." she said lamely and stopped.

Her pale, distraught face touched Mark, and he despised himself for it. Harshly, wanting to cut her, hurt her, and punish himself, he said acidly. "That was over two weeks ago. Maybe I have changed my mind since then. Maybe now I would have you only as my mistress."

Analise flinched; her chest felt as if it had been pierced by a knife of ice. So this was what he wanted: her final, complete humiliation. Why was he so cruel? Was it not enough for him that he had broken her heart? Her eyes filled with tears, and she looked down so that he could not see them. Her public degradation or her brother's life—

what a choice he had given her. She swallowed, trying to push down her rage and pain. Don't let him see, she told herself, don't give him the satisfaction.

She forced herself to look up at him, her face as bloodless and unyielding as a statue. "All right."

"What?"

"I will be your—" She clenched her hands and willed herself to continue. "Your mistress, if you will let Emil go free."

Mark was silent for so long that Analise was afraid he was going to refuse her again, but finally he said tonelessly, "Do you love him that much?"

"Yes, I do," she replied evenly.

Mark's face paled, and he clenched his jaw. He hardly knew whom he hated most—Analise, her lover, or himself. He wanted her even now, wanted her so much he would pay almost any price to have her. He loathed himself for that weakness, and he loathed Analise for her faithlessness. He wanted to hurt her, humiliate her, and yet the pain he caused her sliced through him as well.

"Well, I can hardly say I haven't sampled the wares, can I?" he said flippantly and Analise blushed. "All right. It is a bargain."

Quickly he came around his desk and took her by the shoulders. Analise looked up into his black eyes, and for a moment it seemed as though the flames of hell flickered in them. Then his mouth came down hard upon hers, bruising and brutal, and his tongue invaded her mouth. For a moment Analise felt again that hot, wild sweetness he evoked in her, and, despite everything, she almost melted into loving passion. But at the last moment she regained control of herself and twisted out of his grasp.

They faced each other like fighters, their eyes bright and their breathing quick and shallow.

"No payment in advance!" Analise said fiercely. "First, you fulfill your part of the bargain."

Mark's features twisted into a sarcastic smile and he said, "Oh, yes, I forgot that a whore always gets her money first."

Rage flooded through Analise, and she raised her hand to slap him. Mark caught her by the wrist, clamping his hand around it.

"Don't try it, Analise; you'll always lose. You are better off sticking to false smiles and soft words and twitching your pretty little tail—that has always worked in the past, hasn't it?"

"Damn you," Analise replied, glaring straight into his eyes. "I hope you rot in hell."

Her hatred felt like salt rubbed into the wound of his love for her, and he said cuttingly, "I am sure you will be there to see it."

He released her and went to the door to call one of his men. "Bring Fourier to me; I have just received some very enlightening information regarding him," he told the soldier.

Mark turned back to Analise. "You still want to go through with it?"

"I have no choice," the woman said bitterly. "Don't worry; I never go back on my word. The crucial question is whether *you* are telling the truth."

Without a word, Mark sat down at his desk and scribbled something on a sheet of paper, then stamped it. "There. I have written him a letter of safe conduct, should he be stopped by one of our soldiers. When I release him, he will be able to leave the city freely with that."

Analise said nothing, merely turned away and waited for her brother's approach. When he entered the room in front of his guard, he stopped, stunned by the sight of his sister.

"Analise!" he exclaimed. "In God's name, what are you doing here?"

Analise looked down at the floor, unable to meet the question in her brother's eyes.

"Leave us—and close the door behind you," Schaeffer said to the soldier. Once the guard was gone, he crossed the room to Emil and handed him the slip of paper.

Emil read it, frowning in puzzlement as he read. "A safe conduct. But—I don't understand."

"I am letting you go," Mark said roughly.

"But why?"

Mark laughed shortly. "Miss Caldwell is very persuasive."

"Mark, please, don't," Analise murmured.

"What do you mean?" Emil demanded suspiciously.

"I mean that she has purchased your freedom—" Mark said evenly, looking straight at the other man, "with her body."

"Damn you!" Emil lunged forward, heedless of his entangling leg irons, and crashed to his knees on the floor. "Liar!" he snarled, struggling to get up.

Analise, seeing the pinpoints of flame in the Yankee's eyes, realized he would welcome Emil's attack as an excuse to hit him. She flung herself between them.

"Emil, no! He is telling the truth," she cried desperately.

Her brother stared at her, shocked realization slowly spreading across his face. "You mean—"

"Yes. I have promised to become his mistress."

"Analise!" Emil's voice was low with horror. "You can't mean it."

She nodded and averted her eyes from his stunned gaze.

"But your family—your name—surely you could not dishonor it so," he pleaded.

Mark snorted—trust a Southerner to think first of dishonor to the name rather than his jealousy or the girl's predicament. It made Schaeffer despise the prisoner all the more. He pulled Analise back against him and held her tightly. His free hand ran casually, intimately down her body, some jealous demon in him wanting to goad and hurt his rival.

Analise flushed with humiliation and closed her eyes. Why did he hate her so that he would subject her to such treatment in front of her brother? He acted as if she were a whore or a slave acquired for his amusement. Tears started in her eyes. That is what she was really—a slave who must do as her master bid. He had purchased her body and soul; the payment was her brother's life.

Fourier flushed with anger and shame; he said in a choked voice, "My God, Analise, why?"

"I had to!" she cried out desperately, unable to bear the look of revulsion in his eyes. "It was the only way I could save your life."

"I would rather be dead than see you a Yankee's whore!" Emil lashed out.

Now Mark thrust Analise away from him and advanced on the prisoner, his face and body electric with anger. "You fool! Have you no gratitude, no regard for the sacrifice she has made? She hates me, and yet she will spend all her nights in my bed, enduring my passion, all because of her great love for you. My God, man, you ought to be on your knees thanking her!"

Analise stared at Schaeffer, her mind whirling. Was he mad? One moment he treated her like a common slut, the next he leaped to her defense.

Emil looked at his sister, ignoring the angry man before him, and said coldly, "Analise, if you go through with this, you are dead to me. I swear I will never speak to you again."

"Emil!" Her voice grated with emotion, and tears began to course down her cheeks. "I have to! Please—"

Stonily he turned away from her; Analise burst into sobs. With an inarticulate cry, Mark grabbed the man and flung him against the wall.

"I'd like to kill you!" he hissed. "I swear to God I would, except for my promise to Analise."

"Mark, no!" Analise cried, grabbing his arm to hold him back. "He's helpless, in chains—you can't. Mark, please, you promised me."

Mark turned to her, his face twisted with conflicting emotions. "You love him, even now?"

"Yes! Please, Mark, I promise I will do whatever you say, only please don't hurt him. Set him free."

He stood looking at her, slowly bringing his rage under control, freezing his fiery emotions. If he had been in the Rebel's place and Analise had loved him that much—dear Heaven, he felt as if he would die to have her love him like that. It was the man who forced her he would have hated, not her. What an idiot this Reb was, and Mark hated him for the hurt he gave Analise. Yet she still would risk everything to save him; she loved him that much. It made Mark tremble with fury.

Mark turned from her and opened the door. "Corporal."

When the young man appeared, he said, "I have found the reason for this man's presence here in civilian clothes. I cannot explain it to you; it is too secret. And you must reveal nothing. But take him out of the chains and release him. Give him this letter of safe conduct."

The soldier stared at him in surprise, then looked from Mark's cold, set face to the prisoner's, set in as hard lines as the major's. For the life of him, he could not figure out what was going on here. Mentally he shrugged; it was the Major's responsibility, not his.

"Yessir," he said, saluting, and stood aside for Fourier to go through the door.

The prisoner cast one last fulminating look around the room, then left. The soldier followed him, closing the door after him. Analise sagged wearily against Mark's desk. Emil despised her for what she had done, and no doubt everyone else would too. She would be an outcast from the society she knew, forced to associate only with the enemy soldiers and the traitorous sluts they kept. For that was what she was—a kept woman, the mistress of an enemy soldier. Yet what else could she have done? She could not stand by and watch Emil die when she had the power to save him.

Now Mark was looking at her with that cold, arrogant look of his, as if she were the one who had wronged him. Belligerently she raised her chin. He had ruined her life, but she was damned if she would let him see how broken she was.

"Well? What are your orders for me now—master?" Her voice was harsh and sarcastic.

Mark's eyes narrowed a little, but his voice was cold as he said, "Go back to your house and pack your belongings. I will send one of my men with a wagon to help you."

"Pack my belongings?" Analise repeated, startled.

"Yes. You will move to my quarters. I am residing in the Lancaster house in the French Quarter."

"I am going to live with you?"

"Of course. Where else would my mistress live? Don't tell me you were hoping to fob me off by spending a few hours now and then in my bed."

The blood pounded sickeningly in her head. He was going to show her no sympathy, allow her not even the least shred of dignity. Nothing less than her total humiliation would satisfy him. Why did he hate her so? Why was he so bent on her destruction?

Mark came to her and kissed her hard, possessively, as if he were placing his brand upon her. Analise stood passive beneath his touch. Her lack of response irritated him further. He stepped back from her.

"Go on, go to your house and pack. I'll have my man there in two hours," he snapped.

Analise went to the door, then turned and hissed angrily, "I hate you for this. I will do as you tell me, for I promised I would. But I will hate you always. I'll never forgive you, never. Remember that every time you take me, I'll never come to you willingly."

With that, she walked out, leaving Mark staring unseeingly at the floor, his chest filled with a cold, hard lump, his face as bleak as winter.

Seven

Hastily, with trembling fingers, Analise packed her things. The soldier would be here soon, and she could not bear to have him in front of her house any longer than was necessary. She tossed dresses, slippers, petticoats, much-mended underthings, and jewelry into her trunks. Her mind was too jumbled, too scattered to sort out things properly. All she could think of was Mark and the life that awaited her. A curious blend of shame and eagerness arose in her at the thought of it.

A Yankee Major's mistress. Why, the whole city would scorn her. She would be the shame of her family; no doubt they would feel, as Emil had, that even his death was preferable to such dishonor. She would be ostracized, unable to show her face in public again. And, too, there would be the hell of living with Mark Schaeffer. She had agreed to submit to him; besides, now she would have no one to whom she could turn for help. He could do anything to her he wished; a shiver ran through her at the thought. No doubt he would be cruel and demanding and subject her to all sorts of base desires. And yet—her heart began to beat rapidly in her chest at the thought of the murky, vague licentiousness in store for her. What would he do to her? How would it feel? She thought of his hot, demanding kisses and the fiery touch of his skillful hands. Would he make her feel the way he had then?

But no, that was impossible, she told herself. Then she had been a naive, susceptible girl. Now she knew what a villain he really was. She despised him and knew his tricks. No doubt all he thought he had to do was take her to his bed and she would fall into his hands like a ripe plum. Well, this time he was in for a rude awakening. She would not be so easy now.

Analise closed the last trunk lid and locked it. No doubt she had left something behind, but she could not think what. She clenched her hands to steady them. There was nothing left to do except tell her mother. Analise closed her eyes against the pain; she would rather endure almost anything than the shock in her mother's eyes. But she had to do it; it was too cowardly to just leave a note.

With dragging steps she went to her mother's sitting room, where Theresa reclined on her chaise longue, still crying and worrying over Emil.

"Mama, it is all right. Major Schaeffer released Emil," she began.

"What?" The older woman shot up straight, astonishment and relief mingling in her face. "But how—what happened?"

"I struck a bargain with the Major," Analise said bluntly. "He agreed to release Emil if I would become his mistress."

Mrs. Caldwell stared at her daughter, thunderstruck. Finally she squeaked out, "Analise, you must be joking."

"No, Mama, I am not."

"Analise! You can't; I won't allow it!"

"It is too late, Mama; it's already done. He has released my brother. Now I—I must move into his house."

"What! You are going to publicly—Oh, my Lord! What has come over you? Why, everyone will know; I won't be able to hold my head up in public any more."

"You can repudiate me, if that will help any," Analise suggested coldly, a trace of bitterness in her voice. "Emil already has."

"Oh, no, I simply cannot bear it. This is too much," her mother cried and began to sob. "How could you? Oh, the shame of it. I wish I were dead!"

Analise felt a heavy lump form in her chest. She had expected this reaction. It was just that the reality of it was so hard. Did none of them care about her or feel sorry for the sacrifice she was making? Wasn't anyone glad she had saved Emil's life? To hear her mother or brother talk, one would think she had done this just for her own pleasure, just to spite them.

"Mother, I had to. I had to save Emil's life. Don't you see that?" Analise pleaded.

"I see that you have broken my heart, and your father's. Please, leave me. I want to be alone."

Analise swallowed back the angry retort that rose to her lips and left the room. Outwardly calm, she walked downstairs and sat down on one of the porch chairs to await her fate.

It arrived in the form of the friendly Northern Corporal who had shown her Mark's office. He jumped down from the wagon and quickly loaded it with her trunks and hat boxes, then helped her up onto the high seat beside him. He said little, but kept slewing his eyes around to sneak glances at her, and she knew he was burning with curiosity.

Analise imagined that a Southern lady moving lock, stock, and barrel into a Yankee officer's quarters was hardly an everyday occurrence. However, Analise kept her eyes steadily to the front and her mouth firmly closed.

Her driver was not the only one curious about her. She could feel the looks shot at her from the street. Doubtless she was seen by some people who knew her, and before bedtime it would be all over New Orleans. Analise's cheeks burned with shame. It would have been so much easier for her to have walked. Mark had made her come in the wagon for the sole purpose of humiliating her, she knew.

They pulled up finally before a small, elegant house adorned with a delicate tracery of black ironwork. The soldier helped Analise down and politely opened the black wrought-iron gate for her. Analise stepped into a tiny graceful garden shaded by a lone tree. Bright flowers grew in every spare inch of ground beside the narrow brick walkway. A small carved stone fountain tinkled coolly in the center of the square, and the high brick walls, draped with waxy green vines and intoxicating honeysuckle, lent an air of intimate privacy. A semicircular wrought-iron bench stood against the trunk of the tree, so that one could sit and enjoy the gentle beauty of the garden. In spite of herself, Analise immediately fell in love with it.

The soldier coming in behind her with one of her trunks broke her entranced contemplation of the garden, and she moved reluctantly inside.

The bottom floor, as in most old Louisiana houses, consisted of the wine cellar, storage rooms, and the kitchen rooms, and Analise passed through it with little more than a glance. The second floor was the living area of the family, containing the parlor, study, music room, and sitting room. Although the house was small, its rooms were wide and airy, painted in cool pastel colors, with the long louvered doors open to the breeze. All the rooms were sparsely furnished, which added to the light, spacious look of the home.

Analise strolled through the second floor rooms while the corporal carried her trunks in and up the stairs to the third floor, where the bedrooms were. She was reluctant to follow him there. She wondered if Mark was still at the headquarters. Certainly he was not here, unless—unless he waited for her like a spider upstairs. When the Corporal bounded back into the wagon and clucked to the team, Analise stood for a moment, feeling the silence of the house settle around her. Slowly she walked to the stairs and mounted them.

A bedroom door stood open to the right of the stairs. Analise glanced in and saw that the soldier had set her belongings there. A door connected the bedroom with a small sitting room beyond, and Analise walked over to it.

Mark sat in a high, wing-backed chair at the opposite end of the sitting room, a glass of whiskey on the small drum table beside him. It was a warm evening and he had unbuttoned his shirt and pulled off his boots. He was a shadowy, menacing figure in the evening gloom, and Analise clasped her hands nervously behind her. She told herself that he was only trying to get the upper hand with her by being so rude as to not come downstairs to meet her.

"Is this the way you usually greet a lady?" she asked scornfully, in an attempt to put him on the defensive.

"Lady?" he repeated, raising his eyebrows a little; and Analise flushed. Actually he had stayed up here to save her the embarrassment of meeting in front of the Corporal, and also—though he would not have admitted it—because he felt guilty and sorry and a little nervous about seeing her. She obviously loved another man and loathed him; Mark knew he had been cruel and crude earlier today. Yet he could not stem the flood of desire that rushed through him at the thought of her. No doubt he would hate himself for what he was doing but he could not help it. He had to have her—any way he could.

"Surely rape does not change one from being a lady," Analise snapped back, furious at his slur.

"You call it rape?" he said and laughed. "Then you have a very convenient memory."

Again Analise blushed and her eyes shot disdain at him. "I was not speaking of the past, only of today. Force does not have to be physical."

Anger coursed through Mark, and he said, "Since you have known me, and by your own admission there have been others since me, I hardly think you qualify as a lady. As for rape—as I remember, it was a sale, whore to customer, not force."

"I hate you!" Analise snarled.

The words hit him like a physical blow, but Mark said evenly, "Take down your hair."

"What?"

"You heard me."

Her fingers shaking violently, Analise pulled the pins from her hair arrangement, sending the long curls tumbling.

The man watched her, bright pinpoints of fire in his eyes. When she was through, he said, "Now, undress."

"No!" Analise exclaimed, her face paling.

"Yes!" His voice was as brittle as glass, and as cold.

"You belong to me now; you promised that you would be mine, if I set free your beloved Fourier, mine to do with as I pleased. And it pleases me for you to strip for me. Strip!"

With a last outraged look at him, Analise bent her head and reached back to undo the myriad tiny buttons. Under his piercing gaze it seemed to take forever before she was through unbuttoning them and could shrug the dress off and let it slide to the floor. Still without looking at him, she untied her hoop and petticoats and sent them after her dress. She kicked off her shoes and rolled down her threadbare stockings. Then, taking a deep breath, she untied her chemise and pulled it off, exposing her full, rosy-tipped breasts.

At Mark's quick intake of breath, she looked up for the first time. His face, too, was flushed, and his eyes were riveted to her breasts. He had the look of a hungry man at a banquet. She realized, with a sudden rush of warmth, that he desired her. So it had not been entirely all lies—his lovemaking not solely to gain her father's plans. Moreover, it meant she had some power over him, at least the power to goad him.

Teasingly, she drifted her hands down to the strings of her pantalets and ever so slowly untied the bow and pushed them down lingeringly over her hips. She watched his hot black eyes follow her hands greedily, and saw beads of sweat pop out on his forehead.

Mark suppressed a groan when at last she stood completely naked before him. The tease: she knew what she was doing to him. It excited him that she would play a game with him like that, but jealousy stabbed through him—he had not taught her that.

"Turn around," he said hoarsely.

Analise obeyed him, thinking uneasily that she had really not had much power over him, only what he had wanted her to have. Now he was looking her up and down, as if he were coolly evaluating her, as one would a mare.

"Stop it!" she snapped. "You make me feel as if I were—"

"A slave on an auction block?" he finished for her smoothly. "A piece of property? You are, you know. My property." He rose and crossed the room to her. "Except that when I am through with you, I won't sell you to another man. And I won't beat you—as long as you obey me." This last was said in a light, caressing voice, but his words chilled Analise—"When I am through with you." How long would it be before he tired of her and kicked her out into the night? And what would she do then?

He tilted her face up to him and stared deeply into her eyes. "Say my name," he whispered.

"Clay," she said defiantly.

He flinched and then clamped his fingers cruelly around her jaw. "Say my real name, damnit."

"I don't remember."

His fingers dug in harder with each word: "Mark Schaeffer. Say it—Mark."

"Mark Schaeffer." And then, almost a whisper, "Mark."

He pulled her to him and his mouth came down hard on hers. His hands on her back seared into her, blazing hot with passion.

Mark tore his mouth from hers, only to kiss her again, wrapping his arms around her and pressing her into his body.

"Analise. Oh, God, Analise. So sweet, so long," he mumbled against her flesh as his mouth roamed her face and neck.

Quickly he scooped her up into his arms and strode into the adjoining bedroom. Shoving aside the sheer mosquito netting, he laid her on the bed, then stepped back to hastily disrobe. Then he was inside the haven of the bed too, his lean, hard body astride her. He cupped the globes of her breasts and stroked them, circling the nipples until they stood hard and dark.

"Touch me," Mark ordered, his voice ragged and close to pleading.

Hesitantly Analise put her hands on his shoulders and ran the length of his body slowly down to his thighs. He drew a long, shuddering sigh and closed his eyes against the exquisite agony of it. He had not specifically said to, but Analise wanted to know how it felt, so she brought her hands back up and drifted down the length of his engorged manhood. A moan broke from him, and Analise began to stroke it. His body quivered at her touch and he moaned aloud again.

Finally he said, "No more; I cannot bear it."

Mark stretched out full length, covering her, and pressing her legs apart, slowly moved his thick shaft into her. Analise had forgotten the delightful satisfaction of it; now it was she who could not suppress a moan. The sound stirred him, and Mark began to thrust himself into her, stroking until something began to build in her. Suddenly he shook and cried aloud, and then he rolled away, leaving that something in her building and unsatisfied. Analise bit her lip—she would not tell him that she needed him.

* * *

When Analise awoke the next morning, Mark was gone. For a time she lay staring up at the mosquito netting above the bed and feeling sorry for herself. However, she was not one who could occupy herself with that for long; she got out of bed. She dressed and then began to unpack her clothes and put them away in the wardrobe and chests. By the time that was done, she had worked up a healthy hunger. She decided to descend to the kitchen in search of food and servants.

She found at last a black woman in the parlor, cleaning. The servant was neither surprised or curious, and Analise assumed Mark must have warned her of Analise's arrival— or was it just that Mark so often had a woman staying with him that it was nothing new to his maid?

"There's coffee and rolls downstairs in the kitchen," the woman said, her voice surly. "My name is Martha, and the Major hired me to clean his house and cook his meals and that is all I do. I don't do no waiting on high and mighty little white girls."

Analise stared at her, shocked by Martha's rude, abrupt manner. Despite the way the world had been turned upside down by the Northern occupation, she had not until now been treated with anything but subservience from a black. Trust Mark to come up with such a servant. No doubt he had told the woman she could be as rude as she wished to Analise. Tears stung her eyes as she swept off to the kitchen.

The day passed slowly. Mark did not come home for lunch, and Analise had to forage about the kitchen for a cold, light lunch for herself. She spent the afternoon trying to read, although her mind kept wandering to her own problems. At last, with a sigh of exasperation, she flung the novel aside. Damn that man—why did he have such power over her? How could he create such turmoil in her?

She ought to hate him; she did hate him. Just thinking of the way he had humiliated her the night before made her burn with anger. He was a despicable, hateful man, and he had deliberately ruined her. And yet—a smile curved her lips as she thought of his lovemaking. His kisses, his touch, just the fiery glance of his eyes still set her trembling with passion. How could she hate him so and just melt into his arms like a lovesick schoolgirl? Even now, as she sat dreading his homecoming, bracing herself for his scornful glance and sarcastic words, her stomach also danced with excitement and anticipation. She did not love him still; surely she could not, after the things he had done to her. But then, what did love have to do with reason? Firmly she pushed that thought away. Analise was certain that her love for him had withered and died. It was simply physical: He was so practiced and expert in his lovemaking that her body responded to him against her will. And against her heart, too, she assured herself.

She would not allow the same thing to happen tonight. Tonight she would be cool and in control. Carefully she planned what she would do and say to Mark, the way she would show him how far above it all she was.

However, when Mark did arrive, she was unable to control the wild thud of her heart when she saw him. It struck her anew how handsome he was, his body lithe and firm in the close-fitting blue uniform, his thick black hair falling carelessly across his forehead. His black eyes flickered over her, as cold and hard as marbles, and his angular face remained expressionless.

For a moment, Analise had almost forgotten her resolution. She had started to rise and go to him, but then she saw the indifference on his face and she stayed where she was. From where she sat, she could not see the tiny light of hope that flickered and died in his deep black eyes.

Mark greeted her formally and she acknowledged it with a brief nod. After a few moments they went into the dining room. The meal was simple, but the small table might have been a banquet table for the stiff formality of their manner. Mark's face was hard throughout the meal, as if it were a penance he must endure.

After dinner, Analise rose to retreat to the sitting room, but Mark grabbed her wrist with fingers of iron and said, "No, come upstairs with me. I want you to tend to me."

Analise flushed and dropped her gaze. Mark's fingers bit deeper into her wrist. He wanted to scream at her, to seize her and shake her, to wrap her in his arms and crush her to him until all thought of the other man was driven from her. Instead he turned abruptly and pulled her after him up to their bedroom. Once there he dropped her wrist and sat down, stretching his legs in front of him and casually crossing his legs at the ankle.

"What do you want?" Analise asked sullenly, shifting uncomfortably under his gaze.

"I can see you have not had much training in being a mistress."

"Well, it was hardly what I envisioned as my life's work," Analise snapped back.

Mark laughed and said, "It is quite simple really. Your role is to see that I am comfortable. After dinner I like to relax—take off my boots, and have a drink, smoke a cigar. First, the boots." He extended one leg.

"You mean I am supposed to take it off? I am not your servant."

"You are my mistress, and you are here to give me pleasure."

Analise's eyes flared bright with anger, but she crossed the room and jerked his boot off and flung it to the ground. The other one she disposed of just as noisily. Then she strode to the wardrobe, pulled out his dressing gown, and threw it at him. Mark began to chuckle, enjoying her angry beauty and spirit, which aroused her ire even more. She poured a snifter of brandy from the decanter on the table and shoved it at him, so that it sloshed over the rim onto his hand. Mark's chuckle grew to full-fledged laughter as she threw open the cigar box, grabbed one of its contents and threw the lid back down with a bang, then clipped off its end furiously and hurled it into his hand.

"Wait! Wait!" he gasped between laughter. "Do you plan to throw the light at me as well?" He stood, quickly discarding the things she had thrust at him, and reached out to grasp her by the shoulders. She stood rigid in his clasp, glaring at him fiercely. "My God, you are lovely. You turn a man into liquid. Oh, Analise!"

He pulled her hard against him, wrapping his arms around her like steel and buried his face in the soft fall of her hair. "Love me, please, love me," he murmured against her hair, and his hands began to roam her body. His desire raged inside him like a torrent, and he tore away her clothes, his hands burning to touch her bare flesh. This time, her anger spent, Analise could summon no resistance, and his warm lips and eager, exploring hands aroused an answering passion in her. He kissed her mouth, her throat, and nibbled gently at her ears, sending tremors of delight through her. Analise gave a soft cry of pleasure and her soft lips sought his eagerly. Surprised and pleased, Mark kissed her, their lips blending in a honeyed, mutual sharing of passion. His hands pushed against her back, pressing her body into his, and a soft moan escaped him.

Still locked in their embrace, Mark pulled her to the floor with him, his pounding need for Analise too great, too immediate to even seek the softness of the bed. And this time, when his maleness filled her and he rode the white-hot crest of his passion in her, Analise's own pleasure did not lag behind, but matched him thrust for thrust, until at last they exploded together in a fiery union. Spent, Mark collapsed upon her, and Analise lay beneath the satisfying weight of him, hearing his shuddering breaths, smelling his hot male scent, and feeling on her lips the salty taste of his skin.

Tears welled in her eyes, and Analise wanted suddenly to sob. Oh, God, she was lost, utterly lost. For she knew now that she had deceived herself: No matter what he had done to her or how he had betrayed her, she loved Mark. In truth, she did belong to him; her own emotions left her exposed and vulnerable to whatever hurts he might choose to inflict on her. Her own heart was her worst enemy.

Eight

Analise had not wanted to venture forth in the city because of her new disgraced status, but her agitation the next day was so great that the petite garden could not contain her pacing, and she decided to go for a walk, praying fervently that she would see no one she knew. She hoped the exercise and the familiar sights and sounds and odors might somehow restore order to her jumbled mind.

Now she had really delivered herself into the hands of her enemy, she knew. She loved Mark, and she wanted him. Even though he had deceived her, even though he had shamed her and used her, she loved him. Worse than that, last night she had reveled in his use of her. Her own treacherous body was conspiring with him for her downfall.

He had proved himself to be a selfish, cruel, unfeeling man, one who would use her natural love for her brother to force her to his bed, one who desired not just her body, but her public humiliation as well. Mark wanted to have his pleasure and hurt her too. As if he had not hurt her enough already! It was as if he hated her, but why should he despise her so? She had done no wrong to him.

Whatever his reason, he obviously enjoyed her pain. Yet she, like a fool, loved him. She yearned for his love-making, trembled with love and longing at the sight of him, wanted to be near him and drink in the look and sound and scent of him. And he, all the while, wanted only to debase her. Dear God, what would he do if he knew his effect on her? No doubt he would tease and torture her with it, use her love to degrade her even further, just as he had used her love for Emil.

So her thoughts drove her to walk, and she roamed through the streets of the Quarter, too preoccupied to notice the leering stares of the soldiers and the men loitering around the taverns, or even to pay attention to where she was going. She did not notice that her steps turned automatically toward her home, and it was not until a horrified gasp brought her from her reverie that she realized she had wandered into the familiar Garden District. Analise looked up to see the disapproving glare of Mrs. Blackburn, a friend of her mother's. Ostentatiously the woman turned and crossed the street to avoid walking past Analise. Analise blushed up to her hairline, and wished that she could simply sink through the ground and disappear. She had known that this was the sort of reception she would get, but still it hurt.

Hurriedly she turned and walked back toward the business district, but she was not able to escape quickly enough, for as she turned a corner she came face to face with Becky Oldway. Analise thought she detected a brief gleam of triumph in her former friend's eyes before Becky turned her face coolly away without speaking and swept past Analise, her wide skirts held back to avoid any contaminating touch with her.

Tears welled up in Analise's eyes and she blindly stumbled on, almost running back to the Vieux Carré and the shelter of Mark's little house. There, her heart pounding and her face flushed with the exertion, she flung herself down onto her bed for a good cry, but she found that the soothing tears would not come. The hurt had gone too deep to be healed with tears.

Shakily she sat up. This was to be her situation for all the years to come; for the rest of her life she would be a scorned woman, outside the pale of decent society. Analise rubbed her hand wearily across her forehead. What would happen when Mark grew tired of her? When she no longer interested him and he turned her out on the street? How would she live? What could she do to feed and clothe and house herself? Insidiously, the thought crept into her mind: Seek the protection of another man who would pay her bills in return for her favors.

"No!" Analise cried aloud, hurling herself off the bed. "I will not let him make me into a whore."

Angrily, she began to pace the floor. Even if she starved, she would not seek the security of another man's bed. No, nor would she meekly submit to Mark, no matter how she felt about him. If she let him know she loved him, if she gave in to the wondrous pleasure his lovemaking brought her, she would be giving him the means to destroy her. Soon he would make her his willing mistress, submissive to his every desire, striving to please him, degrading herself to gain his caresses. No, she would give no man that kind of power of her. No matter how she had to lie and pretend, she would never reveal her love for him.

So deep in her thoughts was she that Analise did not

hear the slight tap at her door. After a moment the door opened cautiously.

"Miss Analise?" A dark head peered around the door at her.

Analise looked up, startled, and stared for a moment in disbelief. "May?"

The black woman answered with a smile and opened the door all the way. "Yes'm, it's me."

"May! Whatever are you doing here?"

"I came to work for you—if you need me, that is."

"But what about Mama? The family?"

May shrugged. "Now the Yankees are here, I figure I can leave if I want, like the rest of them. I got no call to stay with your Mama. But I didn't have anywhere else to go until you left. I think it was a fine thing you did, saving Master Emil like that."

Impulsively, Analise ran to her maid and hugged her. "Thank you, May. You don't know how I've wished someone would say that." She stepped back and smiled. "And I would love for you to come and live here. Thank you."

Again Analise hugged the woman, feeling buoyed by this familiar presence in the house. She felt as if May's presence would somehow be a support, a buffer between her and the alien world she now lived in. Analise no longer felt quite so cut off from her past.

Mark came home that evening whistling, a package for Analise under his arm. Her response last night had him hopeful that somehow things might work out between them, despite what he had done to her, despite her love for that fool Fourier.

Analise was stiff and remote at supper, which set Mark back, but he told himself that it was just the awkwardness of the situation. He would give the present to her later, upstairs, where she would feel freer and more responsive.

However, when he handed Analise the package later in their bedroom, she seemed reluctant to take it. Holding it out from her, she said suspiciously, "What is this?"

"A present, you silly girl," Mark responded good-humoredly.

Analise shot him a measuring glance, and unwrapped the package. Folds of soft peacock-blue material spilled into her hands, and she gasped, eagerly pulling it from the wrappings. Softly, lovingly, she felt it, rubbing it against her cheek, letting it flow across her hands and down to the floor.

"It's beautiful!" she breathed. Imagine—material for a new dress. It had been so long since she had had one. Eyes sparkling, she darted to the mirror above the dresser and draped the material across her shoulders and down her front. Oh, it would make a lovely dress; the strong color was a perfect foil for her black hair and white skin, and it turned her blue eyes a most arresting color.

"Oh, Mark," her voice bubbled happily for the first time in a long time. "Thank you. It's gorgeous, absolutely lovely. Why, I will be the envy of every woman in New Orleans. This is the first new dress I've had in—"

Suddenly her voice stopped and her warm expression froze and hardened. A new dress. She would not be the envy of the women of New Orleans, but the scorn. Even now that the blockade was gone and commerce haltingly restored, no one in the city would be able to buy a beautiful new piece of material like that except a Yankee, and any woman appearing in it could be only one thing, a Yankee's mistress.

Her eyes filled with tears. For a moment she had been carried away by the gift, but now she understood its significance. It was the sort of thing a man bestowed carelessly on his mistress, part of the payment for her favors. It branded her immediately a whore and a traitor to her people. It had not been a kindness from Mark; quite the opposite. It was added proof of her shame.

She flushed dully and turned to toss it on the bed. "Give it to one of your other sluts. I don't want it."

Her sudden refusal was like an unexpected slap in the face. Mark stared at her. "What?"

"I sold my soul to you for Emil's life. I will not cheapen that price by taking gifts of your Yankee plunder!"

Mark's face went dark with rage. "Damn you! You lying, sanctimonious little bitch!" He crossed the room in two quick strides and grabbed her arm, bruising her skin with his harsh fingers. "What was that performance last night? You seemed to be my willing bedmate then. Or do you have the gall to say that you moaned and writhed and cried my name, all 'to save Emil?' " He mimicked her viciously.

"Let go of me!" Analise demanded, ignoring the tight, crushing fear in her chest.

"No! By God, I'll not—not until you admit that you hunger for me just as I do for you."

"Never!" Analise hissed, her head high and proud.

Savagely he pulled her to him and kissed her, forcing her head back with his hard kiss. His lips were hot and hard against hers, his tongue probing her mouth. Analise felt as if he were trying to stamp his possession on her with his kiss. Painfully he dug his hand into the soft, thick mass of her hair, holding her head still with an iron grip. His other arm went around her waist, molding her to him, and he bent her farther and farther back while his searing lips moved down over her throat and breasts.

"No. Mark, please, you will make me faint. I cannot breathe," Analise protested faintly.

He raised his head and stared down into her eyes. "Admit it! Say it! Say you want me!"

"No!"

Mark's lips came down upon hers, cutting off her denial. He lifted her and carried her to the bed, roughly tossing her down beside the bright crumpled cloth she had rejected. But there was no roughness in his hands as they unfastened her clothes and moved lightly across her body. Expertly he caressed her breasts and stomach and thighs; while his mouth played over her breasts, his hands touched and aroused her in all the places he knew pleased her. Analise bit her lip and held herself stiff against his advances, even though the raging tide of passion swelled inside her.

When at last he came into her, she wanted to cry out at the sweet satisfaction of it. For a moment she felt filled, completed, and then he began to move within her, and despite all her efforts, she felt the passion inside growing, pounding, building until at last she could restrain it no longer. With a cry, she shuddered as the heart-stopping ripples of pleasure swept over her. Mark rested on her for a moment and she realized that his manhood still lay stiff within her. He was not through, she thought, amazed at this new experience. Then slowly, gently, he began his stroking movements again, and the pleasure was so intense it was almost painful. He pulled her from her languid peace, making that something start to build. Hazily her mind protested that it could not be, that he could not overcome her will again. But soon the fires were burning as hotly as before within her and once more he brought her to the trembling heights of passion. This time Mark reached his own quivering zenith with her, and when it was over, he rolled from her.

Mark looked at her, his eyes agleam. "Do you still dare to deny it?"

Helplessly Analise shook her head and tears of frustration slid out from beneath her closed lids.

Mark awoke the next morning early, sick with remorse and the dregs of anger. Damn his temper! He loved Analise, loved her strength of character, her will; it was what made her so different from the other women. Yet he tried to break that spirit, to bend her to his own will out of his bitter jealousy and anger. Afterward, like now, he felt like an animal for behaving brutally toward her just because she did not love him. God knows, the way he treated her was not likely to inspire any love in her heart!

The guilt would eat at him like acid, and jealousy, and the raw need inside him for her love, until he was stiff and awkward around her and his nerves were like an open wound. Then her slightest rejection or some reminder of her love for the other man would stab him, and he would burst into his roaring anger. Nothing else had ever so jolted him out of his iron control. Always before his mind had ruled his emotions, keeping those bubbling, conflicting forces in check. But Analise could cut his governing reins with merely a scornful glance, and he would blaze with pain and lash back blindly, wanting to hurt her in return.

Poor love. Mark raised himself on his elbow and gazed down at Analise, who lay curled away from him, her hair a frothy tangle of curls across the pillow. A smile touched his chiseled features and tenderly he smoothed the hair back from her face. God, but he loved her. He felt that he would kill anyone who harmed her—and yet he himself had harmed her most of all. Was it a trait of the Schaeffer males, he wondered, this jealousy and rage? Had his father treated his mother like this? Was it that treatment that had turned her to other men? Mark closed his eyes against the thought. Everything was in such confusion now, his parents and himself and Analise all tangled up somehow, and his anger with Analise laced with his pain from his mother's infidelities. The only thing he knew for sure was that he hated himself for what he did to Analise—but he would sooner cut off his own arm than set her free.

When Analise awoke later, Mark was already gone. She flushed with shame and anger when she thought of the night before and how he, as remote and cold as ice, could make her respond like a bitch in heat. Analise knew she would see that knowledge in his eyes for a long time to come.

The beautiful peacock-blue material had slid off the bed during the wild night and lay in a crumpled heap on the floor. Analise picked it up and threw it on the bed wrathfully. Then a thought flickered in her mind, and she smiled a little. Picking up the offending cloth, she sought May out downstairs and gave it to her. May stared at her in disbelief and protested, but Analise was firm; at last the black woman took it, with a broad grin of thanks.

Mark did not come home that night, and fear stabbed through Analise. What if he had been so vexed that he did not return? What would she do then? She shuddered at the thought.

He returned the next evening, and Analise went weak with relief, although she was careful not to let it show on her face. His manner was constrained for the next few days, and he was more polite to Analise and less demanding. He did not free her from her duties in his bed, but neither did he torment her by trying to fire her passions. He took her quickly, releasing her as soon as his swiftly aroused lust was satisfied. Analise told herself that she was grateful for that, but the hasty couplings left her strangely irritable and with an aching void in her loins.

May quickly sewed up the material into a dress of Sunday finery. When Mark saw her in it going off to church, his face went livid with fury. He shot Analise a glance so filled with rage that she swallowed and stepped back from him. He left the house with a fierce slamming of the door and did not return until late that night, after Analise was already in bed and asleep.

"Wake up," Mark commanded and shook her shoulder roughly.

Analise blinked up at him, sleepily bemused. "What? What time is it?"

"Never mind," he growled and flung the sheet back from her body. "Get up. I have a present for you."

His words were sneering and they sent a little flash of fear through Analise; somehow the bitter scorn was far more frightening than his full-blown rage. Quickly, her heart pounding, she slipped from the bed and stood before him. This close Mark reeked of whiskey and cheap perfume. Anger wiped out Analise's momentary nervousness—he had been out carousing with some cheap harlot.

She thought of his hard brown body atop another woman's form and those long, skillful fingers that usually caressed her floating lovingly over another woman's skin.

"Is one mistress not enough for you?" she asked tartly.

Analise regretted her remark instantly, for he grinned wickedly and said, "Jealous, my love? I would have thought you welcomed the respite."

"No, I am not jealous," Analise flashed back. "It is insulting for you to come to me stinking of a whore, to touch me with the filth of her still on your hands!"

Mark shrugged, and asked insolently, "Do you think one slut's skin would corrupt another's?"

Her sapphire eyes sparkled with anger.

"What a complete cad you are! To label me a slut when it was you who disgraced me!"

Mark's eyebrows rose lazily. "As I remember, you made no objection that night in your study."

Analise's eyes stung with tears at the unkindness of his remarks, and she choked out, "You deceived me. I thought I loved you and that you loved me."

"Oh? And what about the others? What is your excuse for them? Did they force you, as you claim I do? Or did you think you loved them too?" Mark asked sarcastically, his eyes glittering in the darkness.

"Others! Why, you low—" Analise sputtered wildly, not even remembering the taunt she had flung at him in her furious desire to hurt him that day in the Market. "There have been no others! You were the first, and well you know it!"

"The first," he admitted, his smile thin and tight with pain, "but not, it seems, the last."

Analise lashed out at him with her hand, and the sound

of her slap against his cheek crackled through the air. Mark's face went still as death and a muscle jumped convulsively in his jaw. Slowly he took her by the shoulders and his hands bit cruelly into her flesh.

"Tell me," he said harshly, "what were they like, the others who had you! Did you couple with them, too, on the floor of your office, or did you welcome them in your bed? Did you moan beneath them as you did with me?" His fingers dug in painfully, and his face was grim and tortured. "How many were there, Analise? How many others tasted the delights of your flesh?"

Analise stared at Mark in surprise and terror. He was talking like a madman, and the look on his face was chilling. When she spoke, her voice came out in a shaky whisper. "There were no others."

His mouth twisted and he flung her violently away, sending her sprawling onto the bed. The movement sent her nightgown flying up, revealing quite a bit of her shapely legs. Analise looked up at Mark, too shaken to move to pull her gown down modestly, even though she knew her position was provocative.

"Take that silly gown off," Mark said hoarsely. "I have brought you something to wear."

He strode to the chair and grabbed something from the seat. Analise stood and obeyed him; he had frightened her too badly for her to balk at his order. Mark came back to her, a froth of gauzy red material in his hand.

"This time I brought you the proper gift for a mistress. Here, put it on. I want you to model it for me."

Hesitantly Analise took the material from his hands and held it up in front of her. She could see now that it was a nightgown made of such sheer material as to be almost nonexistent. Why, it would reveal more than it hid, she thought with shock. Scarlet, the color for loose women—and so indecent that only such a woman would wear it. Indignation flooded her as she wondered if he had gotten it from the woman whose perfume clung to his clothes.

"Put it on!" he snapped.

Carried by the sudden flood of her anger, Analise pulled the gown over her head and faced him brazenly. Mark leaned against the poster of the bed, seemingly languid, but his breath came in short, shallow bursts. His black eyes moved over her body, burning her skin as much as if he had touched her with his hand. Something quivered in her abdomen at his gaze; he looked as though he wanted to consume her.

Analise looked away from him, afraid of how those hot black eyes could melt her, and she caught sight of herself in the mirror across the room. The sheer gown clung to the curves of her body, concealing nothing, but adding an enticing touch of mystery to her nude body. It was slit from the waist on both sides, exposing the sides of her legs—and far more than just the sides, if she made any movement at all. Her breasts pressed against the gauzy red stuff, clearly revealing the brown circle of her nipples. Even more embarrassing, the points of her nipples stood out proudly, hardened by the quiver that shook her when his eyes greedily roamed her body. She felt torn with shame—he dressed her like a prostitute and studied her lewdly, and instead of recoiling modestly, her treacherous body made it obvious that she was aroused.

"Analise," Mark's voice came out almost a groan. "I burn for you. Come ease me. Please come."

His voice shook with desire, and it sparked an answering need in her, but rage coursed through her, sweeping aside her desire. He reviled her and taunted her and dressed her like a common slut; then he expected her to meekly go to him and serve as the receptacle to slake his desire.

"How dare you!" she snarled at him, the tide of her anger rising and drowning all her fear of him.

"How dare I?" he mocked. "You are mine, remember?"

"Never!" Analise cried, the red mist of rage clouding her vision. "Never in my heart! I hate you."

Suddenly she sprang at him, wild with pent-up emotions, no thought in her mind but the animal instinct to strike back. Furiously she attacked him, clawing and kicking and biting at him. Mark caught her wrists and threw his weight against her, and then they went down heavily onto the bed. Wildly they rolled and wrestled across the bed, as Mark fought to restrain her. He wrapped his legs around her and pinned her arms above her head, but still Analise bucked and strained against his heavy weight, past reason or caring.

At last his weight stilled her, and she lay taut beneath him, her mind gradually returning as her fury receded. She heard Mark cursing softly, vividly, words that she had never even heard before, and she looked up at him. His face glistened with a sheen of sweat and his eyes gleamed avidly. She realized suddenly that her struggles had aroused him even more. Why, he had enjoyed it!

His breath came in quick pants, and his smile was an animalistic baring of teeth. Analise was painfully conscious of his legs clamped like iron around her and the hard bulge pressing into her thigh.

"Sweet Heaven, woman, you'll pop the buttons off my trousers if you keep this up," he said crudely.

Analise tried to summon a look of disgust, but found instead that his words sent a stab of heat through her loins. She knew that she had awakened the pure animal lust in him, and she found to her amazement that it excited more than scared her. Dear God, what was she turning into?

His dark head bent and he nuzzled her breast through the sheer cloth. He mumbled against her flesh, his voice husky with passion, and though she heard only part of what he said, she trembled at the ache of desire in his words. Analise knew that she had excited him past anger, past civility, almost past reason.

Mark shifted his weight from her and stood beside the bed. Analise was too tired, too languid now to move; she merely turned her head to see what he did. Slowly, deliberately, he unbuttoned his belt, and slid it smoothly from its loops. For a moment Analise thought he meant to beat her; God knows, he was wild enough now to be capable of anything. She sucked in her lower lip between her teeth, but did not move, only watched him, her eyes speaking her acceptance of what he chose. Mark's eyes locked with hers and with the same slow deliberation of movement, he raised his hand and let the belt drop, coiling onto the bed. The look on his face bespoke both triumph and generous relinquishment.

Analise watched as Mark steadily, unhurriedly, removed his clothes while his eyes feasted on her scantily clad body. She knew that his slow actions were a test and a proof and a pleasure all in one, not a sign of disinterest. Had she made even a move to leave the bed, he would have pounced on her like a cat.

"What are you going to do?" she whispered, more from a desire to hear him than from curiosity.

Again there was the tight, animal grin. "I am going to teach you how to pleasure me."

Naked now, he crawled into the bed beside her, and there, for one long passion-filled night, Mark taught her the secrets of the male body. And for the first time Analise served him, as a mistress would her man, using her mouth and hands and body on him as he showed her, time after time bringing them both to paroxysms of passion.

Nine

There were times afterward when Analise thought of that night with a faint shudder of fear. She had capitulated to him so completely, accepted his domination so passively—no, not passively, but actively participating in her own degradation. He had made her do things no decent woman would do, made her submit to his every wish, and not only had she not fought or even protested, she had actually enjoyed it! She had reveled in the feel and smell and taste of him, glorying in the gasps of pleasure he made at her movements.

Analise wondered if perhaps she really did have the soul of a harlot. And it was that thought that terrified her, the realization that Mark could call forth her basest nature, and she would not have the control to stop it, or even the desire to. She found herself all too easily doing the things he required of a mistress—lighting his cigars, bringing him brandy, making him comfortable in his chair every evening—without thinking, without resenting it. In fact, she realized that she actually wanted to. Just as she obediently did what he requested in bed—and loved doing it.

Oh, she had enough control of herself still that she did not let on to him that she enjoyed it. She managed to stop herself when she started to run down the stairs smiling to greet him every evening. And she betrayed no more than passive obedience to his requests. But she feared that soon she would break and sink herself willingly into this life, becoming his wholehearted mistress and lover.

Days slipped into months, and still Analise retained her slender control of her loving passionate nature. Mark, though he found life more pleasant with her surface submission, longed for the spark of love that was missing. He did not want to return to the elemental self he had been that night, nor did he want a cowed woman. What he wanted was her love and trust; he wanted the skills he had taught her to be performed lovingly, joyfully, not dutifully. Because everything went more smoothly, he fell into anger less and less often. But the more peaceful he became, the more he missed the tumult of love and the more he wished that he had done things differently. He was afraid that he had ruined it by forcing her into his bed as his mistress. Her heart was what he wanted, not her docility.

Mark noticed that she never ventured outside. So, feeling that she had grown too pale and sickly, Mark urged her to go out for a walk or ride. Sometimes she demurred and other times put him off with the promise that she would, but in fact she never did. So finally one Sunday, he firmly insisted that she accompany him on a stroll about the city, despite her wide-eyed, almost fearful protest.

He soon discovered the reason for her reluctance, as well as the extent of the damage his demand that she live with him had brought her. More than one lady had stared at Analise with shock and disgust, as though she were a particularly loathsome insect. His nerves crawled with sympathetic mortification for the woman he loved, and it was all he could do to keep himself from cursing one woman who conspicuously held her skirts away from Analise. Mark could feel the trembling of Analise's fingers on his arm and a dull flush mounted in her face. Adroitly, he turned their walk back home, and there Analise sank down gratefully onto their garden bench.

"Can you understand now why I don't like to walk?" she asked shakily.

Mark was white around the mouth as he answered, "Yes. I didn't realize. I am sorry."

Analise shrugged, and Mark knew how totally inadequate his apologies were, considering the humiliation she had suffered.

"I was selfish and cruel; I did not think. Are—what about your friends? Your family?"

Analise laughed mirthlessly. "I have not seen Pauline Beauvais. Becky Oldway cut me on the street, and so have some other acquaintances. Papa—I don't know; he is not here, but Mama told me never to darken her door again."

Mark swallowed, feeling sick with guilt. Fourier, the dunce, had repudiated her in front of Mark. So she was without lover, friends, or family. Dear God, he had not meant to do this to her. He had wanted her to stay with him forever, but not because he was the only person who would speak to her. He stared down at her bent head helplessly; he could not undo his careless, willful destruction of her life.

"I—I am sorry," he repeated.

"Please don't—" Analise said, her voice strained. She wanted only to fling herself at him, sobbing, and beg him to love her, but she refused to give in to the impulse.

Mark swallowed miserably, then turned on his heel and

walked into the house. Anxiously he paced the sitting room, pondering how he could make it up to her. If he could convince her to marry him—and there was certainly nothing to say he could bring that off—that would at least make her "an honest woman." However, knowing these damned stiff-necked Southerners, he doubted whether being a Yankee's wife was little more respectable than being his mistress. But if he married her and took her away from here, back North where no one would revile her for being a Yankee or know that she had lived with him without benefit of marriage, then she could live a normal life. Maybe, if he was lucky, once she grew happy again, she might come to love him once more.

Of course, the problem in all this was whether she would marry him, considering how she felt about him. Oh, he could make her respond sexually, all right; he had ample proof of that. But he knew just as certainly that he did not possess Analise's heart. When he thought of asking her to marry him, he could imagine her biting, scornful answer, and it made his stomach churn. Mark knew he was being cowardly, but he could not quite bring himself to broach the subject to her. Perhaps if he tried first to win her over with kindness . . .

Analise had more reason to be unhappy than Mark realized. This afternoon's walk had reminded her quite forcefully that she had no friends or family she could turn to now, when she most needed someone. For Analise was certain that she had become pregnant.

Woefully Analise huddled on the garden bench. For two months now she had missed her time, and most mornings found her with a queasy stomach. She had not yet begun to show, but her waist had grown thicker, so that she had had to let out all the waists of her dresses a little. Doubtless she could hide her condition from the world for quite some time, what with the full-skirted fashions, but she could not hide it long from Mark. He knew her body intimately and saw it naked nightly. Her flat tummy was already softening and rounding; it would not be long before Mark noticed the change. He was too experienced a man not to know what it meant. What would happen then? Would he kick her out because she would lose her appeal for him as she grew heavier? Or would he marry her out of some sense of duty toward his child? Or—more likely—would he pension her off as she became unattractive, giving her a little house and money to keep her going?

Whatever course he chose, none of them appealed to Analise. If he threw her out, there were the obvious horrors: no money, nowhere to go, and a baby on the way. The thought made her shudder with fear. But neither did she wish to force him into marriage because she bore his son or daughter. Analise could not stand the thought of living with him the rest of her life knowing he did not care for her, enduring his barbs and slights and his pursuit of other women, loving him and fighting always to conceal it—no, that was too horrible to contemplate. As for the third option: living on his charity, herself and her child stigmatized by her obvious status, her baby a bastard, and no hope for her of any relationship with another man except that of mistress.

No, a thousand times no, to all of them. If only she had someone to go to, someone who would take her in and help her until the baby was born. Then she could move somewhere else and pretend to be a war widow and support herself and her child somehow. It would be difficult and poverty-stricken, but at least she could retain some honor, some dignity. She could leave before Mark even discovered her condition; that way she would never have to face the decision he would make. But she was friendless and alone, scorned by the only world she knew. There was no one to whom she could turn. Analise stifled a sob as she envisioned Mark's face, dark with fury, when he found out. Oh, dear Heaven, what was she to do?

Analise had never been religious, despite her schooling by the nuns, and ever since she slept with Mark, she had avoided Mass, all too conscious of the stamp of sin on her. But now she prayed frantically, stumbling through her rosary, dwelling most fervently on the Hail Mary, for surely the Holy Mother would have sympathy for another mother's plight.

So it seemed a miraculous answer to her prayers the next morning when Martha brought her a note, saying it had been left at their door by a servant. Analise's heart leaped in her throat when she saw the familiar handwriting on the envelope. With trembling fingers, she tore open the envelope and pulled out the note, her eyes darting to the signature at the bottom to confirm her suspicions. She was right; it was from Pauline Beauvais.

Hurriedly she went back to the salutation and began to read:

Dear Analise,
I have been most dreadfully upset because I have received no word from you. When Becky told me what you had done, I refused to believe it, but I went to your house and your Mama confirmed it. However,

she would not speak of you beyond that nor give any explanation for what you did.

Knowing you as I do, I cannot think you went to the Yankee Major willingly. I am confident that he must have forced you in some way, that you must have had good reason. I know he is that insidious spy who masqueraded among us as Captain Ferris, and I am sure he must be truly a villain. I shudder to think of you at his mercy, and I wish most desperately that our beloved Emil were here to rescue you.

Only yesterday I finally discovered where you live. I wanted very much to come to you, but I could not bring myself to enter that man's home. So I am sending Josephine with this letter instead.

Please come to see me or at least write me a note. I want so much to see you and understand why you did this. If I can help you in any way, I will. Please, please answer.

Love,
Pauline

Analise sat still for a good while, staring down at the sheet of paper clutched in her hand. Dear Pauline—she could sense the desperate anxiety and much-tried loyalty that lurked in her letter. Never had she seen Pauline write anything so emotional. At least, she had one friend who had stood by her. Perhaps she would even understand what Analise had done to save her brother and not condemn her, since Pauline herself loved Emil so. Maybe—maybe she would even be compassionate enough to take her in until the baby was born. She certainly sounded quite willing to hide her friend from Mark.

Analise crumpled the note nervously between her fingers; here was probably her only chance. She could go to Pauline and explain about Emil and throw herself on the other girl's mercy. And if Pauline took her in, she could be gone before Mark suspected her condition. She would never have to know whether he would react kindly or cruelly. But now that this golden opportunity had presented itself, she found herself strangely reluctant to seize it. Analise thought of leaving this dainty, cozy home, of never returning to the soft bed that had held so many passionate nights, of never seeing Mark again or hearing his deep voice and the tremulous sighs of his desire.

It would mean an end to her life with Mark if Pauline received her. No longer would he be the center of her existence. Her heart twisted inside her, crying out that it was too much to ask. Life here might seem a hell at times, but it would be unbearably empty without him. Tears stung her eyes, but she brushed them away and told herself sternly to stop this nonsense. This was what she had wanted to do, what she must do. She must remember the alternatives.

Stiffly Analise rose and went upstairs to the bedroom. She got the meager contents of her jewelry box—those pearls and the garnets might bring enough to see her and the baby through the worst times—and emptied them into her reticule. Then into a shopping bag she stuffed a few essentials: another dress, some underclothing, a gown. She did not want to attract anyone's attention by carrying luggage as she walked to Pauline's.

May came in as she was packing and Analise stopped in consternation. May's dark face was expressionless, and she did not bother to ask what Analise was doing.

"Where are you going?" was all she said.

"No. I can't tell you. If Mark questions you, I don't want you to have to hide anything. It's better if you don't know." There was every possibility, Analise thought, that Mark might simply shrug and accept her leaving, not even bothering to look for her. However, it was just as likely that he would be enraged by her breaking her word to him and depriving him of a bed partner. He might try to find her and bring her back, just to prove his mastery of her. At least he was likely to question May and Martha as to her disappearance.

"I'll come with you," May said firmly, but Analise shook her head.

"No, it may not work out and then I will be back here this afternoon. But if it does, I will send for you."

"You're carrying that blue devil's child, aren't you?" May asked bluntly.

Analise turned away and said nothing, but her silence confirmed the servant's suspicions as well as words could. Analise picked up her reticule and the bag, then impulsively reached out to hug her maid.

"Thank you, May, for standing by me," she said and quickly left the room.

Her escape was remarkably easy. She did not even see Martha as she slipped out of the house, and no one she encountered on the street gave her a second glance. It was not very far from Mark's house to Pauline's, and within minutes she was opening the wrought-iron gate of the Beauvais garden and stepping inside.

The black butler who opened the door looked surprised and a little disapproving at the sight of Analise on the doorstep, clutching a shopping bag nervously. But he led her into the sitting room without comment, merely announcing her to the lady of the house. Pauline looked up, shocked into silence for a moment. Then she leaped to her feet, joy spreading across her face.

"Analise!" she cried, rushing forward to embrace her friend.

"Oh, Pauline," Analise returned her hug fiercely. "I had to come and explain. Please help me; you are the only friend I have."

"Of course I will help you if I can," Pauline said, stepping back from her. "What can I do?"

"Well, first, let me explain about—about Mark Schaeffer."

"All right. Here, sit down." Pauline motioned to a chair close to her own.

Analise took a deep breath. "You are right; he was a spy. He—he wooed me in order to get to Papa's plans of the torpedoes. The thing was: I fell in love with him. I thought he loved me, and I was so crazy in love with him; I thought there was something different about us, something wonderful and uncommon. So I—I slept with him." Analise's voice dropped to a whisper and she glanced hesitantly at Pauline. "I was such a fool!"

Pauline sighed. "There, it's all right. All of us make fools of ourselves over a man at one time or another. I don't blame you. If I had thought Emil loved me, who knows what I would have done."

"Except, of course, that Emil is a gentleman and would not have asked you to dishonor yourself," Analise added bitterly. "Anyway, after the city was captured, he came to see me. He said he loved me and wanted to marry me. I don't know what kind of game he was playing. To make it short, I refused and he left in a rage. Then one night Emil sneaked home to see us before his troops left for Vicksburg."

Pauline drew in her breath sharply. "Oh, no!"

"Yes. You know Emil, he has no thought for danger. Major Schaeffer must have been spying on our house, and the next day he stormed in and arrested Emil. They were going to try him as a spy, and you know they would have hanged him! Well, I had to do something to save him; so I went to Mark to plead for his life. And he agreed to let Emil go free if I would publicly become his mistress."

"Oh, Analise, no! What a monster he is! And to think you did that to save Emil's life. How can your mother be so idiotic?" Pauline's eyes welled with tears and she clasped the other woman's hands in hers. "Thank you, Analise. I think it was a noble thing you did. I am eternally grateful to you for sacrificing yourself to save Emil."

"Oh, thank you, Pauline, you have no idea how much that means to me. It's so horrible, being utterly friendless and ostracized."

"Well, now you know you have one friend who will stand by you," Pauline said firmly. "But what is it I can do to help you?"

Analise swallowed and looked down. "Let me come to live here."

"But of course," Pauline responded quickly. "Have you left him then? Don't tell me that he actually—"

"Threw me out?" Analise finished drily. "No, at least not yet. You see I am—in the family way."

"No! Oh, Analise, you poor dear!"

"The problem is: I was never able to stop loving him.

No matter what he did, like a fool, I continued to love him. Even now I do."

Pauline smiled sadly. "I know, Analise. I know."

"I knew you would; you are the only person who would have any inkling of my feelings."

Pauline wrinkled her brow. "But if you still love him, why are you escaping from him?"

"Because I am afraid of what will happen when he sees I am pregnant. I haven't begun to show yet, but soon—"

"You mean, you think he would be so callous as to turn you out?" Pauline asked.

"I don't know what he will do; I never do. He flies into the most horrible rages, and I don't understand what causes them. He accuses me, totally without reason, of having been with other men."

"Mon Dieu, he sounds like a madman!"

"He seems almost tortured, driven; I don't know why. And at times he can be so tender or humorous or gentle. He might discard me, but then he might marry me, to give the child a name. I just don't know; neither one appeals to me. And I could not bear it if he gave me a little house and a stipend, like a quadroon!"

Pauline murmured sympathetically. "Well, of course you shall stay here. I can think of nothing better than having you here to talk to all the time. It will seem like the convent school again."

Analise managed a dry chuckle. "Hardly, with me ballooning out like an elephant in a few months." She smiled and said earnestly. "Thank you, Pauline. Thank you."

Mark did not realize at first that Analise was gone. When he came home that evening, he had steeled himself to propose marriage and face her ire; so, when he found her not at home, his first reaction was relief. However, when she had not appeared by time for supper, he began to grow worried. Where could she have gone? He knew she almost never ventured out into the streets. Once more, and more thoroughly this time, he searched the house, but she was nowhere to be found. Martha disclaimed all knowledge of her whereabouts, saying that she had not seen her leave, but also had not seen her around the house all afternoon.

May claimed the same lack of knowledge as the other servant, but Mark detected something furtive in her tone, and he suspected she knew more than she was saying. It did not take much of his icy questioning for May to admit that she had seen her packing a few garments and leaving.

"Where? Where was she going?" Mark snapped.

"I don't know. Truly I don't. Miss Analise would not tell me where she was going for fear you would force it out of me." And how right she had been, too, May thought ruefully.

"You mean to say that she was running away from me? That she did not want me to follow her?"

May nodded and Mark exhaled loudly with exasperation. "But why? Do you know? Damn you, tell me! Was she going to meet another man?"

Sir!" May exclaimed. "How can you say that? Miss Analise would never be unfaithful! You must know that."

"I don't know anything!" Mark retorted. "But you do; I can tell it. You had better tell me, May, because you must know I would stop at nothing to find out what I want to know."

May eyed him warily. Mark was undeniably good-looking and she suspected that he could be a smooth charmer if he wished. But he frankly scared her.

"I suspect it's the babe."

"Baby? What baby?"

May sent him a meaningful glance. "Why, your baby, of course. The one Miss Analise is carrying."

Mark went pale and still. "Analise? Analise is carrying my child?"

May nodded and Mark sank wordlessly into a chair. He noticed dispassionately that his hands were trembling. He thought of Analise, swollen with his child, and felt a surge of excitement.

His head snapped up. "But why would she run away, then? Now, of all times? She needs me now—doesn't she?"

May shrugged. "Maybe she thought you wouldn't want the child, wouldn't want to know about it, even."

"That's crazy!"

"Maybe she figured you would turn her out, not wanting her after she got fat."

"That's even crazier!"

Again May shrugged. "Most like, she just wants to get away to where nobody knows her, so as her baby won't be branded a bastard."

"A bastard!" Mark cried. "Good God, could she really believe that I would not marry her?"

He clenched his jaw until the muscles jumped. Why should she think otherwise, when he had been cruel to her, punishing her by making her his mistress rather than his wife?

"I have to find her. May, where did she go? I must find her and marry her. I won't let my child be born illegitimate. Where is she?"

"I told you the truth. She would not tell me."

Mark slammed his fist against the wall. He believed May; it sounded like something Analise would have thought of—protecting her maid against his wrath, even at her own expense. Where could she have gone? Not to her mother, surely, nor to any of her friends; she told him yesterday that they had all turned against her. Where, then, could she go?

But of course! Where else but the welcoming, forgiving church? Had she not said she had been schooled by the nuns? In a flash, Mark was out of the house and hurrying toward the Ursuline convent.

It was hours later when he returned to the house, exhausted and worried. The sisters had denied stoutly that Analise was there, and he could not believe they would lie when he explained her condition and his desire to marry and care for her. They had smiled at him sympathetically and shaken their heads. No, quite definitely Analise had not sought refuge with them. They remembered her quite well from school, and swore she was not there.

From there, he had tramped all over the city to every Catholic church he could find, questioning each priest and receiving always the same negative answer. He even went to her parents' house, rousing at the late hour an old butler who declared stoutly that Miss Analise had not returned and that even if she had her mother would not receive her.

Mark was inclined to believe the man, but he was too wild with worry to let even the slightest chance slip through his fingers. So he firmly shoved the man aside and searched the house himself, room by room, sending Mrs. Caldwell into a strong fit of hysterics.

For a long time he stood in Analise's old room. Even

stripped of her presence, the memory of her clung to the place. Unbidden memories of that one sweet night of mutual love in the house crept into his mind. Had he wantonly ruined that? Had he destroyed the only one on earth he truly loved?

Haunted by thoughts of Analise alone and helpless out in the dark somewhere, Mark turned slowly home and there slumped into a chair. It was past midnight. Where was she? Huddled out in the open, hungry and alone, an easy prey for rapists or murderers? Harsh, scalding tears rose in his eyes.

Mark blinked them away determinedly. He must not give way; he had to keep a clear head and think, if he was to find Analise. Could she have taken it into her head to leave the city and travel up to her plantation? She had seemed very fond of the place, and her father was there, she said. That was a definite possibility; she would be strong-willed enough to think she could make it there on foot and escape harm. Now if only he knew where it was . . .

What was the name of the friend of hers? Pauline something. She would be able to tell him; he would make her tell him, if it meant breaking her neck. Resolutely he went back out into the night, oblivious of the late hour.

It took some time to find Pauline's house, especially in the darkness of night. It was not until he recalled her last name and inquired at one of the taverns that he was able to reach it. By then it was well after one o'clock, but he thundered at the door without compunction.

A frightened old black man cracked the door a fraction and peered out at him. Mark put a hand on the door and pushed firmly.

"I want to see Miss Beauvais. Pauline Beauvais."

"But, sir, she is asleep," the old man whispered.

"Damn it, wake her up! I demand to see her. I am a Major in the United States army, and I must question the young lady immediately. I think it is better here than marching her back to headquarters under guard, don't you?"

The old man gaped, relaxing his hold on the door. Mark looked past him to see Pauline coming quickly down the staircase, a flickering candle in her hand. She stopped and stared at him above the old man's head.

"It is all right, Josephus," she said quietly. "I shall see the Major in the sitting room."

She swept regally into the next room, despite the casualness of her frayed wrapper and the long braid of hair hanging loose down her back. In the sitting room she turned coolly and sat, raising her eyebrows in question.

Mark almost chuckled. He had always marveled at the friendship between the beautiful, lively Analise and the plain spinster, but now he could understand the attraction. She was as cool as a cucumber in this decidedly unorthodox situation; few women possessed that sort of calm courage.

"I must ask you not to frighten my butler, Major; he is an old man."

"Miss Beauvais, let me be direct."

"Please do." Pauline regarded him coolly. The man looked awful, ragged with exhaustion and worry. For a moment she wondered if Analise had mistaken his feeling for her. He seemed to have been through some kind of hell this evening.

"I have come to ask directions to the Caldwell plantation."

"The Caldwell plantation!" Pauline repeated, completely thrown by his words.

"Yes, I think Analise has fled there, and I must find her."

Pauline gaped at him. "Are you mad?"

"I think she may have tried to go there, and I must find her as soon as possible. There is no telling what danger she could run into out there."

Pauline opened her mouth to give him the directions and so send him off on a wild good chase, but something in his face stopped her. He was a despicable man, surely; but Analise loved him, and if he had some feeling for her, would it not be better to let him find her?

"Why should I tell you?" Pauline asked. "If Analise wants to hide from you, why should I help you find her?"

"Look, I know you have no reason to think me anything but a scoundrel. In many ways I am. But I love Analise. I just found out today that she is pregnant—" At Pauline's look of distaste, he said scornfully, "Forgive me. I haven't time for polite evasions. The woman carries my child, and I must find her so that I can marry her. Please. Miss Beauvais, I beg of you. I have never begged for anything in my life, but I beg you now. Help me."

Pauline felt a traitorous sympathy seep through her at the evident pain on the man's face, but she took herself firmly in hand and said crisply. "You love her? You wish to marry her? Forgive me, Major, but I find it a little difficult to believe that a man who loves a woman would so cruelly force her to become his mistress, so expose her to public scorn in that way.

"I will tell you frankly, Major, that I have spoken to Analise and she told me much of your treatment of her, and it hardly sounded as if you loved her," Pauline said accusingly.

Mark stared at her. "You talked to her? Today? You mean you know where she is?"

A soft voice behind him said, "Stop bullying Pauline, Mark. Here I am."

"Analise!" He whirled and stared at her, shaken with relief. "Analise." He swallowed, not sure how to proceed.

Analise moved slowly into the room. When Mark had awakened her with his mad pounding, she had known then that in her deepest heart this was what she had prayed for: that Mark would care enough to pursue her and demand her return. She had trailed down after Pauline and eavesdropped unabashedly on their conversation. With a quickly beating heart, she had heard his words and she knew she must face him.

Mark wet his lips and said nervously, "May told me you are pregnant. Is that true?"

She nodded and he cried, "My God, why did you not tell me? Why did you run and hide?" When Analise did not reply, he said in a low voice, "Marry me, Analise."

"Why? So that you may continue to torment me?"

His face twisted with pain. "No. Analise, please, forgive me. It is just that I get so jealous when I think of you and other men. It hurts so to know that you despise me and love another."

"But there is no other man, let alone several!" Analise exclaimed. "I cannot bear this insane, unfounded jealousy! You say you want to marry me. How can you, when you have given me nothing but pain? You told me before that you loved me, but that was a ruse to get to the torpedoes."

"No! I loved you. It was the truth. I love you still."

"You call it love to force me into your bed, to make me promise to submit to you and accept whatever indignities you put upon me?"

"You chose that!" he snapped back, prodded far enough. "You bargained for it."

"Yes!" Analise hissed. "And what a fair bargain it was—my public humiliation for my brother's life!"

Mark stared at her, stunned. "Your what! What do you mean, your brother?"

Analise looked at him oddly. "Yes, my brother, Emil."

"But—but his name is Fourier. He disclaimed any connection with you or your family."

"But of course he is my brother; you must know that. You met him, surely—no, I guess perhaps you did not . . ." her voice trailed off.

"But the name—" he said almost pleadingly, clinging to the last defense.

"He is my half-brother, my mother's son. She was married to a man named Fourier and he died; later she married my father. But Emil and I have always been as close as full-blood kin."

The color drained from Mark's face. "Is this true, Miss Beauvais?" he asked woodenly.

"Of course," Pauline responded, amazed at his manner.

"My God." Mark raised his hands shakily to his face. "My God, what have I done?"

"Mark, what is it?" Analise cried, her alarm for him chasing away all other considerations.

Fourier was her brother; what he had thought was her passion for a lover was really sisterly love. And he had been so blind, so jealous that he had not bothered to ask her what her relationship to the Southerner was. He loved her more than anything in the world, and yet he had not had faith enough in her to even give her a chance to explain. His jealousy had been unfounded, and out of that jealousy he had hurt and humiliated her. Mark thought of Analise's anguish at the bargain he had demanded of her—her pride, her very self in return for her brother's life.

"How you must hate me," he said, steeling himself to look at her.

Analise gasped at the sight of his face, worn and pale, lines of sadness biting deep into his face. "Mark, what is wrong? Why are you looking at me like that?"

Slowly he turned to Pauline. "Miss Beauvais, could I speak to Analise alone? I promise you that I shall not harm her. Ever again."

"Of—of course," Pauline stammered and quickly left the room.

"Analise, please, sit down and hear me out. I know I've been a blind fool; if there was any way to undo the harm I have done you, believe me, I would. It's no excuse, I know, but I did not know that Emil Fourier was your brother. When he was discovered in your house and when you begged so for his life, I thought—" his voice sank lower. "I thought he was your lover. I was crazy with jealousy, and I wanted to hurt you back. So I forced that bargain on you, and it made me even more furious and jealous that you loved him enough to do that.

"And ever since then I have been punishing you because of my suspicions. I know I have been hard and cruel; I have no excuse for it except my damned selfish blindness. I won't ask you to forgive me; it was unforgivable. But, please, give me another chance; let me make it up to you. Analise, please marry me."

Analise gulped and said, "I—I don't understand. You want to marry me because you wronged me?"

"Analise, I love you! I want to marry you because you are the only thing in my life that's ever been good or right. I gave you a false name when I was here before, but my love was real. I loved you then so much that I almost forsook my country in order not to kill your trust in me. I have loved you ever since, no matter how I acted. Please, Analise, believe me."

She stared at him, numb with shock. He loved her. He thought Emil was her lover and he had been jealous. Analise felt hysterical laughter begin to bubble in her throat, and she fought it down.

Mark was desperate at her silence. "I don't expect you to still love me. I know your love could not have survived what I did to you. But, think of your child, Analise. A child needs a name, a father, money, security—I want to provide that. For the baby's sake, marry me. I swear to you that I will accept whatever restrictions you place on me. I won't compel you to share my bed. If you wish, I won't even come near you."

Analise looked at Mark's face, drawn and tired and stamped with anxiety. Bright tears softened his hard black eyes, and when Analise saw them, something within her snapped. With a sob, she threw herself against his chest and his arms clamped around her convulsively.

Her voice was muffled and incoherent amidst her sobs, but he heard quite clearly a few of her words: "Yes, yes, I love you, Mark!"

Trembling with emotion and relief, Mark laid his cheek against her hair, reveling in the warm, soft feel of it.

"Oh, my love," he whispered. "My love."

EXILE

Ten

$\mathcal{A}$nalise had never known such happiness existed as she experienced for the next few weeks. They were married the next day in a brief ceremony by the army chaplain, with Pauline and one of Mark's soldiers as witnesses. Once Analise had dreamed, as all girls did, of a beautiful church wedding, a grand and glorious affair with herself radiant in a beautiful gown. Now, she gave it no thought; all that really mattered was their discovered love.

It was amazing how her world changed overnight, now that she knew that Mark loved her. Hope returned and, with it, much of her former spirit. She went for walks daily and often stopped off at Pauline's house for a cozy chat. Her chin high, she ignored the shock and disapproval of New Orleans society. She only regretted that no one spoke to her outright, thus giving her the opportunity to air her feelings on the attitudes of society and her love for her husband.

Mark was the center of her world, and she spent every day simply passing the time until his return. He brought her gifts that once she would have scorned, but that she now fell upon with cries of delight. Quickly she fashioned dresses from the material he gave her and modeled them for him proudly. And at night in bed, she received and returned his love joyously, delighting now in exciting him with all the tricks she had learned. No longer did her ministrations seem degrading, for now they were outpourings of her love for him. Once she even donned the enticing red nightgown he had given her and stood before him proudly, luxuriating in the fires of passion that sprang into his eyes as he explored her body.

And Mark, freed at last from his suspicions and anger, was able to enjoy Analise's supple, lovely body undetracted by the pricks of jealousy and hurt. They came together in all the fresh, unbridled joy of newly experienced love, and each pounding, searing explosion of desire seemed greater than the last.

A month of such unfettered love passed, and then suddenly the news came, shattering their world: Mark's request for transfer, placed so long ago in the despair of Analise's rejection, had, ironically, finally been granted. He received orders to report for duty in the Virginia campaign.

"No!" Analise gasped in dismay. "Not now! They can't do this. Couldn't you explain, ask to get out of it? Can't you refuse it?"

Mark's lips twisted in a wry smile. "My dear, one does not 'refuse' an order of the U.S. army. I have no choice: I practically begged to be sent back to the Virginia campaign; I can hardly tell them that I've changed my mind. No, I think we are stuck with it."

"You want to go," Analise accused him.

"I would rather fight in a real war than sit around here overseeing conquered women and children. And, as I told you before, I do have a few ideals, and winning this war is one of them."

"Then you do want to go!" she cried, tears swelling in her eyes. "You don't even care!"

"I care," he said soberly and pulled her into his arms. "Oh, I care so much. I don't want to leave you. I want to be with you and sleep with you and be at your side when our child is born. It will be hell being without you, not getting to touch you or see you or hear that beautiful laugh. I'd have to be insane to prefer sleeping on the hard ground to sleeping in a bed with you. Don't you know I would rather love you than fight a war?"

"But—"

"But I have a duty, Analise—to my country, to the human beings enslaved down here, to myself as well. I have to see this thing through. I want to be part of it. I told you before that I could not betray my principles for you; I still cannot."

Argumentative words tumbled to Analise's lips, but she bit them back. It was useless to try to persuade Mark when he had his mind set on something. And she did not want to shatter the bliss of their love with an argument.

"All right," she said. "I promise not to plague you. I know you must go. But, oh, Mark, how am I to bear it?"

Mark caught her to him tightly, burying his face in her thick, soft hair. What a sweet, sharp pain it was—to see her sad because he would leave. Poor Analise: he at least would have the fighting to occupy him, while she could only wait and worry.

Finally he kissed her hair and sighed, releasing her. "Now, let's return to practicalities. There is a ship leaving here for Maryland Thursday; I shall book our passage on it. Can you be ready by then?"

Analise blinked in surprise. "You mean that I am going too?"

He smiled lazily. "Of course. I mean to keep you as close at hand as possible."

"Oh, Mark!" the girl's face lit up.

He laughed. "Now, don't get excited—you are *not* going to come to Virginia with me. I am sending you to my father's home in New York."

A shadow of doubt crossed Analise's face. "But I don't know them. And you said your father was so stern; he may dislike me, Mark. I am a Southerner, after all."

"You are my wife, and he will agree that you belong with my family, especially since you are pregnant. Besides, for all his morality, my father has a soft spot for beauty; I am certain he will dote on you."

She crinkled her brow. "But I don't know anyone in New York. Why couldn't I just stay here in this little house; I will have May to take care of the child. And Pauline will keep me company."

Mark shook his head firmly. "I would be in constant worry if you were here. Except for Pauline, you are friendless. The city dislikes you; you are a traitor in their eyes. I can't leave you here without protection. And what if the Rebs should counterattack and regain the city? No, I want you safe in New York, under my father's protection and with the best medical services available. I'm not taking any chances with you and that baby."

Analise agreed reluctantly, not at all anxious to live so far from everything she knew. Mark smiled and kissed her gently, trying to raise her spirits.

"Come, it is not so bad. You will probably love New York. No one there will ostracize you; you will make friends. My sister lives at home with Father, and she will take you under her wing. Just think, you will have a family again."

Analise smiled a little more brightly then. Surely she would like Mark's sister; she was probably a daring, quick-witted girl, a female version of Mark. It would be good to form friendships and go out in society again. And the idea of a family eagerly awaiting the birth of a grandchild, cosseting and pampering her, was most appealing. Besides, if Mark got a furlough, he would have enough time to go to New York, but not all the way to New Orleans. That alone made New York worth living in.

To Analise's amazement, she quite enjoyed the sea trip to Maryland. Rather than gloomily contemplating their future separation, Mark and Analise spent their time wrapped in a tight warm cocoon of love, savoring every moment. In New Orleans, their love had been a fireworks of passion, but on board ship they attained a deeper, more sober understanding. During the long empty hours they talked, spilling out their hopes, their pasts, their fears, and they never tired of exploring each other's minds and histories.

For the first time in his life, Mark found himself talking about his mother. In an expressionless voice he related the beauty of Thalissia Ferris Schaeffer, the vivid, sparkling personality and lively wit that enthralled every male she met, including her young son. He talked also of her many infidelities, which shamed his father and broke his heart, until at last, he left his faithless wife and returned to the North. Mark's sister Frances, several years older than he, had gone with him. The enchantress Thalissia had had little kindness for a daughter. But Mark had stayed with Thalissia; the boy loved his butterfly mother too much to leave. However, Mark grew to despise her too. The sly laughter and vulgar innuendos that circulated through the local society shamed him; young as he was, he could not even defend her honor by calling out her detractors.

"Defend her honor—what a joke!" Mark said bitterly, his face dark with remembered pain. "Her name was in shreds, anyway. She was growing older and her beauty was melting with time and dissipation. So she grew less discriminating in her lovers. She allowed lower and lower types into her bed." His lips curled with distaste. "She even began taking slaves; I can remember her riding out to the fields and her eyes would roam over the black bucks, choosing the one she thought would best satisfy her desires. And if he did not perform well, it would be the whipping post for him."

Analise shuddered. "You can see why I am no saint myself. I learned to lust at my mother's knee, so to speak."

"But you left."

Mark sighed and lay back on the narrow ship's bed, crossing his arms behind his head. "Yes, I left. When I was fourteen, I found that I could stand it no longer. That house was like a web of decay and decadence, and she was the spider at its center. The whole countryside was like that—rotting at the core, moldering in its wealth and genealogies, slimy with the corruption of slavery. I hated it, and I hated Thalissia. God help me, I still loved her, but finally I came to detest her more. So I ran away and boarded a ship to New York."

Analise was silent for a moment; nothing seemed adequate to say in the face of his story. Finally she whispered, "I am no Thalissia."

Mark pulled her down beside him, his arms a tight circle around her. "I know, my love, I know. But sometimes in the past, when I flared with anger and jealousy, it was partly because of her. It is hard for me to believe in a woman's faithfulness."

Analise smiled and said, lightly mocking, "Oh, a *woman's* faithfulness, eh? I suppose that men, on the other hand, are above that."

He grinned at her. "I confess I spread my seed quite liberally across half the world. But then, a *man's* faithlessness is of little concern to me."

"Well, mark my words, Major Schaeffer," Analise said with mock severity, "you better have a care now. I'll not stand by and patiently ignore your infidelities."

Mark laughed. "No, I am sure not." He put his palms up to her face and kissed her thoroughly. "Don't worry, I may have the Ferris streak of wildness, but like a Schaeffer, I love one woman only for all my life. I have no need of anyone but you."

"Mark," she breathed, and her voice was drowned in his hard, searching kiss.

When they landed in Baltimore, Mark put Analise aboard a train and wired his father the time of her arrival. He could not accompany her because he had to report for duty immediately, and Analise did her best to be stalwart and understanding about it. In truth, she felt frightened, cold, and alone. The freezing air crept beneath her skirts and cut through the thin material of her dress, despite the short cape she wore. Used as she was to the warmth of New

Orleans, she shivered uncontrollably and almost cried at the sight of her cold-reddened nose. It seemed awful that this was to be the memory of her Mark would carry with him: red-nosed and shaking all over and thick-waisted with child.

Analise began to cry and threw her arms around him. Mark enfolded her lovingly, an unaccustomed lump in his throat. He had never found anything as difficult as parting with her. It seemed as if all the light would leave his life when she left.

"Analise, I love you," he murmured against her hair. "I love you more than anything."

She hugged him tighter, gulping back her tears. Then her train pulled in, and Mark settled her in a seat, fussing over her like a mother hen until the conductor made him leave. Analise gripped her reticule tightly and peered out the window as the train began to rumble beneath her feet. When she saw Mark standing forlornly on the platform, she tried to smile reassuringly. But her lips trembled so she was afraid it did not look much like a smile.

The clacking and rumbling increased, and the train gathered speed. Mark's figure receded ever faster, and was gone. Stubborn tears began to fall, even though she hated to weep so publicly. A woman patted her hand and said in a kindly voice that she knew well how Analise felt. Yet when Analise politely thanked her for her concern, an odd look crossed the woman's face and she seemed to pull away. It was a reaction to her soft slurred accent that Analise would become quite familiar with.

Analise had not often traveled by train, and the trip made her uncomfortable. She decided that she far preferred the more familiar steamboat or sailing ship. Even an old-fashioned flatboat was better than this—at least it was smooth.

When the train finally reached New York and Analise emerged nervously onto the platform, she was almost overwhelmed by the bustle and noise. It seemed as though everyone was moving at twice the pace she was used to. Rapid nasal voices assaulted her ears, speaking so fast and sharply that she could understand only about half of what was said. And here and there in the clamor she heard the thick brogue of an Irishman or the guttural sound of German. She felt a strange panic begin to rise in her at the unfamiliar movement and noise. She wished desperately that Mark had been able to get passage for May on the same ship with them; she would feel better if only she had May with her.

Then someone said, "Mrs. Schaeffer?" and she turned quickly.

The man who addressed her had dark hair shot through with gray and black eyes very similar to Mark's, though without their fire.

"Yes?" she said. "Are you Mark's father?"

"Yes," he replied and a thin smile touched his wintery countenance. "And you must be my new daughter-in-law."

"Thank goodness you came. I confess the babble quite intimidated me."

The older man smiled, but a shadow briefly touched his eyes.

"I'm sorry. Did I say something wrong?"

"No, my dear. It's just that your voice reminded me of someone I knew long ago."

Analise felt a flash of pity for the man. Did he still love his pretty, faithless Southern wife?

Prentiss Schaeffer guided her quickly through the train station and into his waiting carriage while his coachman got her luggage. Analise gratefully put her frozen feet on the warm bricks kept in the vehicle for that purpose, and proceeded to stare out the window. A soft whiteness lay over everything, and it fascinated Analise: she had never actually seen snow before.

"I can see you are dressed for a hotter climate. Tomorrow you and Frances must go shopping for some warm clothing," Mr. Schaeffer told her.

Analise nodded. She had thought Baltimore was cold, but this city was bone-chilling. It was beyond her how people could stand to live in such a climate.

"It pleases me that Mark married finally. I was beginning to despair of him. Marriage will settle him down, I think, make him give up some of the foolishness he has indulged in the past. I confess that I was somewhat taken aback when I received his letter saying that he had married you five months ago."

Analise felt a little clutch of fear—did he suspect the date was moved back considerably?—but also a warmth that Mark had tried to protect her in that way.

"I feared he might have acted in haste and to his detriment. But I can see now that was not so. Welcome to the Schaeffer family; you are a welcome addition."

The ride to the Schaeffer house was silent and cold and Analise was glad to see it end. Mr. Schaeffer was a taciturn man, and, having said his piece, he spoke no more. Analise occupied herself by looking out the window at the bleak landscape. Her heart went to her feet when she thought of spending several months here. The Schaeffer home, a large, dark brick house, did little to lighten that feeling, and her introduction to Mark's sister made it even worse.

Frances was a thin, plain woman who did nothing to soften her looks. She was dressed in a dark navy-blue dress with a high, stiff collar and long sleeves. Her black hair was drawn back into a severe knot at the nape of her neck, and her mouth was set in prim lines. Spectacles hid dark eyes much like Mark's and their father's, thus obliterating her best feature. Her manner was stiff with Analise, even remote, and Analise found it hard to believe that this dry spinster was related to Mark.

Frances showed Analise to her room and left, not saying anything more than was absolutely necessary. Analise tried two or three times to start a conversation with the woman, but her replies were short and dismissive. She began to think that Frances must have something against her, though she could not imagine what. Analise sat down, feeling miserable, and wrote a long, tearful epistle to her husband, begging him to get her out of the house.

Rest refreshed her spirits, however, and the next morning Analise tore her letter up. Things would be bad enough for Mark without her burdening him with her troubles. Surely she could handle a surly sister-in-law by herself.

With renewed confidence she went downstairs, only to find that she had not been wrong in her impression of Frances. The woman was as chilly as ever. At Prentiss' insistence, she took Analise shopping for wool cloth and heavy cloaks and warm undergarments, but she said hardly a word, damping every attempt by Analise to carry on a conversation.

Late that afternoon they had a caller, a pretty blonde woman a few years older than Analise. She was a sophisticated, well-turned-out woman, but Analise took an immediate dislike to her. Although Philippa Carter smiled and chatted with her, Analise sensed an underlying dislike that bordered on hatred.

It became clear when Frances sighed after Philippa left and said, "Poor Philippa; it has been quite a shock to her, your coming here. Mark was engaged to her when he left for the war. We all considered her a part of the family already. She is such a dear person. But then Mark's letter came about you . . ."

There was such distaste in her voice that anger flared in Analise. "All right, Frances," she said bluntly, "would you like to tell me why you dislike me?"

"Dislike you?" the other woman said blankly, her eyes unreadable behind her glasses.

Analise snapped, "Don't be coy with me. You have hardly disguised the way you feel about me. Or is a total absence of conversation your usual social attitude?"

Frances looked at her evenly. "If you insist. No, I don't like you. You are a Southerner, and I know Southern women. They are vacant-headed, lying, treacherous females, a disgrace to their sex."

"Don't you think that indictment is a little broad?" Analise asked, her lips twitching with amusement; surely she could not be serious.

"You think that statement is funny? I might have expected that from you."

"I know about your mother; Mark told me that you disliked her—"

"Mark told you about her?" Frances interrupted, obviously offended.

"Well, it is not as if I were a total stranger; I *am* Mark's wife," Analise said with some asperity, annoyed by the woman's attitude.

"Under rather peculiar circumstances," Frances countered.

"What do you mean by that?" Analise asked, her voice dangerously low.

"I mean, it seems rather odd that Mark did not write us of his marriage at the time, rather than several months after the event."

Analise raised her brows coolly. "I gather Mark is a rather poor correspondent."

Frances pressed her lips together until they were merely a slash in her face. She was certain that this beautiful Southern woman had turned Mark's head. Men were so susceptible to beauty; a shallow nature mattered little if the face was lovely. Of course, foolish creatures, they realized their mistake too late and then they were sorry for it. No doubt this Analise had dazzled Mark, seduced him, and gotten herself in the family way so that Mark was forced to marry her. He would regret it, just as their father had regretted it, and he would be in pain for years, too, just like Father.

Analise could see that the plain spinster suffered from a case of galloping jealousy. She had met women like her before, poor frustrated creatures who clung to a brother or father with all the emotion and jealousy of a wife. It was not surprising that she should dislike Analise, especially since Analise was a pretty Southerner like her despised mother. Oh, she could understand it, all right, but it certainly would not make the time she had to spend here very pleasant.

Abruptly Analise went upstairs to her room; it seemed

to her that the best thing to do was to avoid the poisonous woman. She sat down and took up pen and paper to write Mark as cheerful a letter as possible.

At the dinner table that evening, she asked Mr. Schaeffer what to do with her mail to Mark, and he replied that she had only to leave her letters on the entry hall table and they would be taken when the mail was delivered each morning. So after the meal was over, Analise placed her letter on the table he had designated.

The next morning Analise stayed in her room until the noon meal, to avoid Frances. She did not, therefore, see Frances go into the hall and stare down at her letter. Mark's sister hated the thought of Analise writing to Mark, extending her hold on him while he was so vulnerable there on a lonely, frightening battlefront. That was why Analise did it, Frances was certain; she was a calculating vixen and she doubtless knew Mark's infatuation would quickly die if she did not keep it going by writing.

Frances glanced around her: there was no one watching. No one would know if this one letter was not sent. And it would save Mark so much sorrow and pain if his love died now, quickly and cleanly, instead of struggling through her lies and infidelities in all the long years ahead. After another furtive look around, Frances picked up the letter and stuck it in her pocket, then hastened out of the hall.

Eleven

$\mathcal{T}$he winter crept by with agonizing slowness. The cold seemed to Analise to penetrate to her very bones, and she began to think that she would never be warm again. Even huddled before the fire in her new woolen dresses with thick wool stockings underneath and wrapped around with shawls, she could not get warm all over. Her face would be flushed with the heat from the fire, but her backside would freeze. Drafts crept up under her skirts wherever she walked or sat. And if she bundled up for a walk outside, when she returned her face would be chapped and her nose red.

Because of the cold and because she feared slipping on the ice or snow and injuring the baby, she rarely went outside. However, staying cooped up in the house with only the dour Frances for company nearly drove her to distraction. Frances never lost her spiteful, rude manner toward Analise, and it was even worse when her friends came to call. The dainty Philippa Carter prattled constantly about "dear Mark" and never failed to comment on the way Analise's figure was ballooning. All of the other friends were like Frances, "prunes and prisms" intellectual old maids. They spent their time knitting socks and mufflers for the soldiers (which Analise judged would reach the men right at the beginning of the warm Virginia summer) talking abolition, General Grant, and the defeat of the South. Personally, Analise thought Grant a drunken boor—how great did a general have to be to defeat ignorant Tennessee backwoodsmen?—and it was constantly on the tip of her tongue to ask them why they never spoke of the Virginia campaign, where the Southern army reigned supreme.

However, she bit back her words and tried to ignore the barbed words and sly glances that were sent her way. If she retorted, it would just mean a bitter row and the situation would be more impossible than ever.

Mr. Schaeffer seemed to be the only person who had any liking for her. In the evenings, he often played chess with her or discussed books they had read. But even though he was kinder to her than Frances, he was home only in the evenings and he was a reserved, remote man. Analise could not really regard him as a friend. Worse by far than the unfriendly atmosphere of the Schaeffer household was the fact that Mark did not write her. At first she scolded herself for expecting letters sooner than they could possibly come from the war front. Even if it was winter and therefore they were not fighting, there were bound to be many delays. Doubtless Mark, like most men, was not inclined to be a faithful correspondent. Analise ignored the voice inside her that cried that he would write if he truly loved her, knowing how unhappy she was here.

After months had passed, still without word from him, she could no longer quell her doubts. In the last days of her pregnancy, heavy, clumsy, and scared, miserable from the slights and insults Frances aimed at her, and feeling desperately alone, she poured out her feelings to her husband in her letters. She begged him to write, even a few lines, to assure her that he loved her and would return to her. Surely, she thought, he would write her now, but she waited patiently day after day, and still no letter came for her.

It would not have been so unbearable if she had not seen a letter or two from him to Frances and his father lying on the table. He wrote them, but he would not send her even the slightest word! How could he be so cruel?

The obvious answer was that he no longer loved her. He regretted marrying her; perhaps he even hoped that if he ignored her, she would leave his life after the baby was born. No—he could not have been lying; she knew he had loved her! Ah, but, that insidious little voice would say, he had merely been infatuated with her, as Frances was always hinting; and now he had discovered that it was only infatuation, not love, and it had withered away.

That thought made her frantic. What was she to do? How could she win him back when he was so far away? She was so miserable without him, and she could not bear to think of living the rest of her life that way. Analise wondered if she should take her pride and simply leave, setting Mark free to do as he wished. The idea of doing that, however, sent her into a flood of tears.

Her abdomen grew fatter, but daily her face grew thinner and paler, and blue circles formed beneath her eyes. Prentiss Schaeffer looked at her kindly, worriedly, and once he even went so far as to pat her hand and assure her that Mark had always been a very poor letter writer. Analise smiled at him sadly and said nothing. He was trying to be kind, but they both knew it was sheer neglect on Mark's part.

Late in May, the baby was born. It was a boy, a little black-haired, dark-eyed boy, and Analise named him John Prentiss, for his two grandfathers. The labor was long and debilitating; Analise had never felt so alone and frightened as she did during that pain-wracked time in the house of strangers.

Analise wrote to Mark of their son's birth, giving him all the marvelous details about the child. Surely, she thought, he would send his congratulations or ask after her health or at least acknowledge in some way the presence of his boy. But all through her long convalescence, Analise received not a word from him, and she sank daily into greater depression.

If Frances did not like the mother, she doted on the child. Both she and Mr. Schaeffer thought that John Prentiss was probably the most miraculous thing that had ever happened. Frances quickly assumed charge of him. Analise's loss of health during the last stages of her pregnancy and the long, difficult labor had left her weak and sickly. She spent most of her time in bed on the doctor's orders, and she saw the baby mostly at feeding time. Frances played with it and gave the orders to the nursemaid and put it to bed; Analise was too tired and depressed to care.

Gradually she grew better; the warm days of early summer beckoned her, and she made herself leave her bed and dress and move about the house, until at last she could move outside and take brief walks. As she regained her health, she began to realize how completely Frances had taken over her baby. It was irritating to her, the way Frances would come to carry the baby back to his room when she felt feeding time was over or the way she ordered his schedule. One day Analise was in the nursery cooing to Johnny and playing with him, when the nursemaid entered and told her she must leave.

"What?" Analise stared at her.

"It is time for John Prentiss' nap. Miss Frances says he must always take a nap at this time."

Analise's eyes sparked dangerously, but she said as sweetly as possible, "Well, I think today we can delay it a little. Johnny seems quite awake and happy; he and I are having fun together."

"No, you must leave now," the nursemaid said firmly, oblivious to the storm warning in the other woman's eyes. "Miss Fran said he must sleep now, and there are to be no exceptions."

Analise glared at her, her eyes sparkling like blue diamonds. "Since I have been ill and not with my son much, I shall be charitable and assume that you did not recognize me. I am Mrs. Mark Schaeffer, the baby's mother. *Miss* Schaeffer has no right to order my son's life—or mine. In the future you will follow my orders, not hers—that is, if you wish to remain Johnny's nurse. Now, kindly leave this room and let me play with my son in peace!"

Her words came out staccato and stinging, each one a sharp pellet, and the nurse backed away before them, turning and fleeing at her last sentence. Analise continued to play with Johnny, but her anger kept her from enjoying it. Finally she swept out of the room, sending a brief nod at the nurse cowering in the hall. Quickly she plunged down the stairs and out of the house, walking rapidly, trying to burn off her anger. She paid little attention to where she was going, and her steps led her along a familiar path to a little park she often visited. There she flung herself down on a bench and began to brood about her situation: Mark did not love her, did not even acknowledge his child's arrival; she was alone among enemies; and Frances was usurping her place as the baby's mother. Involuntarily, tears began to slide down her cheeks.

"Oh, but please, you must not cry," a soft male voice said, and Analise looked up, startled, straight into kind blue eyes.

"I beg your pardon," she gulped out. "It's terrible to act like this in public. I am dreadfully ashamed."

"No, no, do not be ashamed," he protested, his voice strangely accented. "But it is not right for a lovely young woman to be crying like this. What has made you so sad?"

Analise looked at him, her curiosity slightly aroused. He was a blond man, of medium stature, a little too heavy, perhaps, but nice-looking all the same. He was obviously foreign, and his clothes were of an expensive cut and cloth. But none of this added up to any reason why he should take an interest in her, a total stranger. She wondered briefly if he took her for a common woman, crying on the bench like that, and meant to accost her. One look at his concerned face made her dismiss that notion. He was just a kind person, which she had become unaccustomed to, living among these unfriendly Yankees.

"Forgive me," he said anxiously. "I hope I did not startle you. I have seen you here before, walking; I felt almost as if I knew you and when I saw you crying just now, I had to see if something was wrong."

Much to her amazement, Analise found herself pouring out her tale of woe to this kind stranger, telling him of Frances and her father and the chilly emotional atmo-

sphere in which she lived. She told him abut her homesickness for her native city, about her husband's apparent
uninterest, and about the way Frances had taken over her
baby. Barely in time she stopped herself from blurting out
her entire history with Mark.

"I am sorry," she said contritely. "You don't even know
me, and here I have been talking your ear off."

The man chuckled. "Ah, but I feel I know you very well.
My name is Maximilian Schleyer, so now you know me, as
well."

Analise smiled. "I am Analise Schaeffer, and I am very
pleased to meet you."

They chatted politely for a few moments about the city
and the weather, and Mr. Schleyer kindly did not refer to
her previous outburst. Soon they parted, feeling like old
friends.

After that, Mr. Schleyer often appeared in the park
during Analise's walks. They would walk and talk desul-
torily, exchanging information about themselves. He told
her of his upbringing in Germany and his immigration to
the United States as a young man. He had worked diligently and had been clever, and now he owned one of the
largest stores in New York City.

"Schleyer's! But, of course; I knew that name sounded
familiar," Analise exclaimed. "It is a lovely store. I bought
quite a bit of material there when I first moved here."

"Ah, the next time you come into the store, you must
come up to my office and see me. I shall give you a personally guided tour over the whole store."

Another time they met, Analise told him of New Orleans, describing the unusual city and mixture of people—
"Quite a few Germans settled there in Louisiana," she told

him—and relating her own family and upbringing. She spoke of Belle Terre, the Caldwell family's plantation, and the way she had managed it for years. He seemed quite delighted at her business experience and one day even suggested that she come to work for him.

"But what would I do? I know nothing about a store," Analise protested. She also knew, but did not add, that it would be quite shocking for a lady to so openly engage in commerce.

"What could you do? Why, you told me you knew book-keeping, and you would be a real asset to my Ladies Dress Department; they would think they would look as beauti-ful as you in one of my dresses."

Analise laughed. "You are very kind, but I can't, really. I have a baby to look after."

"Well, if you ever find you cannot bear it another mo-ment in that dreadful place, remember my offer. A working woman can be independent."

That idea took root in Analise's head. If she had a job, she could find a place for her and Johnny to live, and she would not have to endure Frances any longer. She could bring up Johnny without interference; she would no longer have to be dependent on someone else, tossed here and there by their whims. It began to seem a kind of heaven to her: independence, release, and an opportunity to let Mark show what he felt for her. If he did not love her, she would be gone, no longer his unwelcome responsibility. But if he came to her there, with no duty pushing him, then it would mean that he really did love her.

As the weeks passed, the situation at the Schaeffer house grew worse. Frances and Analise quarreled fre-quently over the baby's handling, and Frances seemed more insulting than ever, now that Analise no longer carried Mark's child. No letter came from Mark, and Analise felt more and more the heavy certainty that Mark's feelings for her had died. She had tried to come up with a reasonable excuse for his not writing. Infrequent letters were explicable, but no letters for over six months! It strained one's credulity to think he would do that to a woman he loved. Her heart resisted what her mind knew, but gradually her faith was being ground into dust.

Many nights Analise lay awake, thinking of her husband and crying. She tried to accept the fact that he did not love her, telling herself that it would be easier if she simply believed what was plainly before her face, took the sharp pain, and got over it. This dance of hope and doubt was like a continually throbbing wound.

The only thing that stopped Analise from leaving the Schaeffer house was the fact that on the kind of salary she would receive, she could not pay a nurse for Johnny. It would be all she could handle to house, feed, and clothe them. This obstacle was removed, however, in August, when her maid May arrived at the house. Seeing at last a familiar face, Analise plummeted downstairs and threw her arms around the woman.

She had been worried by her maid's absence, since she was supposed to have followed them on the next boat. May explained that she had had difficulty leaving New Orleans, since she was still a slave of Mr. Caldwell's until the Emancipation Proclamation had made her a free woman.

Frances was clearly disapproving of the maid's loyalty, and Analise had to laugh. May did not fit her picture of a proper slave, and, moreover, for all her vaunted liberality, Frances had never come face to face with a black before, and the very foreignness of the woman frightened her. She seemed to not quite know how to speak or act with her or where to place her. May obviously felt much the same sort of distrust for Frances, which deepened to active dislike after she had been there for a few days and seen the antagonism between Frances and Analise.

Now, Analise knew, she was free to follow her plan for independence, if she wished. Fear of the unknown held her back, however, until one evening after supper, when Frances brought up the subject of Maximilian Schleyer. Analise and Prentiss Schaeffer were playing chess, and Frances was quietly sewing.

Suddenly Frances said, "Who is the man you have been sneaking out to see, Analise?"

Analise and Schaeffer both turned to her, open-mouthed in astonishment. Finally Analise recovered her voice enough to splutter, "Whatever are you talking about? I haven't been—"

Frances smiled maliciously. "It is no use denying it, Analise; I saw you myself last Sunday afternoon at the little park with him."

"Oh, Mr. Schleyer. He is just a friend of mine. And I have not been *sneaking* out to meet him."

"You certainly haven't told anyone here about him."

"Who would I tell? You? You have never seemed exactly to relish conversing with me. I can't imagine telling you anything about my life!"

"I think it would be proper to inform your husband's family," Frances murmured.

"See here, Analise, who is this man? Is this true?" Mr. Schaeffer interjected, his voice ponderous and puzzled.

"It is true, I have a friend named Maximilian Schleyer,

whom I quite often meet when I take a walk. He happens to walk there at the same time I do."

"How fortuitous," Frances said sarcastically.

Analise flushed. She knew that her frequent meetings with Schleyer would not be considered proper for a young married woman, but she had looked forward to them so much that she had been unwilling to stop them. She knew, as well, that after the first meeting the others had not been by accident. Each of them had come because they wanted to see and talk to the other. But there had been nothing wrong with it; they were just friends.

Defiantly she said, "He is my friend. Nothing happened that was at all sinful or false to Mark. It is Mark who has ignored me, as you well know, but I have written him devotedly in spite of that. Never, never have I been in the slightest way unfaithful."

Prentiss Schaeffer frowned. "I know that you have written Mark, and it is unpardonable that he has not written back. When he comes home, I shall take him to task for it. However, even if this friendship is quite innocuous, you must see how it appears to the world."

"Appears!" Analise flared. "Is appearance all you care about? What about the truth? You are just like your son; he acted on assumptions about 'appearance' and never bothered to find out the truth."

"Analise, I am not accusing you of anything, and I know how difficult my son can be. I believe you when you say that your friendship is innocent. However, I cannot allow you to continue to meet him; it is most improper. The Schaeffer name must not be exposed to such a scandal."

"Damn the Schaeffer name!" Analise exploded. "What about me? Since I came here, I have been miserable. You are cold and ungiving, and Frances hates me. She has insulted me at every opportunity, and encouraged her friends to do the same. No one has been in the least kind to me except Max Schleyer. I refuse to give up the one friend I have here. I shall continue to see him."

Schaeffer's face closed into rigid lines, and his eyes were as cold and hard as onyx. "Analise, I strictly forbid it. You are not to see this fellow again."

His domineering tone fed his daughter-in-law's anger. Now she flared out. "Just a moment, Mr. Schaeffer. You have no right to demand that I do anything. You are not my father or my husband, and I am not a child. I am a grown woman, a mother and wife, and I can make my own decisions."

"While you are under my roof, you will—"

Analise interrupted heatedly, "But I shall no longer be under your roof, Mr. Schaeffer. I am tired of your commands and coldness; I am tired of your daughter's hatred and maliciousness. My son and I will leave here as soon as possible."

Both Frances and her father burst into protest at that pronouncement, but Analise was adamant. She had finally been pushed too far. Secretly she was grateful for the scene; now she would be able to leave without feeling guilty. It was the only thing to do if she was not to lose her spirit entirely. It suddenly dawned upon Analise how much she had been meekly accepting and how her will had been sinking more and more into a quagmire of submission and hurt. The loneliness and uncertainty had made her bend over backward to be amiable, and she realized now how frighteningly her personality had been slipping away from her.

But no more! Analise set about packing her things and

finding rented rooms for May, her son, and herself. Frances alternately stormed and pleaded with her not to take the baby away, even going so far as to threaten to take John Prentiss away from her by a court order. Analise ignored her and ignored as well Prentiss' condemning silence. What they thought was not really important. What was important was establishing a life for herself and little John away from this house. She knew she had to be strong now, had to stand on her own—because Mark seemed unlikely to ever return to her.

Twelve

*A*nalise found that her indepen-
dence was to be hard won. Max Schleyer gave her a job,
just as he had promised, but, though she suspected he was
out of kindness giving her a higher salary than most clerks,
it was still difficult to provide the necessities for her little
family. Her working hours were long; she went to the store
at 7:30 and did not leave until 6:30 in the evening, every
day of the week except Sunday. Most of her time at work
was spent on her feet, which meant that by the end of the
day her feet were sore and her leg muscles ached. Moreover, she left the store each day mentally and emotionally
drained from the long hours of smiling, cajoling, and ob-
sequiousness that were necessary to sell her products.
Never had her management of the house and plantation
involved this kind of boring, tiring effort. She was not
really prepared to do it, and many times she wanted to give
in to the cowardly impulse of returning to the Schaeffers
and begging readmittance. She hung on grimly, however,
and things began to slowly improve.

Analise quickly discovered that her Southern accent
offended many of the staunch Northern ladies with whom
she dealt. Therefore, she began to speak with a French

accent, which came easily to her lips, since she had grown up among Cajuns and learned proper French as well at school. Gallic gestures and intonations were as natural to her as breathing. After that, she immediately assumed the authority of a *couturier* on ladies' dresses in the eyes of her customers. Since she had a good eye for color and style and a certain flair for bringing together the woman, dress, and accessories, it did not take her long to achieve success with the customers. Her sales spiraled, and, to her delight, she received the reward of a raise in salary.

Max Schleyer did not speak to her in the store, not wanting to rouse the antipathy of other employees toward Analise. However, he began to call on her at home two or three times a week. Analise suspected that he was falling in love with her, and she knew in good conscience that she should nip the relationship in the bud. She was a married woman and still unhappily in love with Mark; there was no possibility of Schleyer's hopes being fulfilled. But Max was never pressing or forward with her, and she found his company so easy and pleasant that she could not bear to cut him off.

They talked together comfortably, often discussing the store. Max broadened her knowledge of the merchandising business, explaining his policies and methods, the economics of selling and buying. Analise caught on quickly, having a natural flair for business. Soon she was making suggestions for improving the Ladies Dress Department—enlarging the displays and making them more colorful, adding chairs and tables for customers to relax around while fashions were modeled or materials shown to them. Max followed many of her suggestions and, upon their success, made Analise the head of the department and turned the entire operation of it over to her.

After that, Analise worked harder than ever. Now, however, she had more scope and more creative avenues to explore, and she began to become fascinated by her work. She experimented with the dress department, failing sometimes, but more often succeeding grandly. By late February of 1864, the Ladies Dress Department was flourishing more than ever before, and Analise was becoming interested in the entire store. She began telling Max of her ideas for changing the display windows: uncluttering them and putting up arresting thematic displays with fewer items in each window. Moreover, she had done so well that now Max tried her suggestions without hesitation or doubt. When the display windows proved to attract greater numbers of customers, Max began to hint of moving Analise up into general management of the store, an unprecedented idea.

It was then, late in the winter, just before the thaws of spring, that Mark reappeared in her life. She had given up writing him since she left the Schaeffers; she did not have the time any longer to waste in writing a man who so obviously cared not at all if she lived or died. She missed him still and her body ached for the feel of his. Far too often she cried herself to sleep in bitter, unhappy loneliness; and her few free hours were marred by doubts and questions about him.

So she could not say she had forgotten him. However, he had become in a way unreal to her—almost a dream or fantasy—and she did not really expect to ever see him again. Therefore, it was with stunned amazement that she looked up at the crash of her door flying open and found herself face to face with the blazing fire of her husband's eyes.

Analise sat speechless, staring at him, and he laughed roughly. "So this is it? You left my home for these squalid little rooms in a boarding house?"

"I am moving next week to a house of our own!" Analise said the first thing that popped into her head, then cursed herself for responding to his sarcasm.

Mark moved farther into the room, and Analise rose to meet him. Numb with shock, she noted that he looked thinner, older; deep lines around his mouth bit into his angular face. Incredibly, she caught herself worrying about him, and mentally shook herself. This was no time for weakness; she must keep control, not let him manipulate her. She would not run blindly back into his arms, even though her heart leaped at the sight of him. First he would have to account for the cruel way he had ignored her for so many months.

However, Mark, seized by a black rage, swept aside all her firm intentions. He was filled with a roiling mixture of desire, disillusion, jealousy, and anger that he had never felt before. It was worse than when he thought she loved Emil. This time he had fallen from the heights of love; this time he and Analise had had one beautiful month together; he had come to trust her, to believe in her love for him. That had made it all the worse during those long, lonely months when he had not received a letter from her, when he had written her so often, pouring out his love for her and never getting a word in reply. Each day when he had waited anxiously through mail call, only to be defeated yet again, was etched into his heart with acid. Slowly, painfully, he began to realize that Analise had lied to him; she had merely wanted a name and home for her baby. Now that she had it, she would not go to the bother of keeping up the pretense by writing.

Lately he had had Frances' letters to torture him further. She had written him about the birth of his son, and mingled with his happiness was anger that the mother had not even seen fit to inform him. Then Frances had begun recounting Analise's secretive meetings with a German man. Later she wrote to say that Frances had taken John Prentiss and left their home. Her letters informed him that the German man, Mr. Schleyer, had given Analise a job in the store he owned, that he was a wealthy man (wealthy enough, she hinted, to shower presents on another man's wife), and that he called on Analise frequently. Cattily Frances reported that Analise was rising amazingly fast in the company.

Mark could easily see the implications: his wife had become this Schleyer's mistress. He tried to deny it, to have faith in his wife, as he had not had before, but the canker of jealousy ate at him. What else could her actions mean? Sick with despair and yet torn by flashes of hope, Mark sought a furlough during the winter encampment. He had to see Analise, to talk to her and establish the truth of the situation. Finally he had obtained a leave and came rushing home, only to be met by the most crushing blow he had yet received: Frances had evidence that his wife was unfaithful.

Mark's homecoming had frightened Frances badly. To her amazement, Mark's letters had continued persistently; he wrote of his love and pleaded to Analise for a letter. Each time a letter came from him to Analise and Frances

sneaked it off the hall table, she had ripped it open hopefully, thinking this time he would renounce her. But she
found over and over that her brother had not abandoned
his love for the Southern woman. Frances began to regret
her treachery: it was nervewracking to keep it up, but she
could not stop intercepting the letters for fear that would
lead to an embarrassing exposé of what she had done.
When Mark arrived home on leave, she realized in panic
that she must not let their father take Mark to task for not
writing, as he had said he would. Nor could Mark and
Analise be allowed to talk it out calmly. The truth would
come out then; Frances was certain of it. And she could
not face the condemnation from her brother that would
follow.

So she dropped a bombshell designed to ally Mark and
his father against Analise, upset them so that they would
never discuss the letters and so that Mark would storm out
on Analise without giving her a chance to explain. After
all, Frances reasoned, what she told them was undoubtedly
true; it was just that she had not yet been able to catch
Analise in the act.

As Mark and Prentiss sat visiting with Frances immediately after Mark's arrival, Frances said quietly, "I don't
know how to tell you this, Mark. I hope you won't be angry
at me for dabbling in your affairs. I only wanted to protect
you."

"What is it?" Mark tightened involuntarily.

"One day, I followed Analise to her rendezvous with
Schleyer, keeping well out of sight. She left with him and
I pursued them. They went into his house; I waited for an
hour and they did not come out. So I hired someone to
follow her discreetly after she moved out of our home.

Frankly, I suspected that she was faithless to you, and I thought you might need proof in order to get John Prentiss away from her. I got his report: at least twice a week Analise visits Mr. Schleyer and stays very late, long after the lights are turned out, until two or three o'clock in the morning."

Their father had been shocked and shaken, but Mark had sat, impassive as a stone, feeling his world crumble around him. So it was true: he could no longer even question or deny it. Frances had proof of her infidelity. Analise did not love him; she was the mistress of another man. No doubt she had decided he was richer and more pliable than Mark.

It was then that the seething rage hit him, and he had run from the house to Analise's rented rooms and burst in upon her. His wife's beauty hit him like a physical blow, and his anger was fanned by the involuntary leap of desire within him. She stood there, calmly facing him, no guilt or fear on her face, and no love either. He trembled with rage.

"How could you?" Mark hissed, his fierce eyes stabbing into her. "How could you take my son and leave my home?"

"I had every reason to," Analise began her counterattack.

But Mark interrupted savagely, "Damn your adulterous hide! You beautiful bitch, I believed you! What a joke."

Analise stared at him in astonishment, and her silence infuriated him even more. "My God, you don't even try to deny it! What kind of a woman are you? Are you flesh and blood, or is that ice water in your veins?"

That insult flicked her anger into being, and Analise

snapped back, "You dare to accuse me of being cold? You, who—"

"Yes, I accuse you, and I accuse you of quite a few other things as well. Good Lord, Analise, couldn't you have spared even a few minutes to relieve my misery a little? Couldn't you at least have written me a line to tell me of my son's birth?"

Now Analise's head was reeling. She felt as if she were in some crazy dream where she was supposed to know something and yet was ignorant. Mark was accusing *her* of not writing—it was insane! She fought back her bitter laughter.

Again Mark took her silence as admission of guilt, and it twisted his guts. "Why did you do it? Why did you pretend you loved me? I would have married you without that. At least my pain would not have been so great."

"What are you talking about?" Analise cried. "I did love you!"

"Don't lie to me, Analise," he spat scornfully. "I am no gullible German, remember. Even you can't persuade me that it is love you feel when you run straight to the bed of Max Schleyer."

"What! How dare you? Why, that is insane! I never—"

"No more lies!" he thundered, and in the back room Johnny woke and began to cry. Mark glanced in the direction of the sound and then quickly away, almost as if to disavow his presence. "I am no cuckold," he said quietly, his face ravaged with anguish.

Analise was thoroughly bewildered. He made it sound as if it were all her fault, as if she were the one who had not written, as if she were unfaithful to him. Tears stung her eyes—what kind of crazy game was he playing?

"I can't talk to you when you are acting like this," she snapped in frustration. "You are wild and irrational, and until you can calm down and speak like an ordinary human, I refuse to discuss it."

"Oh, you play that nicely, dear wife," Mark's voice dripped sarcasm. "However, it doesn't fool me a bit. I held out a little hope up until the last minute, but now I see. You cannot even come up with a lie to justify yourself."

"Damn you!" Analise's control burst and she began to hurl harsh invectives at him, her words stumbling over each other in anger and hurt. She screamed at him that it was he who had deserted her, that his family had driven her from the house, that she was innocent of his accusations, but she was so infuriated that her tirade came out choked and largely incoherent.

Suddenly, like a man driven beyond his endurance, Mark pulled Analise to him roughly and kissed her. His fingers dug cruelly into her shoulders, and his lips bruised her mouth, as he inexorably forced her to the floor. Analise was frightened at his behavior, and she struggled against him. Mark ran his hands over her body, rediscovering the planes and curves. Wild with pent-up desire, he tore at her clothes, ripping her dress heedlessly. She twisted beneath him, and he had to hold her down and force her legs apart. Silently they fought, and he subdued her with savage triumph, possessing her body with his hands and tongue and flesh. He mastered her and rode to his fiery burst of pleasure, but when he finished, he felt suddenly sick and empty, as though he would never be satisfied again.

Analise glared at him, and Mark rose shakily to his feet. His world was spinning, and he wanted to drop to the floor and cry like a child. The anger and revenge were gone, and all he felt was a deep, empty despair.

White-lipped, he said, "I am going back to Virginia immediately. It is my duty to support you, and I will. But I never want to see you or hear from you again. If you wanted to destroy me, you have done so. Goodbye, Analise."

Mark turned and walked out the door, closing it with a gentle, final thud. Analise stared after him, and then she began to cry, the wracking sobs of desolation.

RECONSTRUCTION

Thirteen

"The war is over! The war is over!" The babble began in the streets, growing louder, spreading into the stores in ripples of whispers, even moving up into the offices on the top floor of Schleyer's Department Store. Analise, frowning over her plans for the next change of the show windows, looked up impatiently at the buzz of conversation beyond her office. Quickly she went to her door and threw it open to see bookkeepers laughing and talking excitedly, some even executing a few snappy dance steps.

She had had a few problems with the men working for her ever since she came, but never such total chaos. Angrily Analise brushed some straying hairs back from her face and demanded, "Just what is going on here?"

"Mrs. Schaeffer!" the office boys cried out, "It's over! Lee has surrendered; the war is over!"

Analise stared at him, surprised. Some of the men remembered that she was from the South, and a sudden hush fell upon them. It occurred to them that perhaps she would not be so pleased as they at the South's capitulation.

She had known for years now that the Confederacy was doomed, had accepted it, just as she had accepted her own exile from her beloved city. So there was no reason why tears should suddenly well in her eyes at the news—but they did. Sternly she blinked them away and said, "Good. Perhaps now things can return to normal."

Hastily she went back into her office; it would never do to break down in front of her male employees. She closed the door quickly behind her and sagged against it, shutting her eyes to the rush of memories. How long it had been, how empty and achingly long. Her son—Mark's son—Johnny was two years old now; she had passed from naive hope and love to bitter disillusionment and humiliation to the blissful heights of love, only to plunge down into this blank, lonely life she lived now. She had been rejected by her own people and become an outcast among these New York strangers. She had borne a child and raised it alone, had worked and succeeded on her own. So long.

And yet, somehow, so brief, too. If she closed her eyes, she could smell again, as if it were yesterday, the sweet cloying scent of honeysuckle in the Caldwell garden and feel the warm, damp spring air against her bare skin. She could remember the scent drifting through the louvered screen doors into her office, where she and Mark lay entwined in passion.

Hot, bitter tears squeezed out between her eyelids. Dear God, would she never be able to rid herself of those sweet, painful memories? It had been almost a year and a half since Mark had stormed out of her house, swearing never to see her again. She sighed—he had certainly kept his word on that score. In all that time, she had received no letter from him, and even though his father came by regularly on Sundays to take his grandchild for a ride in his carriage, Prentiss Schaeffer had never mentioned his son to her. In fact, he had rarely spoken to her at all; he had remained in his carriage and she in the house, and the baby John had been passed from May's hands to Mr. Schaeffer's coachman.

She supposed it was a Schaeffer characteristic: that stubborn, stiff-necked pride, that single-minded selfishness that made no allowance for other people's feelings or wishes. The old man had to have his daughter-in-law and grandson completely under his thumb. If she stood up to him, he cast her off completely. Just as Mark had done. Only with Prentiss it had not hurt so.

Analise thought of Mark's angry, rigidly controlled face, his black eyes spitting wild sparks of fire at her. He seemed to hate her for leaving his father's house; surely he did not really believe those other accusations he had flung at her; so that must be the actual source of his anger. Could he really abandon his wife and son over such an issue?

Well, not abandon exactly—after all, he sent her nearly all his army pay every month, and his father sent her a stipend too (grudgingly and only to save his grandson from poverty). But he had abandoned her in every other way—spiritually, mentally, physically. And that was what mattered, not the money.

She had not received even a note from him. Only the payments that arrived each month with such regularity informed her that he had not been killed. Every check was proof that he was still alive, and if one was later than usual, she worried about him until it arrived. Once, a few months before, a whole month went by without a payment, and she was so frantic that she was on the verge of going to his father and asking him about Mark. But then the next month a double payment arrived, and she breathed a sigh of relief; it was just that he had forgotten, that was all.

The monthly payments she put in the bank, saving them for Johnny when he grew up. She did not need his money or his father's to live. At first it had been difficult; her money hardly stretched over the rent and the food and clothes for the baby. But she had risen quickly at Schleyer's, and Max had rewarded her clever ideas with steady raises. She was good with figures and even more adept at salesmanship. After her ideas about displays in the store windows and installing a tea room for weary shoppers proved so successful, Max had entrusted Analise with more and more authority, until now she was his second in command. She suspected that her raises had been more ample and came more quickly than normal, for Max was always pressing expensive gifts on her, which she steadfastly refused. But at least she knew that she had earned the raises; her ideas had brought in a great deal more revenue to the store.

Every bit of money she could spare from her salary she had invested wisely. Even though she sometimes had to scrimp, she knew she must not let pass the opportunity of cashing in on the wartime boom. Max had allowed her to buy a fractional share of some loans he made to shipbuilders and mills, and when the loans were soon repaid with substantial interest, Max meticulously gave Analise her proportion. Under his tutelage, she soon tripled the profits she had made. She then began to purchase land; soon the war would be over and men would be returning home. They would be moving, expanding, increasing the population, and they would need property. Also, immigrants were arriving in a never-ending stream. The city had to grow, and people would have to buy land. Analise's instincts and intelligence told her that the country was poised on the edge of a huge economic boom, and she calculated that the land prices in New York City would soar.

Considering her investments, her salary, and the savings she had built up from Mark's payments and his father's, she was now rather well-to-do. She was pleased with herself for that. While she was not obsessed with a thirst for great power and riches, neither was she willing to again be in a position of want, as she had been during the blockade and early in the Yankee occupation or when she first left the Schaeffer household. But more than the comforts money could provide, she felt a great pride in her abilities and her independence. She could take care of herself, provide for herself and her son quite adequately. She did not have to depend on the good graces of father or brother or husband or lover. Never again would she feel the palm-sweating fear of her days as Mark's mistress, knowing that if he cast her off she was utterly destitute and friendless.

Analise sighed and wiped the tears from her cheeks. If only her successes could do away with her loneliness and the dull ache that occupied her chest day after day. She loved her son and enjoyed the all-too-short time she spent with him each day, but the company of a baby could hardly provide the intellectual stimulation that she had felt when she matched wits with Mark. Nor could Johnny provide the warm, understanding companionship that lay between a husband and wife.

How she missed those things, and how bleak the future looked, empty of them. But even worse was the physical ache within, the hot, passionate hunger that Mark had awakened in her. She remembered the excitement, the pleasurable tension when he was close to her, the way her heart leaped and her blood coursed fast and hot at just the sight of him. And she thought of the wild, sweet passion of their lovemaking, reliving the touch of his hands and mouth that brought her to that mindless, abandoned burst of pleasure. Having known those moments, she ached bitterly at their loss.

It seemed that no one could take Mark's place. Not that there had been any lack of candidates. She met many men in the course of her business, some of them quite attractive and charming. But none of them set her pulse racing as he had done. Even Max, good, kind Max, who had helped her so and been such a dear friend to her. Ever since Mark stormed out on her, Max had patiently bided his time, courting her steadily but without pressuring her. There was nothing wrong with him: he was good-looking in a quiet, sturdy, blond way; he was intelligent and capable, easily her match in thought and conversation; at every possible opportunity, he offered her his aid; and he was deeply in love with her. Analise knew she could not ask for more than that in a man, and she frequently resolved to forget her wild, hurtful husband and try to fall in love with Max. However, she was never able to bring her willful heart and body under control. No matter how sternly she set her mind to it, she could not wipe out the image of Mark—his face, his hands, his voice, the wild blackness of his eyes. Nor could she cease to feel hurt and loneliness every time that image crossed her mind.

It did not matter that he had steadfastly ignored her, never writing her a letter in the entire time they had been apart. Nor did it matter that he had insanely, unjustifiably accused her of infidelity and of not writing to him, or that he had cast her aside because she had moved from his father's house. None of that carried any weight with her heart. Analise knew that, despite it all, she still loved him, just as she had so long ago, when she was a belle in New Orleans.

Sighing, Analise stood and began to pace her office. She could not concentrate, plagued as she was by her thoughts, and further disturbed by the sounds of jubilation still going on outside. When a knock sounded at her door, she was grateful for the interruption.

"Come in," she said and Max Schleyer entered the room.

"Have you heard the news?" he asked in his softly accented voice.

Analise smiled. "How could I help it?"

"And how do you feel?"

"Oh, Max, trust you to remember that I am a Southerner," she said, taking his hand and squeezing it gently. "I don't know really. I am a little stunned, I guess, even though I knew a Union victory was inevitable. Total defeat of one's homeland is a bitter draught to swallow. More than anything, though, it has made me think about all the things that have happened since the war began, the changes in me. It made me think of New Orleans and how beautiful and warm it is and how much I missed it. I thought of the cold, bitter winter days here in New York and how they chill my blood. I wish I were home again, Max."

"I know that feeling. We have always had that bond— being exiles in this land."

Analise paused and then said in a low voice, "And it made me think of Mark."

A brief look of pain touched the man's face, and he said, "You still love him."

"I don't know. I have done my best not to. There is no reason why I should and every reason why I should not. And yet—" she stopped and sighed.

"Be patient," Schleyer said and patted her hand. "That is my advice. You try too hard to forget him; it only fixes him more firmly in your mind. Just relax and live your life, and someday you will realize that he has vanished from your heart."

Analise wanted to cry, "But when?" Instead, she smiled and squared her shoulders and said, "You are right, of course, Max. I shall do just that."

"Good. Now, what I came here to tell you is that in honor of the end of the war, I am closing the store and giving the employees the rest of the day off. They are so excited they will be perfectly useless anyway, and who would go shopping on a day like this?"

"Good. That gives me a chance to look at the housewares department undisturbed. I have been thinking about rearranging it so that there are some eye-catching displays there. It is much too dull."

"No, you are not!" Max stated with playful sternness. "You and I are going to take the day off as well and treat ourselves to a lazy ride up the Hudson."

"But Max—" Analise began in protest, then stopped abruptly. A slow smile spread across her face. "You are right. It would be just the thing to lift my spirits. Just let me put on my bonnet."

* * *

They sailed up the Hudson to Yonkers and back. A festive air prevailed on the boat, what with the spontaneous singing and shouting of many of the passengers and the frequent blowing of the ship's whistle. All around them was the gaiety of a victory celebration, and even Analise was infected with the general happiness. They stood on the outside deck, feeling the refreshingly brisk spring breeze tug at them.

"Oh, Max," Analise said, her voice soft with bittersweet reflection, "how I have changed the past few years. I used to be so full of life, so happy, full of feeling for people. And now—"

"Now you are a beautiful, mature woman, not a foolish girl."

Analise smiled a little at his staunch praise of her. "Now I am old and tired and bitter. I am hard and sarcastic. A dried-up neuter that cares for nothing but the store and making money."

"And your beautiful baby?" Max suggested. "War ages all of us, Analise; some of us it cripples and some it makes better. Perhaps you were happy then, but what would you be doing now if there had been no war? Would you still be happy? You are a creative person, a hard-headed business woman, full of all sorts of potential. Is it so wrong to use your skills? Is it so bad to be knowledgeable rather than naive? You have strength; you have character. And that gives you far greater beauty than the placid, innocent face of a schoolgirl."

"But I feel so dead inside, almost incapable of feeling," Analise argued, trying to make him understand her inner desolation, the yawning emotional void.

"Analise," the blond man said seriously, taking her

hands between his. "I love you. You know that, don't you?"

She nodded, tears welling in her throat. He was so good, so kind, so utterly—inadequate. *I want Mark!* her heart cried treacherously.

"Marry me, Analise. Let me give you all the lovely things you deserve. Let me make you happy again."

"But, Max, I am already married!" Analise protested.

"To a cold-hearted, lying scoundrel," Max said scornfully. "You can get a divorce from him; from what you have said, we can easily catch him in adultery."

"But the scandal—I can't involve you in something like that."

"I am already involved in whatever concerns you. I choose to be involved."

Analise frowned and turned to look out across the river. To be free of Mark—wasn't that what she wanted? Here was Max offering her kindness and love and wealth, all the things most women wanted. And yet, she knew she would not be happy.

"Max, even though I might end my marriage in a court of law, I would still be married in the eyes of my Church. I am Catholic, you know."

"It is possible to get an annulment, is it not?"

"Sometimes," Analise admitted.

"Well, my Heavens, he forced you to marry him. Then he deserted you. Surely somewhere in all his despicable treatment of you, there must be an acceptable reason for an annulment."

His companion was silent for a moment, staring moodily down at the water. Finally she sighed and said, "I will think about it, Max, I promise. Just give me a little time; I don't want to act hastily."

The German smiled. "Of course, *mein liebchen*, you may have all the time you want. As you know, I am a patient man."

Analise's rare, warm smile lit her face. What a kind man he was. Too good for her, she suspected; would he be able to accept the darker side of her personality? Sometimes she feared that his perception of her had no reality to it.

Schleyer left the next day for Boston to discuss contracts with several New England cloth manufacturers. He said that he wanted to catch them while they were still unsettled at the thought of the end of their wartime uniform contracts. However, Analise suspected that he was also cleverly absenting himself from her to give her a taste of how lonely her life would be without him.

For she was discovering that it was indeed quite lonely. Because she was a woman who had risen to such a high place in the company and because she was friends with the owner, no one in the store was friendly to her. All of them either resented her or were in awe of her, or both. Since she worked all day, she had no time to cultivate the friendship of the housewives who lived around her. Besides, they all thought her suspect and strange: she was a Southerner and had a black maidservant and looked almighty haughty; besides, no one ever came to visit her except that foreigner—it all added up to a pretty strange situation.

Analise found that when it came right down to it, she had no friend other than Max. When he was gone, there was no one to talk or laugh with, no one to admire her, no one to listen to her ideas. At night, when she went home, she could romp some with her baby, but a two-year-old, no matter how loved, could not make up for the dearth of adult companionship. And once he was whisked off to his early bed, there was no one but May or the housekeeper to talk to, and their company was hardly stimulating.

God knows, Max would never be to her what Mark had been, but then, her choice was not really between Mark and Max. Realistically, her choice was Max or this gaping nothingness Mark had left in her.

When Max returned, there was a question in his eyes, but Analise ignored it. She babbled away, too happy to have her friend back to spoil it by getting into the subject of their love relationship. He did not press, merely listened with interest to her report on the store and the new schemes she had in mind and baby Johnny's funny antics.

But, Analise thought, as she walked home that evening, she would have to give him some kind of answer soon. She could not continue to string him along this way. If she did not want him, she must set him free so that some other woman could make him happy. Sighing, she stepped into her home and was greeted by the tiny storm that was her son.

"Mama, Mama!" he cried, his steps thundering down the stairs: and launched himself at her recklessly.

"Johnny!" She staggered a little from the force of his greeting but wrapped her arms tightly around his wiry little body.

How small he was, and yet, how awesome, this little chunk of humanity that was her son. Perhaps her love was enough for him now, but later—how could she teach him all the ins and outs of the masculine world? He needed a father, a man to model, and she could never fill that need.

"Guess what I found today!" he said excitedly, squirming out of her embrace, his baby tongue tripping over the words.

"I don't know. What?" She smiled down at him and lightly caressed his curling black hair. He looked so like his father, with his black eyes and hair and his angular little face. How could Mark just walk away and leave him like that? Did he not care at all for his son?

"Snail!" the boy exclaimed proudly.

"Oh, let me see."

Johnny shook his head. "Secret."

Little fingers of jealousy pricked at her heart: already he was hiding things from her. Immediately, she regretted the thought; a child had a right to his privacy too. Analise refused to be one of those mothers who always had to be the center of their children's lives.

But he's all I have, she wailed inside in protest. Suddenly, horrifyingly, she saw a picture of herself twenty-five years from now: lonely, middle-aged, her looks gone, still clinging to her grown son, lecturing him, prying into his life, trying desperately to live through him.

"I won't," she whispered to herself. "I won't." Yet, if she stayed in this empty life she lived now, wasn't that all too likely? She ought to marry Max, give Johnny a father and herself some interest in life besides her son. Max would be a good father to the boy, someone he could emulate, someone he could trust. Far better than his natural father, she thought bitterly, who obviously did not care whether Johnny lived or died.

"Johnny," she said seriously. "Do you like Uncle Max?"

"Uncle Max?" he said and nodded, beaming. "Horses."

Analise smiled. Of course, the most important thing to him was the beautiful team of horses that pulled Max's carriage.

"Like Grandy," Johnny added and then a brief troubled look shadowed his smoothly innocent face.

"What is it?" Analise saw the look and was suddenly anxious.

"Man at Grandy's house."

His mother's heart began to thud. "A man at your grandfather's? What man?"

"Not nice. He yelled at Aunt Fran."

"Who was the man?" Analise knelt to look him in the face.

"Surprise, Aunt Fran said." His face clouded over and his sturdy little chin began to tremble. "But he yelled. 'No! Get him out!'"

"Did he scare you?" Analise asked sympathetically, her throat clogging with feeling for her son.

He nodded and said, "Looked funny. He scared me. All mad."

"Well, there was nothing to be scared of. Grandy and Aunt Fran wouldn't let him hurt you."

"I know," he sighed, "but Aunt Fran cried."

"Don't let it worry you," Analise reassured him and gave him a kiss. "I will talk to Grandy about it and he will make sure that the man doesn't scare you again. All right?"

The boy nodded mutely, and Analise added, "And next time, don't stew about it. Just tell me, and I will do something."

He smiled sunnily and his mother hugged him. "Now run and wash your hands for supper."

She watched him dart off, her mind whirling. An angry

man at the Schaeffers, someone whose anger could cause Frances to cry, someone whom she told Johnny was a "surprise." It had to be Mark, had to be. No doubt Frances would think meeting his father a delightful surprise for Johnny, and no doubt she would be crushed at his angry rejection of the boy and her efforts. Of course it was Mark. He was already home from the war—and had not made the slightest effort to see her. It was obvious that he meant to keep his promise to never come near her again. And he hated even the sight of his son!

Angrily Analise clenched her fists. She was a fool to cling to this mockery of a marriage. He did not want either her or Johnny, and by refusing to give up on the dead marriage she was depriving Johnny of a father and herself of any kind of happiness. It was not fair, it was not right! She had to rid herself of Mark, had to push him out of her heart as surely as he had pushed her.

Abstractedly she ate supper and pretended to listen to Johnny's childish prattle. After the meal, she rushed through a song and story for the boy and sent him off to bed. Then she scurried upstairs and grabbed her cloak, pausing only long enough to inspect herself in her mirror and with trembling hands pat her hair into place. Taking a deep breath, she started downstairs. She had to do it now, before she lost her nerve, or else she might never do it at all.

Outside her house, she hailed a cab and gave him Max Schleyer's address. It was highly improper, of course, for her to be out at night unescorted, even enclosed in the horsedrawn cab. And to be calling on a man at this hour would be the height of scandal. Analise smiled faintly at the thought. Now it seemed slight compared to many of the outrageous things she had done.

Max's well-trained butler recognized her immediately and led her to the study, betraying by not even the slightest twitch his amazement at her unescorted presence on his doorstep at this hour. When he announced her to Schleyer, his employer's face was less impassive. Delight, astonishment, and concern ran rapidly across it.

"Analise," he exclaimed, rising as the servant discreetly left the room. "What in the—is something the matter? What happened?"

"Nothing, Max; honestly, there is nothing wrong," Analise assured him and paused, feeling suddenly uncertain. "Max, I came to a decision tonight. Johnny told me that Mark is living at his father's house. He also said that Mark refused to even see him. I finally realized how foolish I have been. Max, I came here to accept your offer. I want to divorce Mark and marry you."

For a moment, the blond man stood still, too stunned to speak. Then joyously his features brightened. "Analise, my love," he said and crossed the room to enclose her in his tight embrace.

Fourteen

$\mathcal{M}$ark awakened with a start, his face beaded with perspiration. He had been dreaming about Analise again. In the dream she had stood before him, dressed in white, her hair falling free over her shoulders, as she had looked the first night they made love. She had smiled at him, and he had started toward her, but then a soldier in a blue uniform was between them, blocking Mark. The soldier walked up to her and she began to scream and run, trying frantically to elude the soldier, but he ran after her. The other man caught her and tore her clothes from her and pushed her to the ground. Mark struggled to go help her, but he could not move. Vainly he pulled and strained, but he could not budge from the spot. She looked at him, pleading with him to rescue her, her blue eyes wide and soft with entreaty. But he could not move. In helpless frustration he watched as the soldier pinned her to the ground and raped her. And even in his murderous rage, he felt prickles of desire run through him at the sight of her naked body. Then the soldier rose, leaving her limp and bruised on the ground. He turned, and for the first time, Mark saw the man's face: it was himself.

Cursing softly, he ran his hand across his sweating face. Was he never to stop dreaming of her? It was bad enough that all his waking hours were plagued by the thought of her; it was sheer cruelty that even in his sleep he could not escape. With his good arm he felt for the nightstand beside his bed, listening for the satisfying clink of the bottle. Ah, there it was. He felt his way up the bottle and began to uncork it. There, he thought bitterly, and they said I couldn't take care of myself.

Slowly, encumbered by the bottle in his hand, he struggled to a sitting position in the bed and took a long swig from the bottle. He sighed with relief as the fiery liquid burst in his throat. That was the problem: the pain was not so bad any longer, so that he did not have to drink to ease it, but if he forgot to drink himself into a stupor, he dreamed about *her*.

The door opened, and the burly figure of his aide filled the doorway. "Sir, are you all right?"

"Ah, Jackson, you are as faithful as a wife—more faithful than some." Mark saluted him sarcastically with the bottle. "You must have the ears of a cat. They should have made you a scout."

Jackson did not answer; he had heard it far too often now to even offer a rejoinder. Instead he entered the room and lit the kerosene lamp on the dresser, then settled into his usual chair. The Major—the Colonel, that is—would not besot himself as much if he had a companion.

"You been dreaming about her again?" the Sergeant stated, more than asked.

Mark's answer was a short, bitter laugh, and he took another slug from the bottle. It was beyond Jackson's understanding that a woman—any woman—could turn a man inside out like that for so long. If it had been any man other than the cool-nerved Major who had led him safely through battle after battle, he would have written him off as insane months ago. But Schaeffer had saved Sergeant Jackson's life once in a battle, crawling out in the middle of enemy fire to pull the wounded man to safety, and to Jackson that meant undying loyalty in return. Schaeffer was the stuff of legends to him, a steel-nerved, cool-headed leader, a hero who took the most dangerous assignments and yet pulled his men out of them safely. So Jackson idolized him and despised the woman who had turned his Colonel into the wreck he now was.

From the very first he had seen the Major's anxious daily search of the mails and his quickly masked disappointment. He had seen the bitter, hopeless lines set deeper in his face. But it was after his furlough home that the man went wild. He had always been the sort to seek the hottest part of any battle, but after he returned, he seemed to be actively seeking death. Mark volunteered for the most dangerous assignments and in battle flung himself heedlessly at the enemy. Though he was always protective of his men, he constantly left himself vulnerable. It was only from the sheerest good luck that he had not gotten seriously wounded before he did.

He survived the terrible Union slaughter at the Wilderness in May, but in the fall, at Cedar Creek, a shell had exploded near him, sending shrapnel flying into his left side. At last Schaeffer went down. For his daring, they made him a Colonel; only Jackson and his doctor knew how close the promotion had come to being posthumous. Jackson, who was right on his heels, had carried him back to the medical unit. There the doctors operated on him, removing most of the shrapnel and patching him up as best they could. For weeks he had lain delirious, and in his babbling Jackson heard bits and pieces of Mark's love for Analise and his bitter sorrow at her infidelity. More than once the doctors cautioned that they would lose him, but somehow the man's iron will would not let him die, even if he wanted to. He survived the infections and fevers of the field hospital to be sent back to Baltimore and operated on once more to remove more of the shrapnel. Here his recovery was less dramatic and far slower. Recently, after several months there, he had been discharged and Jackson had brought him home.

Schaeffer's left arm hung useless, and his left leg was so weak and dragging that he could limp along only with a crutch and then only with great pain and effort. A long jagged scar—really two barely separated scars—ran all the way across his left cheek, puckering his skin until his left eyelid drooped badly and his lips seemed always drawn back in a sardonic half-smile. Gone like magic was the strong, handsome man the Major had once been.

At first, he had been racked with pain, and the doctors had drugged him to combat it, but before long they had stopped the drugs for fear he would become addicted. The pain lessened over the months, but very gradually, and when the drugs were stopped, Schaeffer had drunk to ease the pain. During those long, lonely, aching nights, the Colonel had let out, bit by bit, the story of his love. Dry-eyed, his face drawn and twisted, he talked of Analise's beauty and the way he loved her, of his ruinous jealousy and her bitter hatred. He recounted the months that passed without even one letter from her. She had abandoned him entirely and, taking their infant son, moved out of his home. He recounted in halting tones their last angry meeting, when he had accused her of sleeping with the German, and she had not denied it.

It was because of her, Jackson knew, that the Colonel had given up. He had no desire to live; otherwise, a strong man like Schaeffer would not have just lain there, a helpless invalid who was drinking himself to death. Somehow the torment of *her* and the torment of his injuries were all mixed together, compounding each other, until Schaeffer had become a mere shell of a man, hopeless, useless, and wallowing in bitter grief and self-pity.

Deciding to try a different tack, the Sergeant said, "That sure is a fine-looking son you have."

Mark's face twisted. "Damn Fran—why in the hell did she bring him in here? Christ, he doesn't want to see a father who looks like this. I'm likely to give him nightmares."

"Well, for sure you did, screaming at him like that."

Mark ignored him and continued drinking. "Fran keeps yammering at Father to take the boy away from her." Jackson noted that as always Mark was reluctant to speak his wife's name. "What an idiot Fran is; as if I would want my son to be raised in this gloomy household." He smiled thinly. "Besides, I imagine it would break his heart; no male would prefer a lifetime with Fran to a life with—her."

He stopped speaking, his mind filled with images of Analise. He could see her smiling, lovely, bending with outstretched arms to hug her son. What a handsome lad he was—Mark felt a surge of pride. He was nicely dressed and well-mannered, but there was no sign of fear about him, none of the womanish timidity one might expect from a boy raised by women alone. But, no, not women alone;

he was forgetting the German shopkeeper. Yes, no doubt the boy had all the father he needed; it was stupid of Frances to think John Prentiss would have any feeling for him.

The blessed alcohol was having its effect; he felt almost able to sleep now. "Need to move," he mumbled. "Fran's driving me crazy with all that crying."

Jackson could certainly understand that. Ever since they had returned, the Colonel's sister had been a veritable waterfall of tears; the slightest reminder of her brother's condition would set her off. Couldn't the blasted woman realize that her constant crying only deepened his depression and strengthened his conviction that he was a useless, ugly cripple? She might be an intellect, as they all claimed, but she sure didn't have a shred of common sense. As if her crying were not bad enough, the dimwit had brought that pretty blonde fluff named Philippa here to meet her brother. It was obvious that she had not told Philippa about the change in Mark, or at least had not made it clear how bad it was. The blonde had half-screamed when she saw him and then stammered out her apologies, hardly able to back out of the room quick enough. That incident had sent the Colonel into a black mood for over a week.

Mark sighed and his heavy eyelids drifted almost closed. "I can see why Analise had to get away. God, they're dead bores."

In the next instant he was asleep, and his aide quietly rose and tiptoed from the room.

Analise sat by the window, waiting for the arrival of Prentiss Schaeffer's carriage. She intended to have a word with him about the fright Johnny had gotten when he saw his father. If Mark was so unnatural as to dislike his own son, well, that was his loss, but she would not have him upsetting Johnny. It was not good for the boy to have his father forced upon him. Before too long he would have a good father in Max, and it would be just as well for him to never know about Mark Schaeffer.

She sighed—if only she had never known Mark Schaeffer. No, she could not really say that, for then there would have been no Johnny, and she would not give him up for the world. It was just that, well, Mark had spoiled her for other men. Analise doubted that she would ever again feel the bliss that she had felt in his arms.

The other night when she had gone to Schleyer's home, he had wanted to hold back, to wait until she managed to obtain the divorce and could marry him before he took her to his bed. But Analise, fearing that future doubts and her unbidden feelings for Mark might work on her again, wanted to commit herself, to bind herself to this course. Therefore, she had insisted that they make love. She realized later that she had also hoped that the other man's lovemaking would satisfy her longings and erase her need for Mark.

But even though Max had taken her gently, with love and wonder, trying slowly, steadfastly to arouse her, Analise had felt none of the bursting joy she had known with Mark. The German's kisses and caresses had not been clumsy, but somehow every touch reminded her of Mark and the way his hands and lips had set her skin on fire. When the loving was done, and Max lay back, satiated, Analise lay awake, feeling empty and painfully close to tears.

Well, doubtless desire would come with time; after all,

Mark Schaeffer had been under her skin for a long time, and she could hardly expect to change that quickly. She would become accustomed to Max, and his tender efforts would pay off. And if it never happened, if she never again felt that raging pleasure, she could accept it. There was more to love and marriage than the bed. With Max she would be happy and content; she would be secure, and so would her child. Analise was convinced she had followed the correct course.

Max had already found a good attorney for the divorce and introduced Analise to him. After listening sympathetically to her story he had promised to set a detective on her husband's trail in order to find evidence of the requisite infidelity. With a pang, Analise assured him that he would have little trouble coming up with that. It surprised her to realize that it still could hurt so.

No doubt he would soon have the evidence, and then they could proceed with the divorce trial. That would be a painful experience, Analise knew, particularly if Mark and his family decided to try to take Johnny from her. Then she would have to fight the allegations they would throw at her. For that reason, if nothing else, she and Max would have to be very discreet. Any meetings outside the store would have to be few and very innocent, with witnesses to back up their stories. There was no telling when they would have another opportunity to make love, and Analise had to admit that she was not really displeased.

In a year or so, it would be all over, and then she would be able to take her rightful place beside Max. They would go to the opera and to plays. She would be able to dance and laugh and have fun again. And by then, surely she would have succeeded in obliterating Mark from her mind and heart.

"Johnny," she said now to her son, who sat kicking his heels, waiting for his grandfather, "how would you like to go live at Uncle Max's house?"

The boy beamed. He liked the spacious rooms of the Schleyer house, where a boy could run about practically unimpeded, and better than that was the fat German cook who fed him strudel and apple dumplings and marzipan cookies. And best of all were the horses—big, beautiful dapple grays for the carriage and a sleek sorrel for Max to ride.

"I'd like that," Johnny announced. "When? Tomorrow?"

Analise chuckled. "No, not quite that soon. A few months."

"Can I have my own horse?" the boy continued, uninterested in time.

"Oh, I suspect you might—when you are old enough and if you act properly. First we would have to be convinced you would not fall off and break your neck."

Johnny began to protest such reckless action on his part, just as Analise heard a carriage pull up in front of the house. She rose and looked out the window as Johnny scrambled to the floor, crying, "Grandy!"

"Now, wait," Analise cautioned. "I must speak with your grandfather first. You go wait with May until I tell you. All right?"

Reluctantly Johnny nodded and went slowly off to find the black servant. Analise went to the front door and stepped out, only to see to her surprise that Mr. Schaeffer had left the carriage and was coming up the steps to her door. She barely suppressed a gasp at the change in him: he looked exhausted and years older than he was. Deep lines of pain had set around his mouth and eyes, giving him a constantly worried look. Analise felt a swift stab of pity; despite their differences and his unyielding attitude, she had some feeling for him. He was well-intentioned and had always been much kinder to her than Frances.

Stiffly Schaeffer bowed to her and said, "May I come in? I wish to talk to you."

"Of course," Analise moved back into the house and led him into the parlor which she had just left.

"Please, sit down," she said and took her place by the window. "Would you like some tea?"

"No, thank you." He looked nervously away from her. "Analise, I have come to ask you a favor." He looked at her and glanced away, as though at a loss as to how to proceed.

"Go on," Analise encouraged him. "Is it something to do with Mark?"

The older man nodded and sighed, and then, as though his soul came out in the sigh, he began to talk. "Mark came home about a month ago. He—he had been injured in a battle." Analise turned pale and one hand flew to her throat. Was he saying that Mark was dying? No, he couldn't be; not Mark. Not Mark. "He is, well, to put it bluntly, he is crippled. His left arm is useless and he can barely drag himself around with a cane. And his face is badly scarred. He is not the man we knew, Analise, he is broken. Broken." He stopped and buried his face in his hands.

Analise clenched her hands together and said in a tight, controlled voice, "Is he dying?"

Schaeffer raised his head. "Dying? No. At least not physically. He survived the operations and the fevers, and the doctors say he will live a good many years yet. That is, if he cares to."

"If he cares to?" Analise echoed, puzzled.

"He has no interest in life. In anything. Frances and I have tried and tried to find something to light a spark in him: books, old friends, magazines, games. But he does nothing, just sneers at them all with the same black, contemptuous look. Mark makes no attempt to adjust, to accept; he just drinks and drinks and drinks. Every night he swigs down that filthy liquor until he is finally in a stupor. Frances even took little John Prentiss in to see him, hoping he would rouse some feeling in him, but Mark just swore and shouted at them. I'm afraid it must have frightened the boy."

"I think it puzzled him more than scared him, really," Analise said abstractedly, trying to ease the man's mind. Mark crippled! Her stunned mind could hardly accept it. She could not imagine that strength diminished, that vitality quenched.

"Frankly, I am at my wit's end. We simply cannot reach him; every day he grows more sullen, more remote. Frances cries constantly over him."

Analise grimaced; Frances' tears would elicit no sympathy from her. "Mr. Schaeffer, I don't quite understand exactly what it is you want from me."

"Analise, I want you to return. Come back to the house, to your husband. Please, I beg of you. He loved you so; I know—I could see it in his eyes when he came home to find you gone."

"Mr. Schaeffer, you are badly mistaken. I did not leave

my husband—only your house, where I was so unwelcome. It was Mark who left me; he came to me and told me he wished never to see me again. I can think of no plainer indication that he does not love me. What could I do that you or his sister could not? How would I, the rejected wife, have more influence with him?"

"Analise, you know his temper. It flows quick and hot, and he often regrets what he does in anger. One angry outburst does not necessarily reflect his true feeling. Surely you must know that."

Analise raised her eyebrows slightly. "One angry outburst following months and months without any word from him? Never, in the whole time he was away, did he write me a letter. Is that the act of a man in love?"

The old man sighed. "I cannot excuse his actions. I cannot even fathom them, much less explain them. There is too much of his mother in him—and too much of me," he admitted hoarsely. "He does strange, wild things to hurt people and, I suspect, to hurt himself even more. Mark is a divided man, constantly at war with himself. Sometimes when he was younger he would do things he knew would hurt me, as his not writing hurt you, and I think he did them to test my love. Perhaps he has always been afraid that I would cease loving him if he displeased me, that I would leave him as I left his mother. I suppose I should not have left—for his sake."

Analise felt a wave of pity for the man. "Don't blame yourself, Mr. Schaeffer. You did the best you could."

"I acted selfishly. I could not bear any longer to be near Thalissia, to suffer her infidelities and her contempt. It was not that I did not love her, but that I loved her too much. I hoped Mark would come to me, as Frances did, but he loved Thalissia too. So he stayed and I guess he felt that I had left him as well as his mother."

"Mr. Schaeffer, we start out with what our parents give us, but in the end, we are each responsible for what we do with that. You can't take credit for his weaknesses any more than you can take credit for his heart-rending smile or his ability to shoot."

"Don't you see, Analise? I know now that I failed him, that I cannot ever make up to him for his early life. But I cannot stand by and let that happen to his son too. I know how important it is for a child to have a home with two parents who love him; don't take that chance away from John Prentiss. Please, remember, Analise, you are his wife. You owe him some duty; remember your promises to love and honor him? He needs you; he needs little John."

Analise chewed thoughtfully on her lip. She was sorry for the poor old man. She felt like snapping that Mark deserved no duty from her and that it was clear he had no need of little Johnny, since he had shouted him out of his room. But Mr. Schaeffer was not up to such honesty right now. He had to believe someone could help Mark or he would be drowned in guilt. Whatever the old man's reasons were, one thing was clear to her: if she refused to see Mark, crippled and reduced as he now was, and make one last stab at her marriage, could she marry Max and feel justified and guilt-free? She had loved Mark; she was still his wife. Surely she owed him that much.

"All right, Mr. Schaeffer, I am willing to give it a try. I will visit Mark, and you and I will see what his reaction is. If I can help him, I will. But that does not mean I am meekly returning to your house. If Mark shows the antipathy for me which I have seen, I am not going to sacrifice myself by moving in with him. That is too much to ask of anyone. Also, I will not take Johnny with me: Mark has been rude and obnoxious to him once, and I will not allow that to happen again."

"I agree," Schaeffer conceded quickly.

They rode back to the Schaeffer house immediately; Analise suspected that he feared she would not keep her promise if she put it off. When she saw the house where she had spent those miserable months her heart began to thud wildly in her chest. Mark lay inside that house, and she was afraid to meet him again. Would he revile her? Or would he be still as the grave? Schaeffer had said he was crippled—would she even recognize him?

Mr. Schaeffer got out and reached back to help her from the carriage. For a moment Analise froze. Then she took a deep breath and stepped out. Back straight, she followed the older man into the house and down the corridor to her husband's room. They had made the downstairs study into a bedroom for Mark so that he would not have to climb the stairs. The door to the room was closed. Schaeffer stopped and turned to her.

"I think this is a private moment between you and Mark. I will leave you here."

Analise nodded, her throat dry. Before she could move however, the door across the hall opened, and Frances appeared in the doorway. Analise noticed with a certain satisfaction that time had certainly not improved the other woman's appearance. She looked pale and haggard, and her eyes were red-rimmed from weeping. Mark's sister stared at Analise, her eyes wide with dismay, antipathy, and a sort of strange furtiveness. Analise thought she looked like a woman teetering on the edge of a breakdown.

"Papa!" she hissed, her tone accusatory. "You brought her!"

"I told you I would if I could persuade her," her father replied evenly.

"But I never thought—" she began and broke off, glancing at Analise.

Analise smiled slightly and said, "That is the surest way to lose, Frances."

Frances turned to her father frantically. "Papa, you can't. Mark will be so angry. He will go wild."

"Sometimes I think that would be better than the bitter apathy he nurses now."

"It will set his recovery back. All our weeks of careful nursing will go for naught."

"Frances, you know my opinion on this subject. We could argue about it until Doomsday, and you would not change my mind. It is quite obvious to me that you and I have been able to do nothing with Mark. Analise is the only person who has any chance with him."

The woman swung to Analise wildly. "Did Papa not tell you that he is crippled, disfigured? Why, the very sight of him would repel you!"

"No, Frances," Analise returned quietly, her voice smooth and hard as glass. "It is *you* who repels me. Do you want your brother to yourself so much that you are grateful for his scars?"

A flame burst in Fran's dark eyes, and she started for Analise, but her father grabbed her firmly by the arm and led her away. "No, Fran, now be reasonable. Analise is going to speak to Mark; and you and I are going to leave them alone."

Analise watched them thoughtfully; she suspected

strongly that she had touched a nerve there with Frances. Then she shrugged and turned back to the door. Now she had to face seeing Mark again. With a rapidly beating heart, she reached for the doorknob.

At the sound of the opening door, Sergeant Jackson looked up from his chair by the window, but Mark did not bother to glance away from the book he was reading. Jackson's jaw dropped open with stunned amazement as he stared at perhaps the most beautiful woman he had ever seen. Her pale white skin contrasted sharply with her bright, sapphire-blue eyes and the smooth mass of shining black hair that framed her face. Dressed in a bright red dress topped by a gaily military red jacket with black frogging, and a saucy red hat perched on her black hair, she was a vision of beauty and vitality. Jackson knew without being told that this was Analise; it could be no one else. And at last he began to understand the hold she had on the Colonel. She took her first sight of her husband well, Jackson thought. Her hand tightened convulsively on the knob and a tiny gasp escaped her lips, but her expression did not change. It was the barely suppressed gasp that caused the Colonel to look up, and at the sight of her his whole body stiffened.

"Analise," he breathed, and for a moment their gazes locked in silence.

When she first opened the door and saw Mark sitting on the sofa, his legs stretched out before him on the couch, Analise was swept with horrified disbelief. This could not be Mark, this thin, pale wreck of a man, whose face was torn by a livid scar and stamped with lines of bitterness and pain. He was so gaunt, so old—why, his hair was even streaked with gray.

Then he looked up and suddenly the dull, dark eyes had blazed alive, and in that instant Analise felt once more his force, his magnetism, and her knees went weak and wild emotions whirled inside her. She clung to the doorknob for support and smiled tremulously.

"Hello, Mark."

The man remembered then all that had passed between them, remembered too his present condition, and his eyes turned coldly blank and his face fell into its usual sarcastic lines.

"So my 'loving wife' has returned," he said spitefully. "Did they tell you I was on death's door?"

Conflicting emotions tore at Analise, crushing the air from her lungs. She could not really even sort out her feelings, let alone express them, but her disciplined mind and the habit of months of jousting with Mark made her snap back without thinking, "No, actually they told me that you had changed greatly, but obviously they lied."

Her sharp retort made the Sergeant gulp and sneak a look at Schaeffer, but oddly enough his superior's face lightened a trifle and a smile hovered about his mouth.

"Nor have you," he said. God, but she was lovely, more beautiful than he remembered. Maturity had increased her looks, erased the round softness of innocence and substituted the planes and edges and depth that gave real beauty.

Analise crossed the room toward him, impelled by the old need to be near him. He followed her movements, his hungry eyes devouring the details of her appearance. For the first time in months he felt the searing flood of desire, and he wanted to reach out and pull her down to him. She was his, and he wanted to claim her, take her back from that damned German merchant and make her love him. A spasm of pain crossed his face. Cripple, he jeered at himself, you couldn't take a piece of candy from a child or get any woman in your bed except for money.

"May I sit down?" Analise asked and he nodded shortly toward a chair. She sat gracefully and regarded him for a moment. Pain and pity stabbed at her; she wanted to cry for the loss he had suffered, for the marring of his strong lithe body, for the awful agony he had endured.

"Well? Did you just come to gawk?" he asked roughly.

"No," Analise swallowed past the constriction in her throat. Even now, he was so hard and hurtful—had his own pain not given him any more sympathy? "I came because your father asked me to. He wants us to live as husband and wife again."

Mark's lip curled sardonically. "Hopefully you are not silly enough to agree."

His words and voice cut her anew, and Analise wished that she had never agreed to come. He hated her, and his wrathful hatred was almost more than she could bear. "I agreed only to give it a chance, to see if you wanted to try it again."

His laugh was dry and humorless. "Why? So that you can cuckold me again? Oh, I can see the advantages to you—it is so much easier, after all, to be unfaithful to a *crippled* husband."

"How dare you!" Analise jumped up, anger flaming red in her cheeks.

"No, let me finish. You ask if I want you back. The answer is no. I did not want you a year ago when I left your house, and I do not want you now. You are a lying, heartless, faithless bitch, and only a fool would set himself up for the kind of heartache you give. And I, lady, am no fool."

Analise stood staring down at him, rigid with anger and embarrassment, her eyes great blue pools of emotion. "No, Mark, you *are* a fool. You are probably the greatest fool I have ever known. Because I loved you, and yet you broke my heart time and time again. And I was an even greater fool to let you. But I, at least, have gotten smarter. I have closed my heart to you, and I have at last released myself from the love I felt for you. I no longer want you either. And that is why I am filing for divorce. And when I get it, I shall marry Max Schleyer. Goodbye, Mark."

Fifteen

$\mathcal{A}$nalise turned and strode quickly out the door, slamming it behind her. Mark stared bleakly after her. His aide sat stunned for a moment, then exploded from his chair.

"Sweet Lord in Heaven," Jackson cried, "what do you think you're doing? There's the woman you've been eating your heart out over for two years, practically offering herself to you, and you tell her you don't want her!"

"Do you think it was easy, Jackson, giving up the one thing I want in this world?" Mark asked shakily. His hand trembled as he reached for the whiskey bottle and poured himself a drink. "But, good God, man, what was I to do? Look at me—how could I hold her? A useless cripple with a face that frightens children. And if, through pity, she would stay, I could not sentence her to spending the rest of her life with half a man."

His love for her shone obviously on his face, and his eyes burned with anguish. Quickly he gulped down a drink and poured another. He laughed shortly, harshly.

"Oh, hell, who am I trying to fool? I would take her any way I could get her—pity, force, whatever. It is myself I'm protecting. She does not love me; once she did, I think, but

I killed it. I hurt her and used her and humiliated her—small wonder she left me for another man. I thought when we married that she had a feeling for me, a feeling I could nurture and turn into love. But now I see that her only feeling was dislike; she married me to get a name for her child and maybe to pay me back for what I had done. Once she had that, I was no longer of any use to her, and she dropped any pretense of feeling for me.

"So if she came back to me, the best reason I can see is pity, the worst is that it is a move in some devious game of hers. Pity is not much to keep a woman satisfied, and I haven't the charm to make her love me or the strength to make her faithful. She would stray, go back to that Schleyer or find another man, other men. And I could do nothing but take it. The humiliation of her returning out of pity is bad enough, but, sweet Jesus, I could not endure sitting here, *knowing, imagining* and unable to do anything about it."

Jackson sighed. It was hard for him to sort out what Schaeffer had said. He could see the sense in what he said about not wanting the pain of her infidelity when he, crippled as he was, could do nothing about it. And he knew her to be unfaithful and heartless—after all, she had never written and the Colonel's sister said that she had been having an affair with Schleyer. Jackson had despised the woman for a long time for the hurt done to his idol. Yet, seeing her just now, she had not looked heartless. Hadn't he seen the melting look in her eyes when she first saw Schaeffer and hadn't he seen the hurt mixed in with the anger when the Colonel repudiated her? Perhaps there was more feeling in her than Schaeffer realized.

But however painful and bitter the exchange had been

between the couple, Jackson had noticed one thing that made him certain Mark was cutting his own throat by getting rid of his wife: When Analise entered the room, life had suddenly bloomed in Schaeffer's face. There had been love and hunger and anger in him; for the first time he had emerged from his haze of apathy and self-pity. And his aide was not about to stand by and let the Colonel throw away his chance to become a living, thinking, feeling man again. Quickly Jackson left the room.

He was afraid he was far too late to catch her, but when he stepped into the hallway, he saw her in the music room. She stood by one of the windows, looking out, holding herself against the sobs that wracked her body. Sunlight glinted on the tears that ran silently down her cheeks. Mark's father sat in dejection across the room from her, and beside him stood Frances, her expression a mingling of malicious pleasure and, strangely, relief. Jackson had never liked the sister much; she was too high and mighty for him. But now he felt a definite antagonism for her and, suddenly, a sense of distrust. How accurate were the statements of a woman who so obviously hated the person she was gossiping about?

"Mrs. Schaeffer?" he said and she turned toward him. He could see that she had bitten her lips till the blood came, trying to subdue her tears, and he felt a grudging admiration for her. She was as proud as the Colonel was. He hoped to Heaven she was not as stiff-necked. "I wanted to ask you to stay with Colonel Schaeffer, to not do what you said."

The woman's eyes widened and she said bluntly, "Are you insane? You were in there; you heard him say that he did not want me."

"And I have also heard him tell a mother her boy died a hero when he was really shot in the back running from a battle."

"Meaning?" Analise said.

"Meaning the Colonel can lie quite well when it serves his purpose."

"You don't have to convince me of that," Analise said dryly, but a faint look of doubt flitted across her face.

"He is afraid of having his heart broken again by you," Jackson began.

"*His* heart!" Analise cried.

Firmly Jackson plowed on. "I know, though, that inside it kills him for you to leave. And I know, too, that when you were with him tonight, he was closer to being alive than I've seen him since he was injured. Mrs. Schaeffer, he doesn't care about himself or anything else. He doesn't try to use his crippled limbs, although the doctors said there was a possibility he might regain some use, at least in his arm, once he was healed. He just drinks himself into an early grave. He has given up on life."

"And what makes you think I can change that?"

"Ma'am, I saw the change in him the minute you walked in the door. He gave up a long time ago, you see; he gave up when he lost you."

"Lost me! Why, of all the—" Analise began to sputter angrily.

"Yes!" Jackson interrupted harshly. "When he came back from that furlough, he was in a black mood. It was as if he didn't want to live any more. He did not want to live because he had lost you!"

Behind them a muffled cry broke from Frances, but the Sergeant did not pause to look at her. "He took every dangerous thing that came along, was in the front of every fight, looking to get killed. And finally, he got what he was looking for, only it didn't kill him, just maimed him for the rest of his life!

"You owe him something, Mrs. Schaeffer. It's on account of you that he is in the state he is in now."

"No," Analise breathed, backing away from the Sergeant, her face pale. It was all too much; her head was whirling wildly and she felt that she might faint. First there had been the shock of seeing Mark and the sudden resurgence of all the old feelings of love and anger and pain that she had thought she had finally killed, followed by Mark's cold rejection of her. And now here was this man shouting that she was responsible for Mark's being crippled. It was too crazy, too much; she could not deal with it. "No, it can't be true. You are insane. Mark did not love me. Not at all, certainly not enough to be suicidal."

"Didn't love you! I saw him when he came back; I saw the utter despair he was in because you had left him for another man. I heard him get up at night when all the men were sleeping and go sit out in the field and just stare. When he was delirious after he was shot he talked and talked about you. I know. Oh, I know. And before that, when you never wrote him, I saw the hopelessness, the disappointment, the sheer pain—"

"When I never wrote him!" Analise cried, pouncing on one point she was sure of in all the crazy things he was saying. "Sergeant, I do not know whether you are a liar or just plain insane. But I do know you are dead wrong; I wrote Mark often—two or three times a week at first. It was he who did not write to me. I did not stop writing until he came here and told me he was never going to see me again.

And I don't think it was horribly cruel of me to end then. Do you?"

Jackson gaped at her. Lord, but the woman was a cool liar. If he did not know better, had not actually heard the mail calls, he would have believed her himself. "There's no point in lying to me, Mrs. Schaeffer. I know that—"

"Sergeant!" Mr. Schaeffer's voice cracked out. "I will not allow you to abuse my daughter-in-law in my own house."

"But sir—"

"She is not lying, Sergeant. I can vouch for that: many times in the morning when I left for the office, I have seen a letter from Analise to Mark lying on the hall table, waiting for the mail."

Now Jackson stared at the older man, bug-eyed with astonishment. He felt suddenly as though he were in the middle of an insane asylum. "But—but, sir," he began to stammer, "I saw it myself. The Major never got a letter from her. I have seen him turn away from mail call, hands empty, hundreds of times. Ask him yourself. Why should he lie?"

"And why should I lie? Or Mr. Schaeffer?" Analise said scornfully.

"Perhaps you had them addressed wrong," Jackson said slowly.

"They were never returned here. Surely if they were misaddressed—"

"Stop it!" Frances' shriek cut through the air, and they all swung to look at her. She stood, pale and trembling, against the wall, her eyes wild and hunted, her mouth screwed up in an agony of grief. "I hated *her*; she was so like Thalissia, and she had her hooks in Mark, just like

Thalissia did in Papa. I could not bear for Mark to be miserable all his life, like Papa.

"I knew if I broke them up, if I made him realize the kind of woman she really was, that he would be better off. Maybe unhappy at first, but he would get over that. I never meant to hurt him! I love Mark. I didn't dream he would react that way, that he would be so unhappy, that he would throw himself in the path of death!"

"Frances," Prentiss Schaeffer's face was grim, his voice stern as death. "Are you saying that you intercepted Analise's letters to Mark?"

"Yes! I destroyed them. I would take them off the table just before the mail came and burn them." Suddenly she began to half-sob, half-laugh hysterically, and she swung on Analise. "You were bad for him! Bad! I just wanted to save him."

Analise stood white-faced, numb with shock. Mark had never received her letters! He had not read those first eager letters of love or the later heartbroken cries for word from him or the joyful letters about his beautiful son. He had not known how she felt, how she longed for him, how she waited anxiously for his return. Quite the opposite—Mark must have thought she cared so little for him that she did not even write a single letter. The waste, the appalling loss overwhelmed her, sent her reeling. Shakily she stumbled to a chair and sat down.

"Sergeant," Analise said, her voice trembling, "did you say Mark wrote to me?"

"Yes, ma'am, often—at least at first."

"And you took those too, Frances?"

"Yes! Yes!" Her words came out in short gasps in the midst of her flood of tears.

Now her father went to Frances and grabbed her by the shoulders, and said harshly, "And what you told me—and Mark, too—about Analise and that German fellow, was that a lie too?"

"No!" she cried and glared at Analise. "I know she was having an affair with him. Why else did she move from here?"

"But when you said you followed them one day from the park to his house and saw her enter the house, were you lying then?"

"Yes," her voice was sullen and reluctant.

"And what you said about hiring a detective and his following her to Schleyer's house, where she stayed all night?" Schaeffer's voice was like steel and his fingers bit cruelly into his daughter's shoulders.

"It was not true; he never followed her there," Frances admitted, then lashed out frantically, "but I know she was having an affair; I know it! She was just too clever. I couldn't catch her."

"My God!" Schaeffer dropped his hands from her as if she were molten lead. "I can't believe you could be so—so vicious, so unprincipled. My own daughter!"

Analise rose, her entire body rigid with contained anger. "I can't think of anything bad enough to call you. To ruin your own brother's life! To hurt him so callously. Not to mention ruining my life and little John's. You are not a woman; you're a viper! I was not sleeping with Max Schleyer, and you know it, if you set a detective on me. I left here simply because of your coldness and cruelty to me; it had nothing to do with Mark.

"And you also know that concern for Mark never played a part in your schemes. The fact is, you have a consuming, unnatural love for your brother, and you went to any lengths to get him all to yourself. No doubt you laughed with joy when you learned that he was returning home a cripple and you would have him dependent on you the rest of his life!"

"No, no! I never meant for anything to happen to Mark!" his sister protested agitatedly.

Analise lashed out with her hand, slapping Frances hard across the cheek. The two women stood staring at each other for a moment, Analise sparkling with anger and the imprint of her hand bright red against the other woman's chalky face. Then Analise broke and whirled and ran from the house.

Wearily Prentiss Schaeffer said, "All right, Frances, come; now you are going to tell Mark the truth."

The woman gasped and began to cry. "No, oh, Papa, please don't make me."

"You've done your brother a grievous wrong, Frances, and now you must face up to it. You can never repay him for the misery he's been through but at least I'll not let you off scot-free."

Mark took the news silently, not moving a muscle, but he went deadly white around his lips, and his eyes had the look of a mortally wounded animal.

"Did you destroy my letters, too?" he asked and Frances shook her head. "Then please do so now."

"No, wait!" the elder Schaeffer cut in. "Mark, you can't do that. Analise has a right to read those. Don't you want her to know what you felt for her? After all, she was living with the same bitter belief about you—that you did not care for her enough to even write."

"I don't want her to know! I don't want her to read the hurtful, bitter things I said toward the end. I don't want her to know how much it hurt me or how much I loved her. It's been over a year, and she has had plenty of time to get over me. Analise no longer loves me; she has already made plans to marry Schleyer. Let it stay that way; it is better. If she reads those letters—I poured out my soul to her in them, and no doubt she would be filled with pity for me and maybe even return to me."

"But that is where she belongs," his father protested.

"No!" Mark shouted violently. "Damn it, don't you understand? I still love her. And I won't have her tied to a useless shell of a man. I refuse to subject her to a cripple's clumsy pawing. And, God knows, I cannot bear to see the disgust and fear in her eyes when she has to crawl into bed beside me."

"Give the girl a chance, Mark. How do you know she does not still love you, as you love her? How do you know she would be disgusted?"

"Look at me! The man she loved was strong and whole, not a weak, mangled piece of flesh. My face alone was enough to send Philippa into spasms. Think what it would be like to have to look upon my naked arm and leg! To see that multitude of purple, twisted scars, the deep pits where chunks of flesh were torn away—"

He stopped at the sound of a strangled cry from Frances and looked at her. "Not very appealing, is it? Just think of having to live with it."

Frances turned and ran quickly from the room. Mark followed her with bitter eyes. "Father, keep her away from me. I don't want to have to look at her again. And get those letters from her."

"All right, I will. But, please, reconsider what you said about Analise. A husband and wife belong together. And John Prentiss needs a father."

"Let Schleyer be a father to him," Mark snarled. "I would scare the kid silly."

His father sighed and left the room, going up to Frances' bedroom to recover the letters Mark had written Analise. He would take them, as Mark requested, and he would not show them to Analise, at least not yet, but he could not bring himself to destroy them either. It seemed to him that what Mark wanted was wrong, and he would have to think about it before he took any move on the matter.

Behind him, Mark closed his eyes and leaned back against the sofa. Analise! He saw her again in his mind as she had stood before him, so vibrant, so alive, her cheeks as flaming as that red dress, her waist small, her breasts thrusting proudly against the cloth. He bit back a groan of desire. She had always been a beauty in red. Mark remembered the red diaphanous nightgown he had given her that had clung revealingly to her every curve. A shudder of elemental passion shook him now, as it had then.

A kinder God, Mark thought, would have taken away his desire, too, when he had condemned him to being the repulsive thing he was now. But, no, that much of his former self remained, at least where Analise was concerned. He still pulsated with lust at the mere thought of her. And there was no way to relieve it even if he could persuade Jackson to sneak a whore in here for him. A brief smile touched his lips: imagine what his puritanical father would say to that.

No other woman would really slake his thirst for Analise; it certainly never had in the past. He had tried quite a few of them in those long months when Analise did not write and after his disastrous furlough. But none set him aflame as she did nor satisfied him so completely.

What a fool he had been! If only he had not been so consumed with anger and jealousy when he went to see her that time, if only he had given her a chance to explain; but no, even if she had explained, he had to admit that he probably would not have believed her. No doubt he would have taken his sister's word over hers; he had always been so eager to disbelieve her, so wildly jealous. Like a fool, he had thrown away his chances at every turn: first betraying her, then humiliating her and alienating her from all friends and family, getting her with child and compelling her to marry him, then angrily accusing her of infidelity and leaving her without giving her the slightest chance to defend herself. She had loved him a long time ago, before he blew up the torpedoes, and when they were first married, she had seemed to have some feeling for him again, to be happy. But after all that time when she thought he did not write to her—and God knows what other little spiteful tricks Frances had played to convince Analise he did not love her—and then his blind, erroneous repudiation of her, well, every spark of affection she had for him must have been stamped out. And no doubt Schleyer was always hanging around, all too ready to comfort her. Mark knew he had practically handed her over to the other man.

No, Mark told himself, there was probably no love for him left in her at all. He would not fool himself. And what would she feel, discovering how Frances had deceived them? The same bitter gall of regret? The same kind of guilt? Pity for his ruined state? A duty to return to him? He wondered if her pity and duty would be great enough to send her back to him. For a moment he thought longingly of the sweetness of having her with him; she would make life bearable again, touching it with beauty and pleasure, filling his lonely days and agonizing nights.

Proudly, he turned his mind away from the vision. He was not going to use his crippled state to tie her to him. He would not, could not let her see his maimed limbs; he simply could not stand to see the revulsion in her eyes. More than that, he loved her too much to let her waste her life on a wreck like him. If she did come back, he would have to make her leave; he could do that much for her.

After she left the Schaeffer house, Analise walked. She had no sense of time or distance, only the confused maze of her emotions, which needed sorting out, and the drive to expend her anger and frustration. She walked and walked, blind to everything about her, until finally she was exhausted. Wearily she hailed a cab, for the first time aware of what was around her and how far she was from home.

Once home, Analise dropped into bed, not even taking the time to eat, and slept straight through until early morning. She sat up, conscious of a thrill of anticipation and excitement, and then she remembered: Mark was home and he had written her; he had loved her so much he had not wanted to live without her. Tears sprang into her eyes—how horrible it must be for him to be crippled like that; he had been such a strong, vital man.

Quickly she flung on a wrapper and went silently down to the kitchen to make herself some coffee. She was glad she had awakened so early, before anyone else. She needed some time alone to sit and sip her coffee and make plans. It was strange how the exercise and sleep had resolved and clarified the wild, turbulent emotions of the day before. All the anger and futile regret, all the guilt and accumulated pain, all the overlay of coldness and indifference that she had used to seal her wound had burned away, and she was left with one clear, overriding truth: she loved Mark, and could not be happy without him.

Yesterday when she walked into that room and saw him, the old uncontrollable love and passion had surged up in her. Crippled as he was, he was still able to overpower her, still able to spark desire in her with his fiery eyes and set her trembling with anger with his sharp, sarcastic words. She knew now that he was the only one for her, no matter how at times he might wound her. Her heart and body responded only to him. How pale and weak was the pleasure of Max's lovemaking compared to the flame that Mark's mere glance awakened in her.

Analise sighed: poor Max. Hurting him was the only thing she felt hesitation about. He had been so kind to her, so good; he loved her deeply, she knew that. And in a way she loved him—as one might love a friend or relative. But not in the wild, rapturous, consuming way she loved Mark. Analise smiled a secret little smile; it seemed so wondrous that after all this time and after all the things they had done to each other that love should survive, overriding all the hurts and doubts. She had not wanted to love him, had fought it for a long time, but she had finally come to realize that she could not escape from it. She loved him, and she must accept the fact that she always would.

And Mark loved her. He had written her and had been crushed when he received no letters from her. Then when he broke with her because of the lies Fran told, he had been in such despair that he had not cared about living.

Surely that proved he loved her. If only they could forget the past and start clean and fresh—Analise knew she had to try.

Taking a final sip of coffee, Analise went up to her room to dress. Wanting to look her best, she searched her closet and finally pulled out a sapphire-blue dress, which, though plain, showed off her figure nicely and deepened the blue of her eyes. Her dangling sapphire earbobs and that new little white toque with the blue net and cascade of a dainty, blue and white flowers would complete the picture. Carefully, she primped in front of her mirror, her stomach jumping in nervous anticipation. What would Mark say when he saw her? What would he do? She closed her eyes, imagining him reaching out for her, pulling her down into his arms, their lips meeting hungrily. A shiver ran through her. It had been much too long, but at last she and her husband would be together again.

Sixteen

$\mathcal{A}$nalise went first to see Max Schleyer. She felt that she could not, in good conscience, delay telling him of her decision, no matter how much she dreaded it. He was too fine a person to keep dangling on a string. Knowing that Schleyer was always in his office by seven o'clock and that there would be no one else there, Analise went to the store.

Max looked up and smiled when she first entered his office, but he must have seen some indication of her purpose there, for his smile turned hesitant and faintly apprehensive.

"You are here earlier than usual. Is something the matter?" he asked.

"Yes, in a way. I came to tell you something that I am afraid will hurt you, and I am too fond of you to do that."

"What is it?" His voice was quiet, calm, almost as if he expected what was coming.

"I—I cannot marry you after all, Max. I was a fool to decide to. I wanted to forget Mark, to make myself not love him, and I wanted so much to love you, that I thought I could force myself to do it. It was stupid of me and cruel to you, but I truly did not mean to be. You see, I believed that there was no hope left where Mark was concerned, and I wanted to live again and be happy again. I knew that Johnny needed a father. So I came to you. Now I realize how wrong it was, and I cannot go through with it. I'm so sorry, Max, so sorry." Tears formed in her eyes as she looked at the man's face; though he had not changed expressions, the lines of his face had subtly shifted into sorrow.

"You have heard from Schaeffer?"

"His father came to see me," Analise began and poured out the whole story to him. He listened quietly, nodding a little now and then at something she said.

It was no great shock to Max. He had felt that Analise's agreement to marry him had been too good to be true. For a few days he had been the happiest of men, but now he must return to reality. Analise had always had an obsession with that man, and he had feared that she would return to him if Mark ever asked her. And now he had the added emotional appeal of being a cripple. From what he had heard, Max thought Schaeffer a scoundrel, but now it would take tremendous effort and luck to pry Analise from him.

"I am sorry to hear of his injuries," Max said when she had finished. "Is there any possibility of his using the arm or leg?"

"I'm not sure. His aide said yesterday that one doctor had said he might be able to use them when he had healed. So perhaps there is hope."

"I know of a very fine doctor, Dr. Kranze. If you wish, I could persuade him to have a look at your husband and tell you how much—or how little—can be done to help him."

"Oh, would you, Max?" Analise glowed. "You are such a good, generous man. I might have known you—"

"Now, wait. Before you get carried away with my generosity, let me tell you my motive. I love you and still want very much to marry you. As long as your husband is a cripple, I know that I shall be facing tremendous odds. If he were restored to normal, all his bad qualities would become visible to you again. Then I might have a chance—fighting a whole, real man, not a ghost or a cripple. You see how selfish I am?"

"I see," Analise replied and smiled.

"Now, will you be staying on here at the store?" His question came out something less than casually.

"I don't know. I would like to, of course. I really haven't made any plans; I have not even talked to Mark yet. Give me a few days to think about it and decide what to do. All right?"

"All right. I hope you decide to return. And if you need anything, call on me. I shall send a note to Dr. Kranze today."

"Thank you, Max." Analise rose and extended her hand. "I wish there was some way I could make it up to you."

He took her hand and squeezed it. "There is no need."

Once she left the store, Analise's spirits began to rise, and by the time she reached the Schaeffer's house, she had recovered her earlier buoyancy. Although it was by then after eight, the butler informed her that Mark was not yet awake. Prentiss Schaeffer greeted her warmly and invited her into his study for a cup of coffee. He apologized for his son's late sleeping, explaining that Mark often had difficulty sleeping through the night and then overslept the next morning. Carefully he avoided mentioning that Mark had gotten roaring drunk the night before and doubtless overslept for that reason.

It was Sergeant Jackson, who ushered her into Mark's room an hour later, who told her about the drinking session. "Don't let him rile you, Mrs. Schaeffer. He is in a black mood—got one hell of a hangover. So don't take anything he says too much to heart."

Analise frowned a little at his words. Getting drunk hardly sounded like the proper response for a man who had learned his wife loved him. Perhaps, she told herself, quelling the spasm of fear in her stomach, perhaps he had been joyfully celebrating.

Mark looked anything but joyful when Analise stepped into the room. He was again sitting on the couch, his legs out in front of him. His clothes looked as if he had slept in them, and he was scowling darkly at Analise.

"What the hell did you let her in here for?" he growled at Jackson. "I don't want her here."

Analise felt shaken. Obviously her happy expectation of an easy reconciliation was false. Something was wrong, but what? Had they not told Mark of his sister's deception? Or had he heard and refused to believe?

Analise turned to the sergeant. Her voice trembled slightly as she said, "Sergeant, I would like to speak to my husband alone, if you don't mind."

"Yes, of course, Mrs. Schaeffer." He left the room quickly, grateful for the escape from the Colonel's wrath.

"I see you now have Jackson under your spell as well," Mark said sarcastically after the man left.

In the blue dress and coquettish little hat, Analise was

dazzling, Mark thought. It was irritating that the one thing he had never been able to feel for her was indifference. Right now he wanted to throw all pride and honor to the winds and beg her to stay with him, to play on her pity or duty or whatever motivated her. Only the greatest self-control kept him from groveling before her. He had to send her away, he told himself—and soon, or else he would fall apart.

"Mark," Analise ignored his last remark and moved closer to him. "Did your father tell you what Frances said yesterday?"

"Yes."

Drawing a breath, Analise tried again. "Did you believe her?"

He shrugged. "I suppose."

Analise sank down into a chair, dismayed. She could not understand what this attitude of his meant. Why was he so aloof? All the things she had intended to say seemed ridiculous and impossible to say in front of him now.

"I—I thought we might begin again."

"Begin what again?" Mark said harshly. His head was pounding murderously and his insides quivering from the effort of his deception. "Begin fighting? Trying to destroy each other? That has always been our pattern."

"No!" Analise exclaimed and watched, horrified, as Mark poured himself a strong shot of whiskey from the table beside the couch. "I meant, begin our marriage again. Forget what happened and what we thought happened. I want us to live together as a family; I want Johnny to have both parents."

"Johnny? Hah! My face scared the boy half silly!"

"You shouted at him, that's what scared him!" Analise

retorted hotly. "But if you would give him a chance to meet you, without yelling or being nasty, just quietly introduced to him, I am sure he would not be scared of you. Probably he would be curious about your scar for a little while, but he would become used to it quickly."

"Don't you understand that I don't care!" Mark shouted. "I don't want the boy! And I don't want you!" Wildly he threw the half-empty bottle against the door, where it crashed and scattered.

Analise stared at Mark, her stomach churning. He looked away from her. There were running footsteps in the hall and Sergeant Jackson opened the door.

"Colonel? What's the matter? What happened?"

"I broke a bottle of whiskey. Send a maid in to clean it up, and fetch me another bottle," Mark said, his voice surly.

"My God, Mark, it's still morning. Surely you are not going to have any more to drink," Analise cried.

"The hell I'm not!" Mark snapped. "Look, damn it! Get out of my life. I don't want you or the kid. Get the divorce like you said and marry that German. I am sure he will be a much better husband and father than I ever was. I was not cut out to be a family man."

"What were you cut out to be? A drunk?" Analise's voice was sharp.

"I am a cripple, Analise. Can't you see? I cannot ride a horse or dance or cut up my own food or make love to a woman without sprawling all over her. What else am I to do but drink? I'm not even a man, let alone a husband."

Pity flashed across Analise's face and she went to him. Gently, firmly, she put her hands on his face, turned his head to look at her. His eyes were bleak.

"Oh, Mark, do you think I care? Do you think I loved you only because you were handsome or sat a horse well? I knew hundreds of men like that, and I never fell in love with any of them."

Mark heard nothing of what she said, his mind registering only the pity on her face. "No! Get away from me," he croaked. "Let me rot in peace. Can't you get it through your head? I don't love you!"

Analise stepped back, her eyes suddenly pools of hurt. He did not love her; he did not want her or their son. That thought had not occurred to her, but she could see now that it was perfectly likely. Just because he had written her letters did not mean he loved her. Even if he had, as his aide claimed, loved her so much he did not want to live without her, his absence, his wounds, his pain had somehow all combined to kill his love.

Shakily she turned and left the room, not seeing the agony in Mark's dark eyes as he watched her go. Analise went to the music room and sat down to collect herself. All her newfound dreams had been shattered. What was she to do, now that she knew there was no one else for her but Mark; now that Mark did not want her? She could not just return to the solitary life she had been living, apart from her husband, ignorant of all that happened to him, having no effect on his life at all.

Analise stayed at the Schaeffer house the rest of the day, observing the comings and goings in Mark's room, hearing his angry voice, watching him drink himself into oblivion. It soon became obvious that everyone in the house—family, servants, even Sergeant Jackson—spoiled Mark outrageously. No one made the slightest attempt to curb his drinking. Though they might sigh or lecture, they gave him another bottle when he asked for it. If Mark wanted something, someone always fetched it. They coddled and cosseted him and did everything for him.

No wonder he is crippled, Analise thought furiously, and likely to become even more so, the way things were going. Mark had absolutely nothing to do—imagine him without a single challenge, Mark Schaeffer, who liked nothing better than to take up a challenge or accept a risk. He was bored; he had nothing to do but drink. Anyone in that position would have felt gloomy and self-pitying; anyone would have decided he was useless. In short, people were indulging him to death.

Her analysis was confirmed by what Dr. Kranze told her the next evening. Although Mark had at first objected strenuously to being seen by Analise's doctor, after much pleading from his father and Jackson, he had submitted to an examination by Dr. Kranze. The doctor reported to Analise that while Mark had received severe wounds, his problems were more spiritual than physical.

"He has given up," the doctor sighed in his heavily accented English. "Which is too bad, since I think there is some possibility of his using his injured limbs, at least more than he does now. There has been some permanent impairment of the muscles, particularly in the leg. I doubt that he will ever be able to walk completely without a limp, and doubtless his arm will not regain its full strength. However, I suspect that his muscles have atrophied through disuse, and the degeneration will become greater if he continues not to use them.

"Of course," he continued, "I cannot say exactly how much use he could regain. You see, when the nerves and muscles were so injured initially, he could not use them, but the longer he did not use them the weaker the muscles became. Also, even after healing took place, any movement caused such pain that he did not use the muscles; so the weakening continued."

Analise interrupted excitedly, "So all Mark needs to do in order not to be crippled is to exercise?"

"No, wait, don't rush off like that. Besides the weakness, there has definitely been nerve damage—how extensive it was, I don't know. I also do not know to what extent the nerves have regenerated. If the nerves are gone, he cannot do it. If some of the nerves have regenerated, then it could be that they only need to be retaught what to do. The amount that could be retaught depends on the amount of damage."

"Well, how bad is Mark's damage?" Analise asked.

"That I cannot tell. I know there is more capability for movement than he exercises, but exactly how much—" the man gave an expressive shrug.

Analise sighed. This was all so vague. She was a person who liked exactitude, measurements, tangibles that one could work with. After all, they were not discussing theories, but the practicalities of Mark's condition. What good was the doctor if he could not tell what should be done?

"Dr. Kranze, tell me this: How could Mark get better? What should we do?" Analise asked bluntly.

"Well," the doctor said, looking a little taken aback at her directness, and mused a little. "Colonel Schaeffer should start trying to use his injured limbs. It may be a trifle painful at first, and it may take some time to achieve any success. But it is essential that he attempt it." He paused, then said, "Also, I recommend bathing in mineral waters; somehow the waters seem to relax and soothe pain. As far as alleviating the pain goes, a move to some warmer locale would help Colonel Schaeffer most. I am afraid that these cold New York winters will be quite painful to him. Perhaps, if the Colonel is a wealthy man, that might be possible, at least during the coldest months."

New Orleans! Analise thought, and a flash of warmth coursed through her. She thought of the thick, humid air, redolent of honeysuckle and flowers. The low buzz of flies and mosquitoes, the enveloping heat, the sharp smell of beignets and chicory coffee that the street women sold by the Market. And, oh, most beautiful of all, the noise: the lazy, slurred drawls of the people she had grown up with; the bustle of the docks; the musical cries of the fruit vendors; the rich jumble of the blacks' voices. A wave of homesickness swept her, bitter and longing.

Oh, if only she could take Mark back there, where their love had begun, where their passion had burned so bright and hot—surely there he could get well; surely there they could rediscover their love. It would be like a second chance, an opportunity to go back to the place of beginning and start over again.

They could manage it financially. She had saved all the money Mark and his father had sent her, and she was sure she could sell her land interests to Max. Mark had a tidy sum left from his adventuring, and she was sure that Mr. Schaeffer would help support them if they needed it. But wait! Suddenly her mind went swinging back a couple of thoughts. Max. Only the other day she and Max had been toying with the idea of opening up a new store in another city, Boston, perhaps. Why not New Orleans?

Analise's mind was off on this wonderful idea, exploring the possibilities, weighing advantages and disadvantages, considering the site, the builder, the contracts with ship-pers, the—she came back to reality with a thud. First she would have to convince Max of the profit in it. But worse than that, she would somehow have to convince Mark to go. That was doubtless the biggest stumbling block. Every-thing else looked easy next to that: convincing an apa-thetic, bitter, self-loathing Mark, who did not love her, to move with her to the place of their former love and there attempt painfully to use the limbs he was convinced were damaged beyond repair.

Analise looked at Dr. Kranze; she was aware that he was watching her strangely. No doubt he wondered at her silence and the succession of emotions that had crossed her face. She smiled at him tentatively, excused herself for her absent-mindedness, and got rid of him as quickly as eti-quette permitted. She had to think.

She went upstairs and rang for May to help her undress and take down her hair. It was always easier to think seriously in a loose wrapper and with the heavy weight of her hair flowing free down her back. Her best thoughts for the store always seemed to come in this brief time of relaxa-tion before bed.

"May," she asked her servant casually, "what would you think about returning to New Orleans?"

"New Orleans!" The other woman's face lit up. "Do you mean it, Miss Analise? Oh, that'd be Heaven."

"Don't you like the free North, May?" Analise teased.

"No, ma'am, it's too cold and too many white folks for me," May said bluntly. "I'd like to go back where my family is and my friends. Where your blood don't freeze up in the winter and people don't talk so fast you can't understand them. 'Sides, ain't no slaves in New Orleans now either."

Analise sighed as May picked up her brush and began to pull it through Analise's tangled curls. "I would like to go back there too, May, and I think it would be good for Mark's injuries. The doctor said so. Only Mark's so set against me now, I don't see how I will ever get him to move. Why, he doesn't even want to see me, let alone go off to New Orleans to live with me."

May continued to rhythmically brush Analise's hair. She had seen her mistress through all her ups and downs with Mark, and though Analise was not given to pouring out her troubles to May, there was little May did not know about their relationship. She was well aware of Mark's attitude now, but she was also sure, from her more detached viewpoint, that Mark was concealing his true feelings. May had seen his face when Analise ran off that time in New Orleans, and she did not think that a love that strong had just died away.

"Remember that little Penoit boy?" May asked. "The one that fell off his horse and was paralyzed?"

Analise frowned. "Vaguely. What does that have to do with Mark?"

May sailed on. "And Mr. Sieber, that got his arm caught in his presses, and it was so mangled up?"

"Of course. That woman, Tante Monique, cured him." Suddenly enlightenment flashed across her face. "Mark! You're thinking she could help Mark."

"She's got some powerful cures," May said noncommittally.

"But isn't that all black magic, and that sort of thing?" Analise asked doubtfully.

May shrugged. "Tante Monique knows voodoo. She has powers. But it's more than that. She don't just say words over them; she works with them. She heals them. The doctors gave up on that Penoit boy before Tanta Monique got hold of him."

Analise narrowed her eyes in thought. All her life she had heard of Tante Monique and her miraculous cures. She was a free woman of color, a quadroon whose squat frame and ugly face had destined her not to be a wealthy white man's mistress. She had begun by being a midwife and by dealing in voodoo dolls and potions. Soon she spread into other areas of health, where it was said her curatives were more effective than doctors' medicines. Her most famous cures were in the area of restoring life to paralyzed limbs, like the Sieber man and the Penoit child. Doubtless her reputation was exaggerated, and Analise had no patience with black magic, but she knew the woman had had a great many successes and there were those who swore by her. For instance, that distant cousin of Emil's who had been struck by a childhood illness that left his legs paralyzed. The doctors couldn't do anything for him, but Monique had made him able to at least get about on crutches. Surely if anyone could make Mark walk again, she could do it.

"Well," Analise said, "I guess that I will just have to make Mark go to New Orleans, won't I?"

"Yes'm, but how?" her maid responded.

"I will come up with something, May, never fear."

After May had finished Analise sat down in her large overstuffed chair, her slippered feet on the cushioned footstool, and put her mind to her problem. Now that she had at least admitted that she loved Mark for good and always, she had to accept the fact that he did not love her and that, despite that, she still loved him. She wanted the best for him; she must do all she could to help. Analise was his wife, no matter how he felt; and it was up to her to provide him a home and the comforts of living. Most of all, it was up to her to make him better. First, it would require some discipline and sternness on her part. His family's weak indulgence was making him worse. One had to get his back up, challenge him, give him something to work for—or against.

To do that, she had to get him out of the Schaeffer house and under her control. Otherwise Mr. Schaeffer and the servants would continually undermine her efforts. Suddenly a thought came to her—now she knew the strategy to use to pry Mark out of his lethargy. He might hate her for it, but, then, what did she have to lose? Mark did not love her anyway. Yes, definitely that was the thing to do, whatever the cost to herself. She would begin it tomorrow.

Seventeen

$\mathscr{I}$t did not take Analise long to persuade Max Schleyer that he needed to open a new store in New Orleans. Once she pointed out that land and labor should be cheap, since many of the Orleanians had been bankrupted by the war, he began to soften to the idea. Then she reminded him that since the South had been destroyed, it would have to rebuild, and fortunes could be made in the rebuilding. Surely New Orleans would be the center of much of the wealth, and where would be a better place to have a beautiful new store?

"People from all over the South would come there to shop," Analise said enthusiastically. "We can carry all the latest fashions, and acres of expensive laces and china and the knickknacks, just the sort of thing to appeal to the nouveau riche. I will have a very exclusive dress design section, and I will find some suitably aristocratic woman with a French accent to deal with the customers. We can call it the Parisian Room and the prices will be so outrageous that people will flock there to have their clothes designed. Of course, we will have all our usual sections of dishes, pots and pan, shoes, gloves, hats, materials, and then in the back we'll have a hardware section—nails, lanterns, tools, work clothes, work boots, etc. After all, people will have to be repairing their houses, and if you buy here and send them to me, I am sure we can offer them for less than other places there. After all, things will have to come from Northern factories, and they are sure to be at a premium."

Laughing, Max had capitulated, telling her to go to New Orleans and find out the exact facts and figures. If it still looked profitable in the face of reality, she could begin the work. Analise then explained that as manager of a whole new store, she should certainly have a considerable raise.

"What? You get me to open a new store in New Orleans, at a considerable expense, which takes you far away from me and places you more in Schaeffer's control. And then you have the gall to ask me to increase your salary for this?" Again Schleyer laughed, but there was pain in his eyes. "Oh, all right—how about a share of the profits of the new store? Half and half?"

Analise smiled and put out her hand. "A deal."

Schleyer shook her hand and kept it in his grasp. His voice and look were serious as he said, "Analise, I want only the best for you. I can hardly bear to let you go, but I truly hope it will bring you happiness."

The woman smiled a little bleakly. "I doubt that it will bring me much happiness, but it is something I must do."

"Analise—" Words tumbled to his lips, but he bit them back and smiled. "If you ever need me, let me know. I will always come."

"I will remember, Max. Thank you, oh, thank you for everything you have done for me. I would never have made it without you."

Quietly she turned and left his office and—he thought sadly—his life.

Analise set busily about preparations to go: packing, getting passage on a ship for her party, giving notice to her servants, settling accounts, and doing the thousand and one things that seemed to crop up. It would be best, she told herself, to put off approaching Mark until the last moment; it would give him less time to squirm out of it. Sometimes she wondered, though, if it was not simply fear of facing him that made her wait so long.

She went to Mark's father and explained her plans for rehabilitating Mark. He obviously found it hard to accept her removing Mark from his family, although he was forced to admit that their leniency had only worsened his condition. Besides, with what Frances had done, there was a terrible strain in the household. Mark refused to see her or speak to her, and it was driving Fran to the edge of sanity. But New Orleans! Why did it have to be so far away?

"Because the doctor said he would feel better in a warm climate. And, as I told you, I am hopeful that Tante Monique can help him." Mr. Schaeffer made a grimace of disbelief, but Analise went on. "Besides, New Orleans will have some pleasant memories for Mark. It is where we met and fell in love; and, for a while, we were very happy there. And New Orleans is so alive, all filled with sounds and scents and colors—it is bound to lift his spirits."

Mr. Schaeffer sighed. Analise was Mark's wife; certainly she had a legitimate right to take him from this house. Moreover, she was obviously correct when she pointed out how little he and Fran and their servants had done to help Mark. Anyway, Analise was determined to do it, and he had discovered what a strong-willed young woman she was.

That beauty and soft-voiced femininity covered a mind like a steel trap and a character about as soft as an avalanche. Inwardly, Prentiss Schaeffer doubted if anyone other than Mark had ever been able to control her—or even to hold his own against her.

"All right, all right," he said. "I give in. Perhaps Mark would be better off there. I hope, I really hope that you can save him."

Two days before their ship was to sail, Analise returned to the Schaeffer house. Her knees were trembling with dread over what she was about to do, but she managed to maintain a look of tranquil confidence as she swept into Mark's room. She had chosen the most formidable-looking dress she had, a severe dark green silk with a high, formal collar and long sleeves and one of the new skirts, flatter in front and with a long, trailing train in back. Her hair was swept up, curlless, into a heavy knot, exposing the cold jade studs that adorned her ears. Gloves and a wide green hat with a brim that curled down on one side and cleverly shadowed her face completed the imposing picture.

"Hello, Mark. Good day, Sergeant Jackson," she said, keeping her voice brisk and impersonal.

"I—I didn't think you would return," Mark said hoarsely, and the surprised pleasure on his face made Analise's heart leap with hope. Perhaps she would not have to go through with this awful charade, after all. But then his face closed down and he said, "I can't imagine why you did—unless, of course, you enjoy rejection."

Her heart plummeted, but she said cheerfully, "Oh, no doubt you will find that many things about me are beyond your understanding—particularly since you seem to have now decided to pickle your brain with alcohol."

In the stunned silence that followed her remark, Analise sat down in a chair across from the sofa and carefully arranged her skirts around her. She looked up to find Mark scowling at her darkly, and she smiled, letting her lip curl over so delicately with contempt.

"Oh, did I shock you? So sorry. I had forgotten how no one in this house ever speaks the truth to you."

"What the hell do you want?" Mark said gruffly, stung by her light, mocking words.

"I came to tell you that we are leaving for New Orleans the day after tomorrow. Sergeant Jackson, you might want to start packing Mr. Schaeffer's things, and yours, too, of course, if you plan to come."

"New Orleans!" Mark snapped. "Are you insane? I am not going anywhere."

"Oh, yes, you are, my dear. I am your wife, and your father has agreed that you should reside with me, not him."

"I won't go!"

"I don't think you understand. You really don't have any choice. I shall have two strong men come carry you out. What would you do? Fight them? Run away?" Analise said bitingly.

Mark flushed and he stiffened with anger. "Just what do you think you are doing?"

"I will tell you." Her voice dropped its light sarcasm, and she looked him straight in the eye. "I am going to try to turn you into a human being again, that's what. I don't know if you realize what you have become, Mark, because everyone in this house is too lily-livered and too guilt-ridden to be honest with you. However, I am not.

"You are a cripple who could regain the use of his limbs, but refuses to try. I don't know whether you do that out of cowardice or stubbornness or what. Perhaps it is simply that you enjoy so much the self-pity that you wallow in that you can't bear to lose it. At any rate, you lie around in this room like a slug, refusing to help yourself. To pass the time, you drink yourself into oblivion. You have become, in short, a weak, drunken, foul-tempered invalid, and almost no one can stand to be around you."

Scornfully she added, "My God, Mark, at least once you had some charm and strength of character."

Mark's eyes blazed hatred at her, but Analise ignored him and plunged on. "What I propose to do is change the direction you are taking. I am going to try to salvage what little remains of your character."

Jackson swallowed nervously; he felt too much residue heat from Analise's blistering tirade. He wondered if any man, even the Colonel before his injury, had been able to handle her. She had a tongue that could lash the hide off a man. What he did not know was that inside Analise was quaking far worse than he. She knew Mark needed to be jarred from his lethargy and depression, but it cost her a great deal to say the hurtful things she had. After today, she knew that any feeling for her that he might have still held would be gone.

"And just how do you 'propose' to accomplish that?" Mark mimicked her viciously.

"First of all, I am taking away your liquor. We are sailing in two days, and there will be no liquor for you aboard ship. When we reach New Orleans, the servants will be mine and will be instantly dismissed if they bring you any liquor. Nor will the obliging Sergeant Jackson obtain it for you, because if he wishes to stay with you from now on he will follow my rules."

"I pay Jackson, not you," Mark roared.

"If I have to go to court and have you declared incompetent to handle your money, I will. It should not be too hard to prove, considering the fact that you are a cripple and a drunkard. However, I think it would be far easier to hire bodyguards to keep Jackson from being near you if he refuses to cooperate in getting you well."

Mark began to swear angrily at Analise, but Jackson intervened. "No, sir, she's right. I have known for a long time you were killing yourself with drink, but it wasn't my place to refuse you. But if Mrs. Schaeffer is going to stop your drinking, I will stand with her on that."

"Damn both of you, then! I'll get it myself!"

Analise's smile was a taunt as she said, "Not unless you can walk from the house to the store."

The words Mark was about to spew forth died on his lips and his eyes froze. He leaned back and closed his eyes, as though suddenly exhausted. His voice was low as he said, "Lord, what a shrew you have turned out to be. Please go and leave me alone, Analise."

Analise's heart turned sickeningly. Had she failed? Had she pushed him too hard? Too soon? Dear God, all this gut-rending pretense could not go for naught.

"You will be able to do that someday, Mark. The doctor says you can use your limbs far better than now. You can walk if you want to, and I am going to take you to Tante Monique, who will help you to walk and move your arm."

"No mumbo-jumbo black witch doctor is going to make

me well again. Whatever your German doctor says, I am the one who feels my leg and arm, and I know there's nothing there. I cannot move my arm—I've tried. I can shuffle around some with a crutch, if I don't mind the pain or the ugly picture I present. Nothing more. Why can't you accept that? I have."

"You mean you have given up," Analyse replied. "Well, I am not a quitter, like you. Besides, I have a very good reason for wanting you well. As your wife, I have a duty to you. Crippled as you are now, I must take care of you, stay your wife. I simply could not face myself if I left you in the condition you are in. But if I can get you well, make you walk and learn to take care of yourself, turn you from a helpless cripple into a man again, then I will have paid my debt. I will be able to leave you and do as I want without guilt.

"You see, Fran lied when she told you I was having an affair with Max Schleyer. I was not *at that time.*"

She had most definitely caught his attention. He looked at her sharply, repeating, "At that time? Meaning that you have had an affair with him since?"

"Yes. After you left, I eventually recovered. I fell in love with Max and had an affair with him. Now, as I told you a few weeks ago, I want to divorce you and marry Max. But I cannot do that as long as you are a cripple. So, you see, I shall make you work very hard at walking again."

Their gazes were locked for a moment, and then he looked away. His voice came out in a harsh, ragged hiss. "Then, go, go and be damned with you. You have my permission. Leave, and let me rot in peace."

"No, I won't let you. I am not like you; I don't run from

my responsibility. I would not divorce a husband who was a helpless cripple," Analise said brutally.

Mark said through clenched teeth, "Then I swear that I will walk again, if it's the last thing I ever do. Because there's nothing I want more than to be rid of you. Now get out of here!"

Analise leaped to her feet and headed for the door; she did not want him to see the triumphant gleam in her eye. It had worked! Just as she had thought it would, her acerbic comments on his crippled state and her phony tale about Max had brought him to the boiling point. He was so angry and full of hate for her that he would do his utmost to use his arm and leg again, just to spite her.

Firmly she closed the door behind her and then collapsed onto the mahogany bench in the hallway. Never in all her life had she done anything so nerve-wracking—she was shaking like a leaf. She had done it! She had sparked him into life again, no matter how angry and vengeful. But oh, dear God, the look in his eyes—she would never forget the way his eyes had stabbed right through her. Now behind her she heard Mark's harsh, bitter voice, and then there was a thud against the door that made her jump. She pressed her hands to her temples where a blinding pain was growing and sat there, trembling all over, trying desperately not to be sick, while behind her continued the crash of splintering glass and breaking wood as Mark in his impotent rage hurled all the objects close at hand at the door.

Impatiently Analise paced back and forth in her tiny room on the ship. They should be bringing Mark in any time now—unless, of course, Mr. Schaeffer had turned coward at the last minute and refused to send him to the docks in his carriage. Analise bit her lip anxiously, wondering yet again if she should have sent men and a carriage for Mark's conveyance instead of leaving it up to his father.

She looked around the room and smiled faintly, her mind drifting back to the other time she and Mark had sailed on a ship together, when he had taken her to his home from New Orleans. This time would certainly be different. No passion-filled nights in their narrow bed now. They did not even have the same room, for she shared a room with May and little Johnny, while the Sergeant slept in Mark's room so that he could help Mark.

Analise sighed and went up on deck to check on Johnny. She scanned the deck and saw him at the far end, running about excitedly. May held his hand firmly in her grasp to keep him from catapulting into the ocean. Satisfied that Johnny was carefully watched over, Analise went to the railing and searched the docks for a glimpse of Mark. She saw a carriage pull up, and her heart began to speed up. Prentiss Schaeffer stepped out, followed by Sergeant Jackson and a stranger. They pulled out a stretcher and then carried Mark out and laid him on it. Tears misted Analise's eyes. How humiliating it must be for her proud husband to be so exposed to the public eye.

So he would not see her witnessing his crippled entry onto the ship, Analise turned and went down the deck to join Johnny and May. Johnny immediately began to babble to her and she listened inattentively, tensely aware of the progress up the gangplank that took place behind her back. Even long after she was sure it was over and Mark below deck in his cabin, Analise did not turn for fear of meeting his hostile gaze.

She stayed on deck with Johnny while the crew scurried about setting sail, and then May took the boy, pale and tired from the excitement, down to their cabin for a nap. Analise occupied herself by walking up and down the deck until she, too, was exhausted. She spent the rest of the day in her cabin, restraining her urge to check on Mark. His mode of arrival had been hard enough for him, without adding her to his burdens.

For a time, Analise had toyed with the idea of keeping Mark and Johnny separated. Mark had frightened the boy once already, and she did not want Johnny to have to face that again. She had little doubt that Mark would shout at him: his invalidism had turned his temper foul, and he had certainly indicated no tender feelings toward his son. On the other hand, it would be difficult to keep them from meeting, since they would be living in the same house. Eventually the boy would disturb Mark and then he would yell at him. Perhaps it would be just as well to let it happen now; at least she would be close by to comfort Johnny, and maybe it would scare him enough to stay away from Mark.

And there was always the possibility that it might help Mark. After all, he had really yelled at his sister, not Johnny, and no doubt he was worried about his son's reaction to his scar. She could understand his being ashamed for Johnny to see him crippled. It could be that if he got to know John, he would love him like a normal father. Then surely Johnny's childish, cheerful prattle would perk him up; maybe his love for the boy would even give him something to live and work for. Besides, the voyage would no doubt be quite boring for Mark, cooped up in his tiny cabin, especially with no liquor to drink. Johnny might at least entertain him some. Surely those things outweighed the possibility of Johnny getting another fright.

So the next day, Analise took her son aside and tried to explain Mark to him: "Honey, you don't remember him, but you had a daddy who was a soldier and went to fight in the war."

The black-haired boy nodded solemnly. His mother had told him before about his daddy and what a brave, good man he was. Johnny was a little vague as to just what "daddy" meant, as he had rarely been around other children who had daddies, but he knew it was something special and nice, and he was quite pleased to hear that his excelled others'.

"Well, your daddy came back, but he got hurt in the war. He—he can't use one arm and one leg, and his face was cut like this, see? He's the man you saw at your grandfather's."

The boy frowned. "He yelled."

"That was because he was scared. He was afraid you would not like him because of the scar. He wants very much for you to like him. You know how you scream at night when you have a bad dream; you yell because you're scared."

John considered that, turning his head to one side thoughtfully. He, like most children, had a basic understanding and acceptance of fear.

"Would you like to meet him? He would like to see you. He's right next door. For a while he's going to be living with us."

Again the child thought, then nodded his head decisively. His mother smiled, took his hand, and went to Mark's cabin; she knocked, and Jackson opened the door.

Analise pulled him out into the hall and asked him to pass some time on deck, as she wanted to talk to Mark. He complied silently, his expression hostile. Analise shrugged to herself. Her life had not been easy since she met Mark, and she had had to learn to fight to survive. Doubtless the Sergeant thought her a cold, calculating bitch after her display of power the other day. But she had found out other people's approval or disapproval did not help you at all when you had something to accomplish.

She stepped forward into the doorway, Johnny by her side. Mark lay in his bed against the far wall, and now he rolled over and up on his elbow, staring at them. Analise let go of the boy's hand and he stepped hesitantly into the room, in one hand firmly clutching his toy soldier for support.

"Daddy?" he asked uncertainly.

Mark's face went white, and he shot an agonized look at Analise. For a second, Analise almost called Johnny back, but firmly she stopped herself. No pity; no pity. Mark had to take up life again. She stepped back and closed the door.

Mark swallowed and looked at the boy, tensing himself for the terror he knew would shortly erupt in Johnny's face. To his amazement, there was no frightened cry. Instead, the child advanced boldly on him, his gaze steadily on Mark. His father felt a thrill of admiration; he could not fault Analise on the boy—he was a brave little thing.

Johnny stopped about a foot from his bed and extended the toy soldier toward him. "Soldier," he said firmly, as if Mark might mistake it.

Mark wet his lips and said, "Yes, I see. Very nice." He

wrapped his hand around it cautiously and the boy released it.

"You," Johnny said and pointed at Mark.

"Oh. You're giving it to me?" Mark ventured, feeling
out of his depth, and feeling, too, that it was desperately
important that he not fail.

Johnny shook his head impatiently. "No. You a soldier
too."

"Oh, I see. Yes. Yes, I was." He cleared his throat
nervously. What did one say to a two-year-old? He realized
he wanted quite badly to interest the boy so he would stay.

Johnny regarded him seriously, and Mark stared back,
his eyes trying to take in every detail about the boy. It was
amazing to look at Johnny and see himself in miniature—
the black hair and dark eyes, the stubborn chin. There was
familiarity even in the way he stood, feet planted steadily
apart. His son. Mark felt a strange bittersweet ache deep
within him.

Now the child came closer and scrambled up onto the
bed beside his father. He knelt there, looking curiously at
the two scars that bisected Mark's cheek. Mark waited for
the fright or revulsion to appear, but they did not. There
was only curiosity and a hint of concern. Tentatively
Johnny reached out and touched the still-purple ridge; it
was all Mark could do to keep from flinching at the touch.

"What's that?" the boy asked.

"A scar. Some sharp pieces of metal hit my face and cut
it."

Johnny frowned and said with concern, "Hurt?"

Mark's smile was shaky with stunned relief. His son was
not repulsed, only interested.

"Not now. It hurt when it happened."

"Oh. Are you my daddy?" He seemed to have lost interest in the scar.

"Yes, I am."

The child digested this in silence and then said, "What's a daddy?"

Mark gave a short snort of laughter and paused, at a loss for words. He was unused to answering the questions of children. "Well, it's a parent who is a man."

"What's a parent?"

"Your mother is a parent. A mother is like a daddy, except a daddy is a man and a mother is a woman."

The boy looked at him solemnly, and Mark stumbled on, "It means you are my son; I am married to your mama."

Johnny smiled suddenly and said, "Mama pretty."

Mark's eyes went suddenly blank and he said tonelessly, "Yes, she is."

His son slid off the bed and began to explore the room. Mark watched his happy, inquisitive search, and then Johnny came back to the bed, insisting they play with his toy soldier. After that, Johnny wanted to be told a story. Mark could remember no fairy tales from his childhood, so he launched into a story about King Arthur's Round Table, the closest thing to a children's story he could think of. He discovered that Johnny was interested not so much in a story as in the comfortable drone of a voice, for the child's eyelids began to droop, and he soon curled up beside Mark, pillowed his head on Mark's arm, and fell sound asleep.

For a long time Mark looked down at the sleeping child. His thin, blue-veined eyelids and the curving shadow of his lashes against his cheek gave his face a vulnerable look.

Mark found himself seized by a desire to hold him close and protect him from everything that might threaten him. Fatherly love stirred and woke in him, and Mark curled his arm around the sleeping child protectively. Carefully, so as not to disturb Johnny, he laid his own head down and drifted off to sleep.

His last thoughts were: John Prentiss Schaeffer. What a beautiful son. Thank God Analise had raised him by herself, had taken him away from that gloomy, puritanical household of his father and sister.

And then he was asleep.

It was an hour later that Analise quietly opened the door and peeked in. A lump rose and swelled in her throat when she saw her son curled up in her husband's arm, peacefully asleep. For the first time since he had returned, Analise saw Mark's face with the lines of bitterness and pain fallen away. He looked for that one moment like the handsome, vital man she had fallen in love with and so much like Johnny that she turned away, her eyes misted with tears.

Eighteen

Seeing Mark so at ease with Johnny, Analise began to nurture a fragile hope. If he had come to love his son, perhaps there was some hope that he would love her again. At least his feeling for Johnny might make him more receptive to her, more willing to remain married so that he could be around his son. And if they remained married, was there not a chance that she could make him love her again?

Buoyed by these hopes, Analise waited until Jackson left the next day for a walk around the decks, and then slipped into Mark's room. Mark looked up at her, his expression guarded, but not as cold as before. Analise swallowed down the dryness in her throat; her heart was hammering with fear and anticipation. She did not know what to do now; she really had no plan except to see Mark.

It was Mark who spoke first. "Congratulations, Analise, on the way you raised your son. He is a most engaging little boy."

"Thank you. I am glad you like him." Analise was emboldened enough by his compliment to move over to him. "But he is your son as well."

Mark shrugged. "True, but you are responsible for his upbringing and training."

Using his one arm, he squirmed into a sitting position. How galling it was to talk to a woman and have her towering above him. It was better sitting up than lying down, of course, but still . . . As if she had read his thoughts, Analise sat down on the bed beside him. A little quiver shot through Mark. This was the closest he had been to her since he returned; he could smell the faint fragrance of her rose perfume, could see up close the beauty of her skin and eyes and mouth. It had been a long, barren time since he had last kissed her and held her close.

"You are more beautiful even than I remembered," he said without thinking.

As soon as the words were out, he regretted them; that kid had really softened him up. But Analise smiled at him, and he smiled back ruefully. He had the awful feeling that he was slipping, falling, but at the same time there was a certain excitement growing in him. The sight and smell of her were dizzying. Did she know she stirred him? He wished he had a drink to numb his traitorous senses.

He reminded himself that she did not want him, that she loved another man, and that he was an ugly cripple, but his thoughts had little strength against his racing pulse. She leaned toward him, her mouth slightly parted, expectant, her large eyes luminous, and Mark found his breath coming quick and rasping in his throat. Softly she brushed her lips against his, but like a shot, his arm came around her, pulling her against him, and he ground his lips into hers.

Eagerly her lips opened beneath his kiss and her arms wrapped around him. Desire roared through him like a fire, all the fiercer for its long suppression. He kissed her hair, her throat, her eyes, her ears, returning again and again to her mouth in an ecstasy of passion. Analise melted against him, aware of nothing but the tumultuous return of joy and desire after months and months of absence. Lovingly her hands moved over his body, caressing through his clothing the sharp angles and firm muscles of his belovedly familiar body. Mark groaned and a tremor shook his body at her touch.

Analise quickly pulled out her hairpins, ruthlessly destroying her careful hairdo, and shook her hair down. It cascaded like a dark, silken waterfall across her shoulders. She pulled away from Mark and lay down beside him on the bed. He watched her, his eyes black fires of hunger, his chest rising and falling rapidly with short, hard breaths. Analise looked up at him, her black hair spread across the sheets. Slowly she began to unfasten the buttons of her dress, never taking her eyes off Mark's face, naked with desire.

Mark bent, pushing down her chemise, and kissed her breasts, which thrust up proudly, the rosy nipples already hard with longing. Slowly, luxuriously, his mouth and hand played over her breasts, evoking soft moans of pleasure from her. He murmured against her skin, but so softly that Analise could not hear what he said, feeling only his hot breath on her skin.

Analise reached up and unbuttoned his shirt; she ran her hands across his chest and down his stomach. She moved to his shoulders to push the shirt off and suddenly Mark pulled away from her as if he had been stung.

"No!" he gasped, his voice full of horror. He had been so overwhelmed by his desire for Analise that it was not until she moved to undress him that he remembered his mangled arm and leg. Desperately he flung himself away from her, and stood on his good leg, leaning against the bedpost, his back to her. He could not let her look at the scarred, pitted, ruined flesh of his limbs! He would rather die than see that soft passionate glow turn to a look of revulsion. He could not bear for her to remember him like that; he could not stand the humiliation.

"No! Get out of here! Go away! Leave me in peace." His voice was choked.

Shakily Analise sat up; her mind was whirling, bewildered. One moment he was so loving and the next he was rejecting her unequivocally. Something like disgust had crossed his eyes just before he whirled away. What had happened? What had she done that disgusted him?

"Mark? What is the matter?"

His voice was harsh, stabbing. "Can't you understand plain English? I don't want you. Get out of here."

Tears sprang into her eyes as she clutched the front of her dress together and scrambled off the bed. He must have been playing some horrible joke, pretending desire to test her or make fun of her. He must despise her to want to inflict such humiliation. A sob escaped her as she fled to the door, her loose hair streaming out behind her. And then she was gone, the door crashing shut.

Mark collapsed on the bed, his face white and lined with strain. He could not speak or think or even feel. He slid off the bed and hopped to his suitcases, holding onto the bed and the table for support. There he dropped to the floor and opened his portmanteau, searching frantically for the cologne bottle in which he had secreted his whiskey. When he found it, he uncapped it with shaking fingers and gulped a drink. The fiery liquid burned down his throat and hit his stomach like a shock. Mark breathed a sigh of relief and took another swig.

Oh, Analise, Analise—why was he condemned to this hell?

"I finally get the message, Colonel Schaeffer," Analise whispered to her reflection in the mirror, savagely pushing hairpins into her upswept hair. "Believe me, I won't try to approach you lovingly again."

Fortunately, May and little John had been out of the cabin when Analise rushed back to her room. She would not have wanted to deal with the questioning stares at her disheveled appearance. As it was, she was able to cry unwatched. After the tears stopped, she sat up wearily and refastened her dress. She washed the traces of tears from her face and began to brush through her loose hair. Slowly, monotonously, she stroked the brush through her hair, while her mind floated far away. It was therapeutic, and soon it put her to sleep.

When she woke up an hour later and got up to repin her hair, she found that the pain had eased and was turning into anger. If his purpose had been to convince her that he wanted no loving relationship between them, he had certainly achieved that. She would not expose herself like that to his rejection again.

May returned to put John down for his nap. Analise saw the maid glance at her and frown slightly; she knew her tear-reddened eyes had not escaped May's notice. Analise decided to go for a walk herself to escape May's questions. She walked for a long time, trying as hard as she could to think about anything but Mark. Finally she grew tired and went back down to her cabin.

As she passed Mark's door, she heard his voice, angry and slurred, and then he laughed, a high, silly laugh. She stopped and listened suspiciously. Now Jackson was speaking, his voice low and soothing. Then Mark spoke again, and his voice confirmed her suspicions. He was drunk. Quickly she opened the door and swung it back hard.

Jackson jumped and whirled around guiltily. Mark merely looked at her, his face hard and defiant.

"You're drunk!" she snapped.

"You guessed!" Mark said airily.

Analise glared at him and then turned her gaze on Sergeant Jackson. He gulped, feeling as though her look might burn holes straight through him.

"Sergeant Jackson, I believe I made myself quite clear regarding alcohol," Analise said crisply.

Jackson began to stutter, but Mark said, "Don't blame him, General. Jackson did not pack any liquor for me. I hid it away myself."

Analise raised her eyebrows slightly and said, "He is obviously drunk; it must have taken a while. Why did you not inform me of this sooner?"

The Sergeant looked miserably down at the floor. "I'm not a tale bearer, Mrs. Schaeffer."

"Well, I think your ideals are a little inappropriate in this situation, Sergeant, since you are helping the Colonel damage his own health and sanity." She paused and then sighed. The man was too loyal to Mark; though he acquiesced to her demands, he would not volunteer any help. "All right, where did he hide it?"

"He poured out his cologne and put whiskey in the bottle."

Analise went briskly over to Mark and snatched a near-empty bottle from his hands. An empty one already lay on the floor, and she picked that up too. Mark grabbed at her skirt, but she whirled out of his reach and in his drunken state he almost sprawled on the floor.

"You forget, Mark, you cannot any longer make me do what you want by using physical force on me." Her voice was taunting.

Analise went to his luggage and carefully searched every piece, opening every bottle of liquid and smelling it. She succeeded in finding two flasks he had hidden among his clothes and another bottle inside a hat. For good measure, she picked through Jackson's suitcase and found another flask there. When she had searched every nook and cranny she could think of, she swept the bottles up into her arms and stalked to the door.

At the door she turned and said coldly, "I am going to throw these overboard now. I meant what I said, Mark—you are going to sober up, if it's the last thing I do. Sergeant Jackson, I suggest you keep a more vigilant watch, unless you no longer wish to be in our employ. And Mark, if you get a chance to sneak some in, I suggest that you don't do it. As long as you drink, you won't see Johnny. I will not have my son subjected to your drunkenness, and I will not let him be humiliated by having a drunkard for a father."

Mark began to curse her viciously and Analise swung and slammed out of the room. Desolately Mark slumped back on the bed. Well, now she had taken away his only escape. He had no doubt she would make good her threat.

No release in sex. No release in alcohol. He did not know how he would keep from exploding.

The rest of the journey passed without incident. Mark refused to let Jackson carry him up on deck to get some sun and fresh air, declaring that he would not provide a freak show for the other passengers. Instead, he passed away the time sitting or lying on his bed, sunk in sullen contemplation. The only times he brightened were when Johnny came to visit him. Every day and sometimes several times a day, the boy would bounce into his room to show him a toy or hear a story or pester Mark to play with him. Whether it was kinship or simple proximity, Johnny was growing attached to Mark. And daily Mark's love for the boy grew deeper and deeper, until sometimes he wondered how he would ever be able to part with him.

Since Mark had no more alcohol, the boy was his only release from his dark, tormented thoughts. He had lost everything, every dream he had never thought he could have and then had possessed for a brief, beautiful moment, only to have it vanish like early morning mist. But now here was his son, their son, and when he was with him, Mark knew he had not lost everything.

Analise avoided Mark's presence, spending her time on deck or in her cabin. She had a great deal of empty time on her hands, and so, for the first time, she was able to be with Johnny as much as she wished. For her, too, he was a joy, as well as the only thing that remained of Mark's love for her. Analise played with him and read to him and took him on her walks about the decks, indulging herself in being a mother.

There were times when loneliness and regret overwhelmed her, times when she wanted to burst into tears again over Mark's rejection of her. But these she weathered, as she had the other bad times in the past, by plunging into her work. She sat in her cabin and made plans for the new store, jotting down her ideas on luring customers, on organization, on the layout of the store, and on the items to be sold. By the time they reached New Orleans, she had already drawn up an inventory of goods she would stock and designed her window displays for the first six months.

The ship pulled into New Orleans in early September. In New York the days would be turning cooler, but here it was sweltering. Analise, on deck, felt the heavy hot air surround her; her nostrils were assaulted by the smell of the New Orleans docks; in front of her loomed the city. Suddenly she wanted to cry; here the bittersweet memories rose up all around her and she could not push them away as she had in New York. The city itself was a feeling: it was heartbreak; it was love; it was war and anger and passion; it was home.

Eagerly, she leaned over the railing, drinking it all in. At last. At last. Almost running, she went below deck and bustled her party up and off the ship. A hired carriage carried Analise, Johnny, Mark, and Sergeant Jackson to the hotel. May followed in a wagon with the luggage. Johnny was glued to the window, watching in fascination the strange new world he found himself in. He chattered constantly, pointing and exclaiming and asking questions. Analise laughed and looked with him, every now and then glancing surreptitiously at her husband. Mark sat silently, paying no attention to the city outside; there was a pinched, closed look to his face. Analise wondered what he thought—had their return to the city of their love sparked any feeling in him at all?

Registering and getting her party settled in their rooms at the hotel was taxing; it quickly chased away Analise's excitement and left her with a headache. She could take care of things; she was by now used to being in control, being the problem solver and the one with the responsibility. She accepted it, and she did it, but there were times, as now, when she wished it were not so lonely. If only there was someone else there to help shoulder the burden.

There were so many things that needed to be done, and all of them immediately. She must locate a site for the store and negotiate with the owner. They needed a suitable house to live in. And Tante Monique must be found and set to work on Mark's infirmity. Of course, servants would have to be hired for the house, and furniture bought, so they could live in it. It made Analise droop with weariness just to think of all that must be done.

However, she would not allow herself the luxury of resting. She sent May out to find and hire Tante Monique, and, taking little John in tow, she went herself to call on Pauline Beauvais. In all of New Orleans, she could think of no one else who would help her.

To her shock, she found the Beauvais house in a sad state of repair. The delicate fountain in the garden was cracked and no water trickled from it. Flowers grew in wild abandon, straggling over onto the walkway; they were choked with weeds. The grillwork on the fence and balcony was chipped and badly in need of repainting. Tentatively Analise knocked on the door and was even more taken aback when Pauline herself opened it—an older, tired Pauline, whose face was set in tight lines and whose eyes were sad and resigned.

Analise suppressed her gasp and smiled at her old friend. For a moment Pauline stared at her and then her face lit up. "Analise!" she cried and flung her arms around her.

Pauline stepped back and held her at arms' length, looking at her, and tears rolled silently down her face, "Oh, Analise, I never thought to see you again. You look beautiful, more beautiful—" She started to say something else, then checked herself and looked down at Johnny. "And is this—the baby? My, what a big boy you are. Whatever am I thinking of, making you stand outside like this? Come in, come in, and sit down."

The inside of the house showed the same signs of neglect, and Analise saw that Pauline's clothes were old and shockingly threadbare. Her family, never well-to-do, must have been hit hard by the war. And in more ways than one—Pauline's dress was dyed black.

"Pauline, who—not your father?" Analise touched her skirt.

Pauline nodded. "Yes. Papa died at Vicksburg in sixty-three. He never should have gone at all; he was never meant to be a soldier. But I guess he felt because of his gentle, scholarly aspect, he had to prove he was not a coward."

"I'm so sorry, Pauline." Analise paused. "Are you all right?"

Her friend shrugged. "If managing not to starve is all right, then, yes, I guess so. Before the war, we lived mostly on the generosity of Papa's cousin, Raoul Dousson, who lived upriver and had a great plantation. But Dousson was ruined in the war; now he is penniless too. And Papa earned a little bit of money with his writing, but he is gone now. I haven't enough to pay the servants or have the house painted. I do needlework to get enough money to eat." Her laugh was short and tinged with bitterness. "I hate to think what Grandma would say—a Beauvais sewing for a living!"

"Oh, Pauline, I had no idea." Analise said, her heart going out to her friend. "But wait, I have an idea: I can offer you a better-paying job than that." Quickly she launched into her history since she had last seen Pauline, lightly skimming over her personal troubles, but relating her business career, ending with her objective of opening a store in New Orleans.

Pauline stared at her in amazement. "But, Analise, this is so wild. I never expected that you would become an entrepreneur. I can hardly take it all in."

"Well, you better. Because what I am suggesting is offering you the position of head of the dress department."

"Me? Don't be silly. I can sew, but I have no sense of style."

"Style!" Analise dismissed that with a wave of her hand. "I don't need style. I can provide that, or I can hire some penniless artistic woman for that. What you have that is more important is a name. Beauvais is one of the oldest, most respected names in this city. The nouveau riche will flock to you, thinking your breeding will rub off on them. And those of the old line who manage to remain wealthy will come because they know you. And you know they will not come to me."

Pauline hesitated. She suspected that her friend was simply being kind. Then she gave in, nodded her assent;

she needed the money too desperately to stand on pride.

"Good. Then that's settled. I need your help in other ways too. I need to buy or rent a house for us, but I no longer know what is what here. Do you know of any houses? Or could you tell me who deals in real estate now?"

Pauline creased her brow, thinking. Suddenly she smiled. "I know. The Webster house in the Garden District. Mrs. Webster is poor and alone now, and I am sure she would sell. It is a lovely house. Do you remember?"

"I never went inside. But it was pretty on the outside." Analise knew it and approved. It was painted a soft gray with the faintest tinge of blue in it. The shutters and grillwork were the same color of gray, with none of the contrast that was usual, and that gave it a gentle, retiring look. Its large, tree-shaded grounds would be a perfect spot for Johnny to play. "I like the idea. Would you come with me tomorrow to talk to Mrs. Webster?"

A puzzled frown touched Pauline's brow. "Certainly. But—well, I will just be blunt and you can tell me it is none of my business if you want. But why are you taking care of all this? Where is Major Schaeffer?"

"Here. Except it is Colonel Schaeffer now. He was promoted for his bravery in battle, but he was left an invalid."

"Oh, no. Oh, Analise, I am so sorry."

Analise sighed shakily. How good it felt to talk to someone. The story of Mark's injuries poured out. She talked of his attitude, his drinking, of her own determination that he would get well, of her decision to try Tante Monique.

"She is a wonder," Pauline assured her. "If anyone can do it, she can."

Analise would have liked to pour out her heart about her troubled relationship with Mark, but she refrained. All of that was so muddled, such a web of mistake and loss and regret and murdered love that it was too difficult to straighten it out enough to even talk about. All that really mattered anyway was that Mark no longer wanted or loved her. The fact that her own feelings had survived did not change that. And she did not think it fair to burden Pauline with the trials of her lost love. After all, Pauline had loved Emil hopelessly, helplessly, for so long: it was cruel to remind her or to ask for her sympathy.

There was a pause and then Analise asked cautiously, "Do you have any news of my family? Are they—are they all right?"

"They are all still alive," Pauline said. "Though I am sure the war hurt them financially. Emil caught malaria during the siege of Vicksburg, and he is, I think, plagued by recurring bouts of the illness. Your father fled the plantation when the Yankees occupied the city, and he joined the army. I'm afraid he was wounded and they had to—amputate his arm. Your mother is much the same as ever. I don't know quite how any of them survive, without you to handle their affairs. It is sad, isn't it, how useless so many of us are; we were just never tested before."

"Pauline—"

"No, it's true, and you know it. If you had not married Mark and gone to New York, you would be flourishing here, no doubt. You have the spirit and brains to survive."

Analise smiled wryly. "Oh, yes, I survive." I survive and prosper, even; but I haven't the knack for love.

"Emil married Becky Oldway."

"I am sorry, Pauline. I always hoped—"

"No, it is all right. I always knew I would never marry Emil. He loved beauty, and he really did not understand people or see them clearly. And he is so unyielding and harsh about you—ever since he scorned you because you sacrificed so much for him, I have not quite felt the same about him. I did love him, but I know that we would never have been happy together. Anyway, he married Becky when he got back from the war. Mr. Oldway lost everything, too, and they could not afford to buy a house; they had to move out to Emil's land to live all year round."

A smile touched Analise's lips. "I can't quite envision Emil trying to actually operate his plantation. Or Becky away from the social life of the city. And the house—it is lovely and quaint, the old original French planter's house, very long and narrow, raised up on stilts, but rather small and old-fashioned, not at all the sort of mansion Becky is used to."

Pauline smiled back with the same tinge of malice. "No doubt she is miserable. Poor Emil."

Their talk progressed to friends and acquaintances, and Pauline filled her friend in on all that had taken place since she had gone. There were several women who had been forced to take to commerce to feed their families with their men away at war and the enemy at the doorstep. Mrs. Malenceaux, for instance, had turned her huge home into a boarding house. Mrs. Henri Blanchard had developed a booming business selling her pastries and breads to the Yankee soldiers. They were some of the successful ones. Others, like Pauline, had barely managed to scrape by, taking in laundry or doing sewing or raising a subsistence garden.

The hated Yankee soldiers still occupied the city and ruled by martial law. The slaves were all freed, though a few remained with their former masters, having nowhere else to go. There were not enough affluent people any longer to pay them servants' wages, and they were ill-equipped for any other occupations. The result was idleness and unrest. People had been arriving, scavengers from the north, come to "pluck the coins from the dead land's eyes," as Pauline put it. It was a bleak, impoverished situation she described.

Analise finally rose to take her leave. Little John had become quite restive and had begun prowling the house, hunting mischief to get into. Pauline walked her to the door and Analise turned and clasped her friend's hand warmly.

"The worst is over," she reassured her friend. "Now the rebuilding will start. Merchants, shippers, planters—they will all prosper again. And so will you and I, for I will make sure our store is right there to rake in their new wealth. There is prosperity ahead. Trust me—you know I have always had a head for profits."

Pauline smiled and nodded; she watched the woman and her little son walk out of the garden and down the street. Perhaps Analise did have a head for profits where money was concerned. But Pauline had also seen the sorrow in her friend's eyes and heard the conspicuous absence of any talk of happiness or love between her and Mark. Pauline suspected that Analise still had not received any profits in love.

Nineteen

$\mathcal{M}$ay located Tante Monique, but the woman stood on her dignity and insisted that Analise herself visit her to explain the problem. So the next morning Analise set off with her maid for the quadroon woman's home. It was a pleasant little house nestled among many similar houses belonging to other free women of color whose faces and forms had lured wealthy white men. It was on this street that Emil's mistress, Fleur, had lived, Analise remembered. How long ago it had been when she had shocked Emil by mentioning Fleur. So much had happened and she had traveled so far from that sheltered girl she had been. It seemed ludicrous now to think of her being in that role, acting by rules long dead and trampled under the harsh heels of reality.

Tante Monique was a squat, coffee-colored woman with piercing black eyes and a firm jaw. She was dressed in lavender, with a lavender turban around her head. Analise could not judge her age; the wrinkles in her face were timeless, and her essential ugliness did not show age as softer beauty did. Tante Monique walked with a peculiar rolling gait, and she had a way of looking at a person with her head turned to one side that should have made her a figure of fun. However, there was an essential dignity about her, and intelligence gleamed out of her eyes. Whatever laughter rose in one's throat at seeing her, it quickly died unuttered.

When Analise stepped into her house and the woman walked clumsily to her and took her hand, Analise felt a shock of recognition: here was another woman who had learned how to manage things. A warmth seemed to spread from the dark woman's hand into hers and Analise felt the blessed relief of handing over her burden to one who could handle it. Tante Monique nodded at her slowly and smiled, as if she, too, recognized a sister-under-the-skin. Here was no flighty, hysterical rich lady, but one who had known harshness and who was not afraid to fight.

Analise poured out the story of Mark's injuries to Tante Monique, and the woman listened silently. Now and then she nodded, or asked a pertinent question. When Analise mentioned the doctor's diagnosis, Monique snorted, showing her opinion of the theories of the medical profession. Analise finished her description, and waited for the other woman's analysis. Gravely Tante Monique stood and folded her arms.

"You and me," she said, "we heal him. Doctors are no good. But I will call on the help of the spirits, and they will aid us in making him well. Now, you go back to him. I must consult the spirits and make a healing potion for your man. I will come to your hotel this evening and see him."

"Thank you," Analise's voice was full of respect, whatever her doubts of the usefulness of the spirits. "I believe that if anyone can cure Mark, it is you."

* * *

Until Tante Monique arrived that evening, Analise was agitated and restless. She managed to keep a calm front, sending May to find servants for their future house and going herself with Pauline to look at the Webster home. The house was charming and needed little repair, but Analise was far too keyed up about Mark to have much joy in house hunting. It would suit her purposes—she knew she would be satisfied with it in more tranquil moments. Firmly she said that she would take it.

Mrs. Webster was a little taken aback; she knew Analise when she saw her and also remembered the scandal. She would really have preferred not to sell her beloved house to a scarlet woman like that. However, Mrs. Webster badly needed the money and Analise *was* from a good family despite her own misbehavior. And she was accompanied by Pauline Beauvais, who lent her some respectability. Most of all, she was a Southerner, and surely any Southerner was better than letting her house go to the Yankees for want of tax money. So, reluctantly, she agreed to sell her house and most of her furniture to Analise. They agreed upon a price quickly, and Analise went off to find an attorney to draft the deed. Thank heavens she no longer had to worry about money.

After she had seen a lawyer about the deed, she returned to the hotel, still pent up and burning with excitement. May had found several applicants for the servants they needed and brought them back to the hotel. Analise plunged immediately into interviewing them, and by the time supper arrived, she had hired her house servants. After supper, she went to Mark's room and told him that she had found a house for them to live in. Mark seemed remote and uninterested, and Analise felt even less at ease with him. Her greatest desire was to leave his presence, but she did not want to spring Tante Monique on him without warning, so she forced herself to stay and tell him of the woman's impending visit.

Mark's lip curled contemptuously. "Witchcraft! What idiocy."

Analise shrugged. There was no sense in arguing with him. Instead, she went back to her room to await Tante Monique's arrival.

The woman came about an hour later, sweeping in with all the grandeur possible in a short, rotund figure. She was dressed in deep purple, and over one arm she carried a woven straw shopping basket. Analise rose to greet her, her heart hammering with excitement, and led her into Mark's room.

Sergeant Jackson rose, staring at the exotic figure in amazement. Mark fixed a hard glare on Monique, designed no doubt to intimidate her. It made no impression on the black woman, who sailed straight to him. Then she turned to Jackson.

"You," she said, jabbing one fleshy finger at the Sergeant. "Help him lie down on the bed. I need to examine him."

Mark started at these words and cast an agonized glance at Analise. Jackson helped him up and supported his weak side as he hopped and stumbled to the bed. He sat up on the bed and turned to the black woman.

"All right, but not with her in the room," Mark said, pointing at Analise, and Analise felt a little stab of pain.

There was surprise on Tante Monique's face. She said, "No, she must stay," and then she addressed Analise. "Come. I will show you what I do. Then you must repeat it every day, two times. You are the only one here strong enough."

Analise glanced at the Sergeant, obviously much stronger than she, and the black woman snorted. "No, not strong in the muscles. I mean strong in will. This takes much time and stubbornness."

"All right." Analise joined her at the bed.

"Now, take off his trousers and shirt," Monique commanded Jackson.

"No!" Mark held out a restraining hand to his aide, and he looked at Monique in mute appeal. He could not let Analise see his maimed limbs. He had avoided it assiduously, even refusing to take her that time when he was burning for her. Anything was preferable to seeing the shock of revulsion in her eyes. Dear God, he could not bear the humiliation, the pain, the rejection. "No, I refuse."

"So? You are a modest man?" the black woman said. "Somehow I would not have thought so. However, no need to be upset; I have seen the bodies of many men. I hardly notice them; it is the healing I am interested in, not the flesh."

Jackson reached out to unbutton his shirt and Mark batted his hands away, snarling, "Leave me alone!"

"Oh, for Heaven's sakes, Mark," Analise snapped. "Why do you have to be so unreasonable? We are trying to help you recover; you could at least give us a little cooperation. Or have you decided that you enjoy being an invalid so much that you don't want to give it up?"

Mark paled and glared at her, his eyes blazing. Analise returned his gaze evenly and said, "Go ahead, Sergeant."

"But, ma'am—"

Analise swung on the hapless soldier. "Damn it, Jackson, do you remember what I said to you before we left? Either you obey me or you are out. There is no place here for a man who is so soft he obeys a man who obviously cares not at all for his own health. Why, you would let him kill himself if he wanted! Now, which is it to be? Do you do as I say or shall you walk out that door and let me get my new servants up here to undress him?"

Bile churned in Jackson's stomach as he looked at her; he had no doubt that she would make good her threat. He hated to go against Mark, but he could not let some strangers come up here and humiliate him—mock him or hurt him as they overcame his half-strength. With one stabbing look of hatred at Analise, he determinedly attacked Mark's buttons.

Schaeffer did not acquiesce easily. He began to fight, swinging at Jackson with his good fist and trying to lurch away from him. Both Analise and the Sergeant threw themselves on his good side, pinning down his thrashing limbs. Still he struggled and cursed Monique as she unfastened his clothes.

Strangely enough, his wild defiance caused Monique to smile broadly. She looked at Analise with approval and said, "Your man is one hell of a fighter. Good man, he match you."

Her admiration did not deter her from ignoring Mark's preferences. She had decided long ago that what men wanted had little relationship to what was good for them. So she efficiently pulled off his outer garments while Analise and Jackson tussled wildly with Mark, fighting to keep him from lashing out at Monique. As he fought, Mark kept up a steady stream of curses at Analise, Jackson, and the healer.

When at last she exposed his limbs, he ceased to struggle and simply turned his head away from Analise, his eyes glazed and his face rigid with humiliation. Cautiously Analise released him and turned her attention to his mangled body. Two small scars decorated his side, but his left arm was crisscrossed with broad, jagged purple scars and in one place there was a deep indentation where his flesh had been sliced away almost to the bone. His leg was similarly scarred and contained deep pits where his flesh had been gouged by pieces of shrapnel. His lower leg had been broken in two places, and though it had been reset, it was not straight but curved inward, with a slight jutting out at one point of the break. Both limbs, once muscular, were now flaccid and already beginning to grow smaller.

Analise swallowed down the lump in her throat as pity rushed through her. Poor Mark. He had once been so strong and lithe—how hard it must be for him to endure this helplessness, this destruction of his hard masculine beauty. What a hell of pain he must have been through. Hastily she blinked away her tears; it would not do for Mark to see her pity. That would only make him hate himself more.

She forced herself to concentrate on Tante Monique's surprisingly gentle, swift fingers as they expertly ran over Mark's arm and leg. Admonishing Analise to watch carefully and memorize what she did, the black woman began to massage Mark's arm, digging her strong fingers into his muscles and kneading. A spasm of pain touched his face and a low curse escaped his lips.

Tante Monique smiled and said, "Ah, he feels it. That

is good. It is when they feel nothing that it is worst. There is life in his arm. Now, look: here is a bottle of ointment I have made. I will give you several, and you are to rub this into the skin as you work on him. So—"

She uncorked the bottle and poured a faintly green, greasy substance into her hand. Analise could smell the pungent odor of herbs. Skillfully the woman massaged it into his arm and then into his leg. By the time she finished Mark's face was drawn and tight-lipped with pain.

Tante Monique patted his hand and there was sympathy in her voice. "I know you hurt. The course you must follow is difficult, but if you want to use your arm and leg again, you must endure the pain. Open yourself to it. Remember, when you hurt, you know you are alive. But, here, I will give you a little something to ease the pain."

She produced a small vial and poured a tiny amount into his mouth, then handed it to Analise. "Here, you keep this, and don't let him have much, or he will not be able to live without it. Just a few drops whenever the pain gets too bad. Watch what I do now; this is very important. Do this twice a day."

Monique lifted his leg slightly, and holding the calf with one hand, began to rotate his foot with her other hand, then bend it down toward the bed and back up toward his leg. Several times she wiggled, then bent and released each toe. Again and again she bent his ankle. Then she firmly grasped his calf and bent his leg at the knee, pressing it back to his thigh and pushing upward, aiming his knee at his chest. Despite the pain killer, Mark gasped and stiffened and began to curse her vividly and at length. At last, she released his leg, but then started on his arm, moving his fingers, hand, and bending his elbow and wrist much as she had done with his leg. Quite literally she forced his muscles to work.

"Do this two times a day," she repeated to Analise, who had turned the color of paper and felt as though she might be sick—how would she be able to inflict this on Mark? "After a week, start doing it four times a day. Don't worry, the pain will lessen as you do it. Believe me, I have seen it before. You see, his muscles, they got lazy and forgot what to do. Now you have to make them do their job, teach them how to work again. You ever see a child go to his studies willingly? Well, that is how his arm and leg are: reluctant pupils. You are smarter than they. You must bend them to your will."

Analise looked at her a little doubtfully. "Are you sure this will work?"

Tante Monique sniffed. "Did you think such a recovery would be easy? No, it costs a great deal in pain and effort. I saw your son. Did he come to you easily? Or did you not have to wait for him nine months and then be wracked with pain to produce him? Such a miraculous thing comes only when one is willing to wait and work and endure."

Chastened, Analise nodded.

"Now, there is something else you must do: Soak his injured limbs in warm water several times a day. It is best if you can make the water bubble and swirl around him, as in a rocky creek. That is probably not possible, but let him soak. Make sure the water is warm. I will return in two weeks to see how he does. Remember—" She grasped Analise by the arm and looked intently into her eyes. "It is up to you. You must be hard. A soft woman cannot save your man."

Analise smiled at her reassuringly, careful not to let

herself look at Mark's pale, set face. "I can be that. Believe me."

"I know," the other woman said simply and handed the basket of bottles over to Analise.

With great dignity she left the room, and Analise stood staring after her unseeingly for a few moments. Dear God, she hoped she would be able to keep it up. For Mark's sake she had to. Taking a deep breath she went to the bell rope and pulled. Soon one of the neat, white-capped hotel maids appeared at their door.

"I want you to draw a nice, deep, warm bath for Colonel Schaeffer," she said briskly and then turned to the Sergeant. "I will leave it in your hands, Sergeant, to help him in and out of the tub. And make sure both his leg and arm are completely immersed."

For the first time she dared to look at Mark. His eyes were bitter and withdrawn, and he looked away from her without speaking. Analise bit her lip and marched stiffly from the room.

Mark turned his face into his pillow, hot tears of physical pain and broken pride stinging his eyes. He felt degraded, violated; they had moved in and taken over his body, and he had had no control at all. For a moment he wondered if this was what Analise felt when he had forced her to become his mistress. Analise. Oh, God, how the sight and sound and smell of New Orleans had washed over him yesterday as their carriage moved through the streets. It had carried him back three years, thrust him into the sultry somnolent summer he had spent with Analise in their delicate little iced cake of a house. He remembered the diamond-bright sparkle of her eyes and the pink flush of her cheeks when she stormed at him angrily, the cool satin feel of her skin against him, the soft caress of her accented voice. In his mind, he saw her sitting again at her vanity, clad only in a clinging silk gown, her arms raised to pull out the pins from her hair and let it fall in a tumbling black cloud onto her shoulders. The image had shot desire through his body, and he had ached with frustration, wishing desperately that he could be a whole man again.

And now—Analise had seen the horror of his injuries and been revolted; he had read that in the stiff manner in which she held herself and in the way she avoided looking at him. She had stripped him of his last shred of dignity, exposed his mutilations to the one person it hurt him most to have see them. He hated her for that.

The next two weeks were a whirl of activity for Analise. First there were her sessions with Mark, which drained her both physically and emotionally. Each morning and evening she went into his room where he lay, already stripped of his trousers and shirt, looking like someone prepared for the torture chamber or perhaps the sacrificial block. And she found herself feeling guiltily like the Chief Torturer. She massaged his scarred arm and leg, copying Monique's movements carefully, and then forced his muscles to move.

Mark maintained a stoic silence throughout their sessions. It was unnerving, particularly since he kept his eyes fixed on her in a cold, steady gaze of hatred. Now and then a grunt or muffled moan would escape his lips, or drops of sweat would appear on his blanched face, and she would know he was in pain. Analise would feel her own heart twist for him, and yet she had to do it if he was to recover. Many times after a session she went to her room and gave in to a flood of tears. If she had not had such faith in Tante Monique's methods, she would have given up after a few days. She could see that Mark and the Sergeant were totally skeptical, and sometimes she wondered if her faith was merely wishful thinking. But she was committed to this method, and she would see it through to the bitter end.

Her hopes were strengthened by the fact that, toward the end of the first week, Mark's pain was visibly lessening. However, when she increased the sessions to four a day during the second week, as Tante Monique had ordered, the pain was back with a vengeance. The doubling of sessions was a great strain on Analise, multiplying as it did the time and effort she had to expend on Mark's treatment.

Analise was pushed to the point of exhaustion by her heavy load of duties. Besides administering Mark's treatment, she had to deal with all the problems of buying and moving into a house. Since both the attorney and Mrs. Webster needed money as soon as possible, the transaction was completed quickly, and Analise was able to start the repairs and refurbishing that were needed. Besides ordering and supervising that work, Analise had to acquire uniforms for her new servants and instruct them regarding their future duties. She also had to buy furniture to replace the few essential pieces that Mrs. Webster was taking with her to her smaller home.

Although these household chores were quite ample to occupy her time, Analise had business problems to attend to as well. It was essential that she find a site for her store and do it as quickly as possible, so that the workmen could start on it. So by foot and in a buggy she toured the downtown area, searching for the best location for the

store. She did not want to have it right in the middle of
the business district, but more on the edge, toward the
residential district. Near the Garden District would be
best, she thought, since the deteriorating Quarter lay as a
barrier between the downtown area and the wealthy
French Esplanade area. Moreover, she imagined the people
who would acquire new wealth, whether Yankees or
Southerners, were more likely to be American and to gravi-
tate to the Garden side.

Analise really preferred to find an old building that
could be renovated rather than build a new one, since
building was so difficult in New Orleans. Because the city
sat at sea level on marshy land, ordinary foundations were
impossible. Poles had to be sunk and the area filled in with
dirt and brush until it was firm enough to build on. It was
due to this lack of firm soil that New Orleans had its
unique cemeteries filled only with above-ground vaults.

Finally, Analise's efforts were rewarded by finding a
half-block area containing three buildings that she thought
could be renovated and joined to form one large building.
Further investigation revealed that the land had been
owned by the Bouchard family, but had recently been sold
to Joseph Grimshaw.

It was not a familiar name to Analise, but Pauline Beauvais was able to help her. Analise had been taking Pauline
with her on her business expeditions because she valued
her brains and hoped to ultimately place her in the position of her assistant, in which case it was wise for her to
gain as much experience in as many areas as possible. She
also had another motive, which was to start giving her
friend a salary as soon as possible. Pauline had proved to
be quite a help in her knowledge of the area and the

people, including all the twisted family histories and the more recent events that Analise had not known.

When Analise queried her about Grimshaw, a frown shadowed Pauline's face. "He is a Yankee who came here three months ago and began buying land, as much as he could, all over the city. So many people are destitute and forced to sell their property at prices far below its real worth. Grimshaw is a scavenger. He takes advantage of people's misfortunes."

Analise just smiled. "Well, let's see if we can take advantage of him."

She sent him a note informing him of her interest in his buildings and asked him to call on her to discuss buying them. She signed her name and below it wrote, "Representative for Maximilian Schleyer, N.Y.C." She knew that she was more likely to command attention and respect as Max's agent than she would by her name alone, being a mere woman. Analise wanted Grimshaw to realize that she was a person with some degree of skill and intelligence, not an impoverished, naive lady. It put her in a better position, too, if he called on her, rather than her seeking him out; that made him more the supplicant, not her.

Grimshaw called at the appointed hour, and Analise disliked him on sight. He was a big, heavy man with a square, unyielding jaw and narrow, suspicious eyes. When he smiled, there was no warmth in it, only a mechanical movement, and his fleshy cheeks rolled up over his eyes, giving him the look of an animal baring its teeth. His eyes flickered over Analise appraisingly and he wet his lips; all through their interview, he kept glancing surreptitiously at her bosom.

Analise concealed her indignation and irritation behind

a pleasant, formal mask. She was not such a novice as to give her opponent the advantage of rattling her or even of knowing her feelings. She offered him coffee and spent a few moments in polite conversation, then smoothly steered their talk to the subject of the buildings she wanted. Analise wanted to buy the buildings, but he did not really want to sell, preferring to lease. He named a ridiculously high figure, and Analise countered with an equally ridiculously low figure, and they haggled for several minutes, unable to arrive at a mutual price. Grimshaw, with an insulting leer, suggested that he might be persuaded to bring down the price and meaningfully raked her body with his eyes. Analise answered with a cool, damping look and said that she guessed they could not arrive at a price.

Then Grimshaw offered to lease the building to her long-term, and after much haggling arrived at more realistic terms. The rent would not be cheap, but the lease was for ninety-nine years, with Schleyer having the option to renew, and the rent would not increase. Moreover, Grimshaw agreed to renovate the buildings to meet Analise's requirements. Analise disliked the thought of having to deal with the man over the years, but the opportunity was too good to refuse. Analise agreed to meet with him and his builder the next week to discuss the renovations and sign the lease, but she insisted that the lease be sent to her lawyer for inspection before she would sign. Then she smiled coolly and showed him out the door.

Exhausted, Analise sank into a chair. Tomorrow they would begin moving to the house. Tante Monique was coming tonight to judge Mark's progress, and Analise suspected sadly that it had not been good. She got no cooperation from Mark, only acquiescence, and although the pain of the sessions had visibly lessened the last day or so, she could not see any sign that his limbs had improved. Analise sighed and tears of weariness, so often lurking these days, sprang into her eyes. How long could she go on like this, with Mark despising her and her having to hurt him and never any improvement to show for it? There were times when she thought desperately that it was not worth it, and she ought to just walk out and leave Mark to his own devices.

There was a knock on the door, and Analise rose. No doubt that would be Tante Monique. She pushed her doubts aside; there was no time to worry about it now. There were things she had to do. Firmly she walked to the door.

Twenty

Tante Monique's visit did much to lift Analise's spirits. She proclaimed the patient much improved and complimented Analise on the tub with circulating water she had rigged up for Mark. Analise had proved herself her father's daughter by inventing a tub for Mark. She had her servants cut a small hole in the bottom of a regular bath tub and fasten beneath it a smaller tub, which contained a fan. When the tub was filled with water, someone could make the fan rotate by pumping a foot pedal. The fan caused the water to swirl and bubble as Monique had said was more healing, but since it was located under the tub, its blades could not cut Mark. The warm baths in the tub were the only part of his regimen that Mark enjoyed.

Mark was ready to proceed to the next step, Monique told them. He was to continue with the balm rubs and moving the muscles, but now he was to begin using his muscles himself. The black woman described to them the exercises he should follow and the number of times he was to do them. Then, promising to return in four weeks, she breezed out of the room.

The next day they moved into their new house, and

before they could even begin to settle in, Analise had workmen in Mark's room attaching a hand-high rail to one wall and, parallel to it and about three feet away, another rail, which rested on legs attached to the floor. Monique had recommended two bars, although now Mark could use only one.

Twice a day Mark leaned on one rail with his good hand and was supported on the other side by Jackson. Slowly, once down and once back, he moved along the rail, trying to make his lame leg walk. Every step was painful, and usually he had little control over his muscles, so that he often stumbled or his leg went out awkwardly. There were two new arm exercises. One was to bend his arm at the elbow, bringing his hand up to his shoulder. The other was to hold a ball of cloth in the palm of his hand, close his fingers around it, and squeeze.

At first, Mark refused to try any of these exercises, until Analise had to laugh scornfully and call him a coward to spur him into doing them.

"Do you want your son to realize that you had the opportunity to stop being a cripple but were too afraid of the pain to do it?" she sneered.

Anger flooded her husband at that remark, and he set about firmly to prove her wrong. His days became a desert of pain, work, and defeat. For a long time he could not even make his fingers close around the ball or raise his arm an inch, and his attempts at walking were laughable. Doggedly he kept at it, swearing that he would show Analise, somehow pay her back for all her sarcasm and taunts.

One day he was able to close his fingers around the ball and could move on to squeezing. Gradually he was able to lift his arm higher and higher. He even began to make shuffling steps instead of dragging his foot along. Every week he added two more times a day for each exercise. With what seemed to him infernal slowness, he began to improve.

For a long time, he could see what he was doing only as revenge against Analise, something to prove her wrong, to silence her. But one day, as he inched his forearm up, sweat beading on his forehead from the effort, he realized that he was actually moving the arm he had thought paralyzed. It was slow and terribly hard, but at least his arm and leg were not completely useless. Suddenly hope darted through him: if he continued this determined effort, he might be able to walk and use his arm again. No doubt he would never recover the strength he had had, but at least he might be able to function. With even greater determination, he threw himself into his exercises.

Analise could see his progress and was overjoyed. Of course, there were no thanks or liking for her in his eyes, but that really did not matter. All that mattered was that he was improving! That thought gave her renewed energy to continue massaging and bending his leg and arm. It was still tiring, but not so emotionally draining. He cooperated with her now instead of lying inert; sometimes she could feel his muscles pull with her. And the pain was much less. In fact, it seemed as though the lotion rubs were even becoming soothing.

Once they had settled in, Analise was able to devote the rest of her attention to the store. She explained the layout of her store to Grimshaw and the builder, pointing out where to build fitting rooms and where to build counters. The hardware part of the store would be partitioned off, windowless, and with hardwood floors. The rest of the store was to be either marble or parquet tile. Analise insisted that large windows with raised floors for display be set in all the way down the walls. She also required attractive light fixtures and ceiling fans, as well as large carved wooden doors with brass handles at all three front entrances.

Grimshaw protested long and loud at the cost, but Analise remained adamant. After a great deal of bickering and bargaining, he agreed to make the improvements, and Analise agreed to an increase in rent. It was with a sigh of relief that Analise signed the lease setting forth their agreement. She hated having to deal with Grimshaw. At every meeting, his eyes leered at her, and he found excuses to touch her or accidentally bump into her. And one day when they were alone because the builder had been unable to attend the meeting, Grimshaw had the audacity to make her a lewd proposition. Analise answered it with a resounding slap and angrily marched away. But the next day she had to return and act as if nothing had happened; she had put too much time into the building to throw it away in a huff.

While the renovations were taking place, Analise had a myriad of other problems to face. She had to buy equipment for the store and choose and order the goods to stock it. Moreover, she had to comb New Orleans for a talented dressmaker and an artistic person to dress her display windows. Then, of course, there were all the employees to be hired, which meant hours and hours of interviewing applicants, searching for those who were good, loyal salesmen, with that little extra spirit necessary to excel.

Between her job and her work with Mark, Analise had little time left for anything else. However, she was determined not to cut any of her time with her son. Johnny was growing very close to his father, but Analise was still his security. She knew that in these completely new surroundings, he needed her more than before. So she skimped on sleep rather than on time with little John, with the result that as the weeks passed, dark shadows grew under her eyes and hollows formed in her cheeks. It gave her a wan air of mystery and sorrow that was attractive, but Pauline lectured worriedly that she was ruining her health.

Analise did not try to see her parents for a long time, fearing their rejection, but finally one day, as a tongue seeks out a sore tooth, she was drawn to her former home. She stood for several minutes at the gate, looking into the now-ragged garden, delaying the moment of decision. A cold hand squeezed her chest as she looked at the house; like Pauline's home, it was neglected, the paint peeling and the steps beginning to sag. It was obvious that the Caldwells were feeling the pinch of the war.

Drawing a deep breath, Analise pushed open the gate and went up the walk to the front door. Her knock was answered by their old butler, whose face lit up in startled recognition when he saw her.

"Miss Analise!" he cried. "My, how pretty you look."

"Hello, Josiah, how are you? How is everyone?"

"Oh, fine, just fine, Miss Analise. Your mama and daddy are doing as fine as anybody can nowadays."

"Do you think—" the words seemed to stick in Analise's throat.

The black man easily guessed, however, what it was she wished to ask, for he shook his head sadly. "No, ma'am, I don't think that they will see you. I will go ask, if you like."

"Would you?" Analise beamed at him.

It was but a few minutes before he was back, his face set in lines of regret. "I'm sorry, Miss Analise but Miz Theresa, she says 'no'."

Analise swallowed and smiled crookedly. "Well, thank you for trying anyway."

She started to turn away, but stopped. Before she would have just gone unhappily away, but now she was a stronger, different person, and anger shook her. To the surprise of the butler, she suddenly turned and swept past him, and ran to the door of the sitting room, with the butler trotting agitatedly at her heels and pleading with her to turn back.

Mr. and Mrs. Caldwell both looked up in amazement as their daughter burst into the room, her eyes alight with the fire of battle. Theresa gasped and began to fan her face agitatedly, while her husband simply stared.

"Don't worry, I shan't impose my presence upon you too long; I know what your feelings are toward me. However, I just wanted you to know what *my* feelings are. I'll tell you frankly that I am not ashamed of what I have done. I saved Emil's life, and you ostracize me for that. Well, God knows, after the way you and he have acted, I wish to hell I hadn't. You are a selfish, blind, inept group of people. You tell me that I am no longer considered a member of this family. Well, all I can say is 'Thank God for that!' "

Before the others could say a word, Analise was gone in a swirl of sea-blue skirts, leaving her parents staring after her in shock. She swept back to her house on the tide of her fury and stormed up the stairs to Mark's room, startling him from a nap with her slam of the door.

"What the devil!" he exclaimed, his voice thick with sleep.

"Damn them!" Analise exploded, flinging her reticule down and picking up a bottle of the healing lotion.

"Hold it," Mark said, laughter lurking in his voice. "You're not going to start pounding on me when you're in that kind of mood—you'll snap my bones."

Her eyebrows drew together and she sighed. "I suppose you're right."

"Now tell me, what put you in such a snit?"

Analise sank into a chair and rubbed her face wearily. "Oh, I went to see my parents. I thought maybe something had finally knocked some sense in their heads, but obviously not. They refused to even see me."

For the first time in a long while, Mark felt a tug of sympathy for his wife. He was responsible for the rift between her and her family. "I am sorry, Analise."

"Well, I'm not," Analise said stoutly. "They are a couple of pig-headed, antiquated, hypocritical old fools! It's their own throats they are cutting; I am the only one who could and would help them financially. Well, I told them what I think of them. I just hate to think that I come from a family of such idiots."

Mark laughed out loud at that, and Analise ruefully joined him. It was a moment before they realized how easily and naturally they had been talking, just as if the barriers of the last few months were gone. Analise glanced at Mark to see the same realization in his eyes, and immediately they fell into silence. Suddenly the new mood was gone.

Awkwardly Analise stood and went to the door to call Sergeant Jackson. When the Sergeant had removed Mark's outer clothing, Analise poured lotion in her palms and began to massage Mark's arm. She studiously avoided his gaze as she rubbed, for she felt uneasy about the sudden

change in their behavior. Mark, who felt much the same
way, closed his eyes to block her out. Then she began on
his leg, gently kneading the muscles, and a treacherous
warmth crept through Mark's loins. There was no longer
any pain when she massaged his limbs, and suddenly the
intimate touch of her firm, cool fingers excited him. Her
hands dug into his thighs, and Mark could feel his manhood stiffening. He hoped the sheet that lay over all but
his leg would conceal it from her.

For a long time now, Mark had lived on his anger with
Analise; it was disconcerting to discover that she still had
the power to arouse him. Underneath the layers of pain,
anger, and vengeance, his love for her remained, scarred
perhaps, but still very much alive. Stubbornly Mark fought
it; he did not want to feel love or even desire for Analise
any more.

When Analise finally left, unconscious of her effect on
him, Mark beckoned his aide. "Jackson, I want you to do
me a favor."

"Yes, sir?"

"Take some of my money and go over to the Quarter.
Find a good whorehouse and bring a girl back here for
me."

Jackson started. "But, sir—here?"

"Yes, damn it. Don't look so shocked. Surely you realize
I have never been a monk."

"No, sir, of course not. And I am glad to see you feeling
good enough again to want a woman. It's just—why seek
out a whore when you've got a wife who's the most beautiful woman I've seen right in the same house with you?"

"Perhaps you don't remember that she told me she
would divorce me?" Mark said dryly.

"Of course I do, but begging your pardon, I have noticed that Mrs. Schaeffer is not above bending the truth a little to get what she wants." He ignored Mark's snort of sarcastic laughter and went on. "Anyway, I think she might have been lying that day, just to goad you into working on your injuries."

"And just what has brought you to that improbable conclusion?" Mark asked.

"Sir, you haven't seen the lady when she leaves this room after your treatments. Back when you were in so much pain, she would be white as a sheet and shaking all over once she got out of your sight. One day I even saw her sit down out in the hall and burst into tears."

"How touching."

Jackson continued heatedly, "It doesn't make any sense that she is in love with some guy in New York, but she's down here nursing you instead of being up there with him!"

"She feels it is her duty."

"Huh! That don't make sense, either. If she has such a strong sense of honor and duty, what's she doing being unfaithful in the first place?"

"You don't know Southerners, Jackson. They have a peculiar sense of morals."

"Yeah, well, it must be highly peculiar, then, for a faithless wife to work herself to a frazzle getting her crippled husband strong enough that he can stop her infidelities! She will make herself ill at the rate she's going, with all the time she spends on you, and then running that store, not to mention managing a household and mothering her boy. Haven't you seen the way she looks? She has lost weight, and there are dark circles under her eyes. Or are you just too wrapped up in yourself to notice anyone else?"

"Damn it, Sergeant, that is enough!" Mark roared. "I don't have to justify myself to you or anyone else. My wife does not love me—you have no knowledge of what has happened in the past. I do, and I know she has no reason to love me and every reason to love that German. But even if she did love me, I refuse to subject her to my love again!"

"Are you going to begin that excuse again? She has seen your arm and leg several times a day for quite a few weeks now. She has touched your scars over and over. How can you think she would be repulsed by them now?"

"She has seen them impersonally, as a doctor might see them. That is a far cry from lying naked against them and allowing that horror to caress you. But there is worse than the scars. It is what is inside me that she needs protection from. Ever since I met her, I have harmed her in one way or another. I always let my jealousy and my damnable temper get the best of me. I loved her and yet I hurt her. She makes me so angry I could strangle her, but the very thought of her makes me quiver with passion like a schoolboy. In other words, Sergeant, our life together is a hell for both of us, and it is best to make a clean cut. Oh yes, I am burning for her right now—why do you think I require the services of a whore? But if I somehow coax Analise into bed to ease my hunger, it only prolongs the painful end for both of us."

"I just can't believe you would step aside and let another man take your wife from you, especially such a wife as she is," Jackson argued stubbornly.

"Damnation, are you deaf?" Mark exploded. "I love Analise, yes; I want her to be happy; I want to get off this merry-go-round of love and hate and desire and jealousy. If I loved her less, I would not hurt so, and I would not hurt her so much, either. Maybe then I would do what you want. But I love her too much to keep her tied to me and the bitter, twisted love we shared."

Jackson stopped, nonplussed. The Colonel had delved too far into complexities that his own simple values of love and marriage could not absorb. Schaeffer was a dark, convoluted man, and his wife was not exactly straightforward and simple herself. Perhaps Mark was right; no doubt he had a better understanding of their complicated relationship. He still felt guilty about bringing another woman into Mrs. Schaeffer's own home, but the Colonel would be hard put to go to a cathouse himself, and God knows he deserved some enjoyment after all the torment he had been through.

"All right, sir, I will go," he capitulated. "What sort of girl do you want?"

"Lord, man, do you think I care? Anything but a black-headed girl or someone as ugly as sin."

The girl Jackson found and sneaked up the back stairs to Mark's room was a lively, vulgar redhead with a certain coarse, full-blown handsomeness. He let her into Mark's room, then stationed himself on guard outside the door.

What he did not reckon with was Analise deciding it would liven Mark's spirits to take a ride through the city with her in an open carriage the following day. Buoyed by the congenial atmosphere between them earlier in the afternoon, she went to Mark's room to ask him if he would care to join her. His aide was sitting outside his door and barred the way effectively by jumping up and beginning to chatter to her foolishly. It was so unlike the usually stolid

Jackson that Analise's suspicions were immediately aroused. Not guessing the truth, she thought that the Sergeant must have yielded to Mark's pleas and sneaked him in some liquor.

"Sergeant, I am trying to go into my husband's room. Would you please step aside?" she said firmly.

Jackson stammered helplessly, but he did not budge from the doorway. That confirmed Analise's suspicions, and she marched furiously back to her room and straight across to the connecting door, which was never used. She was livid with anger that Mark had backslid when he seemed to be doing so well, and her fury carried her several steps inside his room before the scene in front of her actually registered. Then she stopped dead in her tracks, too surprised and hurt to even gasp.

There was a woman in Mark's bed: completely nude, she sat astride him, her pelvis pumping up and down. Beneath her Mark groaned and jerked and his hands roamed over her body. His face was turned toward Analise and she saw that his eyes were closed and his face twisted in an ecstasy of passion she knew well. As though he sensed her presence, Mark opened his eyes and for one long moment their gazes locked. Then deliberately Mark turned his head away and went on with what he was doing, just as if she had not been there. The color drained from Analise's face at that calculated insult, and she ran from the room.

Jackson, who sat in the hall congratulating himself on keeping Analise ignorant, saw her emerge from her room and walk toward him. One glance at her paper-white face and leaden walk made him realize she had discovered the truth. He rose, expecting her to order him to leave the house.

But she simply said in a colorless voice, "Sergeant, please do Mark's treatment for me in the future. I really have not got the time, and I believe Mark will manage quite well without me."

Twenty-One

*A*nalise saw little of Mark through the months to come. She no longer massaged his legs; Jackson did that now. Rarely did she even stop by his room to inquire after his health, although she questioned Jackson daily about Mark's progress. She played with Johnny for a couple of hours in the evening, and the rest of the time she devoted to the new store.

As for Mark, he grew stronger daily. He became maniacal about his exercises, working at them as though success in moving his dead limbs would somehow heal his emotional wounds as well. He progressed rapidly enough so that by Christmas he was able to surprise his family by walking downstairs to join them, supported only by a cane.

At his entrance, Analise's face lit with joy and she took a few involuntary steps forward, crying, "Mark! Oh, Mark, you've done it!"

Tears of happiness and pride sprang into her eyes, and she wanted to run to him and throw her arms around him. However, she remembered in time that her husband would not welcome her embrace. No, he preferred the touch of any common slut to hers. So she stopped and clasped her hands in front of her and subdued her radiant smile.

"Hello, Mark, I am glad to see you doing so well," she said coolly.

"Thank you." Mark's manner was equally stiff, and his black eyes did not betray that they searched his wife's face eagerly for any hint of forgiveness or love.

Not that he really wanted her forgiveness, he told himself. He had done the right thing, forcing her to break with him. They would both be better off apart. Still, he could not quite suppress the hopeful surge of his heart when he saw her smile at him, her face bright with pride at his achievement.

Winter turned into the wet, muddy days of early spring. Mark trained himself to handle a fork and knife, to write, even to shoot a pistol creditably. Daily he strengthened himself, taking longer and longer walks, and using his arm more. He could not recover full strength in his arm, and because of the bad breaks in his leg, he walked with a limp. But he no longer needed a cane to support him and he could resume all the activities of a normal man. Except for the slight limp and the scars, he could have passed for his former self.

Analise swelled with pride whenever she saw him, and she longed to throw her arms around him and tell him of her love and admiration. But even as she rejoiced in the return of Mark's abilities and self-respect, she dreaded the conclusion that must soon follow. Mark no longer needed her and she had failed to win back his love. Soon she would either have to leave him, as she had promised, or admit that she had not planned to divorce him. She could not force herself to leave, nor could she humble herself so before his dispassionate dark gaze. Not that it mattered what she did—Mark could leave under his own steam now.

However, Mark was not anxious to initiate the parting, either. As he regained his health, his spirits returned also. The stronger and more confident he grew, the more he wanted Analise and the less imperative it seemed to set her free. Once he was free of pain and less absorbed in the movement of his limbs, he realized how much Analise had done for him, how hard she had worked, and how effective her sarcasm had been where loving sympathy had failed. His anger with her and his thirst for revenge faded into nothingness, and he found himself left with only his persistent love for her and the void of his life without her.

He took to eating downstairs, sometimes even sitting quietly with her and Johnny during the evening, watching the beauty of her face as she laughed and played with her son. At those times he ached for her with a need long unfulfilled, and he wanted to carry her up to his room and make violent love to her until all thought of the bland German was eradicated from her mind. There was nothing to separate them now, he told himself, and the long months of pain and helplessness had changed him into a calmer, more sober man, one who would not impulsively flare with jealousy. This time they could make it.

Later, though, he would call himself a blind fool. He had always been certain that the next time he would change, and yet his wrath and jealousy still bubbled quickly to the surface. There was no proof that it would be any different now. Besides, if he had really changed, he knew he must accept the fact that he could not force Analise to love him—that he had tried far too often and failed miserably. Face it, he told himself, too much has happened. Analise had been hurt too often, and she now loved another man. Let her go. Do the right thing: set her free.

So, caught in his dilemma, loving her yet plagued by his conscience, wanting to let her go to her future happiness yet unable to cause the break, Mark drifted, much as Analise did, saying nothing and waiting for the ax to fall.

One day in March when Mark returned from his morning walk, he found a visitor waiting for him in the parlor. With a start of surprise, he recognized John Caldwell, Analise's father. Smoothly he hid his amazement and greeted the man impassively, but inside his mind raced: What the devil was the man doing here? Had he finally decided to forgive Analise and make his peace with her?

"No doubt you wonder why I am here," Caldwell began hesitantly. When Mark made no effort to ease the situation, merely raised his eyebrows silently, the older man cleared his throat nervously and stumbled on. "The fact is, I have come to ask you a favor. As you no doubt know, I was ruined by the war, utterly ruined. Belle Terre, my plantation, is completely unproductive; I haven't the money to hire workers and set it on its feet again. It is good land, but useless to me in the state I am in. Since Mrs. Caldwell and I badly need the money, I am forced to—to sell it. I came to you in the hopes that you might buy it."

"Me?" Mark's voice rose in astonishment. "Why did you not go to your daughter, Mr. Caldwell? I am sure she would be happy to support you and your wife, so that you would not have to sell Belle Terre. Or if you are too proud for that, I know she would purchase the plantation and put it back into production."

"No, I could not go to Analise," Caldwell said firmly. "She broke her mother's heart, disgraced the family."

"Yet you can come to me to beg a favor—me, a Yankee, the man who forced Analise to become my mistress, the man who entered your house under false pretenses and stole the plans to your invention. I confess I find your principles somewhat hard to comprehend." Mark's brows drew together thunderously. "Your own daughter, who sacrificed herself to save her brother, is beneath your touch, but you will ask a favor of her seducer, her betrayer, an enemy spy and saboteur!"

"Your sins do not dishonor the Caldwell name, sir. Analise's do."

"God save me from a Southerner's sense of honor!" Mark exclaimed.

"I—I understand that you have a son. I would like for him someday to have the land, so that it will at least be kept in the family. That is why I came to you."

"I would like to toss you out on your ear," Mark said, his voice deadly calm. "As far as I am concerned, I would not lift a finger to keep you from starving, for the wrong you have done to Analise. But because Analise treasures Belle Terre and because I want my son to have his heritage, I shall purchase it. I shall have my attorney call upon you to arrange the sale; I have no wish to deal with you personally. Now I shall ask you to leave my house."

Caldwell rose nervously and turned to go; those icy black eyes were enough to freeze a man.

"Oh, and Caldwell," Mark interrupted his flight. "Until you come to beg forgiveness of Analise, you will not be received at my house. Is that understood?"

His only answer was a nod and the other man's flight from the room. Mark's lips twisted scornfully: the heartless, cowardly fool! He dropped into a chair. Now, what the hell was he going to do with a broken-down plantation?

As he thought about it that afternoon, Belle Terre

seemed more and more a perfect solution to his problems. He had been raised on a plantation; rebuilding and managing one was something he was qualified to do. The warm climate suited him; somehow during the war and his marriage to Analise, he had become reconciled to his Southern upbringing. Just because he had been pained by his mother and had hated the hypocrisy and the slavery, he did not have to deny his love for the warm, fertile, sweet-smelling land. His time in New Orleans had brought home to him how much he missed the land he was raised in.

He no longer wanted to return to his life of adventuring. He wanted to be near his son, and he wanted to occupy his time in some satisfying way. Taking a run-down farm and making it productive again appealed to him. After the destruction of the war, it would be good to be a part of a renewal of life.

Most of all, he could avoid facing Analise's departure. His removal to Belle Terre would show her plainly how completely he had recovered and set her free to pursue her own life. He would not have to live with the daily torture of being near her, wanting and not having her. Nor would he have to watch her leave him. All he had to do was move to the plantation, give her grounds for a divorce, and let her do as she wished. She could go to Max, or stay, or even come to him—no, he must not let himself think like that. He would not trick himself with false hopes.

That night at supper Mark dropped his bombshell: "Analise, I have decided to buy Belle Terre."

She stared, dumbstruck. "Belle Terre! My Belle Terre?"

Mark recounted her father's visit of this morning, carefully avoiding his comments regarding Analise. But Analise was too clever not to fill in what he had left out; only dislike of her would have sent Caldwell to Mark. Her eyes sparkled with tears.

"Thank you," she said softly. "I am glad Johnny will have it. And thank you for helping my parents; it was very kind of you."

"I can hardly let my wife's parents go to the poorhouse." Mark passed it off lightly. "Besides, I've recovered so well that I am bored. I need something to do, and the plantation seemed a perfect opportunity."

"You mean you are going to rebuild it?" Analise asked, surprised.

"I am not entirely a novice at it, you know."

"Well, of course, but, well—I'm just surprised," she said lamely. "I guess I did not realize how well you have become."

"I know that I have you to thank for it," Mark said soberly, looking straight into her eyes.

Analise shifted uncomfortably beneath his gaze. What did he mean by that? And how should she respond?

"What I am trying to say in my own clumsy way is that I realize how much you have done for me. I want to apologize for all the crazy, abusive things I said to you when you were trying to help me."

"That's all right. I understand; you were depressed and in pain." Analise felt her pulse quicken. Was he about to ask for a reconciliation? Invite her to accompany him to the plantation?

For a moment they were silent, waiting anxiously for some word of hope, some sign from the other. Then the moment passed and Mark stood up, smiling stiffly, and excused himself from the table.

* * *

The sale of the land went quickly. Mark occupied himself in the meantime with inspecting the land and making plans for recapturing it from the grip of nature, with hiring workers for the fields and carpenters and painters to repair the deteriorating plantation house. The house had once been a beauty, and Mark was determined to restore it to its former grandeur.

It was a huge white mansion in the typically Southern style, with a verandah running around three sides, both first and second stories supported by tall, graceful columns. There was a third floor, as well, where dormer windows protruded from the sloping roof. A little ornamental cupola adorned the high center of the roof. A spacious lawn surrounded the house, dotted with giant, spreading oak trees. On the back side of the house a wide bricked walkway stretched between the main house and the small, original planter's home behind it. A trellis covered the walkway and formed doorways at each end, and on the trellis roses and honeysuckle, untended for years, ran riot, forming a cool, lush, dark enclosure, almost overpowering in its intoxicating scent. Though its exterior was reminiscent of plantation homes across the South, its interior construction was typical Louisianian, wide and open to the air. Also stamping it as Creole-built were the tall cisterns painted to match the house and the round white *garçonierres*, the small two-story edifices built to house the sons of the house when they emerged into their raucous teens.

Mark could easily understand Analise's love of the place—the house, the gardens, and the fields that stretched beside the flat brown Mississippi. As he rode over the fields, sticky from the spring rains and overgrown with weeds and rivercanes, he felt more at peace than he ever had, and when he approached the square, heavy house, he felt as if he were truly coming home. Sometimes he imagined Analise sitting on the verandah waiting for him; that would make it complete. If only she would say she wanted to move out to the plantation with him; if only she would join him in his reclamation of the land . . .

But she did not. Analise kept herself busy at the store, readying it for opening. Though she waited all through Mark's preparations for departure, hoping against hope that he would turn to her and ask her to live with him at Belle Terre, he did not do it. And she, after all his rebuffs, had too much pride to beg him to let her come, only to receive yet another rejection.

So the days passed, and Mark left to live at Belle Terre, with never a word said between them about Analise joining him. Little Johnny cried and said he missed his new-found daddy. Analise, holding him close, admitted that she did too. At least Johnny would be allowed to visit his father, she thought bitterly, whereas it was quite clear that she was unwelcome. She told herself that she should be grateful that he had not pushed her to that final scene she so dreaded. At least he had not demanded that she fulfill her threat to divorce him. He was near and they were still married; John could see his father often, and she would be able to catch a glimpse of him now and then. That was more than what faced her months ago in New York.

She had her work at the store, and she must concentrate on that. The hardware section at the back was complete, and she opened it while the rest of the store was still under renovation. Analise wanted its necessary items to be available to the public as soon as possible; and luxurious surroundings were not important here. Every day found her at the store, supervising her employees and the renovation. She had received a letter from Max Schleyer saying that he planned to sail to New Orleans for the opening of the store, and Analise was determined that he would be presented with a jewel of a store, as well as profits already made in hardware.

Joe Grimshaw no longer plagued her at the store, but since Mark had gone, he had taken to dropping in on her in the evenings. Hearing the rumors of Mark's departure, he assumed, like many others, that Mark no longer considered them bound and that Analise was now fair game. Though, true to Analise's orders, her servants refused him admittance, coolly and untruthfully swearing her either out or indisposed, Grimshaw stubbornly continued to call on her. Once, seeing his angry face as he left, Analise wished fervently that the burly Sergeant had not gone to Belle Terre with Mark; she had the uneasy feeling that she could use a little protection.

There were times when Sergeant Jackson echoed Analise's wish that he had remained in New Orleans. Mark attacked the run-down farm like a maniac, working from dawn to dark without ceasing and expecting the same from his workers. Since Jackson had carpentering skills, he was appointed the task of repairing the old house—which he far preferred to any sort of work in the fields. However, he could not quite join in Schaeffer's fanatical belief that the house should be immediately and perfectly restored.

Mark himself worked in the fields, stripping down to the waist to struggle and sweat right alongside his employees as they pulled the lush overgrowth from the land. Under the rays of the hot sun, Mark's unhealthy pallor vanished, and his skin turned nut-brown. The heavy work completed the recovery of his strength, hardening his muscles to the iron they had once been and burning away the excess flesh that months of inactivity had added to his frame.

His goal was to recover and plant one third of the plantation, leaving the rest to be cleared during the winter months next year. Right now time was of the essence, for spring was passing quickly. Once the land he had chosen was cleared, he set his workers to planting the sugarcane. Untiringly he rode through the fields supervising, inspecting, dismounting to demonstrate what he said or to help with a difficult task.

One afternoon late when he rode wearily back to the house he was surprised to see a shabby buggy pulled up in front of the mansion. For a moment his heart leaped with hope: Analise had come! The next instant he knew it could not be her; her buggy was spanking new, not old and worn like this one. He supposed it must be some neighbor come to pay a call. With a sigh he went into the parlor.

A blonde young woman in a faded, once-fashionable dress sat on the green velvet love seat. She smiled up at him, and he recognized her as faintly familiar. As he obviously stumbled over her name, she pouted coyly.

"Colonel Schaeffer, how terribly ungallant of you to forget me. You were known by a different name when we first met, but I am still named Becky," she teased playfully.

Of course, Becky Oldway. He had met her once at Analise's house. She was still a vapidly pretty thing, though lines of discontent were beginning to settle around her mouth. In a few years the pout would not be teasing pretense, nor very pretty.

"Of course, Miss Oldway," he said.

"Yes, you remembered! Except that it is Mrs. Fourier now."

"I stand corrected. But what a surprise to see you. What are you doing out here?"

Becky giggled. "Why, I am your neighbor—or nearly so. Emil and I live on his family plantation now. Of course, it is not so fine as this house, just one of those horrid old long planter's houses. The original house there—imagine. But then the Fouriers never lived on their land." She sighed elaborately. "The war has changed life for so many of us."

"Of course," Mark replied, trying for a tone of sympathy, although he wished the flighty minx anywhere but here. He was sore and tired and badly needed rest. "May I offer you refreshment?"

To his annoyance, she accepted readily, and Mark had to ring for a servant and order iced drinks for both of them. Gaily she chattered on for nearly an hour, oblivious to her host's tired silence.

At last she left, but for the next two weeks, Mark saw her many times more, for she continued to pop in on him on one pretext or another. Mark realized with amusement that Emil's wife was trying to captivate him. He felt no particular desire for her; compared to Analise, most women were rather ordinary. However, he felt the need of sex, especially when dreams of Analise plagued his night, and he supposed that Becky would do as well as any. She certainly seemed quite ready and willing. And it amused him to think of cuckolding the man of whom he had been unjustifiably jealous for so long; it would serve the prig right, he thought, for the nasty way he repaid Analise's sacrifice for him.

Had Becky known of his cold analysis of her, she would have been quite horrified. Never the most subtle of people, she was quite certain that she had hidden her intentions well. She had flirted with him but in a way she thought cleverly concealed her intentions, hoping to drive him to such passion that he would sweep her off her feet. She, of course, would protest with great innocence but at last succumb to the powerful force of love. She must not appear loose, for then he might not marry her.

For marriage was Becky's ultimate aim. She was not sure yet just how she would get around the inconvenience of her marriage to Emil, but it was obvious from his presence here that Mark's marriage was quite dead, and rumor had it that Analise would divorce him. Why Analise would throw away such wealth was beyond Becky's understanding, but Becky felt sure she would be able to persuade Mark to pursue the divorce should Analise fail to do so. Of course it would all be the most terrible scandal, but, then, it would be worth it. Just the thought of Mark's money made her heart beat faster.

When the war ended, Becky had married Emil, partly because it had been her plan for years and partly because there were now so few men around that she felt she must latch on securely to the one she had. And foolishly she had assumed that having been wealthy once Emil would become so again. Unfortunately, Emil had inherited all his money; his talent had been for spending money, not making it. They had been forced to retire to the plantation, where Emil was quite unsuccessful at getting money from the land. Becky had been unbearably bored with the dull country life and quite put out by its inconveniences. She was bound and determined that she would not spend the rest of her life here watching her clothes fray and her looks fade.

When Mark came to Belle Terre, it seemed heaven sent. For one thing, it would be quite satisfying to take away the husband of her old rival. For another, Mark was rich, and even if she could not manage to disentangle herself from Emil and marry him, he would doubtless give his mistress expensive gifts. Once again, Becky had miscalculated her man. She thought that only an extremely rich man would spend so much recovering Belle Terre. But Mark, obsessed with the land and house, had sunk nearly every penny he had in it. Moreover, he was most unlikely to be fond enough of a mistress to get her anything, and he would have scoffed at the idea of marrying anyone when Analise divorced him.

However, Becky, blithely unaware of her mistakes, pursued her quarry diligently. That wretched scar on his face made her shudder, and once when she came upon him working, with his sleeves rolled up, it was all she could do to suppress a gasp at the sight of his left arm, scarred and pitted as it was. Still, the money would make that bearable. Except for the scars he was quite good-looking and his lean, tanned body set off a tumult in her loins. Becky suspected that he was an adroit lover, and, after all, one could always close one's eyes.

Becky was frustrated, though, that Mark was so slow about picking up his cues. Why, one would almost think he wasn't interested in her! Finally she had to resort to an outright play on his jealousy to get him going.

Casually she mentioned one day as she strolled through the garden with him that she had heard Joe Grimshaw had been paying assiduous attention to Mark's wife.

"Who?" Mark asked, his brow knotting.

"Oh, a boorish man, one of those carpetbaggers. Of course, I know that Analise would have nothing to do with a man like that . . ."

Mark snorted with laughter. "Good Lord, no! I remember the fellow now. Analise despises him."

He had heard Analise more than once making a sneering comment about the man, but, until now, he had not heard of Grimshaw's making advances toward her. Mark wondered if perhaps he ought to send Jackson back to the city to protect her. Or better still, perhaps he should go back himself and pay this Grimshaw a visit, just to let him know Analise was not some unprotected female whom he could annoy without consequences.

Lost in thought, he did not hear what Becky was chattering on about, but a familiar name brought him up short. "Who? What did you say?"

Becky grinned inwardly—*that* had caught his attention. "Why, nothing, just that Mr. Maximilian Schleyer, the owner of that store Analise spends so much time on, is visiting her."

Mark's voice came out choked. "You mean—he is actually staying at her house!"

"Why, heavens no, Mark!" Becky gave an amused, sophisticated laugh. "One must observe the proprieties, after all."

So Schleyer was here, and it was clear to all what his relation with Analise was, from Becky's laughing comment. Far exceeding Becky's hopes, anger stabbed through him. So Schleyer was what she wanted—well, let her have him! Schleyer could take care of Grimshaw for her, since he was so patently her new protector.

Mark's face went dark with rage, and the scar stood out whitely on his cheek. Becky felt a little icy stab of fear. Then suddenly Mark turned to her and pulled her to him. Expertly he kissed her, and even as he kissed her, his fingers traveled down her back, undoing her buttons. Becky was so taken aback by his abruptness that she forgot her act of innocence until Mark had already dragged her behind a concealing hedge and pulled her dress down off her shoulders.

Then she recalled her role and gasped, "Colonel Schaeffer, what do you think you are doing! You can't—I mustn't—"

Mark laughed and said, "Come off it, Becky, you have been angling for this for two weeks, and we both know it. Don't play the fool with me."

He cut off her cry of indignation with another hard kiss, and Becky decided she did not wish to protest any further. Quickly she helped him unfasten her garments, and they tumbled to the ground together. And Becky found, quite pleasantly, that if indeed she kept her eyes closed, it was quite the most exciting lovemaking she had ever experienced. The only thing that marred it was the fact that she distinctly heard him whisper "Analise" at the height of his passion.

Twenty-Two

"Analise," Max said warmly, beaming at her. "It is perfect. Absolutely perfect. I salute you for the job you have done."

"Thank you." Analise flashed her lovely smile at him. The opening of the store had gone beautifully, and Max had been filled with praise for her. "But I could never have done it without Pauline."

Analise took her friend by the arm and pulled her in closer to them. "Now, what I have in mind is a victory dinner for the three of us, at my home. Now, don't excuse yourself, Pauline, I have already told the cook there will be three of us, and she would be quite furious."

Skillfully Analise guided them out the door of the building. Funny how things would just suddenly make sense—like yesterday, when she had introduced Max to Pauline, and it had come to her in a flash how perfectly suited for each other they were. Their calm, quiet personalities, their quick minds, their kindness and reserve were like peas in a pod; Analise was certain they would be comfortable and happy together. Oh, Max might be attracted to a flashier person like herself, but if they had married, she feared that the unconventional, impetuous side of her character would have driven him to distraction. Analise and Mark, for all their clashes of will and misunderstandings, matched each other, just as, Analise was certain, Max and Pauline would match. If only the two fools would forget their ill-fated loves and just notice each other!

So Analise had decided to play matchmaker. Today she had included Pauline on most of their tour around the store and given her friend every opportunity to talk to Max. It was obvious that, when given a little push, they enjoyed talking to each other; Pauline even exhibited little of her habitual shyness. Analise planned to continue the rapport by hosting a cozy little dinner for the three of them. She was sure that she could maneuver Max into escorting Pauline back to her house after the meal.

Supper went well, and Analise was pleased with the growing friendship of Pauline and Max. The only jarring incident was the noisy and drunken arrival of Joe Grimshaw on Analise's doorstep. As the three of them sat in the drawing room after supper, enjoying a glass of liqueur, the sounds of an angry confrontation in the front hall interrupted their conversation. Analise lifted her eyebrows questioningly and went to investigate, closely followed by Pauline and Max. Augustus, the butler, was struggling to close the door on the burly form of Joe Grimshaw, while Grimshaw tried to thrust himself inside, snarling insults at the black.

"So your mistress is out, huh?" Grimshaw bellowed at the sight of Analise. "Damn it, boy, I'll have your hide for this."

Analise sighed and said, "I am entertaining some old and dear friends, Mr. Grimshaw, and I left express orders

that I did not wish to be disturbed. Now, if you will please
go . . ."

She turned pointedly and began to walk away, and
behind her the enraged Grimshaw exclaimed angrily and
threw himself against the door. Surprised, the butler went
staggering back, and Grimshaw burst into the hall. Analise
turned, rigid with fury.

"Mr. Grimshaw, I believe I have made myself perfectly
clear. Your attentions are most unwelcome. I am a married
woman, and—"

"Hah! A married woman? Yeah, married to a scarface
who doesn't even live in the same house with you!"

Analise went deadly white, and her eyes blazed blue fire
at the man. "How dare you! You ignorant scum, you aren't
fit to even breathe the same air as Mark Schaeffer! Get out
of this house, and never, never set foot in it again."

Augustus took the man by the arm to eject him, but
Grimshaw flung him aside.

"Oh, high and mighty, aren't you? Defending your
noble husband! Well, let me tell you something, lady. That
precious husband of yours is sitting out at your plantation,
having a fine time with your brother's wife. Yes, sir, your
husband is dallying with that little blonde flirt, Becky
Fourier."

Analise was so furious that she could not speak; without
a word, she swept back into the drawing room. The butler,
now aided by Max, succeeded this time in pitching the
intruder out the front door. Pauline followed her friend
anxiously.

"I'm sorry, Analise . . ." she began.

"Don't worry, Pauline. I would not believe anything

that lecherous villain told me," Analise reassured her, then stopped at the look on Pauline's face. "Then it is true?"

"No, no! I don't know; it is only a rumor," Pauline stumbled.

Analise sighed and sat down heavily. "There is no need to protect me, Pauline. I am well acquainted with Mark's habits. The only bed he shuns is mine."

Pauline blushed at the other woman's bluntness and was grateful for the distraction of Max entering the room.

"Who was that rude fellow, Analise? Does he bother you like this frequently?" Max asked worriedly.

"He has never acted quite that low," Analise admitted, then explained quickly who he was and how he had been calling on her. "Tonight was the first time he has gotten inside the door, but I confess that he frightens me a little."

"Why the devil doesn't Schaeffer—" Max began, then bit off his words.

"Come, let's forget it. I am amply protected here, and Grimshaw is nothing more than an annoyance."

They tried to resume their previous conversation, but Grimshaw's interruption had unnerved them all. Soon Pauline rose to take her leave. As Analise had hoped, Max politely offered to escort her home. While Pauline got her reticule and light evening shawl, Max turned to Analise.

"You still love him, don't you?" he said quietly, and Analise nodded. "So there is no hope for me?"

"No, Max," Analise said sadly. "I am afraid there is no one for me but Mark. It is my misfortune that he does not care for me, but I know I will never be happy without him."

Max sighed. "I guess then that I must face reality."

Analise smiled. "There are other charming Southern ladies around, Max."

"You mean such as Miss Beauvais?" Max asked and smiled. "Don't tell me you have taken up matchmaking now, as well. Well, perhaps you have something there. Perhaps you are right."

Pauline reentered the room, and the three of them said their goodbyes. After Max and Pauline had gone, Analise sank down into a chair. So—Mark had taken up with Becky Oldway. A flash of anger shook her. Of all the people to choose! He might at least have picked someone she did not know. No doubt he had done it out of spite, knowing how it would anger her to imagine him lying with her own brother's wife, who had once claimed to be her friend and then had cut her so coldly when Analise became Mark's mistress. Analise closed her eyes against the pain. Why did he want to hurt her so? Why did he hate her?

Mark was surprised the next morning to see a blond stranger riding across his fields toward him. He stopped his work and stood looking at the man, who pulled up beside him.

"I am looking for Mr. Schaeffer," the man said in an accented voice.

"I'm Mark Schaeffer." Mark's stomach turned icy at the sound of the German accent.

"I would like to speak to you. I am Max Schleyer."

No doubt he had come to discuss the divorce arrangements, Mark thought. Keeping his face expressionless, Mark said, "I will ride back to the house with you."

For a few moments the two men rode in an antagonistic silence. Finally Schleyer cleared his throat and said, "I do not know what Analise has told you about me . . ."

Mark chuckled humorlessly. "Enough."

Max raised his eyebrows a little; he could not tell if Schaeffer was jealous or simply unconcerned. He was a hard, unreadable man, and that vicious scar certainly did nothing to soften his looks.

"I will be honest with you, Herr Schaeffer," Max plunged in, emotion thickening his accent. "I think the world of your wife. I would marry her in an instant if she would have me."

Bitterly Mark said, "Since she is quite willing to sleep with you, I can't see why she would not marry you. Or has Analise found better fish to fry?"

"How dare you speak of Analise that way!" Max exclaimed, anger flushing his face.

"It takes no daring; Analise told me herself that she had slept with you, and she intended to divorce me and marry you."

"Analise and I had one night together—when she had received no letters from you for a year and a half, after you had told her you would never come back to her, when she knew you had returned from the war but made no effort to contact her. Can you blame her for trying to get a little happiness for herself? Are you so blameless yourself? Didn't you sleep with other women? Are you not now having an affair with Analise's own sister-in-law?"

"I fail to see what business it is of yours." Mark's tone was icy.

"Analise refused to marry me when she discovered that you had returned home a cripple. She said she knew she could love only you. She wanted to restore your health. I lost her to you; I think that makes it a concern of mine."

"She told me she would divorce me once I was well, so

I can't see why you have anything to worry about," Mark sneered.

"Then she lied to you. Only yesterday she told me she still felt bound to you and refused to marry me."

Mark shot him a surprised glance, but said nothing.

Max continued doggedly. "Believe me, I had little desire to come here today. I think you are a scoundrel and a fool for the way you have treated Analise. It is beyond my comprehension how any man lucky enough to be married to Analise could shun her. However, for Analise's sake, I felt I had to come. A man named Joe Grimshaw has been bothering her. He has called on Analise constantly, even though she has made it clear she does not wish to see him. Last night he even forced his way into the house. He was drunken, rude, and vulgar; he shouted at Analise and informed her of your affair with Mrs. Fourier, in front of two other people and a servant. I fear for Analise's safety and reputation, but I have not the right to protect her. That is a husband's right and duty; so I came here to urge you as strongly as I can to speak to Grimshaw and make it clear that the lady is under your protection. Even if you have no concern for Analise, surely you must feel compelled to protect your name and honor."

"My name and honor are of little importance to me," Schaeffer said bluntly. "However, I will take care of Grimshaw. Thank you for telling me about the situation. Analise had not informed me that the man was annoying her. I do not think she regards me in the light of a husband as much as you do, Mr. Schleyer."

"You are blind then, if you cannot see how Analise feels about you," Max returned heatedly.

Mark looked at him scornfully, and said, "Excuse me,

Mr. Schleyer. I would love to sit here and discuss with you my wife and my marriage, but since you have reminded me of my marital duties, I think I had better pay Mr. Grimshaw a visit."

At that, he galloped off, leaving Max staring after him in astonishment. It was closer to cut through the fields to the River Road than to ride back to the house. Besides, there was nothing Mark needed from the house; he carried a gun with him in the fields to shoot poisonous snakes. That and his fists should get his point across.

The flame of his fury sent Mark racing into town. He was not certain at whom he was most angry—Max, for rebuking him about neglecting Analise's safety; himself, for not knowing what was happening and acting sooner; Grimshaw, for bothering Analise; or Analise herself, for not turning to him for help. Damn the woman, she had no use for him; she was supremely confident that she could do everything. Now that he was cured, he might as well not exist.

When he stormed into Grimshaw's office, Mark was a frightening picture in his dirty sweat-damp field clothes, a gun stuck in his belt, and his dark face grim with anger, the scars standing out on his cheek. Grimshaw, seated behind his desk, rose, stammering with fear.

Mark's acidic voice cut him off. "I am Mark Schaeffer; it is *my* wife you have been annoying."

Grimshaw's knees turned to jelly, and he said plaintively, "I didn't know—that is, I thought, the way she goes all over by herself and runs a business, and what with you way out there by yourself, well, I just thought—"

"I don't give a damn what you thought. She is my wife, and if you bother her again, I will come back. And then you'll be lucky if you are left alive. Do you understand?"

Mark's eyes blazed with an unholy fire, and Grimshaw found he was unable to speak. Dumbly he nodded. Mark nodded shortly and left the office, swinging the door behind him with such force that the glass in the upper half of the door cracked.

He mounted his horse, then turned on impulse toward Analise's store. She would not be home yet, of course, he thought; she practically lived at that damn store. His entrance into the store drew a few askance glances, but no one moved to stop him as he strode through the building, pausing only to ask the location of the offices. He opened the door of Analise's office with a crash, and Analise looked up, startled. Framed in the doorway, lean and tough in his casual clothes, the gun tucked into his belt, his face brown and hard, with its disfiguring scar, he looked like danger personified. Analise felt her pulse quicken.

"Why the devil didn't you tell me about Grimshaw?" he demanded and moved inside, closing the door with a heavy thud.

Analise blinked. "Grimshaw?"

"Yes, Grimshaw. Your German lover led me to think the man's attentions were unwanted, or was he wrong?"

"Max Schleyer is not my lover!" Analise responded, rising to his anger as she had always done. "As for Grimshaw, I don't know what concern he is of yours."

Mark's eyes narrowed. "What concern? Have you forgotten that I am your husband?"

"No, although since you seem to want to ignore the fact, I saw no sense in appealing to you. I imagined you would laugh and tell me to handle it myself, in your usual callous way."

"*I* ignore our marriage? It is *you* who live here, spending all your time and efforts on this store. No one would suspect you had a son and husband! It is you who want a divorce so you can marry Schleyer. It is—"

"Wait!" Analise interrupted wrathfully. "*You* were the one who left me to live at Belle Terre, never even asking me to accompany you. What am I supposed to do, trot after you like a faithful dog? Well, believe me, I will not! It is *you* who have a lover, not I. How dare you accuse me of wrongdoing, when you are sleeping with my brother's wife? When you brought a prostitute into our own house to service you?"

"Damn it, I am a man, not a statue. I need release."

"Release! What about me? I waited for you for months and then you left me flat, taking Frances' word above mine. It has been over three years since you deigned to grace my bed. What about my needs? Do you think I have no passion? Do you think I don't want to feel your touch, your kiss?"

Her words fanned the ever-smoldering desire in him. He crossed the room in two strides to pull her into his arms. Roughly he kissed her, months of frustrated desire burning in his fierce lips. Analise's arms went around his neck as he bent her back onto the desk, his weight on top of her. With one hand he shoved her heavy skirts up and caressed her shapely legs, tugging at her stockings and underclothes. He groaned as his efforts revealed her slender white thighs. Feverish with pent-up desire and anger, Mark pressed his burning lips into the smooth white flesh. Past reason or discretion, he unbuttoned his trousers and covered her with his body, thrusting boldly into her.

Analise sucked in her breath and began to wantonly move her hips beneath him. It was so sweet, so beautiful, to feel him again . . . Her body flamed, and quickly she arched against him, waves of pleasure crashing through her. Her movement rocketed him to climax also, and he gave a hoarse cry and collapsed upon her, trembling.

It was then that her head cleared and Analise realized the embarrassment of her position: taken like a slut, fully dressed, atop her desk, with the door unlocked. What if one of her employees had come in? And then quickly on the heels of that thought came the memory of Becky Oldway.

She pushed at him crossly. "Get off me. What do you mean, coming in here and throwing me across my desk like some primitive savage?"

Mark sighed and stood up, reality setting in. Good Lord, he had done it again: attacked and abused Analise in his anger. He felt suddenly sick with regret. Again—he had done it again; he had no control over himself. He could not seem to keep from hurting her. So deep and bitter were his feelings against himself that he paid no attention to Analise's manner, missing entirely the shallowness of her irritation, the slight anger that only begged for an apology or explanation or, best of all, an outpouring of his feelings. Instead Mark stood and adjusted his clothing, avoiding her eyes.

"I am sorry, Analise. Consider that my final act as a husband. Divorce me. I have given you ample grounds with Becky."

Still without looking at her, he left the room. Quickly

he walked through the store and out to his horse, almost running from the bone-melting pleasure he had felt back there. Dear God, why was nothing so satisfying as the tender body of his wife, despite the selfish greed with which he took her? He mounted his horse and rode back to Belle Terre, his thoughts on the lovemaking he had just left, remembering so vividly the pleasure of her that desire throbbed in his loins again. He ached for her again, more strongly than ever, and hated himself for it. Perhaps he would fetch Becky; that might blot out the sweet memory of Analise.

Analise sat down in her chair, stunned. When he had taken her, she had believed he had returned to her. Perhaps she should not have spoken to him crossly; it was just that she wanted him to apologize for Becky, to ask her to take him back. Oh, damn her pride! That was what made her say that.

And yet—surely what she had said would not drive away a man like Mark. No, he must not have intended to stay; he had just wanted to have her one last time and then divorce her. Shaken, Analise rose and walked home. She would not be worth anything now, and, besides, it was almost closing time. All the way home, she went dully over and over his words. She could not escape the facts that Mark wanted a divorce and that he admitted his affair with Becky. He did not love her. He had proven that over and over again. How long would it take to get that into her head?

When Analise arrived home, she went straight upstairs, refusing supper. She could not eat anything now, the way she felt. She slumped into a chair and sat staring out at the approaching dusk. It was almost two hours later that she finally stirred and rang for her maid to help her undress. Her eyes fell on a packet of letters on her dresser, and Analise went over to look at it curiously. The familiar writing on the envelopes made her heart leap.

Her maid entered and she swung around. "May, what are these? How did they get here?"

"Why, I put them there, Miss Analise. Mister Max brought them. He says Mr. Schaeffer in New York asked him to bring them to you. They're all the Colonel's letters to you that you didn't get."

"I see," Analise said and picked up the packet. "That's all, May, thank you."

When May left, Analise hurried to her chair and opened the top letter with trembling fingers.

Beloved Analise

I cannot tell you how terribly I miss you. Nightly I dream of you and waken stiff with desire, like a young lad. You are so beautiful, so tender, that I ache with love and passion. I wish I could tell you how great my love for you is.

If only I could be there to support you when our child is born—though I would probably go mad to see you in pain and be unable to ease it. I worry about you constantly; please take good care of yourself.

Today I was thinking about our time aboard ship. That period was the most wonderful time of my life. Ever since I can remember, I have been haunted by the memory of my mother, driven to do wild, reckless things, hating both her and my father. But in your arms I at last found peace. Your love is my world, my foundation. I think I would crumble without it . . ."

Analise raised her head, tears shining in her eyes. His letter was so sweet, so full of love that it made her swell with bittersweet joy. So much happiness had been snatched away from them!

She read on, swiftly perusing the candid outpourings of love that turned into hurt questionings, and finally into bitter, angry letters that seared her heart as he railed at her for not writing him. Underlying them all was a love whose depth she had never before realized. It was no wonder he had remained bitter and untrusting with her even after he had discovered Frances' treachery. He had built his fragile world on her and he would have been bone-deep scared to entrust his soul like that again and risk another shattering of his world. Crippled and in pain, full of regret and fear, and tormented by the cruel things she had said to spur him to work on his recovery, it was no wonder that Mark lashed out at her and tried to keep her separated from him. He was struggling to find firm footing, and he could not risk the total vulnerability of loving her.

But he did love her; Analise knew now that he did, no matter what he said. The love expressed in his letters could not have died so suddenly. It might take patient effort on her part; she would have to fight Becky and even Mark himself to recover his love. But when had she ever been afraid of a fight?

Suddenly Analise threw back her head and laughed delightedly. Before her lay excitement, challenge, a testing of her powers, and, at the end, a lovely reward. She could think of nothing that would please her more. Quickly she grabbed her riding gloves and a light shawl, then ran down the stairs, calling to her butler.

"Augustus, have the buggy harnessed for me; I am driving out to Belle Terre. Alone."

"But, Miss Analise, it's nighttime!" her servant expostulated.

"I am not blind, Augustus. Quickly, now. I am going, no matter what you say."

There was a mutinous look on the man's face, but he left to follow her instructions. When he returned, however, he carried a heavy cavalry pistol, which he held out to her.

"Now, here, Miss Analise, you take this. The Colonel left it behind, in case you needed protection. Them's lonely, dark roads out there, and all kind of riffraff is roaming around—white and dark. So you carry this, just in case."

So when Analise settled herself into the open buggy and took up the reins, she placed the pistol in her lap. However, the journey passed without incident, and Analise found that she rather enjoyed the ride, despite her impatience to arrive. When at last she turned into the oak-lined driveway and the blocky bulk of the house loomed out of the darkness before her, she felt her throat constrict with tears. It had been so long since she had been here, so horribly long.

The house was dark—and no wonder, since it was now well past midnight—except for one lighted room. Analise knew that was the master bedroom, no doubt where Mark now slept. Quickly Analise scrambled from the buggy, tossing the reins over the hitching rail, and went quiet as a wraith up the steps and into the house. She knew the house well and unerringly made her way to the spiral staircase, then up and through the hall to the lighted bedroom. Outside the door she checked at the sound of soft feminine laughter. Anger flashed through her, and she thought, here is the first of my fights. Cautiously she turned the knob and inched the door open a crack. Mark sat in a metal slipper-shaped bathtub, leaning languorously against the high back, his eyes closed, a thin cigar in one hand and a glass of whiskey in the other. Beside him knelt a naked Becky Fourier, her blonde hair streaming down her back. She had a cloth in one hand and was sensually rubbing it across Mark's chest, working up a soapy lather, then rinsing it off.

Analise stared in silence for a moment, then swung open the door with a crash and stepped inside. Mark's eyes flew open at her noisy entrance, and Becky gaped at her. Analise stood straight and stiff with anger, her blue eyes blazing, letting the drama of the situation soak in. She had without thinking carried the pistol in her hand when she left the buggy, and now she held it down by her side, hidden in the folds of her skirts.

"Well, Becky, once you cut me on the street because I lived with a Yankee, and now here you are kneeling to wash him, like a slave girl," Analise said dryly. "Quite a switch, don't you think?"

Becky's throat was too dry to speak; Analise, with her blazing eyes and cold, calm voice, frightened her. Mark said nothing, just watched Analise with narrowed eyes.

"Becky, I think that you should get up, get dressed, and leave this house—forever. Don't ever come back here or try to contact my husband. Do I make myself clear?"

The blonde woman found her voice then and answered

with false bravado. "I think that is Mark's choice, not yours, isn't it? This is his house, and he wants me."

"Becky, you are a fool," Analise said dispassionately. "Mark uses you to satisfy his sexual hunger—hunger that I arouse in him. I don't suppose he told you that he wanted you tonight because he had been to see me this afternoon. Believe me, he will drop you like a rock as soon as you cease to interest him. I know Mark, and I know you, and it shouldn't be long before he finds you a dead bore."

Mark could not help but smile at Analise's cool analysis. Lord, but she was self-possessed; Becky looked like a frightened child beside her. He could feel the challenge rising up inside of him, and he knew he wanted her.

"How dare you! That's not true!" Becky cried, jumping up. "Mark wants *me*, not you. He loves me; he does!"

Analise laughed, and her right hand came up until the deadly pistol pointed straight at Becky.

"Get dressed, Becky," she said, her voice as hard and cold as glass. "Even if Mark did want you, it really would not matter. Because if I ever hear of your seeing him again, I will come after you. I won't kill you, of course, just maim you so that no man will look at you ever again. Is that clear?"

Becky nodded, dumb with fear, and began to scramble into her clothes. Under Analise's icy gaze, her fingers fumbled nervously, and finally, half-dressed, she scooped up the rest of her clothes and ran from the room. Analise closed and locked the door behind her. Mark watched the proceedings with amused interest. What on earth was Analise up to?

She spoke to him now. "Mark, I have decided to come here to live; I intend to truly be your wife once more."

"Oh, and do I have nothing to say about it?" he inquired lazily.

"No, because you would only say something foolish and false. Your father sent me the letters Frances saved, and after reading them I know you lied when you said you did not love me."

"Damn him!" Mark exclaimed. "I told him to burn them."

"I love you, Mark," Analise said clearly, proudly. "I have ever since we first met. There will never be anyone else but you for me. I love you and I want you. Sometimes I lie awake at night, wishing you were in my bed, longing for the touch of your hands on my skin, aching to feel you filling me—"

"Stop it, Analise, for God's sake!" Mark said in a choked voice.

"No, I won't. I am tired of all the lies and evasions; I am sick of your infidelities. I want to be your wife again."

"Can't you understand that we're not good for each other! It's over, and it is pointless to start it up again. Too much has happened to us; too much hurt, too many lies, too many suspicions."

"I don't believe that; your love is not dead."

"Damn it, it is!"

"Then prove it," Analise said sharply. "Get up out of that tub."

She raised her gun threateningly and he stood. The water streamed off his lean, muscled flesh, and Analise's eyes roamed over him appreciatively. The look in her eyes stirred him unbearably, and he fought against it. Dear Heaven, he wanted her, but he must not give in to it. He must not hurt her any more.

"You have turned into a hard, domineering woman, Analise," he said bitingly. "You've become a tight, unfeeling, desiccated thing. No man could stand your temper or your overbearing ways."

"Oh?" Analise said silkily. "Aren't you man enough to tame me? Am I too strong a challenge for you? I thought you could take me to your bed and make me a woman again."

Mark's breath rasped in his throat. "Are you crazy? Can't you see what I look like? I am scarred, Analise, maimed."

"I stroked those very scars for months," Analise replied. "Can you honestly think they could hold any horrors for me? No, indeed, sometimes I hated massaging your arm and leg because I would go hot and quivering at touching your naked flesh."

A tremor shook him at her words, and Analise smiled. "Do you expect me to believe that you don't want me when your very body betrays you?" She glanced pointedly at his stiffening manhood.

With a little laugh, Analise tossed the pistol onto a chair. Her hands went up to her hair, deftly unpinning it and letting it tumble to her shoulders.

"Analise, don't," Mark pleaded, desperation in his voice. Her teasing was driving him to the brink. "I am trying to help you. I'm bad for you. I hurt you over and over again. My jealousy and my rage overpower me, and then I hurt you. And I hate myself for it. Please, for both our sakes, don't tempt me."

"I don't care," Analise unbuttoned her dress, watching Mark's eyes follow her fingers avidly. "I can handle you.

Believe me, I'll keep you so busy, you won't have the strength for anger or the time for jealousy."

She slipped off her dress, unfastened her hoop, and stepped out of it. Slowly, maddeningly, she advanced on him unfastening her undergarments and slipping out of them one by one. Finally she stopped a foot away, her ripe body naked to his gaze. Mark's eyes blazed with passion and he trembled like a hard-run horse.

"Prove you can live without me," she said softly. "Touch me and then leave me. Prove it."

With a groan, Mark reached out and pulled her to him, burying his lips in hers. Analise stretched up to meet him, pressing her body against his. Finally he tore his mouth away and just held her a moment.

"I love you," he whispered. "I want you to remember that, if I ever hurt you again. I love you more than anything on earth."

"I know," she said, and his mouth descended on hers once again.